E

MW01673798

The Business of Pleasure

Vol. 1

SALZWASSER VERLAG

Edmund Yates

The Business of Pleasure

Vol. 1

Reprint of the original, first published in 1865.

1st Edition 2022 | ISBN: 978-3-75258-984-9

Verlag (Publisher): Salzwasser Verlag GmbH, Zeilweg 44, 60439 Frankfurt, Deutschland
Vertretungsberechtigt (Authorized to represent): E. Roepke, Zeilweg 44, 60439 Frankfurt, Deutschland
Druck (Print): Books on Demand GmbH, In de Tarpen 42, 22848 Norderstedt, Deutschland

THE BUSINESS OF PLEASURE.

THE BUSINESS OF PLEASURE.

BY

EDMUND YATES,

AUTHOR OF "BROKEN TO HARNESS," ETC. ETC.

IN TWO VOLUMES.

VOL. I.

LONDON

1865.

CONTENTS OF VOL. I.

THE BUSINESS OF PLEASURE.

CHAPTER I.

INTRODUCTORY.

IF, as Froissart says, we English take our pleasure sadly after our fashion, it is very certain that we take it coolly. We *will* have it, be it in what shape it may, though dressmakers die in working against time for the preparation of our court-robes, and bakers' lives are sacrificed to our partiality for hot rolls. But when we have got it, we think very little of it, and very much less of those who, some by great natural gifts, combined with much labour, industry, and perseverance, minister to the pleasure of which we make so light. Great actors and singers are, by a certain portion of society, classed with cooks, mountebanks, and horse-jockeys. "That man who wrote the book, you know," is the phrase by which Mr. Tennyson or Dr. Darwin would be designated; and world-renowned artists are "odd persons whom one does not meet about." With that wretched imposition which occasionally in England is known as society—that gathering of vapidity to each component part of which the laws which guide it prescribe a blank ignorance—an uncaring, unquestioning acceptance of matters as they stand; a horror of talent as low, and of unconventionality as not correct,—with this dreary phantasm sometimes regnant among us, Business, however lumpy, coarse, unrefined, can be received, provided it be properly gilt; but Pleasure and her professors, however clever, bright, and decent, are under the ban. Yet the Business of Pleasure is carried on in the most methodical manner, is of enormous extent, employs countless "hands," and avails itself of all the counting-house, clerk, day-book and ledger system, without which respectability cannot understand existence. To carry out the Business of English Pleasure, men and women are at this very time practising eight hours a day in dreary little Italian cities under renowned maestri, labouring against innumerable difficulties, privations, and disappointments, and solely cheered by the hope that on some future day they shall be permitted to minister to pleasure in London, and earn the meed reserved for a few such ministrants. In the Business of Pleasure acres and acres of English ground, and Rhenish mountain, and French and Spanish plain, are set apart and cultivated to the highest degree of perfection: in the same interest hardy Norsemen are salmon-fishing; heavy Westphalian boors, preposterously accoutred, are boar-hunting; blue-bloused Alsatian peasants are fattening bilious geese; dirty Russians are oiling cod-sounds. Those engaged in the Business of Pleasure are of various stations, of various temperaments, of various degrees of usefulness; but from all is there required as strict honesty, punctuality, and fidelity, as proper and earnest a performance of their duties, as thorough rectitude, as in any other condition in life.

It is my purpose in these Essays to show the inner life of some of those carrying on the Business of Pleasure, and bringing thereto as much energy, honesty, and industry, as great aptitude for business, as much self-abnegation, as much skill and talent for seizing opportunities and supplying promptly the public demand, and in very many cases as much capital, as are required in any other business. It may arise from the fact that I spring from parents who by profession were, according to a generous Act of Parliament only recently repealed, set forth among their fellow-men as "rogues and vagabonds;" but one of whom certainly used-up his life, and killed himself at an early age, from his unceasing labour in a popular, an honest, an intellectual, but a parliamentarily-despised, calling. It may be that in my own career I have seen that those who made it their business to amuse men in their leisure, had very often a much more difficult, and always a more thankless, task than those who coped with men in their active work. It may have been from other causes not necessary to dwell upon; but I have long felt that the "butterfly" notion common among ordinary business people, as applied to those who belonged to none of the recognised professions, or whose trade could not be found entered in the exhaustive list in the *Post-Office Directory*, was a mistake. So that, my family-connection with theatrical life, and my own position as a journalist and writer, favouring the scheme, I determined upon giving specimens of the inner life of some of those establishments where pleasure is carried on as a regular business and in regular business fashion; showing, so far as is practicable and just, the method, manner, and expense of its conduct. To these I have added a few Papers descriptive of the actual business details; the cost and conduct of certain of the sports and pastimes of Englishmen, such as hunting, shooting, &c.; the organisation of an excursion-agent; the inner life of a newspaper-office; some articles descriptive of the behind-the-scenes of the Volunteer movement; and some other papers illustrative of London society.

CHAPTER II.

CREMORNE GARDENS.

REMOVING recently into a new house,—a miserable performance which has once or twice fallen to my lot,—I determined, besides giving a "general superintendence" (which means looking helplessly on, while stout men in carpet-caps balance chests-of-drawers, console-tables, and looking-glasses, and saying to them, perspiring, and in proximate danger of letting every thing drop: "Steady there; mind the corner! a-a-h! the gilt frame!"),—I determined on looking after my books, of which I possess a tolerable number, and arranging them myself. Experience fully carrying out all she had promised in the round-hand copy-slip at school, taught me this plan; for when we made our former celebrated removal from Glum Street, Holstein Square, to Jetsam Gardens, Matilda, my maid, kindly undertook to "put my books straight"—an effort which resulted in an utter impossibility of finding any work of reference, and in the final discovery of the third volume of Rabelais lurking shamefacedly behind Nelson's *Fasts and Festivals.* So I sat down on an enormous pile of volumes in the middle of the library-floor, and I looked at the row of empty bookcases, glaring in a very ghastly manner from the walls, and I began my task; very seldom, however, settling more than a dozen books without again sitting down to peer between the leaves of some volume which I had not seen for a very long time. They were of all sorts: some of my father's old Charterhouse schoolbooks; editions of the Classics, free from all that erudite annotation which has been so productive of headache to schoolboys of more recent date; some of my own schoolbooks with names once familiar, now long forgotten, scrawled on the margin of the pages, and a fancy portrait of Euripides (very fancy) on the fly-leaf of the *Orestes;* Jones's early poems, *Twilight Musings*, with my name inscribed on the title-page in Jones's own hand, "from his devoted friend and cue-fellow." Jones is now principal vitriol-thrower on the *Scalpel* literary newspaper, and is popularly believed to have written that review of his devoted friend and cue-fellow's last book of travels, which caused the devoted f. and c.-f. to spend an evening rolling on his hearthrug in agonies of rage and despair. Here are other given books: *Manna in the Wilderness, or the Smitten Rock*, presented to me at "Crismass 1844," as the written legend records, by my cousin Augustus, who was great at morality, but weak in orthography, and who in the next spring ran away and joined Herr Carlos Wilkinsoni's travelling cirque, after having forged his father's name to a check for twenty pounds. Here is my first copy of Shakespeare, with my name in faded ink, and underneath it two sets of initials in different handwritings, the owners of which, long separated by death, are, I pray Heaven, more happily reunited; and here is a copy of Blugg's collected works, with the sixpenny label of the book-stall still sticking to it. Poor Dick Blugg, who combined so much capacity for writing and gin-and-water, and whose life was divided between a bare room containing a desk, a blotting-pad, an ink-bottle, and a pile of paper, where he did his work, and the night-houses in the Haymarket, where he spent his money. Other books, acting as milestones in one's life: copy of Mr. Thomas Moore's *Lalla Rookh*, with the "young gazelle" bit very much pencil-scored; Byron's *Giaour*, *Childe Harold*, and works generally, with marginal pencilled references expressive of my entire concurrence in the noble poet's views of human nature (by the date it must have been just after J. M. married that stockbroker); and a copy of the *Vauxhall Comic Songster*, with the portrait and autograph of a once-celebrated comic singer. Milestones indeed! Where is the comic singer? Dust and ashes! The Yorick of the orchestra, with his white waistcoat and his thumbs in his arm-holes, his queer merry eyes and thin pursed lips, with his riddles and his jokes and his tol-de-rol choruses—dust and ashes! And Vauxhall? with its thousand of extra lamps, and its gritty arcades, and its ghastly Italian walk, and its rickety firework gallery, and its mildewy Eve at the fountain, and Joel Il Diavolo's terrific descent with the crackers in his heels, and the skinny fowls and the dry ham and the rack-punch, and the enclosure outside Mr. Wardell's house where all the hansom cabs were inextricably mixed together—where are these? On what the bills used to call the "royal property" (at this moment I can plainly see the sticking-plaster portrait of Simpson, life-size, by the pay-place) are reared now suburban villas, wherein the young soap-boiler tosses his son and heir, or the bone-crusher's head-clerk reads the American news with calm contempt. No! the name may remain, but the place has vanished for ever.

'Vanished for ever' is a dreary phrase; but then I recollect that there is yet a place of amusement for summer-nights, and that those lively persons who "to Ranelagh went and Vauxhall" may, if they have a mind (and legs) to do so, go to what I should imagine must be a much pleasanter place than either of them,—to Cremorne; and when this idea came into my head, I remembered that during the previous week I had been at CREMORNE, and I put down my *Comic Songster*, and lay back on the pile of books, thinking on all I had heard there.

Heard at Cremorne! What do people hear at Cremorne? The band and the peripatetic brass-instruments (which indeed are rather too much heard), and the rumble of the bowls in the American Saloon, and the crack of the rifles discharged by the sportsmen at the little tin beasts which slowly revolve, and the whizzing rush of the rockets, and the roar of the final firework explosion (which must be so comforting to any neighbour suffering with sick-headache, and just in his first sleep); and sometimes, I am given to understand, there may be heard by young couples at Cremorne the voice of love! I heard all these except the last (but then I am not young, and on this occasion I was not a couple); but I heard something else. For as I wandered about the grounds and looked in at the open coffee-room windows, and lounged into the theatre, staring for a few minutes at the ballet, as I noticed the thoroughly trim and neat appearance of the gardens, as I marked the extensive preparations for the fireworks, and as I endeavoured to dodge the rather meandering steps of a gentleman in armour whom I encountered in a back-walk, whose vizor rendered him doubtful as to his eyesight, and whose shining greaves rendered him unsteady on his legs,—I began to ponder on the magnitude of the undertaking, and to wonder how the various wheels in the great whole worked with such unceasing regularity. Here must be large capital involved, very many people engaged, constant supervision exercised, and all for the production of Pleasure. Your "man of business" (who, by the way, when he is that, and nothing more, is horribly offensive) would sneer at the application of the word to the conduct of such a place as this; and yet I have no doubt that there is as much labour, capital, and energy employed here as in many establishments whose names are household words in the circle of a mile from the Exchange. Pleasure has its business, which requires to be carried on with as great tact, earnestness, energy, forethought, and exactness as any other; and when patience, prudence, and perseverance are brought to bear in carrying on the business of pleasure, the result is Fortune. When the business of pleasure is carried on as pleasure itself, no one is pleased, and the result to the speculator is Bankruptcy.

The more I thought of the subject the more I wondered; so that presently encountering the master-mind and governing spirit of the establishment, I requested to have some details of its cost and management: he pleasantly consented, and "while the men and maids were dancing, and the folk were mad with glee," I sat calmly discussing statistics, and gleaned the following information anent the wherewithal necessary for carrying out the business of pleasure at Cremorne.

So quietly, orderly, and well is this place conducted, and with such sensible regard to the interest of its frequenters (who, by the way, are of all classes, ranging from old women and children who come for an early tea and a stroll in the grounds, who are possessed with wild desires to see the dogs and monkeys, and listen to the band, down to gentlemanly gentlemen who eat suppers, and are far too grand to express their desire to see any thing at all), that, by its non-frequenters and by a huge class of amiable people who look upon any amusement as emanating from Moloch and beckoning towards the gallows, it would never be heard of, were it not for the practical wit of certain exquisite humorists, who annually mark certain festive days in London's calendar by breaking the proprietor's glasses and the waiters' heads. This amiable class may perchance be strong in its notions of the diffusion of capital and the employment of labour; it may be always publishing pamphlets in which these subjects are paraded, in which it is clearly proved that this wretched country is on its way to destruction, and that the sooner every person with natural strength or mechanical knowledge is on his way to some hitherto unheard-of land—there to set up that log-hut, and to ply that axe which have stood the poetasters in such good stead—the better for himself and for society.

The gardens of Cremorne are twenty-two acres in extent, are prettily laid out, are filled with brilliant flowers, and are kept with as much care as those of the Horticultural Society. Indeed, of the quiet daylight frequenters of the place, were they not properly attended to, there would be a serious falling off. During the season the services of fifteen gardeners are constantly required, in rolling paths, mowing lawns, and attending to the beds. Previous to opening, twenty carpenters, six scene-painters, twelve gasmen, two women to sew canvas, four men to repair the roof, and five house-painters, take possession of the outside of Cremorne and its appurtenances; while two upholsterers, fifteen wardrobe-makers, and ten property-men, look up old material, and prepare for internal decoration. Then the literary gentleman attached to the establishment sits down in his cabinet to compose the announcement of approaching festivities, and eight bill-posters convey the result of his cogitations to an admiring public.

In the season of 1863 the Gardens opened early in the spring with a dog-show; and the estimate for the preparation—for gardeners, painters, roofers, carpenters, smiths, labourers, and gravel-diggers—amounted to 3500*l.*, independent of the cost of material, galvanised iron, timber, ironmongery, wire-work, &c., about 2000*l.* more. While the exhibition was open, the expenses of keepers, police, attendants, and music, were about 300*l.* a week, and a very large sum was expended in advertisements and prizes. This dog-show, however, was an extraneous affair, not calculated in the regular round of expense. In the same category was the tournament, to produce which the services of three hundred "supers," six armourers, thirty-two horses, and ten grooms were specially engaged. When the Gardens are open for the season, the regular staff is very large and very costly. It comprises sixteen money-takers, seven gasmen, two scene-painters, three house-painters, one resident master-carpenter, and seventeen wardrobe men and women. The stage department requires the services of twenty-five carpenters to work the scenes, a prompter, a hundred members of the *corps de ballet*, two principal dancers, three principal pantomimists, several vocalists, and a turncock, without whose aid the fairy fountains would not flow. Add to this a firework manufacturer with seven assistants, fifteen riders, and several horses in the circus; a set of twenty dogs and monkeys, with their master, in the Octagon Theatre; a set of marionettes and their master, in another part of the grounds; twenty-five members of the regular orchestra and two peripatetic bands; a gentleman who delivers a lecture on the Australian explorers; three regular policemen, and on extra nights six others;—and you have some notion of what the management of Cremorne Gardens has to meet on Saturday mornings, as the cost of the amusement it provides.

The hotel department, belonging to the same proprietary, is, of course, worked by a totally different staff. The in-door division has the services of a manager and housekeeper, fifteen barmaids, two head-waiters, eighteen other waiters, a booking-clerk, two hall-keepers, and three porters. The outer division is managed by a head-waiter with fifty subordinates. In the kitchen there are four professed cooks with assistants, a kitchen-boy, a vegetable cook, two scullery-men, two bakers and confectioners, who are all overlooked by a larder clerk. There is also a man whose sole business is the production of soda-water and ginger-beer; and there is a cowkeeper.

A few years ago supper was the great meal at Cremorne; but under the present management dinners have been made a feature of attraction in the programme; and the number of diners is now large. You can dine at various prices, and have almost any thing you like to order, for the commissariat is on the most extensive scale. Regarding the consumption of food at this single establishment at the height of the season, the following list may be taken as a daily average: six salmon, twenty pairs of soles, twelve gallons of whitebait, one turbot, twenty-five pounds of eels, twenty dozen of lobsters, twenty gallons of shrimps, one saddle of mutton, one haunch, six quarters of lamb and six legs, six joints of roast-beef, two fillets of veal, fifty pounds of pressed beef, six dozen pigeon-pies, twenty-four dozen fowls, twelve dozen ducks, twelve tongues, six hams, forty pounds of bacon, two tubs of butter, two sacks of flour, and two hundred eggs. Of vegetable produce, the daily consumption is fifty quarts of peas, three dozen cauliflowers, one hundred-weight of potatoes, twenty score lettuce, one hundred heads of beetroot, thirty bunches of turnips and carrots, and six hundred bundles of watercress. Six hundred-weight of ice, two hundred-weight of sugar, and twenty pounds of tea, are also consumed daily.

Such is the internal economy of Cremorne, confessedly the prettiest and best-managed public night-garden in Europe. That it is not so lively as the Chaumière, Mabille, Asnières, or the Closerie des Lilas, must be ascribed to the different character of its frequenters. We have no Counts Chicard, Brididis, Mogadors, or Frisettes (I am *laudator temporis acti* here! it is years since I was in a French public night-garden) among us. I do not think that loss is to be regretted. I know that in "mossoo" visiting us is to be found the most enthusiastic admirer of Cremorne.

CHAPTER III.

THE GREENWICH DINNER.

When you invite a friend to "dinner," before specifying the when and where, you leave him in a pleasant state of uncertainty as to your intentions and his chances of pleasure. You may mean the domestic dinner, than which, when well done, nothing can be better. By well done I mean not more than half-a-dozen people, all of them knowing and understanding each other; soup, fish, joint, a couple of entrées, a bird, a pudding, and some maccaroni; a neat-handed Phyllis instead of a stupid waiter; sound wine, and a small cigar before going up to the ladies; where you have some really good music, and get away by eleven. This is doing it well: it can be badly done in many different ways. In the "pot-luck" style: a bit of hard loin-of-mutton swimming in coagulated grease, dank dabs of greens, mild beeswax of cheese, warm flat Romford ale, two glasses of fiery sherry, and a tumbler of diluted turpentine called whisky-and-water. In the grand style: where the host and hostess pass two wretched hours in telegraphing to stupid servants; where the funny friend will tell the *mal-à-propos* anecdote which cuts the most-to-be-made-up-to member of the party to the quick; where the guests all hate you for being pretentious and endeavouring to excel them; where conversation is on the revolving-light principle—occasionally bright, frequently hazy, generally dull; and where it is difficult to know which are most delighted when the entertainment is at an end—the people who were so pleased to see their friends, or those who have passed such a charming evening. There is the club-dinner: where you have a grand opportunity of airing your importance, and bringing your social status to bear heavily on your unoffending guest. And there is the tavern-dinner, to which you tell him you take him that "we may have a pleasant, free, jolly evening, old fellow, and be out of the way of all club-formalities." And then there is the Greenwich dinner, which is of itself a thing apart, and at the mention of which the invited one beams with delight.

For any one who knows any thing about a

Greenwich dinner knows he cannot be asked to a bad one. The whitebait get large in July; the salmon-cutlets *can* have been sent up and sent down, and sent up again, too often; the duck may be tough; the waiting (notably when there are three City-companies, the staff of a daily newspaper, and a hundred people in the coffee-room, all clamouring and dining at once) somewhat tiresome; but, on the whole, you cannot dine badly at Greenwich.

The mere fact of dining out of town is agreeable. It is a hot staring June day; the heat reflected from the pavement permeates every where; the air is still and sirocco-like; one side of the way (that on which the sun is shining) is deserted; while on the other, those men who are strong-minded enough are mopping their bald foreheads and carrying their hats boldly in their hands. Vagabond dogs with lolling tongues, unpleasantly suggestive of hydrophobia, loiter at the corners of the streets, and regard the legs of the passers-by with furtive and maniacal glances; boys forget the charms of toffee, buns, and pegtops, and devote their pocket-money to the purchase of clinging dabs of nastiness known as penny ices; butchers' shops, always unpleasant to the eye, become offensive to the nose; while from the gratings of the eating-houses issues a warm puthery steam, which turns me sick as I pass. No dinner in London to-day! No hot joint, tongue-flaying cheese, lukewarm beer, fiery sherry! Across my brain come visions of myriads of fish-dishes, cool cup, ice-water, luxury—Greenwich! Thither we fly, I and thou, shadowy Cleophas, to my more shadowy Asmodeus. What matter whether steam-rattled over ragged-school-containing brick arches from London Bridge; floated-down on board *Waterman* No. 3, "deal-built, dirty-bottomed, and carrying an inexperienced medical student" bound on the same errand as ourselves; or whirled-down in the most reckless and dust-provoking of hansoms! Here we are at The Vessel; and now to look around us. Outside the door stand some thirty carriages of every description, horseless and closely packed together: sly little broughams, radiant in varnish, with pink window-blinds, and a tiny basket strapped opposite the seat to hold the bouquet and gloves of the fair owner; heavy drags, looking so like superior stage-coaches without the plate and the letters, and with much-besilvered splinter-bars attached to the rails of the hind-seat; stock-brokers' high-wheeled mail-phaetons, all brass and lacquer and fresh garish paint; roomy family clarences, dowagers' yellow-bodied chariots, dissipated-looking dog-carts, with the oilcloth on the suspended trap much torn and trampled by unsteady, not to say drunken, feet; rakish hansoms, and even one or two four-wheeled cabs.

A constant stream has been pouring in ever since we have been here, and when we enter the coffee-room we find it nearly filled. Observe that the best tables (those nearest the window, with the good look-out on the river) are nearly all occupied by solitary diners,—elderly big men with bald heads, huge stomachs, stolid expression, and succulent protruding under-lips. These be your City merchants, your magnates of Lloyds' and the Exchange, your lunchers at Garraway's and the Jerusalem, your Gordon-Square dwellers, bank directors, vestry wranglers, charitable-parochial-rate supporters; these be your fathers of Mudie-subscribing daughters, and of club smoking-room-haunting sons; these be your autumnal-touring Britons, who give the notion of the *Milor Anglais* to the Parisian *vaudevilliste* and the Italian libretto-writer; these be your "regular John Bulls," who live but for their business and their stomach. Go to, ye who say that there is no pleasure in the mere consumption and mastication of food! Watch these old men: note the bobbing of their pendulous red cheeks, like the gills of a turkey-cock; see the lighting-up of that dull fishy eye as the waiter advances bearing the duck and peas which follow so pleasantly after the course of fish; mark the eagerness with which that pulpy, shaky, mottled old hand clutches the champagne-glass destined to cool the throat now fired with the devilled bait; listen to the cluckling sound with which these old jaws wag o'er the melting marrowfats,—and then say what is the *summum bonum* of human happiness. To this man you might read the sweetest poem of Tennyson, the most touching pathos of Dickens, and he would not experience an emotion; but let his potatoes be soddened or his gravy burnt, and you shall behold a rage worthy of Marino Faliero, and a grief compared to which that of Rachel weeping for her children was a delusion and a sham!

And now let us glance at the internal economy of this house—The Vessel.

From the 1st of April to the 30th of September, Pleasure's business is in full swing here, and never allows the smallest relaxation. With a view to such business, and nothing else, The Vessel was built. On the heading of its bills it calls itself an hotel; but you might search in vain on The Vessel's basement for the commercial-room; you might pass the remainder of your life hunting without success for the large family bedrooms, or the stuffy cupboards in which bachelors are made to pass the night. There are no baths and no billiard-room, no quaint assembly-room leading up three steps at the end of the first-floor passage, and smelling as if the ghosts of our gavotte-dancing grandmothers still inhabited it. You will never find rows of boots with number-chalked soles standing outside its chamber-doors, nor regiments of bed-candlesticks on its hall-table; no "boots" lurks up its stairs at the chilly hours of the morning to call any one who is going by the first train, nor has such a thing as a "breakfast order" ever been heard within its capacious walls. From its cellar to its attic The Vessel means dinner, and nothing but dinner. On its ground-floor are its hall, a lavatory, and the coffee-room with its numbered tables and its cheery look-out on the river. On the first-floor are the large rooms used for City-companies, testimonial-dinners, and such-like, at which between two and three hundred guests often sit down simultaneously; above are the smaller rooms used for private parties. Each of these rooms is distinguished by a name—the Nelson, the Beaufort, the Wellington, &c.—and the party in each is accredited with the dinner, wine, &c. ordered and consumed, in the following fashion. In the bar sits the booking-clerk at a desk; behind him is a speaking-pipe; at his side are two flexible tubes, one descending to the cellar, the other to the kitchen. Down the speaking-pipe comes a roar: "Wellington —ice-pudding, bottle of decent hock." Book-keeper gives ice-pudding order, but is slightly confounded about wine, so calls up, "Wellington! sparkling hock, did you say?" Answer: "Decent hock, gentleman said." "All right." Then down cellarman's tube: "Wellington—bottle hock No. 3." The principal cellarman has two assistants, who are despatched for wine while he books each order against the particular room named. The system of check is thus treble, and at the end of the evening, when accounts are made up, three entries of every order are brought forward—that is to say, the waiter's who gives it, the booking-clerk through whom it passes, and the cellar-man who executes it. The cellars are perfect marvels of order and systematic detail; and so thorough is the supervision, and so accurate the check, that the superintendent, looking at the last stock-taking, can reckon the consumption to the moment of inquiry, and can at any time give you to a bottle the exact state of any bin in the vast cellarage. While on this subject, it is worth noticing that though the cellar contains numerous specimens of rare wines and curious vintages, it is very seldom indeed that they are called for. Punch, sherry, and champagne with the dinner,—and nearly always champagne,—it seems to be a fixed idea with Greenwich diners, more especially with those who but seldom indulge in such a luxury, that champagne is a positive necessity. After dinner, by men of the present generation, and at parties where ladies are present, claret is generally drunk; but at the great feeds of the City-companies, at the testimonial-presentation dinners, at the annual gatherings of old gentlemen belonging to eccentrically-named clubs—institutions with a superstructure of indulgence springing from a substratum of charity—nothing but East-India brown sherry and sound port ever "sparkle on the board" after the cloth has been removed from it.

On the first-floor is a kitchen, which supplies that and the floor above, while the house is pierced with "lifts" for the speedy conveyance of hot dishes and removal of plates, glasses, &c. One of these lifts penetrates to the cellar, and brings up the wine fresh and cool from the deep dark bins; one fetches the fruit and dessert from that bower wherein a pretty girl passes her life engaged in the dispensation of such luxuries; several are perpetually clattering down into the kitchens, and returning laden with different courses, all set out in order for the particular room, the waiter attached to which is in attendance to receive them. The same order and regularity which pervades the rest of the establishment is brought to play upon the waiters: to each man the plate given out is counted and entered on a record; each has his own particular cutlery and glass; each is accountable for every thing supplied to him; each has, as the first instalment of his day's labour, to cut up a huge brown loaf into that timber-yard arrangement of delicious slices, without which no Greenwich dinner would be complete. Added to this, on every floor in the secret recesses unexplored by the general public, hangs a written code of laws and a table of fines applicable to waiters' irregularities. At the Greenwich houses the majority of the waiters will be found to be foreigners, and they are mostly sons of German innkeepers, many of them men of worldly position, who have come over here to acquire a knowledge of their business, and an insight into the ways of the world. The head-waiter at such a house as The Vessel is a superior man; at large dinners he draws a regular sketch of the table, which is generally in horse-shoe form, and on an average holds thirty-five dishes, seventeen on either side, and a huge centre-piece before the chairman; he arranges them artistically, and can in an instant denote the exact place of any dish. The daily list of eatables is prepared each morning by the superintendent (one of the partners), and nearly every article is purchased in Greenwich. Some of the fish is purchased in Billingsgate, but most comes from two local fishmongers, who each morning supply a priced tariff of what they have to offer. The meat and nearly all the vegetables are purchased in the neighbourhood; and with such exactness are The Vessel's books kept, that the precise amount spent in lucifer-matches during the season is entered, and figures with other equally small items in the grand total of the partnership account. What these accounts must be for fish alone may be guessed, when it is recorded here that between the 1st of April and the 30th of September, there is an average consumption of *thirty-five thousand* flounders.

Whitebait, without which there would be no Vessel, and in the minds of a great many people no Greenwich—whitebait, which Theodore Hook called "curl-papers fried in batter," which most people sneer at as nothing, and which every body eats with delight—are caught where the water is a little brackish, generally between Barking and Greenhithe, with a net thirty feet long and twelve feet wide. This net is cast always in daylight, either at high or low water, and remains two feet below the surface until nearly the ebb or flood, as the case may be. At the commencement of the spring whitebait first appear, but not in large quantities, as these are old fish who escaped the last year's netting; about the middle of April the young fry, perfectly transparent, arrive, and in the first week in May come to perfection. So it continues for a couple of months; then gradually whitebait get larger and larger, and about the close of September are lost sight of altogether. There is a speciality for dressing "bait;" and the fisherman who, assisted by his son, for upwards of a score of years has supplied The Vessel, not only catches the whitebait, but cooks them. On a glowing coke-fire is placed a large frying-pan full of boiling lard; the fish, first thoroughly rolled in flour, are placed in a cloth, which is plunged into the hissing fat. The cook, a perfect Salamander, utterly impervious to the frightful heat which makes strangers wink and beat a hasty retreat, takes the handle of the frying-pan and turns it from right to left, peering in at the seething mass. In two minutes the cooking is accomplished, and the fish are emptied out of the cloth on to a dish. Ye who would taste your bait in perfection, get permission to eat it in the kitchen! Salmon come from the banks of the Severn and Tweed, soles from Texel and Torbay, whiting and mackerel from the South Coast, smelts from the Medway, turbots from Dover, eels and flounders from the Thames, perch and crayfish from Oxford, lobsters from the coast of Norway, trout principally from Loch Leven, red mullet from the Channel Islands.

Here is an example of the manner in which the Business of Pleasure is carried on with the utmost regularity and precision; with every precaution of check and counter-check, book-keeping, and all the paraphernalia of ledger-demain which respectability prescribes (in no Manchester cotton-broker's or Liverpool ship-owner's offices could the accounts be more closely kept); with the liberal diffusion of a huge capital, and the employment of a large number of hard-working persons.

CHAPTER IV.

RIDING LONDON: OF OMNIBUSES.

WEIGHING thirteen stone, standing six feet high, possessed of an indomitable laziness, and having occasion constantly to go from one part of town to the other, I want to know how I am to have my requirements attended to with ease and comfort to myself. If my name were Schemsiluihar, and I had lived ages ago at Bagdad, I should have gone quietly into the garden, and, after rubbing my ring on my lamp, or burning my incense, I should have prostrated myself before an enormous genie, who would have been very much hurt by my humility, would straightway have proclaimed himself my slave, and, after hearing my wants, would immediately have provided me with four feet square of best Turkey carpet, on which I had only to deposit myself to be wafted through the air to my destination; or he would have produced a roc for me to sit astride on; or an enchanted horse with a series of pegs in his neck, like a fiddle, the mere manipulation of which increased or checked his speed. But as I happen to live in the benighted year of peace '63, as my name is Nomatter, and as I reside in Little Flotsam Street, Jetsam Gardens, N.W., the carpet, the roc, and the peggy steed are unavailable. I could walk? Yes, but I won't. I hate walking; it makes me hot, and uncomfortable, and savage: when walking, I either fall into a train of thought, or I get gaping at surrounding objects and passing people, both of which feats have the same result, namely, my tumbling up against other pedestrians, straying into the road under the hoofs of horses, and getting myself generally objurgated and hi'd at. I couldn't ride on horseback, because no man with any sense in his head, combined with any weight in his body, could ride a horse over London's greasy stones. I could ride in a cab, but it is too expensive; in a brougham, but for the same reason doubly magnified, with the additional fact that I do not possess one. Leaving out of the question the absurdity of the proceeding, there is no living man capable of conveying me for several miles in a wheelbarrow; and when I state that I have never yet been the subject of a commission de lunatico, I need offer no further explanation of my declining to ride in a velocipede—a humorous conveyance like the under-carriage of a chariot, the occupant of which apparently rests himself by using his arms as well as his legs for his propulsion.

When I was a boy at school, I recollect in the shop-windows prints of an aerial machine, a delightful conveyance like an enormous bat, sailing over London (which was represented by the dome of St. Paul's and a couple of church-spires), and filled with elegantly-dressed company, who were chatting to each other without the smallest appearance of astonishment. I cannot positively state that there was a captain depicted as in command of this atmospheric vessel, though my belief leans that way; but I perfectly well remember a "man at the wheel," grasping a tiller like a cheese-cutter, and directing the course with the greatest ease and freedom. This would have been an eligible mode of conveyance had the scheme ever been carried out; but the inventor only got as far as the print, and there apparently exhausted himself, as I never heard any thing further of it. And this, by the way, reminds me that an occasional trip in Mr. Coxwell's balloon would be a novel and an exciting method of getting over the ground, only there being no "man at the wheel," there is a consequent absence of definite knowledge as to where you are going; and if I, bent on travelling from Jetsam Gardens to Canonbury Square, were to see Mr. Coxwell looking vaguely out, and were to hear him remarking, "Isn't that Beachy Head?" I should feel uncomfortable.

So I am compelled to fall back on a cheap, easy, and, to a certain extent, expeditious mode of locomotion, and to travel by the omnibus. I am aware that professed cynics will sneer at my use of the word 'expeditious.' There are, I believe, journeys performed in the middle of the day, when the snail gallops gaily past the outward-bound suburban omnibus, and when the tortoise, having an appointment to keep at the Ship and Turtle, prefers to walk, in order that he may be in time; but the middle of the day is consecrated to old ladies going "into the City" on business, while my experience is confined to the early morning and the late evening, when we run "express," and when, I will venture to wager, we go as fast, the crowded state of the streets considered, as ever did the York Highflyer or the Brighton Age. My associations with omnibuses are from my youth upward. As a child I lived in a very large thoroughfare, and I used to stand for hours at the window watching the red Hammersmith omnibuses, luminous with the name of "GEORGE CLOUD," and the white Putney and Richmond omnibuses, and the green "Favourites," boldly declaring the ownership of "ELIZABETH and JOHN WILSON,"—grand 'buses those, with drivers and conductors in green liveries, always renewed (with an accompaniment of nosegay for buttonhole, and favours for whip, and rosettes for horses' ears) on the occasion of the Queen's birthday. I was originally taken to school in a hackney-coach,—I perfectly well recollect kneeling at the bottom in the straw as we (I and a broken-hearted aunt) ascended Highgate Hill, and imploring tearfully to be taken back home, even in the lowest menial capacity,—but I came back in an omnibus, in a high state of effervescence, and with a large stock of worldly experience. I first saw her who, as the bagmen's toast says, doubles the pleasures and halves the sorrows of my life, as I stepped off an omnibus. I first went down to my office on an omnibus; and I still patronise that same conveyance, where, I may incidentally mention, I am a "regular," that I always have the seat next the coachman on the off-side, and that my opinion on the news from America is always anxiously expected by my fellow-passengers. Long since, however, have the omnibuses of my childhood been "run off the road." Mr. George Cloud and his compeers have retired; and the whole metropolitan service, with very few exceptions, is worked by the London General Omnibus Company; concerning which,—its rise, origin, and progress, and the manner in which it is carried on,—I have, under proper official authority, made full inquiry, and now intend to report.

If the present Emperor of the French had succeeded in his memorable expedition with the tame eagle to Boulogne, it is probable that we in England might still be going on with the old separate proprietary system of omnibuses; but as the tame-eagle expedition (majestic in itself) was a failure, its smaller component parts had to escape as they best could. Among these smaller component parts was one Orsi, captain of the steamer conveying the intruding emperor; and Orsi, flying from justice, flew, after the manner of his kind, to England, and there established himself. Years after, in 1855, this M. Orsi bethought himself of a scheme for simultaneously improving his own fortunes and bettering the condition of London omnibus-traffic, by assimilating its management to that which for a long time had worked admirably in Paris. He accordingly associated with himself a crafty long-headed man of business, one M. Foucard, and they together drew up such a specious prospectus, that when they submitted it to four of the principal London omnibus-proprietors, Messrs. Macnamara, Wilson, Willing, and Hartley, these gentlemen, all thoroughly versed in their business, so far saw their way, that they at once consented to enter into the proposal, and became the agents for Messieurs Orsi and Foucard. The division of labour then commenced: the Frenchmen started for Paris, there to establish their company (for our English laws on mercantile liability and the dangers of shareholding were, a few years ago, much foggier, and thicker, and less intelligible, and more dangerous than they are now); and so well did they succeed, that, in a very short time, they had raised and perfected as a "Société en Commandite" the "Compagnie Générale des Omnibus de Londres," with a capital of 700,000*l.*, in shares of 100 francs (or 4*l.*) each; three-fourths of the capital—such was our neighbours' belief in our business talents and luck in matters touching upon horseflesh—being subscribed in France. Meantime, the English section were not idle: as agents for the two Frenchmen they bought up the rolling stock, horses, harness, stabling, and good-will of nearly all the then existent omnibus-proprietors; they became purchasers of six hundred omnibuses and six thousand horses, of an enormous staff of coachmen, conductors, time-keepers, horse-keepers, washers, and other workmen; and, what was very important, they possessed themselves of the "times" of all the important routes in London and the suburbs. These "times" are, in fact, the good-will of the roads, and were considered so valuable, that in some cases as much as from 200*l.* to 250*l.* were given for the "times" of one omnibus. Under this form, then, the company at once commenced work, Messrs. Macnamara, Carteret, and Willing acting as its *gérants* (managers), with no other English legal standing; and under this form, that is to say, as a French company with English managers, it worked until the 31st of December 1857, when, the Limited Liability Act having come into operation, by resolution of the French shareholders the "Société en Commandite" was transformed into an English company, and bloomed-out, in all the glory of fresh paint on all its vehicles, as the London General Omnibus Company (Limited). With this title, and under the managerial arrangements then made, it has continued ever since.

With the exception of some very few private proprietors, and one organised opposition company (the "Citizen"), the entire omnibus service of the metropolis and its suburbs, extending from Highgate in the north to Peckham in the south, and from Hampstead in the north-west to Greenwich in the south-east, embracing more than seventy routes, is worked by—as it is called familiarly—the "London General." In this traffic are engaged upwards of six hundred omnibuses and six thousand horses, the working of which is divided into ten separate districts, each with a head district establishment. Each of these omnibuses travels on an average sixty miles a day, and to each is attached a stud of ten horses, under the care of a horsekeeper, who is responsible for them, and who knows the exact times when they will be wanted, and whose duty it is to devote himself to them. A horse is seldom changed from one stud to another, or removed, except in case of illness; each horse is numbered, and all the particulars relating to him are entered in a book kept by the foreman of the yard. The purchase-cost of these horses averages twenty-six pounds apiece, and the majority of them come from Yorkshire, though agents of the company attend all the principal fairs in England. They are of all kinds: long straggling bony hacks, short thick cobs; some looking like broken-down hunters, some like "cast" dragoon-chargers, some like Suffolk Punches who have come to grief; but the style most valued is, I am told, a short thick horse, low in the leg, round in the barrel, and with full strong quarters, whence all the propelling power comes. They are of all colours,—blacks, bays, chestnuts, browns, grays,—though the predominant shade is that reddish bay so ugly in a common horse, so splendid (more especially when set off by black points) in a velvet-skinned thorough-bred; a colour particularly affected by the manufacturers of the studs in those toy-stables which are always furnished with a movable groom in top-boots, a striped jacket, and a tasselled cap, with a grin of singular vacuity on his wooden countenance. The average work of each horse is from three to four hours a day, and each horse consumes daily an allowance of sixteen pounds of bruised oats and ten pounds of mixture, formed of three parts hay and one part straw. Their general health is, considering their work, remarkably good; to attend to it there are eight veterinary surgeons, who are responsible for the health of the whole horse-establishment, and who are paid by contract, receiving four guineas a year for each stud of ten horses. The shoeing is also contract-work, twenty-five farriers being paid two pounds per month for each stud. At Highbury, where there is a large dépôt of six hundred horses, there are exceptions to both these rules; a veterinary surgeon and a farrier, each the servant of the company, being attached to the establishment. I went the round of the premises—a vast place, covering altogether some fifteen acres—with the veterinary surgeon, and saw much to praise and nothing to condemn. True, the stables are not such as you would see at Malton, Dewsbury, or any of the great racing-establishments, being for the most part long low sheds, the horses being separated merely by swinging bars, and rough litter taking the place of dry beds and plaited straw; but the ventilation was by no means bad, and the condition of the animals certainly good. My companion told me that glanders, that frightful scourge, was almost unknown; that sprains, curbs, and sand-cracks were the commonest disorders; and that many of his cases resulted from the horses having become injured in the feet by picking up nails in the streets and yards. There are a few loose boxes for virulent contagious disorders and "suspicious" cases, but it appeared to me that more were wanted, and that as "overwork" is one of the most prevalent of omnibus-horse disorders, it would be a great boon if the company could possess itself of some large farm or series of field-paddocks, where such members of their stud as are so debilitated could be turned out to grass to rest for a time. Some such arrangement is, I believe, in contemplation; but the company has only a short lease of their Highbury premises, and is doubtful as to its future arrangements there. While on this subject I may state that an omnibus-horse generally lasts from three to four years, though some are in full work for six or seven, while there are a few old stagers who have been on the road ten or twelve.

The coach-building department also has its head-quarters at Highbury, and employs one hundred and ninety men, whose average wages are two hundred and fifty pounds a week. Here all the omnibuses (with the exception of some six-and-twenty provided by two contractors) are built and repaired, as are also the vans used in conveying the forage to the outlying establishments from the central dépôt (of which more anon), and the chaise-carts and four-wheelers in which the superintendents visit their different districts. Every morning at six A.M. three compact little vans leave Highbury for the various districts, each containing three men, and an assortment of wheels, axles, and tools, for any repairs that may be wanted. One of these men is always left behind at the head district-dépôt, to meet any contingency that may arise during the day. When an accident occurs in the street, an omnibus is immediately despatched to take the place of that which has broken down; the "plates" (*i. e.* the legal authorisation of the Inland Revenue) are shifted from one to the other; and if the smash has been serious, a large van arrives and brings off the disabled omnibus bodily up to Highbury. But such accidents are very rare, owing to the constant supervision given to the axles, tons of which are constantly thrown aside. These axles are all manufactured on the premises, and are composed of ten or twelve pieces of iron "fagoted" together. The trade or cost price of an ordinary omnibus is one hundred and thirty pounds; but the large three-horse vehicles, which are of tremendous weight (those from Manchester, in use in 1862 plying to the Exhibition, weighed thirty-six cwt.), cost two hundred pounds. The ordinary time of wear is ten years; after that they are of little use, though some last seventeen years. The wheels require entire renewal every three years, and during that time they are under frequent repairs, the tires lasting but a few months. So soon as an omnibus is condemned, it is broken up; such portions of it as are still serviceable are used up in repairing other omnibuses, but in a new omnibus every bit is thoroughly new. The condemned omnibuses stand out in an open yard abutting on the line of the North-London Railway; and the superintendent of the coach-builders told me he had often been amused at hearing the loudly-expressed indignation of the railway passengers at the shameful condition of the company's omnibuses — they imagining that the worn-out old vehicles awaiting destruction, which they saw from their railway carriage-windows, were the ordinary rolling stock of the London General. The wood used in the composition of the omnibuses is English and American ash, elm, deal, and Honduras; but the poles are invariably formed of stout English ash. The superintendent told me that these poles last far less time than formerly; and this he attributes to the stoppages having become so much more frequent, owing to the introduction of short fares; the strain upon the pole, occasioned by constant pulling-up, gradually frays the wood and causes an untimely smash. Before I left I was shown an ingenious contrivance for defeating the attacks of those universal enemies, the street-boys. It appears that the passengers of a little omnibus which runs from Highbury Terrace to Highbury Barn, and which, for its short journey, has no conductor, were horribly annoyed by boys who *would* ride on the step and jeer with ribaldry at the people inside. To beat them, my friend the superintendent invented what he calls a "crinoline," which, when the door is shut, entirely encloses the step, and so cuts away any resting-place or vantage-ground for the marauding boy.

The dépôt where all the provender is received, mixed, and served-out for all the district establishments, is at Irongate Wharf, Paddington, on the banks of the Regent's Canal; a convenient arrangement when it is considered that the barges bring stores to the doors at the rate of fourpence-halfpenny per quarter, while the land-transport for the same would cost one shilling. Hay is, however, generally brought in at the land-gates, for the facility of the weigh-bridge immediately outside the superintendent's office, over which all carts going in or out are expected to pass. There is no settled contractor for hay, but there is no lack of eager sellers; for the company are known to be quick ready-money purchasers, and a transaction with them saves a long day's waiting in the market. On this same account the company are gainers in the deal, to the extent of the expenses which a day's waiting in the market must involve for rest and refreshment for driver and horses. When a sample-load is driven into the yard and approved of by the superintendent, a couple of trusses are taken from it and placed under lock and key, to serve as reference for quality; and when the general supply comes in, every truss which is not equal to the quality of the sample is rejected by the foreman, who carefully watches the delivery. The whole of the machinery-work of the building is performed by steam-power, erected on the basement-floor, and consisting of two engines of two-hundred-and-fifteen-horse power, consuming four tons of coal a week. By their agency the hay received from the country wagons is hoisted in "cradles" to the topmost story of the building, where it is unpacked from its tightened trusses; to the same floor come swinging up in chain-suspended sacks, the oats from the barges on the canal, and these are both delivered over to the steam-demon, who delivers them, the hay separated and fined, and the oats slightly bruised (not crushed), and freed from all straw and dirt and stones, through wooden shoots and "hoppers," into the floor beneath. There—in the preparation-room—the ever-busy engines show their power in constantly-revolving leather bands, in whirling wheels, and spinning knife-blades, and sparkling grindstones; there, are men constantly allaying the incessant thirst of the "cutters" with offerings of mixed hay and straw, which in a second are resolved into a thick impervious mixture; while in another part of the room the bruised oats into which it is to be amalgamated are slowly descending to their doom. All the "cutters" are covered over with tin cases, else the dust germinated from the flying chaff would be insupportable; while at the hand of every man is a break, a simple lever, by the raising of which, in case of any accident, he could at once reverse the action of the machinery. Descending to the next floor, we find the results of the cutters and the bruisers; there, stand stalwart men covered with perspiration, stripped to the shirt-sleeves, and who have large baskets in front of them at the mouths of the shoots, anxiously awaiting their prey. Down comes a mass of chaff, the basket is full, a man seizes it, and empties it into a huge square trough before him; from another shoot, another basket is filled with bruised oats: these he empties into the trough on the top of the chaff; he pauses for one minute; a whistle, forming the top of a pipe descending into the basement-story, is heard, that signals "All right and ready." He turns a handle, and presto! the floor of the trough turns into tumbling waves of metal, which toss the oats and the chaff hither and thither, mix them up, and finally drop them, a heterogeneous mass of horse-food, into sacks waiting their arrival below. Three of these sacks are sent away daily as food for each stud of ten horses; seven large provender-vans are, throughout the whole of the day, conveying sacks to the different district establishments; twenty-six men are engaged at this dépôt, each from six A.M. to six P.M.; and the whole affair works without a hitch.

I have treated of the horse service, the coach-building service, and the foraging service of the company. I may in conclusion come to its human service, the drivers and conductors.

Each man, before entering on his duties, is required to obtain from the Chief Commissioner of the Metropolitan Police, a license to act. To obtain this, he must give reference to three respectable householders, and deposit five shillings for the expenses attendant on the necessary inquiries and issue of the license. If the references be satisfactory, a license, in printed form, describing the name, address, and general appearance of the holder, is granted, and with it the metal badge to be worn when on duty. These licenses are renewable on the first of June in each year, and as the magistrates endorse on the paper every conviction or reprimand, the renewal of the license is necessarily dependent on the possessor showing a clean bill of health. If the driver have no serious blot on his character, and can prove to the satisfaction of the superintendent that he is competent for the management of horses, he is generally at once accepted; but the conductor's character must stand a greater test. He is virtually the representative of the company on the omnibus, and to him is confided a large amount of discretionary power, such as the refusal to carry intoxicated people, or such persons as by dress, demeanour, &c., may be "fairly objectional to the passengers." He is constituted the arbitrator among "brawling passengers," and has, indeed, a very stringent code of rules laid down for his guidance—one of which is, that he is to "abstain from any approach to familiarity," which—as in the case of a pretty maid-servant with a not unnatural susceptibility to approach—is, I take it, soul-harrowing and impossible to be carried out. As regards the collection of money, each conductor is provided with a printed form of "journey-ticket," on which, at the end of every journey, he is required to render an account, at some office on the route, of the number of passengers carried, and the amount of moneys received. At the end of the day he makes a summary, on another form, of the whole of his journey-tickets, and next morning he pays over, to the clerk in the office, the money he has received during the previous day, deducting his own wages and those of the driver, and any tolls he may have paid. Every driver receives six shillings a day, every conductor four shillings, out of which the driver has to provide his whip and apron, and the conductor the lamp and oil for the interior of the omnibus. Both classes of men are daily servants, liable to discharge at a day's warning, but either can rest occasionally by employing an "odd man," of whom there are several at each district establishment, ready to do "odd" work, from which they are promoted to regular employment.

The receipts of the company are very large, averaging between eleven and twelve thousand pounds a week (in one week of the Exhibition year they were above seventeen thousand pounds), and I asked one of the chief officers if he thought they were much pillaged. He told me he had not the least doubt that, by conductors alone, they were robbed to the extent of *twenty-five thousand pounds a year*; and a practical superintendent of large experience, on my repeating this to him, declared that he believed that sum did not represent the half of their losses from the same source. I asked whether no check could be devised, and was told none—at least, none so efficient as to be worthy of the name. Indicators of all kinds have been suggested; but every indicator was at the mercy of the conductor, who could clog it with wood, and so allow three or more persons to enter or depart, while the indicator only recorded the entrance or exit of one; and unless some such turn-table as the turn-table in use at Waterloo Bridge could be applied (for which there is obviously no space in an omnibus), check was impossible. The sole approach to such check lay in the services rendered by a class of persons technically known as "bookers," who were, in fact, spies travelling in the omnibus, and yielding to the company an account of every passenger, the length of his ride, and the amount of his fare. But it was only in extreme cases, where the conductor was incautious beyond measure, that such evidence could be efficient against him. These "bookers" are of all classes, men, women, and children, all acting under one head, to whom they are responsible, and who alone is recognised by the company. The best of them is a woman, who, it is boasted, can travel from Islington to Chelsea, and give an exact account of every passenger, where he got in, where he got out, what he was like, and the fare he paid.

I think I have now enumerated most of the prominent features of our omnibus system. When I have casually mentioned to friends the work on which I was engaged, I have been requested to bring forward this grievance and that. Brownsmith, weighing fifteen stone, wants only five persons allowed on one seat; little Iklass, standing four feet six in height, wants easier method of access to the roof. But my intention was description, not criticism; and, even if it were, I doubt whether I should be inclined to represent that any large public body, comparatively recently established, could on the whole be expected to do their work better than the "London General."

CHAPTER V.

RIDING LONDON: OF CABS, JOBS, AND BLACK JOBS.

THERE is a very large class of Riding London, which, while not sufficiently rich to keep its private carriage, holds omnibus conveyance in contempt and scorn, loathes flys, and pins its vehicular faith on cabs alone. To this class belong lawyers' clerks, of whom, red bag-holding and perspiration-covered, there are always two or three at the Holborn end of Chancery Lane flinging themselves into Hansoms, and being whirled off to Guildhall or Westminster; to it belong newspaper reporters, with their note-books in their breast-pockets, hurrying up from parliament debates to their offices, there to turn their mystic hieroglyphics into sonorous phrases; to it belong stockbrokers having "time bargains" to transact; editors hunting up "copy" from recalcitrant contributors; artists hurrying to be in time with their pictures ere the stern exhibition-gallery porter closes the door, and, pointing to the clock, says, "It's struck!"—young gentlemen going to or coming from Cremorne; and all people who have to catch trains, keep appointments, or do anything by a certain specified time, and who, following the grand governing law of human nature, have, in old ladies' phraseology, "driven everything to the last." To such people a Hansom cab is a primary matter of faith; and certainly, when provided with a large pair of wheels, a thick round tubby horse (your thin bony rather blood-looking dancing jumping quadruped lately introduced is no good at all for speed), and a clever driver, there is nothing to compare to it. Not the big swinging pretentious remise of Paris or Brussels; not the heavy, rumbling, bone-dislocating droskies of Berlin or Vienna, with their blue-bloused accordion-capped drivers; not the droschky of St. Petersburg, with its vermin-swarming Ischvostchik; not the shatteradan calesas of Madrid, with its garlic-reeking conductor! Certainly not the old vaulty hackney-coach; the jiffling dangerous cabriolet, where the driver sat beside you, and shot you into the street at his will and pleasure; the "slice," the entrance to which was from the back; the "tribus," and other wild vehicles which immediately succeeded the extinction of the old cabriolet, which had their trial, and then passed away as failures. There are still about half-a-dozen hackney coaches of the "good old" build, though much more modest in the matter of paint and heraldry than they used to be; but these are attached entirely to the metropolitan railway stations, and are only made use of by Paterfamilias with much luggage and many infants on his return from the annual sea-side visit. Cabs, both of the Hansom and Clarence build, are the staple conveyance of middle-class Riding London; and of these we now propose to treat.

Although there are, plying in the streets, nearly five thousand cabs, there are only some half-dozen large masters who hold from thirty to fifty vehicles each, the remainder being owned by struggling men, who either thrive and continue, or break and relapse into their old position of drivers, horsekeepers, conductors, or something even more anomalous, according to the season and the state of trade. My inquiries on this subject were made of one of the principal masters, whose name I knew from constantly seeing it about the streets, but with whom I had not the smallest personal acquaintance. I had previously written to him, announcing my intended visit and its object; but when I arrived at the stables, I found their owner evidently perceiving a divided duty, and struggling between natural civility and an enforced reticence. Yes, he wished to do what was right, Lor' bless me! but—and here he stopped, and cleared his throat, and looked, prophetically, afar off, over the stables' roof, and at the pigeons careering over Lamb's Conduit Street. I waited and waited, and at last out it came. Would I be fair and 'boveboard? I would! No hole-and-corner circumwentin? I didn't clearly know what this meant, but I pledged my word then there should be none of it. Well, then—was I a agent of this new cab company as he'd heard was about to be started? Explaining in full detail my errand, I never got more excellent information, more honestly and cheerfully given.

My friend had on an average thirty-five cabs in use, and all of these were built on his own premises and by his own men. There was very little, if any, difference between the price of building a Hansom or a Clarence cab, the cost of each, when well turned out, averaging fifty guineas. To every cab there are, of necessity, two horses; but a careful cab-master will allow seven horses to three cabs, the extra animal being required in case of overwork or illness, either or both of which are by no means of unfrequent occurrence. These horses are not bought at any particular place, but are picked up as opportunity offers. Aldridge's and the Repository in Barbican furnish many of them. Many are confirmed "screws," some are well-bred horses with unmistakable symptoms of imminent disease, others with incurable vice—incurable, that is to say, until after a fortnight's experience of a Hansom's shafts, when they generally are reduced to lamb-like quietude. There is no average price, the sums given varying from ten-to five-and-twenty pounds; nor can their lasting qualities be reduced to an average, as some knock up and are consigned to the slaughterer after a few weeks, while other old stagers battle with existence for a dozen years. In the season, cabs are generally out on a stretch of fifteen hours, going out between nine or ten A.M., returning to change horses between three and five P.M., starting afresh, and finally returning home between midnight and one A.M. Of course there are cabs which leave the yard and return at earlier times, and during the height of the Cremorne festivities there are many which do not go out till noon, and seldom appear again at the stables until broad daylight about four A.M. These are far from being the worst paid of the cab fraternity; as a visit to Cremorne, and a mingling in its pleasures, is by no means productive of stinginess to the cabman, but occasionally results in a wish on the part of the fare to ride on the box, to drive the horse, and to proffer cigars and convivial refreshment on every possible occasion. Each cabman on starting carries a horse-bag with him containing three feeds of mixed chaff, which horse-bag is replenished before he leaves for his afternoon trip. The cab-masters, however, impress upon their men the unadvisability of watering their horses at inn-yards or from watermen's pails, as much disease is generated in this manner.

The monetary arrangements between cab-masters and cabmen are peculiar. The master pays his man no wages; on the contrary, the man hires horse and vehicle from his master;

and, having to pay him a certain sum, leaves his own earnings to chance, to which amicable arrangement we may ascribe the conciliatory manners and the avoidance of all attempts at extortion which characterise these gentry. For Clarence cabs the masters charge sixteen shillings a day, while Hansoms command from two to three shillings a day extra; and they are well worth it to the men, not merely from their ordinary popularity, but just at the present time, when, as was explained, there is a notion in the minds of most old ladies that every four-wheel cab has just conveyed a patient to the Small-Pox Hospital, the free open airy Hansoms are in great demand. In addition to his lawful fares, the perquisites or "pickings" of the cabman may be large. To him the law of treasure-trove is a dead letter; true, there exists a regulation that all property left in any public vehicle is to be deposited with the registrar at Somerset House; but a very small per-centage finds its way to that governmental establishment. The cabman has, unwittingly, a great reverence for the old feudal system, and claims over anything which he may seize the right of freewarren, saccage and soccage, cuisage and jambage, fosse and fork, infang theofe, and outfang theofe; and out of all those port-monnaies, pocket-books, reticules, ladies' bags, portmanteaus, cigar-cases, deeds, documents, books, sticks, and umbrellas, duly advertised in the second column of the *Times* as "left in a cab," very few find their way to Somerset House. I knew of an old gentleman of muddle-headed tendencies who left four thousand pounds' worth of Dutch coupons, payable to bearer, in a hack Clarence cab; years have elapsed, and despite all the energies of the detective police and the offer of fabulous rewards, those coupons have never been recovered, nor will they be until the day of settlement arrives, when the adjudication as to who is their rightful owner—with a necessarily strong claim on the part of their then possessor—will afford a pretty bone of contention for exponents of the law. All that the driver has to find as his equipment, is his whip (occasionally, by some masters, lost nose-bags are placed to his account); and having provided himself with that, and his license, he can go forth.

But there is a very large class of London people to whom the possession of a private carriage of their own is the great ambition of life, a hope long deferred, which, however sick it has made the heart for years, coming at last yields an amount of pleasure worth the waiting for. Nine-tenths of these people job their horses. Those pretty, low-quartered, high-crested brougham-horses, with the champing mouths and the tossing heads, which career up and down the Ladies' Mile; those splendid steppers, all covered with fleck and foam, which the bewigged coachman tools round and round Grosvenor Square while "waiting to take-up;" those long, lean-bodied, ill-looking, but serviceable horses which pass their day in dragging Dr. Bolus from patient to patient,—all are jobbed. It is said that any man of common sense setting-up his carriage in London will job his horses. There are four or five great job-masters in town who have the best horses in the metropolis at command, and who are neither dealers nor commission-agents, but with whom jobbing is the sole vocation. And, at a given price, they can, at a few days' notice, provide you with any class of animal you may require. Either in person, or by a trusty agent, they attend all the large horse-fairs in the kingdom; or should they by any chance be unrepresented there, they are speedily waited on by the dealers, who know the exact class of horse which the job-master requires. Horses are bought by them at all ages, from three to seven. Young horses are broken-in at four years old, and when their tuition is commenced in the autumn, they are generally found ready for letting in the succeeding spring. The breaking-in is one of the most difficult parts of the job-master's business. The young horse is harnessed to a break by the side of an experienced old stager, known as a "break-horse," who does nothing but "break" work, who is of the utmost assistance to the break-driver, and who, when thoroughly competent, is beyond all price. Such a break-horse will put up with all the vagaries of his youthful companion; will combine with the driver to check all tendencies on the part of the neophyte to bolt, shy, back, or plunge; and if his young friend be stubborn, or devote himself to jibbing or standing stock-still, will seize him by the neck with his teeth, and, by a combination of strength and cunning, pull him off and set him in motion.

The prices charged by job-masters vary according to the class of horse required and according to the length of the job. Many country gentlemen bringing their families to London for the season hire horses for a three or a six months' job, and they have to pay in proportion a much higher rate than those who enter into a yearly contract. For the very best style of horse, combining beauty, action, and strength, a job-master will charge a hundred guineas a year, exclusive of forage; but the best plan for the man of moderate means, who looks for work from his horses in preference to show, and who has neither time, knowledge, nor inclination to be in a perpetual squabble with grooms and corn-chandlers, is to pay for his horses at a certain price which includes forage and shoeing. Under these conditions, the yearly price for one horse is ninety guineas; for a pair, one hundred and sixty guineas; and for this payment he may be certain of getting sound, serviceable, thoroughly creditable-looking animals (which he may himself select from a stud of two or three hundred), which are well-fed by the job-master, and shod whenever requisite by the farrier nearest to the hirer's stables, to whom the job-master is responsible, and which, when one falls lame or ill, are replaced in half an hour. Having made this arrangement, the gentleman setting up his carriage has only to provide himself with stables, which, with coach-house, loft, and man's room, cost from twenty pounds to thirty pounds a year; to hire a coachman, costing from one guinea to twenty-five shillings a week; to purchase a carriage-setter (a machine for hoisting the wheels, to allow of their being twirled for proper cleaning), and the ordinary pails, brushes, and sponges, and to allow a sum for ordinary expenses, which, according to the extravagance or economy of his coachman, will stand him in from six pounds to twelve pounds a year. If more than two horses are kept, the services of a helper, at twelve shillings a week, will be required; and it is scarcely necessary to add, that if day and night service have to be performed, at the end of three months neither horses nor coachman will fulfil their duties in a satisfactory manner. Indeed, there are several otherwise lucrative jobs which the job-masters find it necessary to terminate at the end of the first year; the acquisition of "their own carriage" proving such a delight to many worthy persons that they are never happy except when exhibiting their glory to their friends, and this is aided by ignorant, unskilful, and cheap drivers taking so much out of their hired cattle as utterly to annihilate any chance of gain on the part of the real proprietor of the animal.

As a provision for sick or overworked horses, each principal job-master has a farm within twenty miles of London, averaging about two hundred acres, where, in grassy paddocks or airy loose-boxes, the debilitated horses regain the health and condition which the constant pelting over London stones has robbed them of. Generally speaking, however, the health of a jobbed horse is wonderful. In the first place, he is never purchased unless perfectly sound, and known by the best competent judges to be thoroughly fitted for the work which he is likely to undergo; then he is fed with liberality (six feeds a day are on the average allowed when in full work); and, lastly, there is generally a certain sense of decency in his hirer which prevents him from being overworked. This fact, however, is very seldom realised until a gentleman, urged by the apparent economy of the proceeding, determines upon buying a brougham-horse and feeding it himself. On the face of it, this looks like an enormous saving. The horse is to cost—say from sixty to eighty pounds, the cost of keep is fourteen shillings a week, of shoeing four pounds a year. But in nine cases out of ten owned horses take cold, throw out splints or curbs, pick up nails, begin to "roar," or in some fashion incapacitate themselves for action during so large a portion of the year, that their owner is glad to get rid of them, and to return again to the jobbing system.

Although most job-masters profess to let saddle-horses on job, yet—for yearly jobs, at least—there is seldom a demand for them. A saddle-horse is in general a petted favourite with its owner, who would not regard with complacency the probability of its being sent, on his leaving town, to some ignorant or cruel rider. So that the jobbing in this department is principally confined to the letting of a few horses for park-riding in the London season. For these from eight to ten guineas a month are paid, and the animals provided are in most cases creditable in appearance, and useful enough when the rider is a light-weight and a good horseman: heavy men, unaccustomed to riding, had better at once purchase a horse, on the advice of some competent person; as hired hacks acquire, under their various riders, certain peculiarities of stumbling, backing, and shying, which render them very untrustworthy. Some job-masters have a riding-school attached to their premises, and whenever an evident "green hand" comes to hire a hack for a term, the job-master, who reads him like a book, asks, with an air of great simplicity, whether he is accustomed to riding. In nine cases out of ten the answer will be, "Well! scarcely!—long time since—in fact, not ridden since he was a boy;" and then the job-master recommends a few days in the school, which, to quote the words of the card of terms, means "six lessons when convenient, 2*l.* 2*s.*"

Probably the next day the victim will arrive at the school, a large barn-like building, and will find several other victims, old and young, undergoing tuition from the riding-master, a man in boots, with limbs of steel and lungs of brass, who stands in the middle of the school, and thence roars his commands. This functionary, with one glance, takes stock of the new arrival's powers of equitation, and orders a helper to bring in one of the stock-chargers for such riders, a strong old horse, knowing all the dodges of the school, and accustomed, so far as his mouth is concerned, to the most remarkable handling. He comes in, perhaps, with a snort and a bound, but stands stock-still to be mounted—a ceremony which the pupil seems to think consists in grasping handfuls of the horse's mane, and flinging himself bodily on to the horse's back. The stern man in boots advances and gives him proper instruction; off starts the horse, and takes his position at the end of a little procession which is riding round the school. Then upon the pupil's devoted head comes a flood of instruction. Calling him by name, the riding-master tells him that "Position is every thing, sir! Don't sit your horse like a sack! Body upright, elbows square, clutch the horse with that part of the leg between the knee and the ankle, toes up, sir"—this is managed by pressing the heel down—"where are you turning them toes to, sir? Keep 'em straight, pray! Tr-r-ot!" At the first sound of the familiar word the old horse starts off in the wake of the others, and the rider is jerked forward, his hat gradually works either over his eyes or on to his coat-collar, his toes go down, his heels go up, he rows with his legs as with oars. When the word "Can-tarr!" is given, he is reduced to clinging with one hand to the pommel; but this resource does not avail him, for at the command "Circle left!" the old horse wheels round unexpectedly, and the new pupil pitches quietly off on the tan-covered floor. The six lessons, if they do not make him a perfect Nimrod, are, however, very useful to him; they give him confidence, and he learns sufficient to enable him to present a decent appearance in the Row. (Until a man has ridden in London, he is unaware of the savagery of the boy population, or of their wonderful perseverance in attempting to cause fatal accidents.) These riding-schools are good sources of income to the job-master, and are generally so well patronised that the services of a riding-master and an assistant are in requisition, with very little intermission, from seven A.M. till seven P.M. The middle of the day is devoted to the ladies, who sometimes muster very strongly. In the winter evenings the school is also much used by gentlemen keeping their private hacks at livery with the job-master; and being warm, well-lighted, and spacious, it forms a capital exercise-ground. These schools are also much frequented by foreigners, for the sake of the leaping-bar practice, which enables them to prepare themselves for the gymnastic evolutions of "Fox-Ont."

Having treated of the arrangements in force in London for those who ride in omnibuses, cabs, private carriages, and on horseback, we now come to the preparation for that last journey which one day or other must be made by us all, and which has its own peculiar staff of vehicles, horses, and attendants.

The black-job or black-coach business (as it is indifferently called) of London is in the hands of four large proprietors, who manage between them the whole vehicular funeral arrangements of the metropolis. These men are wholly distinct from the undertakers; they will take no direct orders from the public, but are only approachable through the undertakers, whose contract for the funeral includes conveyance. They provide hearse, mourning-coaches, horses, and drivers; and one of their standing rules is, that no horse can be let without a driver,—that is, that none of their horses must be driven by persons not in their employ. These horses are fine, strong, handsome animals, costing 50*l.* a-piece, and are all imported from Holland and Belgium. They are all entire horses, no mares are ever used in the trade, and their breeding—for what reason I know not—is never attempted in this country. They are mostly of a dull blue-black colour, but they vary in hue according to their age; and, as their personal appearance is always closely scanned by bystanders, they are the recipients of constant care. A gray patch is quickly painted out; and when time has thinned any of the flowing locks of mane or tail, a false plait, taken from a deceased comrade, is quickly interwoven. They are for the most part gentle and docile, but very powerful, and often have to drag their heavy burdens a long distance. The black-job masters manufacture their own hearses, at a cost of forty-five pounds each; but mourning-coaches are never built expressly for their dreary work. They are nearly all old fashionable chariots, which, at their birth, were the pride of Long Acre, and in their heyday the glory of the Park; but which, when used up, are bought for the black-job business, and covered with japan, varnish, and black cloth; are re-lined with the same sad colour; and thus, at an expense not exceeding thirty-five pounds, including the cost, are changed into mourning-coaches, likely to be serviceable in their new business for many years.

Among other items of information, I learned that Saturday is looked upon as the aristocratic day for funerals, while poor people are mostly buried on Sunday; that there is a very general wish among undertakers that cemeteries should be closed on Sunday; that very frequently no hearse is employed, the coffin being placed crossway under the coachman's seat, and hidden by the hammercloth; that in cheap funerals one horse has often to convey from eight to twelve passengers; and that, after the ceremony is over, the most effectual thing to stanch the flow of mourners' grief is often found to be a game of skittles at the nearest public-house, accompanied by copious libations of beer.

CHAPTER VI.

RIDING LONDON: OF THE PARCELS-DELIVERY COMPANY, AND "PICKFORD'S."

YEARS ago, not merely when "this old cloak was new," but when this old cloak (which I never possessed, by the way, and which is a mere figurative garment to be hung on pegs of trope or hooks of metaphor) was a short jacket, ornamented with liquorice-marks and fruit-stains, and remarkably puffy in the region of the left breast with a concealed peg-top, half a munched apple, and a light trifle of flint-stone used in the performance of a game called "duck," I was presented with a serviceable copy of Shakespeare, and immediately entered on an enthusiastic study of the same. In a very little time I had made such progress as to identify very many persons with the characters in the plays; thus, a hump-backed blacksmith, a morose ill-conditioned fellow, always snarling at us boys over the half-hatch door of his forge, stood for Caliban;

the fat man with the bald head, who was always taking turnpike-tickets with one hand and mopping himself with the other, was obviously Falstaff; the headmaster was Prospero (somewhat hazy this, but, if I remember rightly, a confused mixture of the former's cane and the latter's wand); the French usher was Dr. Caius; and Sneesh, the tobacconist and newsvendor, whose shop-door was graced by a wooden Highlander, a perfect Tantalus, in the way he was always expecting a pinch of snuff and never got it, was Macbeth. Nor were the minor characters unfilled. I particularly remember that I identified the proprietor of the oil-and-pickle shop in the High Street as Rumour—perhaps on account of his establishment being "full of tongues;" while both the famous carriers of the Rochester Inn-Yard, those good fellows who wanted Cut's saddle beaten, who so heartily abused the oats, who had a gammon of bacon and two razes of ginger to be delivered as far as Charing Cross, and who showed such an invincible disinclination to lend Gadshill a lantern, were embodied in Cokeham, who connected us with the metropolis. A sharp, clever, 'cute man, Cokeham, with a moist eye and a red nose, and an invariable crape hatband, respected by the masters, popular with the boys (we made a subscription for him when his gray mare was supposed to have staked herself in the night in Upton's fields, and bought him a fresh horse, only regretting our money when we learned that Cokeham himself had staked her to trot against a butcher's horse, and won the match, and had then sold her for fifteen pounds to the loser), punctual in his delivery of home-sent cakes and play-boxes, and never "telling" when a shower of stones would rattle against his tilted cart as he passed the playground wall. There was not very much difference, possibly, between the Rochester carriers of Henry the Fourth's time and Cokeham. Until very lately, "carrying" seems to have been a fine old Conservative institution, and with the exception of the substitution of a tilted-cart for Cut's pack-saddle, and a few other minor details of that kind, to have gone on in a very jog-trot fashion. In a small and very humble fashion the Rochester men, even to this day, have their descendants: walking through some behindhand suburb, one may still observe a parlour-window decorated with a small placard bearing a capital letter of the alphabet, a bouncing B, or a dropsical and swollen S—the initial letter of Bolland, or Swubble, the village-carrier, who furnishes his clients with these mystic symbols of indication, to be placed in the window when his services are required.

But so far as London and what is commonly known as the London district are concerned, the old body of carriers has been entirely superseded by the London Parcels-Delivery Company, which was established in 1837, and which, after many severe struggles at the outset, has become a recognised and necessary institution, admirably conducted, serviceable to the public, and remunerative to its shareholders. Its principal establishment is in Rolls' Yard, Fetter Lane, where the whole of the practical detail is devised and carried out under the superintendence of a manager, who has been in the company's service since its earliest days. The plan originated by the Post-office, and in force therein until the recent division of London into districts, is followed by the Parcels-Delivery Company. Every parcel collected for delivery is brought into Rolls' Yard, and sent out thence, even though it was originally only going from one street in the suburb to another a hundred yards off, and this is found to afford the only efficient system of check. In all respectable and thriving neighbourhoods, at graduated distances according to the amount of business to be done, the company has its agents for the receipt of the parcels to be conveyed. These agents, who are paid by a percentage on the number and amount of their transactions, were at the outset nearly all keepers of Post-office Receiving-houses. It was naturally thought that such persons would be the most respectable in their various neighbourhoods, and their holding their little government appointments was a guarantee of their position. But, like other great creatures, the Post-office has its weaknesses, one of which is found to be an overweening jealousy; it ill brooked the divided attention which its receivers bestowed upon the Parcels-Delivery Company; but when rivals started up and called themselves the Parcel Post and Parcel Mail, then St. Martin-le-Grand rose up in fury, called to his aid the services of the redoubtable Mr. Peacock, well-known in connection with dishonest postmen and mornings at Bow Street; and having, with the great hammer of the law, smashed the rash innovators who had dared to appropriate those sacred words "post" and "mail," which a sagacious legislature has dedicated solely to St. Martin's use, St. Martin issued an edict forbidding his servants to have any thing to do with receipt or despatch of parcels for whatsoever company, and commanding them to serve him and him alone. So since then the company have selected the best agents they could find, furnishing them with a blue board, with a well-executed picture of a delivery-cart proceeding at a rapid rate—which board, in many instances, is imitated as closely as possible by the carrier of the vicinity, who places it at the door of a neighbouring shop, and, thanks to the heedlessness and ignorance of domestic servants generally, obtains a certain share of the patronage intended for the company.

Again, following the example of the Post-office, the Parcels-Delivery Company have an inner and an outer circle, one not exceeding three miles from Rolls' Yard, the other extending somewhat over twelve miles from the same point. The farthest places embraced are Twickenham Common in the south-west, and Plumstead in the south-east. In the far-lying districts there are two deliveries a day; nearer localities have four deliveries. There is a small difference in the rates charged between the two "circles;" but in both the collection and delivery are made by the ordinary carts, though in the City, where the general class of parcels is cumbrous and weighty, the collections are made by pair-horse vans.

The company possesses about eighty carts and about a hundred and sixty horses. Although there are some thirty stables scattered about London belonging to it, the majority of the horses, about a hundred, are stabled in Rolls' Yard. They are good serviceable-looking animals, better in stamp and shape than either the omnibus- or the cab-horses, being larger boned, stronger, and altogether less "weedy"-looking; they cost more too, averaging forty pounds a-piece. Each horse works five days out of the seven, and covers in his journeys about thirty miles a day. To every cart are attached a driver, and a boy who acts as deliverer; the former with wages of twenty-five shillings a week, the latter fourteen shillings, with such little perquisites as they may obtain from the public. The general conduct of these men and lads is, I was told, excellent, and never—save at Christmas, when the generosity of the public takes the form of gin—is there any irregularity. Then, looking at the extra work imposed on them, the rigidity of discipline is wholesomely relaxed, and the superintending eye suffers itself to wink a little. For at Christmas the labour in Rolls' Yard is tremendous. During the four days preceding Christmas-day last year, upwards of thirty-two thousand parcels, principally of geese, turkeys, game, oyster-barrels, and cheeses, were conveyed by the company. At such a time the manager does not take off his clothes, and looks upon sleep as an exceptional luxury.

I had proceeded thus far in my "carrying" experiences, and was debating where to turn for further information, when the question was settled for me—as many questions are—by my friends, enterprising creatures who rushed at me, crying "Pickford's!" Old gentlemen told me how this very firm of Pickford's had been carriers by land upwards of a century, even before canals were introduced by the Duke of Bridgewater in 1758; how that they then commenced the water-traffic, and carried it on with the same regularity as they do their present business, but in rather a different manner, as it then took five days to convey goods from London to Manchester—a feat which is now performed in twelve hours. Young gentlemen were full of the reckless daring of Pickford's drivers, the power of Pickford's horses, and the weight of Pickford generally. Ladies, young and old, agreed in condemning Pickford as a "horrid" person, who blocked up the road perpetually, and prevented cabs and carriages drawing up at shop-doors. So I decided on calling upon Pickford—who, by the way, is not Pickford at all—and having been most courteously received, and accredited for all the information I required to a practical gentleman, whose kindness and readily-given information I hereby acknowledge, I set to work to take Pickford's measure, and to find out all about him.

I first called on Pickford—who is not Pickford—in Wood Street, at the Castle Inn—which is not an inn, and which has not the least appearance of ever having been one; for Pickford has so gutted it and twisted it for his own purposes; has thrown out so much yard, constantly resounding with champing horses and lumbering vans; has enclosed so much gallery; has established so many offices, public and private; has so perforated it with speaking-tube and telegraph-wire; and has so completely steeped the place in business, doing away with any appearance of inn-comfort and hotel-luxury, that the idea of anybody's taking his ease in his Castle Inn is ridiculous on the face of it. Here Pickford, who is not Pickford, and of whom it may be further remarked that he is three gentlemen rolled into one, has his head-quarters for correspondence and general management; but here he professes to have nothing to show us beyond the ordinary routine of a mercantile office, of course marked with the special individuality of the carrying business. Wanting to see Pickford in full work, I must go to one of his dépôts—Camden Town, City Basin, Haydon Square in the Minories, which will I visit? I choose Camden Town.

At Camden Town—invariably abbreviated in Pickfordian language into Camden—Pickford, who is the recognised agent of the London and North-Western Railway Company, has enormous premises adjoining the goods-station, and is to be seen in full swing. Employing more than nine hundred horses in

London, he keeps three hundred of them at Camden. Going into these stables, we are at once struck with an air of substantiality in connection with Pickford, which is different from any thing we have yet seen during this tour of inspection of the ways and means of "Riding London." There is special potentiality in his stables, with their asphalte pavements and their large swinging oaken bars, in his big horses, in his strong men, in his enormous vans. Most of the horses are splendid animals, many of them standing over sixteen hands high, and all in excellent condition. They are all bought by one man, the recognised buyer for the establishment, who attends the principal fairs throughout the country; the average cost-price of each is forty-five pounds. They are fed on a mixture of bruised oats, crushed Indian corn, and peas, which is found to be capital forage. Each horse, when bought, is branded with a number on the front of his fore-feet hoofs, and is named; name and number are entered in the horse-book; and by them the horse's career, where he may be working, and any thing special relating to him, is checked off until he dies or is sold. Pickford's horses last on an average seven or eight years, and then they are killed; but in many instances, when no longer fit for roughing it over the stones—for what the dealer poetically described as the "'ammer, 'ammer, 'ammer on the 'ard 'igh road"—they will be bought by some farmer for plough-work; and, after a hard London life, will peacefully end their days in some secluded village. The last duty which some of them perform while in Pickford's service is to pull the trucks which arrive by the line under the shed. These trucks, arriving in long strings from all parts of the line, are shunted into an enormous covered space, and are then unloaded on what is called the "bank," a broad landing-stage, on the other side of which are the empty vans ready to receive the goods, and carry them off to the various districts into which Pickford, in common with the Post-office, has divided London. On this bank are placed at intervals numerous desks, by each of which is a weigh-bridge. By the truck which is being unloaded stands a clerk, known as the "caller-off," with the invoice in his hand; he shouts out the description, destination, and proper weight of each article to the clerk at the desk; the load is placed on the weigh-bridge, and, found correct, is freshly invoiced, and sent off by van. We observed a very miscellaneous collection of articles here—chairs, fenders, barrels, looking-glasses, pottery, and an open basket of Welsh mutton, merely covered by an old newspaper. There are very few accidents here, and, it is believed, very little undetected theft. Printed documents relating to the conviction of recently-discovered culprits—one of whom we read was a "sheeter"—were freely stuck about the walls. The goods, being packed in vans, are then sent off to their destination. The vans are very strong, and, judged by the weight they carry, tolerably light. They are all built by one firm in the Borough, at a cost-price of about eighty pounds each. The foot-board for the driver folds up on a hinge—a very convenient arrangement—and immediately under the seat there is a "boot," for holding the macintosh-cover for goods, with which each driver is supplied. In these vans a ton and a half in weight is allowed for each horse; that is to say, a full three-horse van carries between four and five tons, never more. All the vans, entering or leaving the establishment, pass over a weighbridge, by which, in a glass case, sit two clerks. If the van prove too heavily loaded, it is sent back to be lightened. Each van has a number conspicuously painted on it; and the number, the name of the driver, the number of his invoice, and his place of destination, are all duly entered by the clerks in the glass-case. Each team of horses takes out for delivery and returns with two loads of goods daily. The bulk of the goods arrive by night-trains, and are at once sent out; indeed, Manchester goods are at their consignee's door as soon as the invoice announcing their arrival is delivered by the morning's post. Every van has a driver and a "book-carrier," who acts as conductor and delivers the goods. At night, when his van is unloaded, and after its final journey, the book-carrier goes to his head-office, and "books his work"—which means giving a detailed and statistical account of his transactions during the day. These accounts are then sent to Wood Street, and there duly filed.

Before leaving Camden I went into the vaults, now used as store-cellars for pale-ale by Messrs. Bass, but formerly Pickford's stables. These stables, holding three hundred horses, were full on the night when a great fire broke out, some seven years ago. The horse-keepers go off duty at eleven P.M. About half-an-hour before that time the foreman of the stables discovered that another portion of the premises was on fire. The stables were shut off by large gates still standing. The key of these gates the foreman had about him; with great presence of mind he rushed off and unlocked the gates, and called to the horse-keepers to let loose all the horses. The order was obeyed, the horses were untied, and, amid the whoops and shouts of the helpers, came out three hundred strong, charging up the incline and tearing into the streets. Away they went, unfollowed and unsought for; but of all those horses not one was lost. All were brought in during the succeeding few days from all parts of London, whither they had fled in their fright; but none were stolen, and none were damaged. Only one horse was burnt, a very big beast, known as a "wagon-sitter," and used for backing the wagons under cranes or against the "banks." He was a dangerous brute, and so violent that only one man could manage him. This man unloosed him, but he would not move, and he was burnt in his stall.

Pickford is at home in about ten other places in London, besides having country-houses agreeably situate at Liverpool, Birmingham, Manchester, Edinburgh, Aberdeen, and where not. But I visited him at only one other residence—a little villa on the City Basin of the Regent's Canal, where, before railway times, all his principal business was transacted. Every thing here was carried on much in the same manner as at Camden, the only noticeable feature being what is called the "order warehouse," corresponding very much to the "cloak-room" of a metropolitan railway-station, a receptacle for things left till called for. To this order warehouse are sent Manchester goods or silks bought at a favourable turn of the market, and left in store until required to be despatched for foreign consignment or country trade. Here, among this heterogeneous assemblage, we saw casks of glue from France, bales of stockings and hosiery from Leicester, sewing-machines, their stands and cases, in vast numbers from America, barrels of soda-ash, a large church-organ, the boiler of a steam-engine, baskets of shells, piles of cheeses, two or three hip-baths, a bit of sacking full of bones, several spruce trunks, a sailor's chest, a packet of wire for bonnet-shapes, a parcel of theatrical wardrobes, a packet of vermin-destroying powder, &c. &c. All these wait either a long or a short time, as the case may be, in Pickford's custody; but it very rarely happens that they are not eventually reclaimed.

When I took farewell of Pickford, who is not Pickford, I left him with a smile upon his face—a smile which seemed to say, "You've got a smattering of me, a taste, a notion; but it would take you months to learn all my business." I nodded in reply, on the Lord-Burleigh principle, intending my nod to convey that I knew all that, but that I had got sufficient for my purpose; the rest was his business, and very well he does it.

CHAPTER VII.

MY EXCURSION AGENT.*

VAST numbers of people are, for a comparatively trifling sum, conveyed from one large town to another, or from the heart of a populous neighbourhood to sylvan scenery or picturesque surroundings, and then, after a few days' revel in the unwonted peace and air and freedom, are taken back to their work-a-day life. Wanting to know something of the statistics and general management of the enormous excursion-trains which, during the summer months, convey them, I sought for the longest-established manager of such expeditions, and found him at home nestling in a large newly-fronted house, under the shadow of the British Museum. The front-door of

* The Excursion Agent here described is Mr. Thomas Cook, of Great Russell Street, London, and Granby Street, Leicester. After this article appeared in *All the Year Round*, I had many letters of inquiry from unknown correspondents. I referred them all to Mr. Cook, and I have reason to believe that none of them regretted the recommendation.

this house, on which was a large brass-plate duly inscribed with the excursion agent's honoured name, stood open, and by the side of a glass-door within, where the visitor's bell is usually to be found, I read the word "Office," and entering, found my agent awaiting my anticipated arrival. The house is, as I afterwards learned, a private hotel; but the neighbourhood being severely respectable, and the neighbours objecting to any thing so low as a public announcement on a board, my agent defers to their prejudices, describes his house as a boarding-house, or receptacle for his customers while in town; and, being a Temperance man himself, conducts his establishment on strict Temperance principles. And at the very outset of our conversation my agent let me know that he was not a contractor for excursion trains or trips, that he had no responsibility, and that the work was entirely performed by the railway companies over which the trips were taken; that he made suggestions as to the routes, &c.; that his profit accrued from head-money or percentage on those whom he induced to travel; in fact, that he was a traveller on commission for various railway companies, in which capacity he paid all his own advertising, generally a heavy amount.

For more than twenty-three years my agent has been at this work, arranging excursions between England and Scotland, during which time more than a million passengers have been under his charge. He has arrangements with every railway company that can be made available for Scotch trips, and sometimes begins to gather the nucleus of his company far away in the extreme west of England, then sweeping up the West-Cornwall, the Cornwall and South-Devon, the Bristol and Exeter, the Midland, the North-Eastern, and the North-British railways, he reaches Edinburgh, into which city he will pour more than a couple of thousand people by special trains within a period of twenty-four hours.

My agent does not profess to make hotel arrangements for his flock, but he takes care to advise hotel-keepers of a coming influx; and he thinks that hotel-keepers in the Highlands and elsewhere are kept in order by a list of their prices being published in his programme. At some places far away, such as Bannavie, in the West Highlands by Fort

William, and Braemar, at the period of the Highland gathering and games, there has been a pressure, but *something* has always been arranged; for the hotel-keepers, who at first were disposed to snub my agent as importing the wrong kind of article for them, now eagerly looked for his countenance and recommendation. At Oban he had established a set of lodgings, which he found operated as a wholesome check on the hotels. To carry people, not to feed them, is my agent's business; and, as a rule, he declines to enter into any agreement for boarding and lodging his troop, but, if they wish it, he will settle all their hotel-bills on the road, and present them for discharge at the end of the trip; and it speaks highly for the honesty of excursionists, when he declares that during his whole experience he has never made a bad debt amongst them, or lost a farthing by them. Had he ever been asked to lend any of them money? Frequently; and had never refused. He had lent as much as twenty pounds to one of his excursionists, an entire stranger to him, and had always been repaid. Had he taken any security? Not he. Sometimes a gentleman would offer his watch; but what did he want with a gentleman's watch? He told him to put it in his pocket again.

At Edinburgh the thousands disperse, and start off on different routes, according to the length of their holiday and the depth of their purses. Those who know the country, young men, and spirited people start off alone. Ladies and inexperienced persons remain in the flock, and go the tour, supervised by my agent, in a party, numbering sometimes as many as two hundred and fifty, half of whom are ladies. The ordinary tickets are useful only as far as Edinburgh, but there are offices in all the large towns in Scotland at which fresh tickets for further-extended trips can be obtained. And here my agent, chuckling audibly, informs me that his tickets for coaches always have precedence, where, as is frequently the case, the vehicular supply is not equal to the tourist demand; and the coach-proprietors being, in most cases, also hotel-proprietors, it is not to be wondered at that there is loud and frequent grumbling from the outside public at the best places in inns and on the coaches being given to the excursionists. Of these extended trips, the most favourite is that including Glasgow and Inverness, Staffa and

Iona; the reason, perhaps, being that it is one of the cheapest as well as the loveliest, and with it there is connected a circumstance of great interest. For, with a certain amount of proper pride, my agent tells me that a series of improvements which, during the last few years, has been made in the condition of the poor fishing population of Staffa and Iona, is principally due to his excursionists. When they are inspecting the old cathedral at Iona, my agent takes the opportunity of introducing the subject of the natives' poverty and their hard lives, and appeals to the generosity of his flock; the excursionists, holiday-making and happy, are in proper cue for the reception of such an appeal, and respond liberally; so liberally, that by their subscriptions twenty-four fishing-boats have been built for the poor fishermen of the place. Many poor boys from these desolate regions have also been provided with comfortable situations in large towns. My agent also informs me that, during his whole experience, he has never had an accident with any of his people, that no one has ever been taken ill,—nothing beyond a little over-fatigue, no serious illness,—and that he has had constant cases of love-matches made up on the trip, and has taken the happy couple their honeymoon excursion in the following year.

Asked as to the character of the company usually availing itself of his tickets, my agent responded shortly, "first-rate;" but, on its being explained to him that the social status rather than the moral character of his excursionists is what is inquired after, he became more communicative. The destination of the excursion, he explained, greatly determined its numbers and the social classes from which it was made up. The trips to Edinburgh, and the shorter excursions in England, attract tradesmen and their wives; merchants' clerks away for a week's holiday, roughing it with a knapsack, and getting over an immense number of miles before they return; swart mechanics, who seem never to be able entirely to free themselves from traces of their life-long labour, but who, my agent tells me, are by no means the worst informed, and are generally the most interested about the places they visit. In the return trips from Scotland to England come many students of the schools and universities; raw-boned, hard-worked youths, who, in defiance of the popular belief, actually do return to their native country for a time, probably to make a future raid into and settlement in the land whose nakedness they had spied into in early youth. As to Swiss excursions, the company is of a very different order; the Whitsuntide trip has a good deal of the cockney element in it, and is mostly composed of very high-spirited people, whose greatest delight in life is "having a fling," and who do Paris, and rush through France, and through Switzerland to Chamounix, compare every place they are taken to with the views which formed part of the exhibition at the Egyptian Hall, carry London every where about with them in dress, habits, and conversation, and rush back, convinced that they are great travellers. From these roisterers the July and September excursionists differ greatly: ushers and governesses, practical people from the provinces, and representatives of the better style of the London mercantile community who form their component parts; all travel as if impressed with the notion that they are engaged in fulfilling the wishes of a lifetime, in a pleasant duty never to be repeated. They stop at all the principal towns, visiting all the curiosities to be seen in them, and are full of discussion among themselves, proving that they are nearly all thoroughly well-up in the subject. Many of them carry books of reference with them, and nearly all take notes.

I inquired whether my agent always accompanied his flock, or whether he occasionally permitted them to wander alone. He told me that on the Swiss trips he made a point of being with them from the starting-place to the destination, and that he never considered himself free from responsibility (though of course there could be no kind of claim on him) until they were all landed in England. He should pursue this course on the Italian and all Continental excursions; but in England he frequently did not meet his tourists until their arrival at the first large provincial town on their route, when he "turned up promiscuously as it were." I asked him what was gained by remaining with the large body, and not rambling away by oneself. When, in reply, my agent hinted that his society and guidance were the advantages in question, he looked at me so sternly that I determined to press him with no further questions of that nature.

In the Exhibition years of '51 and '62, my agent, for the first time since 1846, had no Scotch tourist-trips, being engaged by the Midland Railway Company as manager of their Exhibition excursion-trains, in which capacity he supervised the conveyance to London of above a hundred and fifty thousand persons; and in those years my agent commenced business in another line. The excursionists, once landed in London, wanted somewhere to live in, and, with the usual caution of country people, distrusted the touters and advertisements greeting them on every side. Remarking this feature in the first batch which he brought up, my agent immediately engaged six private family houses "furnished for the season," as boarding-houses for the richer members of his flock, who, for six shillings and sixpence a day each, were provided with bed, breakfast, and a meat-tea. For the working people he took a block of new houses, two hundred model-cottages of two or three rooms each, in the neighbourhood of Fulham, furnished them at a cost of about a thousand pounds, and charged their occupants half-a-crown a day each for bed, breakfast, and tea; dinners were not provided. About twelve thousand persons were lodged here during the season; among them three delegations of skilled workmen from Paris, fifty in number, one delegation of fifty from Turin, and two of forty each from Germany. Mr. Foster, the member for Bradford, also brought up five hundred and forty of his workpeople for a three-days' treat, and lodged them with my agent. Several of the railway companies recommended my agent's lodgings on their excursion-bills—a concession never before made.

Although my agent is perfectly amiable on all other subjects, I find one topic on which he is absolutely ferocious, and that is the supposed danger of excursion-trains. Obviously he has expected me to touch upon this point, for I no sooner utter the words, "How about the danger?" than he stops me by holding up one hand, while with the other he produces a written paper, which he delivers to me, and begs me to "cast an eye over." Casting two eyes over it, I find it to be a tabular statement, showing that in the thirteen years between 1851 and 1863, both inclusive, the Midland Railway Company conveyed two millions six hundred and seventy-six thousand six hundred and eighty-eight passengers by excursion-trains, being an average of two hundred and five thousand nine hundred a year. My agent further informed me that the only serious accident which ever happened to an excursion-train on the Midland Railway was in 1862 at Market Harborough, when one life was lost and several passengers seriously injured. This accident cost the company eighteen thousand pounds in compensations, law expenses, loss of property, &c. To insure the safety of these excursion-trains special arrangements are made, the best guards are appointed to conduct them, and in every case an experienced inspecting-guard accompanies the train to see that all the others do their duty. A programme of excursion-trains all over the line is published weekly, a copy being supplied to every station-master, guard, or other responsible officer; besides which, special notices are supplied to all pointsmen and other stationary servants, in anticipation of the coming of the trains. In defence of his system, my agent also urged that all great public demonstrations were encouraged and aided by excursion-trains; and that societies for the promotion of religious, social, and philanthropic objects were often indebted to the railway companies for the crowds brought together to attend them, and in many cases for pecuniary aid, in the shape of percentage on the earnings; that excursion and tourist arrangements constituted the chief support of many watering-places; whilst the benefits derived by the humbler classes is entirely dependent on such arrangements; and that the visits paid by large numbers of excursionists to Chatsworth, and other great houses thrown open to them by their rich owners, did an immense amount of social good, and gave rise to the growth of pleasant feeling between the benefited and the benefactors.

It was in 1855 that my agent, longing like Alexander for fresh worlds to conquer, bethought him that the Paris Exhibition, then being held, would probably prove attractive to excursionists; and thither he organised a trip, which provided for a visit to Paris, thence proceeded through France to Strasburg, and returned home down the Rhine. So successful was this experiment, that ever since he has repeated it annually; but, as he expressed himself, he "was never able to feel his way" to Switzerland till 1863, when, in person, he conducted three parties (one of them three hundred strong) from England to Geneva. My agent's tickets for an excursion from London to Geneva cost, first-class six guineas, second-class four pounds twelve shillings and sixpence; they are available for twenty-eight days, and allow of the journey being broken at Rouen, Paris, Fontainebleau, Dijon, Maçon, and all the principal towns in Switzerland. Supplemental tickets are issued in Switzerland at twenty per cent under the usual prices, and nearly all the excursionists visit Chamounix. There are three regular Swiss trips in the course of the year: one at Whitsuntide ("not a good time," said my agent, in reply to my elevated eyebrows, "but it is merely an extension of my annual excursion to Paris"); one in the first week of July—the largest and best, principally on account of its being vacation-time in the schools, and my agent's excursion being much favoured by ushers and governesses; and one in September. On all these occasions my agent takes charge of and acts as guide, philosopher, and friend to the party. I suggested that his knowledge of foreign languages must be severely taxed. Then he smiled, and told me that was provided for by his knowing nothing but English; but that mattered little, as there was always one of his party at his elbow to explain what he suggested. His hotel-arrangements are all made beforehand; in every principal town in Switzerland he has one regular hotel, with fixed prices, eight to nine francs a day for every thing, attendance included, "And the best hotels too, mind you," said he emphatically, "the best hotels—such as the Royal at Chamounix."

Emboldened by his success, my agent confided to me his idea of, during the following summer, enabling English excursionists to see for themselves what it is that the Romans really do, and which we are all expected to emulate while we are temporary denizens of the Eternal City. In plain words, he purposes taking two special parties to Italy, one in July and one in September, over one of the Alpine passes, Mont Cenis, St. Gothard, or the Splugen, through the Lake district to Como and Milan, with the option of running on to Turin, Florence, Venice, and Rome itself! He is led to expect a very large concession from the Italian railways, and has his plans pretty nearly matured.*

* This excursion was made with very great success. A friend of mine, well known in journalism, was one of the

Now surely this kind of thing is a good kind of thing, and ought to be encouraged. It is right that a hard-working man, labouring in one spot for fifty weeks in the year, should, in his fortnight's holiday, betake himself to some place as far away from and as different from his ordinary abode as lies within the reach of his purse; and this he is only able to do by the aid of such providers as my excursion agent. And each year should, if possible, be spent in a different locality. Ramsgate and Margate are good, fresh, and wholesome; and Southend, though it would be improved if its pier were a little shorter, and its water a little salter, is good too; but as even perpetual partridge palled upon the epicure, so does a constant recurrence to one sea-side place pall upon the holiday-seeker. In the excursion-train he can fly to fresh fields and new pastures; he can see the glorious English cathedrals, the gray Highlands, the quaint Belgian cities, the castled Rhine crags, the glaciers, mountains, and waterfalls of Switzerland, and perhaps the blue plains of Italy,

---

party, and has in an amusing article chronicled his thorough approval of Mr. Cook's arrangements.

for comparatively a very trifling sum; and these seen, he will return with a fresh zest for his home and for his work, and a fresh appreciation for all that is beautiful in nature or great in history.

If these then be, as I fancy they are, some of the results of the work of my excursion agent—work in itself requiring clearness of intellect, and honesty and stability of purpose—I think I have a right to claim for him a position, modest but useful, in that great army of civilisation which is marching through the world.

CHAPTER VIII.

HOLDING UP THE MIRROR.

If the writer of these presents prides himself upon one point,—and he is afraid he prides himself upon a good many,—it is on his possessing an extraordinary stock of theatrical information. This stock is derived entirely from a weekly paper which is dropped down his area every Sunday morning, and the perusal of which is one of his greatest enjoyments. This journal,* well connected and highly respectable, is the chronicle of the theatrical, musical, and "entertaining" world; its columns teem with advertisements from professionals of every description; from it the manager learns what talent is disengaged, the actor what situations are vacant, the author where his pieces are being played, and to whom he is to look for remuneration; it contains a synopsis of all the theatrical performances in this country, and American hints as to new pieces which are coming out across

* *The Era.*

the Atlantic; it gives profuse and erudite criticisms on those which have been recently played; it supports in vigorous language all dramatic charities and institutions; it attacks in fiery terms any short-seeing stiff-necked bigotry,—in a word, it is the actor's hebdomadal monitor and friend.

But woe be to you, O general public, if (not being theatrical) you take refuge in the excellent newspaper that has enlightened the writer, and purpose therewith solacing the tedium of your journey to Bolton-le-Moors or Stow-on-the-Wold! How can you grasp the fact that there are at present wanted at the Belvidere Rooms, Seagate, "Heavy Leading Gentleman, Juvenile Leading ditto, Second Low Comedy to combine Singing, Heavy Leading Lady to combine First Old Woman; also a few good Ability Ladies and Gentlemen"? What do you make of the announcement that "a couple of first-rate funny niggers may write"? What is your notion of a "window-distributor who can insure a large display"? Would any thing puzzle you more than to find "tenants for the Rifle-Gallery, Hermit's Cave, Fancy Bazaar, Tea- and Coffee-Stands and Confectionary-Bar at the Peckham Paradise;" unless it were to discover that you had suddenly obtained the appointment of "stunning, first-rate, go-ahead agent in advance" to the "Lancashire clog-dancer and dulcimer-player, and the comic gentleman (Irish)"? You have to dispose of no paintings on glass of the best description, suitable for a pair of lanterns with three-and-a-half-inch condensers, to use with oxy-calamic and oil lights; you could make but little use of the fighting-tiger, the property of the late King of Oude, and Champion of the Arena; you would stand no higher in the estimation of your serious aunt at Clapham, from whom you have expectations, even though you were to appear at Ebenezer Villa in company with Mr. and Mrs. Jacopo Bligh, the celebrated duologue duetists; neither would your Angelina love you more dearly were you to have "pegtop whiskers," or even the "real imperceptible shape," which is not to be equalled at the price. Worse than Greek, Hebrew, Double-Dutch, or that mysterious language passing under the title of Abracadabra, would be these advertisements to you;—but the writer was cradled in a property washing-basket, was nursed by a clown, was schooled at Dr. Birchem's establishment for young gentlemen (Scene 3d: Usher, Mr. Whackemhard; Scholars, Masters Sleepy, Dozy, Yawn, Sluggard, and Snore; Dunce, Master Foolscap), and has since graduated in the university of the great theatrical newspaper.

An advertisement in bold type, at the top of the second column of the paper, runs thus: "DACRE PONTIFEX.—This popular tragedian appears at Frome, Glastonbury, Yeovil, Lyme Regis, and at Bridport, on the 25th of April. Managers wishing to secure the services of this celebrated *artiste* are requested to apply to the theatrical agent, Mr. Trapman, Rouge Street, Blanco Square." Ah! a very few years ago and the inhabitants of Frome and Glastonbury might as well have wished for a sight of the extinct dodo as of Dacre Pontifex! Managers of the first London theatres fought for him; it was whispered that marchionesses were dying in love for him; to be seen in his company was an honour even for the most radiant gentleman in the crackest of crack regiments. Dacre Pontifex had been but a short time in London when he attracted the notice of Mr. Bellows, the great tragedian, then about to start on his American tour.

Mr. Bellows took Pontifex with him, taught him, polished him, and turned him into a master of his art. When he returned to England, one of those fits of Shakespearian enthusiasm which periodically seize upon the town had just begun to germinate; newspapers were referring to the Bard and the Swan, and several gentlemen were lashing themselves into a state of fury touching the immoralities of the French stage, and the triumphs of vice. Wuff was the manager of the T. R. Hatton Garden at that time, and Wuff was a man of the age. He knew when Pontifex was to return, and no sooner had the fast-sailing Cunard packet *Basin* been descried off Liverpool, than Wuff and the pilot were on board together; and in the course of half an hour a document duly signed by Pontifex was in Wuff's pocket. "I'll bill you in letters three feet long, my boy, on every dead wall in town; and, please the pigs, we'll resuscitate the British drayma, and put Billy on his legs again!"

Shakespeare, thus familiarly spoken of by Mr. Wuff as Billy, proved once more the powers of his attraction, and the success of the new actor was beyond all question. Whether he raved in Hamlet, languished in Romeo, stormed in Othello, or joked in Benedick, he invariably drew tremendous houses, and received overwhelming applause. His portrait was in the illustrated journals, and in chromolithographic colours on the title-page of the Pontifex Waltz (dedicated to him by his humble admirer Sebastian-Bach Faggles, chef d'orchestre, T. R. Hatton Garden). Old Silas Bulgrubber, the stage-doorkeeper, grumbled furiously at the number of applications for Mr. Pontifex, and at the shower of delicately-tinted notes for that gentleman, which were perpetually pouring into Silas's dingy box. The odour of the patchouli and sandal-wood essences from these notes actually prevailed over the steam of the preparation of onions and mutton which was always brought in a yellow basin to Silas at twelve o'clock, and which made the porter's habitation smell like a curious combination of a hairdresser's and a cook-shop. Wuff, the great impresario, as in those days the favourite journal not unfrequently designated him, was in ecstasies; his celebrated red-velvet waistcoat was creased with constant bowings to the aristocracy of the land. He gave a magnificent dinner to

Pontifex at Greenwich, at which was present a large and miscellaneous company, including the Marquis of Groovington, who had married Miss Cholmeleigh, late of the T. R. H. G.; Sir Charles Fakeaway; Four-in-hand Farquhar, of the Royal Rhinoceros Guards, Mauve; Captain Kooleese, Tommy Tosh, well known at the clubs; Mr. Trapgrove, the dramatic author; Mr. Replevin, Q.C., the Star of the Old Bailey, and Honorary Counsel to the Society of Distressed Scene-shifters; Mr. Flote, the stage-manager; Slogger, Champion of the Middle Weights; Signor Drumsi Polstoodoff, the Egyptian Fire-annihilator; and many others. The banquet cost Wuff a hundred pounds, caused the consumption of an immense quantity of wine, and ended in the Fire-annihilator's springing into the middle of the table, kicking the decanters on to the floor, and in a strong Irish accent requesting any gentleman present to tread on the tail of his coat.

From this Greenwich dinner may be dated the beginning of Pontifex's extremely bad end. That little dare-devil, Tommy Tosh, and that fastest of fast men, Four-in-hand Farquhar, who were first introduced to Pontifex at the Wuffian banquet, no sooner made his acquaintance than they showed themselves perfectly enraptured with his company. They pervaded the dressing-room which he shared with Mr. Deadwate, the low comedian, and "stood" brandy-and-water to that eminent buffo; they waited for Pontifex at the close of the performance, and took him away to Haymarket orgies, to private suppers, to where the frequenters of the Little Nick worshiped their divinity with closed doors and on a green baize-covered altar, and to every scene of dissipation which the town could boast (or not boast) of. One sultry day in July, when Wuff was thinking of speedily closing the T. R. H. G., and transporting all his company to some seaside watering-place for the combined benefit of their health and his pocket, Mr. Flote tapped at the door of the managerial sanctum, and entering, informed his chief, that though the orchestra was already "rung in," Mr. Pontifex, who was to appear in the first scene, had not arrived at the theatre. The overture was played and twice repeated, and during the third time of its repetition Pontifex arrived. Mr. Flote, who had been watching for him at the stage-door, turned ghastly pale when he saw him, and followed him anxiously to his dressing-room, then descended to the wing, and waited until he should appear. The British public, which had grown irate at being kept waiting, and which had treated with the utmost scorn the explanation which Mr. Slyme, the "apologist" of the theatre, had offered for the delay, was now softened and soothed by the expectation of their favourite's appearance; and when the cue which immediately preceded his entrance was given, those acquainted with the play commenced an applause which swelled into a tumultuous roar of delight. The effect of this ovation upon its recipient was very singular; he started back, covered his head with his hand, and staggered to a chair, into which he fell. The applause ceased on the instant, and in the sudden lull Mr. Flote's voice was heard urging somebody "for Heaven's sake to rouse himself." Mr. Pontifex then rose from the chair, balanced himself for a few seconds on his heels, looked gravely at the audience, informed them in a high-pitched key that he was "all right," and fell flat on his back. In vain did Mr. Slyme, Mr. Flote, and even the great Wuff himself (that theatrical Mokanna who was never unveiled to the public save to receive their compliments upon his transformation-scene on Boxing-nights) appear before the baize and appeal to the audience; it would not brook Mr. Dacre Pontifex any longer; and hence we find his advertisement in the favourite journal, and his intention to visit the lively localities already set forth.

What next, among the advertisements in the favourite journal? "To BE LET, with extensive cellarage attached, suitable for a wine-merchant, the CRACKSIDEUM THEATRE ROYAL. Apply at the stage-door." The Cracksideum to let again! That old theatre has seen some strange vicissitudes. Once, it was taken by Mr. Stolberg Stentor, a country tragedian of enormous powers of lung, who had roared his way to the highest point of theatrical felicity in the Bradford and Sheffield regions, and who only wanted an opening in London to be acknowledged as the head of the theatrical profession. A good round sum of money, honestly earned by hard work in the provinces, did Mr. Stentor bring with him to London, and the old Cracksideum looked bravely in the new paint and gilding which he bestowed upon it. A good man, Mr. Stentor, an energetic, bustling, never-tiring actor, a little too self-reliant perhaps, playing all the principal characters himself, and supporting himself by an indifferent company, but still a man who meant to do something, and who did it. What he did was to get through his two thousand pounds in an inconceivably short space of time. The public rather liked him at first, then bore him patiently, then tolerated him impatiently, then forsook him altogether. Stentor as Hamlet in the inky cloak, Stentor as Richard in the velvet ermine, Stentor as the Stranger in the Hessian boots, Stentor as Claude Melnotte, Stentor as the Lonely Lion of the Ocean, Stentor as Everybody in Everything, grew to be a bore, and was left alone in his glory. Still he never gave in; he received visitors sitting in his chair of state; after the first word he never glanced at a visitor, but continued practising the celebrated Stentor scowl and Stentor eye business in the mirror; he kept the carpenters at a respectful tragic distance; he awed the little ballet-girls with the great Stentor stride; and he remained monarch of all he surveyed, until he played his last great part of Stentor in the Insolvent Court, the minor characters being sustained by one Mr. Commissioner, and some "supers" named Sargood and Linklater. His appearance here was so great a success, that his audience requested to see him again in six months' time.

An Italian, the Favourite Prestidigitateur of his Majesty the King of the Leeboo Islands; Mr. Lens's Starry Carpet, or the Heavens at a Glance; the Female Wilberforcists, or Emancipated Darky Serenaders; and Mr. Michael O'Hone, the celebrated Hibernian orator,—succeeded each other rapidly at the Cracksideum, and, after a few nights' performance, vanished, leaving no trace behind, save in their unpaid gas-bills. One morning, mankind read in the favourite journal that the house had been taken, and would shortly be opened by Mr. Frank Likely, with the assistance of a talented company. I walked down to the theatre to satisfy myself, and saw in a minute that the announcement was true. A chaos reigned in the interior of the old theatre; all the worm-eaten pit-benches, under which the rats had so often enjoyed a healthy supper of sandwich fragments and orange-peel, were piled up in a heap in a corner of the outside yard; stalls covered with Utrecht red velvet were being screwed down in their place; Leather Lane had emptied itself of mirrors, which paper-capped men were fixing all along the passages; one set of bricklayers were tearing to pieces the old dwelling-house, another was building the portico; pendent from the roof, and straddling across planks supported by flimsy ropes, sat deep-voiced Germans, decorating the ceiling in alternate layers of blue and gold, and issuing guttural mandates to assistants hidden in the dome; carpenters were enlarging the private boxes; scene-painters were looking over the old scenes; and, in the midst of all the confusion, stood Mr. Frank Likely himself, dressed in a dark-blue frock-coat, with a camellia of price in the button-hole, lavender trousers, amber-coloured gloves, and smoking a choice cigar as he superintended the preparations. Under the Likely management, the Cracksideum was something like a theatre: none of your low melo-dramas or funny farces, but choice little vaudevilles, torn up like mandrakes with shrieking roots from the Boulevards, and transplanted all a-blowing to the Strand; comediettas of the utmost gentility, and burlesques teeming with wit and fancy, and giving opportunities for the display of the series of magnificent legs belonging to a picked corps de ballet, and to such brilliancy of scenery as only the great genius of the accomplished Scumble could invent and execute. Filling the house were the great names in which the fashionable world rejoices, princes of the blood, blue ribbons, and gold cordons, heavies of the household troops, wicked wits, old gentlemen living with and on young gentlemen, a few lovely ladies with very brilliant eyes and pearly complexions, but the audience principally of the male sex, and generally to be described as loose. Behind the curtain, and filling the elegantly-appointed greenroom, the literary staff of the theatre; Horsely Collaridge, the young burlesque writer, ragged, hoarse, dirty, and defiant; Smirke, the veteran dramatist, serene, calm, and polished from the top of his bald head to the sole of his evening boots; Lovibond and Spatter, critics who dined on an average three times a week with Likely, and spent the remainder of the evening receiving theatrical homage; little Dr. Larynx, medico in ordinary to the profession, and a sprinkling of the aristocracy, who had panted for his distinction ever since they left Eton, but who, having achieved it, found themselves not quite so happy as they had anticipated. Grand days, glorious days, but not calculated to last; the entertainment was soon found to be of too light and airy a description for the old audiences of the Cracksideum, and the new audiences ran into debt at the librarian's for their stalls and boxes, and very little ready money found its way into the pockets of the management. Nevertheless, Mrs. Frank Likely still kept up her gorgeous bouquets, still put on two new pairs of lavender gloves per diem, and still kept up her Sunday-evening parties at that cottage on Wimbledon Common, which was the envy of the civilised world; likewise, Mr. Frank Likely still betted highly, smoked the best Havannahs, dressed in the best taste, and drove in his curricle the highest-stepping pair of grays in London. But Black Care soon took up her position in the back seat of the curricle behind the high-stepping grays; gentlemen of Hebraic countenance were frequent in their inquiries for Mr. Likely; little Mr. Leopop, of Thavies Inn, had a perpetual retainer for the defence; the manager darted from his brougham to the stage-door through a double line of stalwart carpenters, who sedulously elbowed and kept back any evil-looking personages; and finally Mr. Likely, after playing a highly-eccentric comic character, with a bailiff waiting at each wing, and one posted underneath the stage to guard against any escape by means of trap-door, was carried from his dressing-room to a cart in the hollow of the big drum; and the advertisement just quoted appeared in the favourite journal, announcing the Cracksideum as again To Let.

"Wanted, for an entertainment, a professional gentleman, of versatile powers, age not over thirty. Characters to be sustained: a Young and an Elderly Gentleman, a Modern Fop, a Frenchman, and a Drunken Character in Low Life." Can I not check-off on my fingers twenty gentlemen who could undertake this responsibility? Young Gentleman: blue coat, wrinkled white trousers, stuffed and grimy at the knees, Gibus hat, and brown Berlin gloves; carries an ebony cane with a silver top, and smacks therewith his leg approvingly; talks of his club and his tiger; of Julia and his adoration for her, sings a ballad to her beauty, and regards her father as an "Old Hunks." Elderly Gentleman—"Old Hunks," aforesaid: hat with a curled brim, iron-gray wig, with the line where it joins the forehead painfully apparent, large shirt-frill, Marsala waistcoat, blue coat with brass buttons, nankeen pantaloons fitting tight to the ankle, ribbed stockings with buckle, thick stick with crutch-handle; very rich, very gouty, loves his stomach, hates young gentlemen, speaks of everybody as a "jackanapes," is unpleasantly amorous towards lady's maid, whom he pokes in ribs with stick, and carries all his wealth (which is invariably in notes, to "double the amount" of any named sum) in a fat pocket-book, which he bestows as a reward to virtue at the finale. Modern Fop: brown coat with basket buttons, enormous peg-top trousers, whiskers and moustache, eye-glass—which is his stronghold in life—says nothing but "ah!" and "paw-sitive-ly damme!" except words abounding in the letter "r," which he pronounces as "w." Of the Drunken Character in Low Life it is unnecessary to speak: a depressed eyelid, a hiccuping voice and staggering legs, and there is the "drunken character" complete. The professional gentleman of versatile powers, who places himself in communication with the proprietor of the entertainment, will probably find himself expected to purchase the manuscript, dresses, and properties appertaining thereto, and to start entirely on his own account. He is not unlikely to agree to this. He has been for some time out of employment, and when last engaged at Stow-in-the-Wold he had to play Horatio, when every one knows that Laertes is his right line of business. He thinks it a good opportunity, too, to let the managers see what stuff he has got in him. And then he has a wife, a pale-faced consumptive woman who can play the piano and accompany his songs; and so, finally, he invests the remnant of his savings, or borrows money from his wife's family, who are in the serious book-binding interest, and who look upon him with horror, not unmixed with fear, and commences his tour. Oh! on what dreary journeys does the "Portfolio," or the "Odds and Ends," or whatever the poor little show is called, then go! To what museums and literary institutes, where the green damp is peeling off the stucco, where the green baize-covering is fraying off the seats in the "lecture-hall," where there are traces of the chemical professor who held forth on Acids and Alkalis last week, in pungent-smelling phials and the top of a spirit-lamp; and where the pencil memorandum on the whitewashed wall of the ante-chamber, "coffee, baby, spurs, watch, umbrella, rabbits," with a mark against each item, is evidently attributable to the conjuror who gave such satisfaction the week before last, and was so particular as to his properties! In dull gaunt "assembly-rooms" of country old-fashioned inns, where the unaccustomed gas winks and whistles in the heavy chandelier, and where the proscenium is formed by an antiquated leather screen, which has been dragged from the coffee-room, where for countless years it has veiled the cruet-mixings of the waiter from vulgar eyes; where the clergyman who sits in the front row feels uncomfortable about the "modern fop," as tacitly reflecting upon the eldest son of the lord of the manor; and where the landlord and the tapster, who keep the door a few inches ajar, and are perpetually running to look, when there is no one in the bar, declare the "drunken character in low life" to be out-and-out and no mistake. Poor little show, whose yellow announce-bills are handed-in with such cringing courtesy at the shops of the principal tradesmen, and are seen fluttering in damp strips, weeks afterwards, on all available posts and palings. Poor little show!

The Music-Halls are only of recent introduction among the amusements of London, but their advertisements occupy at least one-half of the front page of the journal. Here they are: the Belshazzar Saloon and Music-Hall, Hollins's Magnificent New Music-Hall, the Lord Somerset Music-Hall, and half a score of others; to say nothing of the old-established house, Llewellyn's, where there are suppers for gentlemen after the theatres. Magnificent places are these halls, radiant and gay as those in which the lady dreamt she dwelt, miracles of gilding and plate-glass and fresco-painting, doing a roaring trade—which they deserve, for the entertainment given in them is generally good, and always free from offence. These are the homes of the renowned tenors, the funny Irishmen, the real Irish boys, the Tipperary lads (genuine), the delineators of Scotch character, the illustrators of Robert Burns, the Sisters Johnson the world-celebrated duologue duettists, the sentimental vocalists, the talented soprani, the triumphant Bodger family (three in number), and the serio-comic wonder, "who is at liberty to engage for one turn." It is curious to observe how completely monopoly has been overset at these places; no sooner does a gentleman achieve success at one place than he is instantly engaged at all the others, rushing from one to the other as fast as his brougham can take him, singing the same song in different parts of the metropolis seven or eight times during the evening, and making a flourishing income.

Change of manners has done away with the theatrical tavern which flourished twenty years ago, with its portraits of theatrical notabilities round its walls, and its theatrical notabilities themselves sitting in its boxes; where leading tragedians and comedians of intense comic power would sit together discussing past and present theatrical times, while theatrical patrons of the humbler order looked on in silent delight, and theatrical critics were penning their lucubrations in neighbouring boxes. Famous wits and men of learning clustered round the dark-stained tables of the Rougepot in Playhouse Court, and half the anecdotes and good sayings which have saved an otherwise dull book, and made many a dull man's reputation, first saw gaslight beneath its winking cressets. But we have changed all that. The famous wits are dead, and the men of the new generation know not the Rougepot; the theatrical critics go away to their newspaper-office to write, the actors' broughams are in waiting after the performance to bear away their owners to suburban villas, and the old tavern is shut up. Still, however, exists the theatrical coffee-house, with its fly-blown play-bills hanging over the wire blind; its greasy coffee-stained lithograph of Signor Polasco, the celebrated clown, with his performing dogs; and its blue-stencilled announcement of Mr. Trapman's Dramatic Agency Office upstairs. Still do Mr. Trapman's clients hang about his doors; old men in seedy camlet cloaks, with red noses and bleared eyes; dark sunken-eyed young men, with cheeks so blue from constant close-shaving, that they look as though they were stained with woad; down Mr. Trapman's stairs, on autumn evenings, troop portly matrons who have passed almost their entire life upon the stage, and who, at five years of age made their first appearance as flying fairies; sharp, wizen-faced little old ladies, who can still "make-up young," and are on the look-out for singing-chambermaids' situations; heavy tragedians with books full of testimonials extracted from the pungent criticism of provincial journals; low-comedy men, whose own laughter, to judge from their appearance, must, for some period, have been of that description known as "on the wrong side of the mouth." There you may see them all day long, lounging in Rouge Street, leaning against posts, amicably fencing with their ashen-sticks, gazing at the play-bills of the metropolitan theatres, and wondering when their names will appear there.

One more advertisement, and I have finished. "To Barristers, Clergymen, and Public Speakers.—Mr. Cicero Lumph, Professor of Elocution, Principal Orator at the various universities, and for upwards of thirty years connected with the principal London theatres, begs to represent that he is prepared to give instruction in public speaking by a method at once easy and efficacious, and that he can point with pride to some of the first orators of the day as his pupils.—N.B. Stammering effectually cured." Many years ago, Cicero Lumph was a dashing captain of dragoons, with a handsome face, a fine figure, and splendid expectations from an old aunt who adored him. His craze was theatrical society, and he was at home in every greenroom, called all actors and actresses by their Christian names, and spent his money liberally upon them. The old aunt did not object to this; she rather liked it, and used to revel in her nephew's stories of those "humorous people, the performers." But when the captain so far forgot what was due to himself and his station as to enter into an alliance with one of these humorists (he married Bessie Fowke, a meek little coryphée of the Hatton Garden ballet), the old lady's rage was terrific; and she only had time to alter her will and to leave all her property to a Charitable Society, before her rage brought on a fit of apoplexy and she expired. Poor Lumph, finding all supplies thus summarily cut off, was compelled to resign his commission, and of course took to the stage; but the stage did not take to him, and he failed; then he became secretary to Mr. Tatterer, the great tragedian, wrote all his letters, made all his engagements, and (some said) prepared all the newspaper criticisms which appeared on that eminent man. When Tatterer came up to London and took the Pantechnicon Theatre, where the early Athenian drama was revived at such an enormous expense, and with so much success, Lumph became his treasurer and continued his toady; and when Tatterer died in the heyday of his triumph, Lumph found that he had netted a considerable sum of money, and that he could pass the remainder of his life without any very hard exertion; so he became an instructor in elocution. He is an old man now, with a small wig perched on the top of his head, bushy eyebrows overhanging little gray eyes, and a large cavernous mouth, with three or four teeth sticking upright and apart in the gums, like rocks. His body is bloated and his legs are shrivelled; but he has still the grand old Tatterer stride, the Tatterer intonation of the voice, the Tatterer elevation of the brow, the Tatterer swing of the arm—all imitated from his great master. He lives in a handsome old-fashioned house in Hotspur Street, Douglas Square, and his knocker all day long is besieged with candidates for instruction. Thither come blushing young curates, who have stammered along well enough in the country parishes to which they were originally licensed, but who, having obtained preferment, think they must be polished up for the London or watering-place congregation which they are to have in care; thither come stout members of Parliament, big with intentions of catching the Speaker's eye, but doubtful of their powers of execution when they have ensnared that visual organ; thither come amateur Othellos, Falstaffs, and Sir Peter Teazles, who are about to delight their friends with private theatricals; and the door is often blockaded by stout vestrymen or obnoxious churchwardens, anxious to show bravely in a forthcoming tournay in some parochial parliament. There, in a large drawing-room do they mount an oaken rostrum, and thunder forth the orations of Sheridan and Burke and Curran; there does the sofa-bolster become the dead body of Cæsar, and over it do they inform Lumph, who is sitting by and critically listening, that they are no orator as Brutus is.

I could go on for pages upon pages about my favourite journal and those whose interests it supports; but no more shall be said than this: Deal gently with these poor players. That they are the "chronicles and abstract of the time" now, whatever they were in Shakespeare's day, I cannot pretend; for perhaps among no other set of human creatures will so pure and thorough a system of conventionality, handed down from generation to generation, be found to exist; but they are almost universally honest, kindly, hard-working, self-supporting, and uncomplaining. And in no other class will you find more zeal, gentle-heartedness, and genuine philanthropy than among those whose life is passed in Holding up the Mirror.

CHAPTER IX.

TOM MOODY AND CO.

WHAT Englishman possessing any share of the national vanity, or any proper self-respect, would declare his ignorance respecting the manners and customs of the hunting-field, and the inner life of that grandest of British field-sports, fox-hunting? We all knew Tom Moody, the whipper-in, well, of course! We know about bright Chanticleer proclaiming the morn, and old Towler joining the cry, and the southerly wind and the cloudy sky, and the

> "Hey, ho, chivy!
> Hark forward! hark forward! tanti-vy!"

with very quick enunciation and very high upper note, and all the rest of it. We know Fores's hunting-sketches, and those admirable woodcuts of Mr. John Leech's, where the "swells" are always flying their fences, and the "snobs" are always coming to grief; where the pretty girls, whom no one else has ever so charmingly portrayed, are rushing at bulfinches; while those glorious boys, whom no one else has ever attempted, are running their Shetlands at raspers. There is a popular style of literature now, the hero of which is always an athletic horsey man; and, notwithstanding his weight, making it a point to be up with the first flight throughout the run, generally winning the heiress and the Great Poldoody Steeple-chase at one and the same time; or reproaching the young lady who has jilted him for a richer suitor, by taking some terrific and horribly-dangerous leap in the very teeth of the pony she has driven in a low wicker-carriage to the meet. Thanks in some measure to the convenience of railways, there are probably but few of us with a sporting turn who have not been out with the Queen's stag-hounds, the Surrey fox-hounds; or who have not, while staying at Brighton, enjoyed a day's sport under the generalship of that glorious specimen of the English yeoman who hunts the Brookside harriers. But notwithstanding all these experiences, I have an idea that very few persons, even those who take great interest in such matters, have any notion of the enormous expense and trouble consequent on the management of a pack of hounds; and it is for the benefit of those who are thus ignorant, and who may be glad of having the whole information in a handy shape, and in a small compass, without the trouble of reference to encyclopædias or heavy statistical works, that these observations, derived first-hand from two of the first masters of hounds in England, and carefully compared with standard authorities, are written.

And first, of the hounds. The number of couple in a pack of fox-hounds depends on how many days in a week the pack is hunted. If twice a week (or with an occasional extra day, called a "bye-day"), twenty-five couple will be sufficient; for three days a week, thirty-five couple; and for four days a week, forty-five couple will be required. The prices of hounds vary according to demand and supply. Draft-hounds, *i.e.* such as have been selected for steadiness and scenting powers, generally average three guineas a couple; but the safest plan for an intending master of hounds is to consult the advertising-columns of sporting-journals, and see whether any well-known and established packs are for sale. At the present time of writing* there is but

* 1864.

one pack in the market, and for them is asked thirteen guineas a couple. Three or four hundred guineas is a common price, and one is not likely to get any thing very special for the money; but a good pack has now and then gone cheap, and been picked up for five hundred pounds. No man with any sporting nous would refuse to give a thousand guineas for a pack of hounds with a thoroughly-established reputation. Much larger prices are on record. From Mr. Blaine we learn that in 1826 Mr. Warde, a well-known sportsman, sold his pack for two thousand guineas; while in more recent times Mr. Foljambe's hounds, sold by auction in lots at Tattersall's, realised three thousand six hundred pounds—one lot of five couple fetching three hundred and eighty guineas, and another of four couple and a half, four hundred and eighty guineas. Here is your preliminary expense.

Having provided your pack, you will, of course, have prepared your kennel for them, which will not be a small item in your outlay. As you can expend fifteen shillings or five hundred pounds on a dressing-case, according to the style of article you require, so will the cost of the erection of your kennel depend entirely on your taste and the contents of your purse. The Duke of Richmond's kennel cost ten thousand pounds. The Duke of Bedford's is four hundred and fifty feet in length. You will probably be satisfied with something less magnificent than either of these; but there are, nevertheless, certain necessaries which it is incumbent on a kennel-builder to provide. Among these are a boiling-house for the meat, lodging-rooms for the hounds, a grass or gravel court into which to turn the dogs while the lodging-rooms are being aired, a plentiful supply of good water, and a lodging-room for either your huntsman, whipper-in, or kennel-attendant, who must be so close to the hounds that, should any quarrelling take place, they can hear his voice, or the crack of his whip, or the sound of a bell, which he could pull, and which should hang over where the dogs sleep. Hounds are very savage in kennel; and after a fight in which a dog has been killed, his body is sometimes devoured by the rest. Old sportsmen have an anecdote, too, of a whipper-in being torn to pieces on going into the kennel at night in his shirt, in which dress the hounds did not recognise him, and without first calling to them. The best food for hounds is oatmeal and horse-flesh, boiled; vegetables, *after* hunting, boiled with the meat, greaves, mashed-potatoes, and skim-milk. Biscuits and greaves, also boiled, form excellent food in the summer or off-season. All food should be given cold, and it should be boiled into pudding one day, and given the next day. The cost of feeding hounds depends on the price of oatmeal; but about twelve pounds per annum per couple may be looked upon as an average, perhaps a low-average sum. Hounds are called by name, and, as it is termed, "drawn," to be fed in three, four, or five couples at a time. The door is wide open, and the meat-trough is in view of the hungry pack; but, until called out, not one attempts to stir. Says Mr. Prior:

> "Abra was ready ere he named her name;
> And when he called another, Abra came."

It is very lucky that Abra was a lady and not a hound. A hound thrusting in or coming out of his turn, not when his name is called, is sent back with a flea in his ear. This is to make them know their own names, and is the only way of teaching them. The late Mr. Apperley (the celebrated "Nimrod") gives a remarkable instance of the discipline at feeding-time, which occurred at Sir Bellingham Graham's. "Vulcan, the crowning ornament of the pack, was standing near the door waiting for his name to be called. I happened to mention it, though in rather an undertone; then in he came and licked Sir Bellingham's hand; but though his head was close to the trough, and the grateful viands smoking under his nose, he never attempted to eat; but on his master saying to him, 'Go back, Vulcan; you have no business here,' he immediately retreated, and mixed with the hungry crowd." Hounds should be fed once a day, with delicate exceptions; that is to say, a hound with a delicate constitution will require a few minutes longer at the trough, and may require to be fed twice in the course of the day. Before quitting this branch of the subject, let us give two important cautions. Build your kennel in a dry spot, thoroughly well drained, and so avoid rheumatism, kennel-lameness, and nine-tenths of the ills to which dogflesh is heir; and feed your hounds late at night, and so insure a comfortable rest for them, their keepers, and you and your guests, if the kennel be at all near the house.

And now of the staff and the stud. Foremost and most important among the former is the huntsman, who should be in the prime of life, combining vigour and experience. Too young a man is apt to be fussy, self-opinionated, and wanting in judgment; too old a man to be slow and incapable of sufficient bodily exertion. Your huntsman should think of hunting, and nothing else; should be submissive to no cap-ribbon; no slave to drink, which would be fatal; no gadabout, taproom loiterer, pothouse frequenter. During the season his exercise will prevent any thing he takes doing him any harm; during the off-season he will find plenty to do in drilling his pack, and acquainting himself with their various peculiarities. He must ride well always, sometimes desperately; and he must be firm, yet courteous, with those terrific strangers who crop-up occasionally at all meets, and who will over-ride the hounds. Your cockney sportsman, and your over-excitable enthusiast, who—the one from ignorance, the other from irrepressible impulse—ride close upon hounds, are the good huntsman's direst foes. Hounds may be driven miles before the scent by the pursuance of such a practice; and it is not to be wondered at if the huntsman sometimes loses his temper. He is a servant, however, and must moderate his language ; but he may safely leave the unhappy transgressor to the remarks of his master, which are generally very full-flavoured. Sometimes the victim declines to bear such language.

The breeding, rearing, and training of the young hounds is entirely to be done by the huntsman ; and in the field he is master of the situation, and directs every step in progress by his voice or his horn, in the blowing of which he must be really scientific. There will be one or two whippers-in, according to the size or status of the pack. If there be two, the first is but little inferior to the huntsman, and should be qualified to take his place in his absence. One of the whips should always remain with the pack, to prevent the younger dogs from running riot, and giving tongue heedlessly. The pad-groom is also an essential adjunct to a hunting-establishment, for it is his duty to follow to cover with the second horse ; and he requires either a thorough knowledge of the country, or an innate appreciation of topography, to enable him to keep the hounds within view, to be able to skirt and cut across the country, and withal to meet his master at the proper place with a fresh and unblown animal. Of course the keep of such a staff is costly. The wages of huntsmen average from eighty to one hundred pounds a year, with a cottage and certain perquisites ; but there is a noble duke, an enthusiast in the sport, who gives his huntsman two hundred pounds per annum. This however, is, of course, an utterly exceptional wage.

The first whip will cost five-and-twenty shillings a week, the second a guinea, the pad-groom a guinea, and the kennel-feeder, if there be one, another guinea a week.

The wages of neither huntsmen nor whips are high when it is remembered what brutes they ride, and that they are never expected to crane at any thing, but to fly ox-fence, brook, any thing that may come in their way. Nimrod relates several anecdotes which he heard from whips of their falls: one complained that his horse was "a dunghill brute," because, "not content with tumbling, he lies on me for half an hour when he's down;" another, having had his horse fall on him, and roll him "as a cook would a pie-crust," got up, and limping off, said, "Well, now I *be* hurt." Another acknowledged to having broken three ribs on one side and two on the other, both collar-bones, one thigh, and having had his scalp almost torn off him by a kick from a horse. Nor, if we may credit the same excellent authority, is there much thought given to these unfortunates. "Who is that under his horse in the brook?" "Only Dick Christian" (a celebrated rough-rider), answers Lord Forester; "and it's nothing new to him!" "But he'll be drowned!" exclaims Lord Kinnaird. "I shouldn't wonder," observes Mr. William Coke; "but the pace is too good to inquire."

In addition to huntsmen's whips, you will require two or three helpers in your stable, at wages of from twelve shillings to fifteen shillings a week, and an earth-stopper, who will get half a guinea a week. In this estimate I have said nothing of the saddler's nor of the farrier's bills, most important items.

And now you have to provide horses for your staff and for yourself—dependent, of course, on the number of your servants and the number of dogs you hunt. A huntsman and two whips will require two horses each for two days a week, or eight horses for the three for three days; the pad-groom will require a horse, and there should be a couple of hacks for messages. The master may do with three, or may be able to afford more—I should say he will require four, barring accidents. The precise cost of hunters is entirely a matter of weight and fancy. A ten-stone master of hounds, with an eye for a horse, good judgment, and talent in bargaining, can, in the country, mount himself more than decently for fifty guineas; whereas in town the price would be doubled. With increase in weight the price runs up frightfully, and an eighteen-stone man would give five hundred guineas for a horse, and think himself lucky, if the mount suited him in every respect. No amount of weight prevents a man from following, or even keeping hounds, if the passion be on him, and he can afford a proper mount; there are masters of hounds of seven and a half stone weight, and there are one or two ranging between eighteen and twenty stone. To get themselves properly carried, men of the latter stamp must expend an enormous sum in horseflesh, requiring, as they do, the speed and jumping-power of the hunter, combined with the solid strength of the dray-horse. The horses for the huntsman and the whips are often good screws, or perhaps horses which, unless in constant work, are "rushers," or "pullers," or "rusty." When these animals are kept in perpetual motion, have a good deal of hard work, and can have any sudden freak of fancy taken out of them by a judiciously-administered "bucketing," they are generally useful mounts for servants. A horse with a bad mouth is often a good horse for a whip, or when an original delicate mouth is lost; for very few uneducated men have light hands.

Horses a little worn are often bought for servants, or very young horses, if the men are good workmen, are bought and handed over to the servants to be made. Forty pounds may be taken as an average price for whips' horses, sixty pounds for huntsmen's mounts; but there is a master in England who pays a couple of hundred guineas for his huntsman's horses: but then the huntsman stands six feet two. These horses are turned out from the 21st of April, and one man can look after and cut grass for six horses; but the average price of their keep throughout the year is twenty-five pounds each; a master of hounds may reckon that the keep of each of his own mounts is forty pounds a year.

In summing-up the question of expense, it will be well to bear in mind the axiom of a well-known sportsman of bygone days, that "a master of hounds will never have his hand out of his pocket, and must always have a guinea in it;" but it may be laid down as a principle that the expense generally depends upon the prudence, experience, and interest possessed by the owner of the pack and the stud. Two men have worked different counties in a season, one at the fourth of the expense incurred by the other, and the difference in sport has been inappreciable. It may, however, be taken as a fact, that the expenses of a fox-hound pack for hunting *twice* a week, including cost of hounds, horses, huntsmen, and stable-attendants, will be about fifteen hundred; and for three times a week, two thousand pounds.

Besides the packs of hounds kept by private gentlemen, there are many subscription packs. About a thousand a year is the average amount of a subscription pack's income, though some have larger revenue. Men of very large means will subscribe eighty or a hundred to the pack; but twenty-five pounds a year is regarded as a very decent subscription from a man whose income is moderate. The system of "capping," *i.e.* the huntsman's touting round with his cap, has fallen into disuse, and would be winked at but by very few masters; certainly no huntsman would be permitted to "cap" a stranger joining the meet, save in such a place as Brighton, where the hunt is attended by very many strangers, and where a "half-crown cap" is the regular thing.

Such are some few particulars of the cost of the noblest of British field-sports; a pastime which lasts from youth to age, and, if we may believe the oft-quoted anecdote, becomes "the ruling passion strong in death;" for it is related that, on its being broken to two sporting-men who were out at sea that the vessel must infallibly sink and they perish, one was silent, while the other, looking at his friend regretfully, only said, "Ah, Bob! no more Uckerby Whin!" naming a celebrated covert where they were always sure of a find.

CHAPTER X.

MY NEWSPAPER.

THERE seems to be something in the mere fact of a man's making a speech which prevents his telling the truth. That language was given us to conceal our thoughts, we know from the subtle wisdom and biting wit of Talleyrand; but it does appear passing strange that while a man is erect on his two feet, his left hand fingering his watch-chain, while his right is tattooing on the table-cloth, he should give utterance to a series of preposterous untruths. Take my own case, for instance. Why did I, last night, at the annual summer dinner of the Most Worshipful Company of Leather-Breeches Makers, held at the Ship Tavern, Greenwich—why did I, in returning thanks for the toast of "the Visitors," declare that that was the happiest moment of my life? Seated next morning in the calm seclusion of my villa at Dulwich, and recalling the exact circumstances under which that assertion was made,

I find that rarely has it been my lot to be more excessively wretched and uncomfortable. I had "come down" on board an overcrowded steamer, under the garish eye of a very hot sun; I had occupied three inches of the wooden arm of a wooden seat, with a very scarlet soldier on my right, and a child labouring under that painful and easily-caught disease, "the mumps," on my left. Revelling in the anticipation of the coming banquet, I had been affronted by the constantly-renewed offer on the part of a boy of "refreshment," consisting of two mouldy captain's-biscuits and three soft shiny cigars. I had been compelled to use severe language to an old person who would persist in offering me "Dawg Toby's Gall'ry o' Fun," a halfpenny broadsheet of villanous woodcuts, which spoke little for Dog Toby's sense of humour or sense of decency. Further, during dinner I had eaten more fish than I ought; to say nothing of the enormity of duckling and peas, Nesselrode pudding, and fondu. I had taken wine with each of the worshipful Leather-Breeches Makers once, with Mr. Master twice, and with myself a good many times. I had drained a very deep goblet of claret to the Leather-Breeches Makers' Company, "root and branch, may it flourish for ever!" (what *does* that mean?) And when I rose to my feet to respond to the mention of my name, I was pale in the face, parched in the mouth, shaky in the legs, weak in the memory, quavery in the voice, and frightened out of my senses. That was what I called the happiest moment of my life! I should be sorry to write the word with which, in strict justice, I ought to stigmatise that expression. I know when the happiest moment of my life really comes off. Not when I receive my dividends from those very abrupt gentlemen who have, apparently, a natural hatred of their customers, across the bank-counter; not when I go to my old wholesale grocery-stores in Lower Thames Street, and smell the tea and taste the sugar, and dip my hand into the piled-up rice, and learn from my sons of the yearly increase of the business in which I still keep my sleeping-partner's share; not when that fair-haired knickerbockered boy who calls me "grandad," makes cock-horses of my knees, and rides innumerable steeple-chases, clutching at my watch-guard for a bridle; nor when his sister, a fairy elf, makes a book-muslin glory on my lap, and kisses me as her "dear dada"—those are triumphs, if you like, but there is something too exciting in them; they are not the happiest moments of my life.

That blissful period is to me, so far as I can judge, about ten A.M. I have had my comfortable breakfast; my wife has gone down to see to the domestic arrangements for the day; if it be summer, I stroll on to the corner of my garden; if it be winter, I shut myself into my little snuggery; but, summer or winter, I find laid ready for me a box of matches, my old meerschaum-bowl, ready filled, and—my newspaper. Then follows an hour composed of three thousand six hundred of the happiest moments of my life. I light my pipe and take up my paper, duly dried and cut, without which enjoyment is to me impossible. I have seen men on the outside of an omnibus attempt to fold a newspaper in a high wind, reading to the bottom of a column, and then suddenly becoming enwrapped, swathed, smothered in a tossing crackling sheet. Call that reading the newspaper! I like to read a bit, and puff my pipe a bit, and ponder a bit; and my ponderings are not about the machinations of the Emperor Napoleon, not about the probable result of the American war, not about the Conference, not about the state of the money-market; but about that much talked-of march of intellect, that progress of progress, that extension of civilisation, which have shown their product in my newspaper lying before me.

Newspapers were first invented by a French physician, who found it his interest to amuse his patients by telling them the news. The avidity with which his daily gossip was received engendered the hope that, if collected and printed, it might do more than reconcile his patients to the ever-unwelcome visits of their doctor. Monsieur le Docteur Renaudot, for thus was he styled, applied therefore to Cardinal Richelieu for a patent, and the first number of the *Paris Gazette* appeared in 1662.

In the interests of my newspaper, men who have taken high collegiate honours have last night wasted the midnight oil, and before me lies the result of their deep thought, masterly scholarship, and special study of the subject intrusted to them; not one single word was dropped by the great orators in last night's debate, finishing at two A.M., which I do not find recorded for my perusal; while the vapid prosings of the dreary members have such pith as was in them extracted into a few lines. For my gratification, and that of a hundred thousand other readers, a gentleman thoroughly competent for his task has recorded his opinion of the merits of the new tenor who last night made his first appearance at our Opera; while glancing a little lower down, one may experience quite a glow of satisfaction in reading the noble names of the superb ones who were present at the Princess's reception. In the next column I can see exactly how stands the latest betting on the coming races, and I also find it chronicled—in a manner which I confess I never could comprehend —how yesterday's races were run, how Cœur-de-Lion had it all his own way to Nobb's Point, closely followed by Butcher-Boy, Gipsy, Avoca, and Tatterdemalion; how, at the distance, Butcher-Boy and Avoca ran out and collared the favourite; and how just before the finish Smith called upon the mare, and, Avoca answering, was hailed the winner by a head. How on earth do they know all this? I believe these racing-reports are exact descriptions of the struggle; but how do the reporters manage to see all this in a lightning flight for a mile and a half, or how do they manage to distinguish the colours of the horses? Sometimes I have fancied there are some things in a newspaper which I could do myself; but assuredly this is not one of them. I find, too, that my journal must have several sporting-gentlemen attached to it; for in the same column I read an account of a yacht-match at Erith, with critical remarks about the manner in which the *Flirt* was sailed by her noble owner; and a vivid description of a cricket-match at Lord's between the elevens of Rutland and Yorkshire, with a laudatory notice of Mr. Bales's "five-er" with a leg-swipe. In a corner of this column I also find quotations from the cotton-market at Manchester; from the corn-markets at Leeds, Liverpool, Scotland, Ipswich; from Messrs. Sheepshanks' trade-circular in regard to the colonial wool-sales; and from the latest prices of hay at Smithfield and Whitechapel, where I find "the market is dull, with fair supplies." There also is spread out for me shipping-intelligence, informing me what vessels have arrived at, or passed by way of, our own ports, what vessels have been spoken with in far-distant latitudes; there I get a meteorological report of the actual and probable state of the weather all over the

United Kingdom; and in the immediate vicinity I find an elaborate report of the state of the mining-market, whence I glean that Wheal Mary Anne advanced twenty shillings, and that Cotopaxis were rather flatter.

Hundreds of others are in the employment of my journal. In its interest a famous writer has taken the pilgrim's staff, and wandered through America desolated by her civil war, has passed through Mexico, and lingered among the islands of the Spanish Main, duly transmitting vivid descriptions of his adventures, and of the result of his observations. In the same interest, at all the principal continental cities,—notably at Paris, Berlin, Vienna, Petersburg, and Madrid,—my journal has its agents: quiet, gentlemanly men; now gay bachelors going into the fast society of the Cercle and the Jockey Club; now steady middle-aged men, regular attendants on the Börsen Halle, now quaffing horchata, and puffing cigarettes on the Puerta del Sol, now colloguing with P.-and-O. captains at Alexandria, or chaffing "griffs" at Suez; but always having ears and eyes wide open, be it for a political "shave," a dancer's triumph, or a rise in the markets, and always transmitting that intelligence instanter by letters or telegram to my journal. In the same interest two gentlemen are attached, one to the head-quarters of the Danish, another to the German army; solemnly precise men are gliding about the Exchange, writing in their memorandum-books the latest quotations from Capel Court, the latest "done" at Gurney's, the latest whisper from the Bank parlour; one member of the staff is flying away in one of the compartments of a royal train, while another is pursuing his inquiries among the starving poor of Bethnal Green; one reporter has just buttoned up his note-book containing the charge of the judge to the jury trying a murderer, while another is taking down the chairman's "speech of the evening" at a charity dinner; the fire "which was still blazing fiercely when we went to press," the murder up Islington way, which was committed late last evening, the new farce, "on which the curtain did not fall till past midnight;" all are recorded in my journal, which also gives utterance to the cries of innumerable indignant amateur correspondents.

From my experience, the outside public which reads and delights in its newspaper has very little idea of all this enormous trouble and expense in preparing the daily sheet, and has not the smallest conception of the powers required in the various leading journalistic men. Take the editor alone. Talk of the general of an army, of his tact and readiness, what is he compared to the editor of a leading daily paper? An editor, if he be worth his salt, must possess the art of watching public taste, the art of seeing what inevitably *must* be, and the power of writing leaders, or getting them written, to say that it *shall* be. He must have the faculty of collecting materials, and finding men to deal with them; the faculty of being able to say *something* at once on any important event which may turn up; the faculty of dining-out well; and when dining-out, the faculty of *not* talking, save to excite discussion and draw out information. Men of ripe middle age make the best editors; too young they are apt to be flippant, excitable, and aggressive; too old they fall into carelessness, laxity, conventionality, and twaddle. And your editor must necessarily be a thorough citizen of the world, and determined to subdue all his own natural tastes and inclinations for the success of his journal. He may look upon the theatre with eyes of loathing; but he should take care that his dramatic criticisms are full, fair, and immediate. He may look with horror upon sporting; but his racing-reporter should be up to every move on the turf. He must never be sleepy between 8 P.M. and 3 A.M.; must never be ill; must observe a strict Mokanna-like seclusion, and not "make himself free;" he must take every step in his business promptly, but with caution; and once having committed himself to any cause, however great, however slight, he must stick to it for ever, and defend it *per fas aut nefas* to the very best of his ability.

One of the golden rules for success in the conduct of a newspaper, and one without the adoption of which it is impossible for any journal to succeed, is—*spare no expense.* Have the very best in the market; and do not mind what you pay, so that you get it good. When the Californian rage for gold-digging began, the *Times* employed a gentleman to go out; and that he might be competent, sent him first to a gold-refiner's in the City to learn all the processes of refining, had him taken over the Mint, and sent him forth thoroughly *au courant* with all that was known of his subject in London. Then the leader-writers should be masters of their craft, *va sans dire;* and to this end it is found necessary to have men of various professions and of various tastes, to each of whom can be intrusted a special subject. Of late years it has been found that great κῦδος, and consequent circulation, has been occasionally obtained for several of the morning journals by some specially admirable descriptive article; and that style of writing has consequently been more sought after and more fostered. The ordinary reporter is now kept to ordinary reporting; and when an article descriptive of any event of peculiar interest is required, a man of higher journalistic rank is appointed to write it. Some of the descriptions of Mr. W. H. Russell and Mr. Woods in the *Times*, of Mr. G. A. Sala and Mr. Godfrey Turner in the *Telegraph*, of Mr. Justin M'Carthy and Mr. Leicester Buckingham in the *Star*, of Mr. Parkinson and Mr. Murphy in the *Daily News*, and of Mr. Williams in the *Standard*, are as good as can be, and utterly different from any thing that would have been looked for in the journals twenty years since.

Although I always wondered in a vague kind of way at the manner in which my journal was produced, when I knew nothing about it, I think my astonishment has even been greater since I saw the working of the vast engine of social progress. Arriving at about ten o'clock in the evening, I found an intelligent guide awaiting me, and by him was first conducted into the library—not necessarily a portion of a newspaper establishment, but here interesting as the depository of the volumes, from their earliest sheet, of the *Times* and the *Morning Chronicle*, once conspicuous in journalism, now defunct. I took down a volume of the *Chronicle* hap-hazard, and opening it at the date February 4, 1792, read a protest of the Irish Parliament on a vote of congratulation to the king on the marriage of the Duke of York with the Princess of Prussia. The Irish gentlemen were "dissentient" because they could not "consistently with principle or honour join in thanking a sovereign whom it is in the highest degree criminal to deceive, on having entered on the government of Ireland as viceroy, a man under whose administration measures inimical to the public welfare had been supported with success, and every measure beneficial to the kingdom uniformly opposed and defeated." The viceroy to whom this special compliment was paid was Lord Westmoreland. Poor Ireland! — well up in the grievance-market even in those distant days. In the same number I found the advertisement of a "Proposal for a complete History of England, by David Hume, Esq.;" a notice of a gallery of pictures, "by Messrs. Barry, Copley, Fuseli, and T. Lawrence;" and an announcement of the performance of *Richard the Third*, —"The Queen, Mrs. Siddons; being the first time of her performing that character."

I proceeded to a suite of rooms occupied by the sub-editor and the principal reporters. In the outermost of these rooms is arranged the electric-telegraph apparatus—three round discs, with finger-stops sticking out from them like concertina-keys, and a needle pointing to alphabetic letters on the surface of the dial. One of these dials corresponds with the House of Commons, another with Mr. Reuter's telegraph-office, the third with the private residence of the proprietor of my journal, who is thus made acquainted with any important news which may transpire before he arrives at, or after he leaves, the office. The electric telegraph — an enormous boon to all newspaper-men—is specially beneficial to the sub-editor. By its aid he can place before the expectant leader-writer the summary of the great speech in a debate, or the momentous telegram which is to furnish the theme for triumphant jubilee or virtuous indignation; by its aid he can "make-up" the paper—that is, see exactly how much composed matter will have to be left "standing over,"—for the tinkling of the bell announces a message from the head of the reporting-staff in the House, to the effect, "House up; half a col. to come." Sometimes, very rarely, wires get crossed or otherwise out of gear, and strange messages relating to misdelivered firkins of butter, or marital excuses for not coming home to dinner, arrive at the office of my journal. The sub-editor has a story how, after having twice given the signal to a West-End office which Mr. Reuter then had, he received a pathetic remonstrance from some evidently recently-awakened maiden, "Please not to ring again till I slip on my gown!" On the sub-editor's table lie the weapons of his order: a gigantic pair of scissors, with which he is rapidly extracting the pith from the pile of "flimsy" copy supplied by the aid of the manifold-writer and tissue-paper, by those inferior reporters known as penny-a-liners; and a pot of gum, with which he fits the disjointed bits together; here also are proofs innumerable in long slips; red, blue, and yellow envelopes, with the name of my journal printed on them in large letters—envelopes which have contained the lucubrations of the foreign and provincial correspondents; an inkstand large enough to bathe in; a red-chalk pencil like the bowsprit of a ship; and two or three villanous-looking pens. At another table a gentleman, gorgeous in white waistcoat and cutaway coat, is writing an account of a fancy-fair, at which he has been present; printers, messengers, boys, keep rushing in asking questions and delivering messages; but they disturb neither of the occupants of the room. The fancy-fair gentleman never raises his eyes from his paper, while, amid all the cross-questioning to which he is subjected, the sub-editor's scissors still snip calmly on.

Next to the composing-room, where I find about seventy men at work "setting" small scraps of copy before them. The restless scissors of the head of the room divide the liner's description of horrible events at a position of breathless interest, and distribute the glorious peroration of a speech among three or four compositors, who bring up their various contribution of type to the long "galley" in which the article is put together. These men work on an average from four P.M. till two A.M., or half-past two (in addition to these there are the regular "day-hands," or men employed in the daytime, who work from nine till five). They are mostly from twenty-five to thirty-five years of age; though there is one old man among them who is approaching threescore-and-ten, and who is reported almost as good as any of his juniors. They earn from three to four guineas a-week each. The room is large, and though innumerable gaslights are burning, the ventilation is very good.

I glanced at some of the writing at which the men were working; and as I thought of the fair round text in which my ledgers and day-books were always entered up, and then looked at the thin jigging hieroglyphics which, in close lines, and adorned with frequent erasures and corrections, lay before the eyes of those poor compositors, I shuddered at the contrast. On inquiring, however, I found that the compositors made very light of cacography, and that it was seldom indeed that a man had to refer to his neighbour to help him in deciphering a word.

Although a printer may be sitting all day, yet in his own way he is a great traveller, or at least his hand is. A good printer will set 8,000 ems a-day, or about 24,000 letters. The distance travelled over by his hand will average about one foot per letter, going to the boxes in which they are contained, and of course returning, making two feet every letter he sets. This would make a distance each day of 48,000 feet, or a little more than nine miles; and in a year, leaving out Sundays, that member travels about 3,000 miles.

From the composing-room I, and a certain amount of type duly set and locked up in a "forme," proceeded to the foundry—a workshop covered with scraps of metal-filings, and with a furnace in the middle of it. Unlike their fellow-workmen of the village of Auburn, as described by Goldsmith, the smiths in the foundry of my journal by no means relaxed their ponderous strengths and leaned to hear, but were obviously far too hard at work to do any thing of the kind. So soon as the type-containing formes arrive, they are hammered all over with a mallet to reduce them to an average level and consistency; then they are oiled, and an exact imprint is taken of them on what is called a "matrix"—a preparation of French-chalk on stiff paper. This matrix is then dried over a furnace on hot metal plates; a mixture of lead and antimony in a liquid boiling state is poured on it, taking the exact form of the indented letters, filling up every crack and crevice, and becoming, in many reduplicated forms, the actual substance from which the journal is printed, and which to that end is sent to the machine-room, whither I followed it.

The machine-room of my journal is a vast whitewashed hall, with three enormous clanging, plunging, whirling metal demons in the midst of it, attended by priests and devotees, half of whom are employed in administering to their idols' appetites by feeding them with virgin paper, while the other half wrenches from them the offering after it has passed through the ordeal. In plainer language, the demons are three of Hoe's most powerful printing-machines, containing together twenty-six cylinders, and in attendance upon them are eighty men and boys, half of whom feed the machines with fresh paper, while the other half receive the sheets after they have passed under the cylinders. The cylinders in these machines make one million four hundred and five thousand revolutions in the course of one night, and for a single day's circulation travel at the rate of nearly nine hundred and eighty-five miles. When its machines are in full swing, my journal is produced at the rate of eight hundred and eighty-four copies per minute. The length of paper used in one day in my journal will make a path one yard wide and nearly one hundred and sixteen miles long; one day's circulation placed edge to edge would closely cover a piece of land of nearly forty-three acres; one week's circulation, placed one on the top of the other, would make a column three hundred and nineteen feet high. The weight of paper used in one day's circulation of my journal is seven tons thirteen hundred-weight two quarters and twenty pounds; there are also three hundred and ninety-six pounds of ink consumed in one night's printing; and the length of tape used upon the machines is a little over four miles. In the midst of all this whirling dazzling confusion, accidents very seldom occur; the ringing of a bell, the movement of a handle, and the rotation of the engine ceases instantaneously. To a stranger the vast room, with its glare of gas, its smell of oil and steam, and its whirring engines, is a kind of orderly Pandemonium. There are galleries whence he can survey all that passes; but a few minutes must elapse before his eyes become accustomed to the tearing of the engine, and his ears to the clanging discord; though those employed seem thoroughly habituated, and pursue their avocations as though they were in the quiet composing-room itself. Indeed the head-engineer, who acted as my guide in this department, had such interest in his work, that he told me he seldom took a holiday or absented himself from his post. He evidently regarded those who did not ordinarily spend their evenings in the company of his machines as inferior beings.

So the demons go clanging through the night, until they are supposed to have had as much as is good for them, and their fires are raked out, their steam is let off, and machinists and feeding-boys go home to bed, whither the compositors and the sub-editor have long since preceded them. Then the advanced guard of the day establishment, in the persons of the publisher and his staff, appear upon the scene. The street outside is lined with light spring-carts, with those peculiarly bony horses which always seem to come into newsvendors' hands; crowds of men and boys fight up the passage to the publishing-office, while inside there is a hullabaloo, compared to which the howling at an Irish wake is silence, and the parrot-house at the Zoological Gardens is a quiet retreat. Right has very little chance against might in such a medley as this, and the weakest usually goes to the wall; but eventually the big wooden tables are cleared, the last load has been carried to the van, the last boy has rushed off with his arms full of damp literature, and the starters by the Parliamentary for Liverpool at seven have my journal on their knees, while merchant-princes resident in Brighton, and coming thence by the "daily-bread" express at a quarter to ten, find it on their breakfast-tables at half-past eight.

Taking such things into consideration, is it wonderful that I regard my newspaper as a marvel, and that I from time to time lay it down to ponder over the capital, talent, and energy involved in its production?

CHAPTER XI.

GUNNING.

GUNNING is my theme; not the patronymic of those three beautiful sisters who fired the hearts (if the dried-up integuments can be so called) of the court gentlemen in the time of the Regent, but the great art of shooting; on English manor or Scottish moor, from the back of a pony or the bows of a punt, in solitary ramble or grand battue; indulged in by my lord with his party of friends, his keepers, his gillies, and his beaters; by Bill Lubbock the poacher, known to the keepers as an "inweterate" with his never-missing double-barrel and his marvellous lurcher; or by Master Jones, home for the holidays from Rugby, who has invested his last tip in a thirty-shilling Birmingham muzzle-loader, with which he "pots" sparrows in the Willesden fields. Gunning, which binds together men of otherwise entirely opposite dispositions and tastes, which gives many a toiler in cities pent such healthful excitement and natural pleasure as enable him to get through the eleven dreary months, hanging on to the anticipation of those thirty happy days when the broad stubble-fields will stretch around him, and the popping of the barrels make music in his ear; gunning, a sport so fascinating, that to enjoy it men in the prime of life, with high-sounding titles and vast riches, will leave their comfortable old ancestral homes, and the pleasant places in which their lines have been cast, and go away to potter for weeks in a miserable little half-roofed shanty on a steaming barren Highland moor, or will risk life and limb in grim combat with savage animals in deadly jungle or dismal swamp. Gunning, whose devotees are numbered by myriads, the high-priest whereof is Colonel Peter Hawker, of glorious memory, who has left behind him an admirable volume of instruction in the art. Not unto me to attempt to convey hints, "wrinkles," or "dodges" to the regular gunner; mine be it simply to discourse on the inner life of the art, showing what can be done, in what manner, and for how much; and giving certain practical information in simple and concise form to the neophyte.

And first to be mentioned in a treatise, however humble, on gunning, are guns. A muzzle-loading double gun by a first-class London maker costs forty guineas, or with its cases and all its fittings, fifty guineas. The leading provincial makers, and those of Scotland and Ireland, charge from thirty to forty pounds complete; most of their guns are, however, in reality manufactured in Birmingham, where the price of a double gun varies from twenty pounds to two pounds five shillings, or even less, according to quality. The second-class London makers charge from twenty-five to thirty-five pounds; but most of their work is made at Birmingham, and only "finished" in London. The London work is much the best; for, as the wages paid are much higher, London attracts the best workmen from all parts of the country. Another reason is, the greater independence of the workmen in London. In Birmingham, especially,—between trade agreements on the part of the masters, and trade unions on the part of the men,—a man who can work better or more quickly than his fellows is continually hampered; and he generally makes his way to London, where he finds a fairer market for his labour, and fewer restrictions. The situation of Birmingham, near to the coal-producing districts, renders the cost of fuel much less than in London; and all the operations which require a large expenditure of fuel, such as the welding and forging of the barrels, &c., are done at Birmingham, even for best guns; and it is frequently asked, since all the materials, barrels, &c. come from Birmingham, why pay the much higher prices of London makers for the same thing? meaning, that as the London makers get their barrels (the chief portion of the gun) from Birmingham, the prices they charge are extortionate. Now, what the London barrel-maker really does get from Birmingham is simply two rough tubes of wrought iron, not fit in their then condition even to serve as gas-pipes. All that makes them of any value as gun-barrels—the boring, filing, putting together for shooting, &c.—has to be done in London at four times the cost, and generally with ten times the accuracy, of Birmingham work. The fallacy lies in supposing that "the same thing" is obtained in both cases. If what a man buys when he purchases a gun be merely the six pounds of wrought iron and steel in the barrel and locks, and the half a foot of walnut plank in the stock, the value of these materials at twenty pounds a ton for the metal and a shilling a foot for the wood is less than five shillings for the whole, and he may well consider he is overcharged if he pay a pound for the complete gun. But what he buys is really the time and technical skill of the contriver, the time and skill of the workman, the waste of manufacture (and how enormous this frequently is, may be judged from the fact that ninety pounds of rough metal will be consumed in making a pair of Damascus gun-barrels weighing about six pounds when finished); these are the real things purchased, and whether the buyer pay ten or fifty pounds, he will generally get only the value of his money, and no more. Skill and time can never be brought to the same close competition as the price of raw material, and the tendency of both is to become dearer instead of cheaper every day.

During the last four or five years the use of breech-loading guns has become common in England. The system adopted is called the "Lefaucheux," from the name of its inventor, and it has been general in France for many years. Twenty-five years ago some guns of this pattern were brought from Paris by Mr. Wilkinson of Pall Mall, who endeavoured to introduce their use into England, but without success; and they were finally sold at one-fourth their cost, as curiosities only. The price of breech-loading guns of best quality is five guineas more than muzzle-loaders; they are sold in Birmingham at from eight pounds to thirty pounds. The advantages of a breech-loader to young sportsmen are, principally, that the guns cannot be overloaded, two charges cannot go into the same barrel; the charge can be taken out in an instant; and though, if the gunner be clumsy, he may shoot a friend, he cannot by any possibility shoot himself. This little distinction is highly appreciated, since accidents in loading from the muzzle were by no means unfrequent.

To a moderate-minded man, three or four thousand acres in England would be a good manor, of which four hundred should be covert. Potatoes used to be good covert, now the best is clover left for seed, mangold, swedes and turnips, beans, &c. The usual price is one shilling per acre; but in the neighbourhood of London and large towns the rent is higher, and the value arbitrary. For four thousand acres, to do the thing well, one should have a head-keeper, whose cost will be as follows: a house, a guinea a week for wages, five pounds a year for clothes, twelve pounds a year for ammunition, a certificate three pounds, and a "deputation" from the lord of the manor, without which he cannot, I believe, legally take a gun away from a poacher. He generally has a pony and a spring-cart allowed him, sometimes the keep of a dog. It has been well observed, that "it is not every fellow with a short jacket and half a dozen pockets, that is fitted for a game-keeper." He must be trustworthy; for he has in the mowing-time to pay a shilling a nest to the mowers, sometimes to pay for the destruction of vermin, &c., and he can cheat if he like. He should be a good, but not a noted or crack shot; not such a shot as keeps his hand in by practice on his master's game; and he should be thoroughly knowing in the habits of all manner of vermin, and in the mode of destroying them. He should not be allowed to break dogs for any one save his master, or to rear pets, or in fact to do any extraneous duty. A game-keeper's situation is a pleasant one when he and his master pull together. There is always enough to do, both in and out of season, to keep a zealous man fully employed. He should be brave, yet not pugnacious; amicable, and on good terms with the neighbouring farmers, yet not sufficiently so ever to wink at poaching, however mild—and the natural instinct for poaching, even amongst farmers of the better class, is something marvellous—and civil and attentive to his master's guests. (N.B. It is usual to give a keeper five shillings for the day, if shooting at a friend's manor, and then he cleans your gun; at a grand battue, a guinea is frequently given, but for a day's *partridge*-shooting five shillings is ample. This, be it remembered, is expected.) Your head-keeper will want a man under him, with wages of twelve shillings a week, and a house, and at certain seasons watchers or night-men. These are generally paid by the night. The beaters employed at battues are very frequently old men or boys on the estate who are fit for nothing else; they get from one shilling to half-a-crown for their day's job.

For such a manor as I have pictured, two brace of pointers or setters, and one retriever, would be enough, and a good close-working spaniel, or a brace or leash, according to fancy. A brace of well-broken second-season setters should be purchasable at from twenty-five to thirty pounds; spaniels at five pounds each; a good retriever would be cheap at twenty guineas, ten pounds being a very common price. If possible, by all means breed your own dogs, or get them bred by your friends; a purchased pointer is a pig in a poke—purchased, I mean, through the medium of an advertisement or from a regular dealer. Some animals so bought have never even had powder burnt over them, cower at the shot, and fly away home immediately afterwards; others have a kind of "crammed" instruction—that is to say, they will be very good when kept in constant practice, but if left at home for a few days will forget all they have learnt, and come into the field wild and ignorant. Pointers are more useful than setters for partridge-shooting, easier to train, less liable to take cold, more easily steadied, and more tenacious of instruction. On the other hand, setters are superior for grouse-shooting, being harder-footed. Spaniels are the most useful of all dogs: there are two classes—the "mute," which are the best for all practical purposes; and those which fling their tongues, begin their noise as soon as they are put into cover, put all game on the alert, and send every jack-hare and old cock-pheasant out of the other end. A spaniel should stop when he rouses a rabbit or hare, should never range more than thirty yards from the gun, should drop when the gun goes off, and should then lie until signalled on. He should go through any furze or brambles like a rat; should be short on his legs, long in his body, have a long head, go to water, and retrieve alive; he should work with his tail down, and the set of the tail should be down also. His ears should be bell-shaped, small at the top and large at the bottom. The best breed is the "Clumber" spaniel, which is always mute, always lemon-and-white in colour, but not generally fond of the water. The next best breed is the Sussex, liver-and-white; the darker the liver, the better; the best-marked have a white blaze down the face, white muzzle, liver nose, lips flecked with liver, and flecked legs, belly and hips white, and white collar and chest. The most fashionable spaniels are mute black-and-white, or black-

and-tanned, legs, feet, and toes well feathered before and behind, and the feet round as a cheese-plate. As to retrievers: when you hear people speak of a genuine retriever, do not place much credit in their assertions, as there is no regular breed, and the best retrievers are generally mongrels, half-poodle, half-spaniel, and sometimes with a cross of Newfoundland. A well-taught retriever combines the qualities of pointer, setter, spaniel, and water-dog, with his own peculiar instinct of fetching a dead bird out of any brake, and carrying him with jaws of iron and teeth of wool. I need not say that such a dog is invaluable.

If you go in for pheasant-breeding, you go in for expense at once. The artificial food for three hundred pheasants, *until they shoot their tails*, would cost fifteen or twenty pounds. By artificial food I mean eggs, rice, greaves, chopped onions, lettuce, &c. I should say that every pheasant shot on any manor costs twelve shillings, for they *must* be reared by hand. The good friend with whom I have had many a pleasant day in the woods, calculates the cost of his birds at a pound each; but he does every thing in an unnecessarily princely fashion, and has a staff of keepers and beaters inferior to none in number or cost.

Grouse-shooting in England can be pursued in Yorkshire, Northumberland, and Westmoreland, in some parts of Wales, in Kerry, Limerick, Wicklow, and Tipperary in Ireland, and in the Scotch Highlands. Within the last few years grouse-shooting has become such a fashionable amusement, that the prices of moors have risen enormously, and have at length attained a fabulous height. Twenty years ago, the highest price for a moor of from twenty to forty thousand acres, fit for four guns, was four hundred pounds; you would be lucky now to get it for double the money. This is owing to the manufacturing gentry, who are tremendously keen grousers, and have a general leaning towards gunning, and can afford to pay magnificently. Here it may be well to call attention to the advertisements of moors to be let for the season, the owner of which stipulates that the tenant shall "be limited to a thousand brace"! He must not shoot more, for fear of thinning the stock on the moor. Caveat emptor. The intending answerer of such advertisement may safely pledge himself to abide by this stipulation, and if he and his friends bag three hundred brace, they may think themselves highly favoured. Setters and pointers (Russian and Spanish preferred by some) are the best dogs to shoot grouse to; the time, between the 12th of August and the 20th of September, though some talk of October and even the early days of November, but you will get better grousing between the dates I have mentioned; a large-bored gun, and, if with a muzzle-loader, No. 3 shot. Colonel Hawker says: "Grouse take a harder blow than partridges."

Also in the sporting journals, under the heading "To Let," you will find the entry, "Splendid deer-forests." A deer-forest is so named on the celebrated *lucus à non lucendo* principle: it does not contain a single tree, but is simply a Highland tract of land from which sheep have been kept off—as sheep and deer will never feed together. The most celebrated are the deer-forests of Lord Lovat, the Duke of Richmond, the Duke of Athol, and, above all, of the Marquis of Breadalbane. For a good deer-forest, a thousand a year is a low price; and every deer shot costs, on an average, from sixty to eighty pounds. Let no man, unpossessed of great bodily strength, with lasting power and patience, undertake deer-stalking. To walk for miles to the shooting-ground, to crawl on all-fours or on the stomach for several hundred yards through brake and brushwood, and then to take steady aim at a distance of over a hundred yards at about the least, requires men in high training and of natural bodily strength. But your amateur, however good, is never equal to your gillie, whose eye is more acute than the best Dollond or reçonnoitrer; whose arm is as steady as a rock, after any amount of exertion; and who goes up any number of the stiffest braes without turning a hair, or apparently without an extra pulsation. A knowing shot, your gillie, and one who never neglects an opportunity. They tell a story of a noble lord who, last year, was out on his moor with his favourite gillie, when he spied a noble stag about four hundred yards off. The nobleman put his rifle to his shoulder, covered the object, then lowered his piece. "Donald!" said he. "Me lard!" said Donald. "That's a fine shot." "Et wad be a faine shot for the mon as wad het it," was the

Highlander's sententious reply. "Take the rifle, Donald, sight it carefully, and give it me back; if I knock over that fellow, the rifle shall be yours." The gillie took the rifle and sighted it, and gave it to his master, who fired, and killed his stag. According to his promise, he gave the rifle to the gillie. Since then he has never been taken nearer than four hundred yards to any deer on his estate!

Never let any ribald "chaff," any denunciation of Cockney sport, prevent you from enjoying a good day's rabbit-shooting whenever you have the opportunity. With a couple of mute spaniels and a sharp terrier, you may have an excellent morning's sport; but you must remember that it is very quick shooting, and you must keep your gun on the cock, and be ready to pull the instant you see the rabbit run, if you would have a chance of hitting him. Be wary, for rabbits are wonderfully "up to trap;" pretend not to be looking after them, and you will throw them off their guard; but if you advance in a business-like manner, gun in hand, depend upon it that a flash of white tails is all you will see of your game—of the older ones, at least; the younger are less knowing, and more easily potted.

For any hints about wild-fowl shooting, go to Colonel Hawker, and consult no other. He is a little rococo and old-fashioned; but in the main he is as right now as he was when he wrote, and his advice is sound, practical, and sensible. Take it all with that "grain of salt" which the old Latin proverb prescribes; for though there lived strong men before Agamemnon, there are not many men strong enough to undergo all the hardships which Colonel Peter Hawker lightly touches upon in his hints on wild-fowl shooting.

It is unusual to take a dog with you when invited to a day's shooting. But in partridge-shooting, when you receive the invitation, it is common to ask the question, "How are you off for dogs?" and to take them if wanted. To take your dogs over without having ascertained the wish of your host, will cause you to be regarded as rather a cool hand. Perhaps, after all, spaniels are the most serviceable animals; setters and pointers are not much used in England, as there is little "laying" for birds under the new system of farming, and now turnips are drilled, birds rise before the dogs.

Finally, do not imagine that you can leave

the London season, the jolly nights in the Club smoke-room, the heavy dinners with ingoted East-Indian uncles, the twenty-one dances winding-up with a never-ending cotillon, indulged in night after night; and then go down to Norfolk, or wherever may be the manor to which you are invited, and shoot. The thing is impossible. You must be, to a certain extent, in training; at all events, your wind must be decent, your muscles braced, and your hand and eye steady. A long waltz may be good for your wind, but it will shake your arm; and a pipe of Cavendish or a couple of extra cigars will spoil your sport for the day. So do not be down-hearted at first if you fire wild, or if the squire and his country friends grin a bit as the birds fly away unharmed; wait—let your faith be "large in Time," as Mr. Tennyson has it; and very soon you will feel your hand getting in, and you will find that, as sweet Will, who has something on every thing, says, "Your shooting then is well accounted."

CHAPTER XII.

THE GRIMGRIBBER RIFLE CORPS: WE COMMENCE THE "MOVEMENT."

It was not until long after this grand patriotic volunteer movement had been started that we began to talk of it at Grimgribber, and it was much later before we thought of joining it. You see we are rather peculiar at Grimgribber—not aristocratic, perhaps, but decidedly rich, and on that account rather high and stand-off-ish. We live in large houses, considerably given to portico; we carpet our halls, and therein do a good deal in the proof-before-letter prints and stag's-horn and fox's-foot hat-rail line; we have very large gardens, with graperies and pineries, and every thing that can cost money; but we are decidedly not sociable. To tell truth, Grimgribber is, perhaps, a thought overdone with Quakerdom, having been selected as the favoured spot in which some of the choicest spirits of the Peace Society have pitched their mortal tents, and the consequence is, that it requires the greatest exertions to prevent our general notions from becoming too drab-coloured; so that when we read in the newspapers of the formation of the various corps, we merely shrugged our shoulders, and said "Ah!" in rather an admonitory tone; and it was not until the announcement that the Queen would probably receive the officers and review the troops, that the possibility of there being a Grimgribber regiment dawned upon us. I am bound to confess that the idea did not originate with me, but with Jack Heatly, a young stockbroker, who was always looked upon as a dangerous character, and who, when at a very early stage of affairs he joined a metropolitan rifle corps, was considered as having booked himself for perdition. Under cover of the darkness of night, and with extraordinary mystery (for even his bold spirit quailed at the audacity of his plan), Jack paid me a visit one evening last December, and imparted to me his ideas for the formation of the Grimgribber volunteers. The first of his large-souled propositions was, that he should be made captain; the second, that I should undertake all the work; the third, that I should mention the scheme to all likely persons, in my own name at first, but if it met with approval, in his.

I was struck with Jack's magnanimity, and fell into his views; so, likely persons were seen, and agreed at once to the rough outline of the scheme—Grimgribber should have a rifle corps; that was decided on; all details could be entered into at a public meeting, which should be forthwith advertised and held in the lecture-room of our Literary Institute. The consternation with which the drab-coloured portion of our population received this announcement cannot be described; the head-shakings, the hand-upliftings were awful, and the accusative case of the second person singular was joined to every verb of monition and reproach, and applied to us rigorously. But we managed to make way even against this, and we held our meeting. One of the county members had promised to preside, and at eight o'clock the room was crammed and beginning to get noisy, but the county member had not arrived; then I, as secretary, explained this to the meeting, and proposed that some one else should take the chair; and some one else accordingly took it, and had just reached a triumphant point in his peroration, when the door was burst open, and the county member walked in, in a white waistcoat and a rage; and we had to begin all over again. But still we had a very great success. I had drawn up a set of rules, based on those of Jack Heatly's former corps, and these met with great approval; an enemy had obtained admission, and he caused some disturbance by uttering a very loud and sarcastic "Hear, hear!" after one of them which inflicted a fine of five shillings for discharging the rifle by accident; and when I sat down, he rose and proceeded to comment on this rule, declaring it absurd to punish a person for an offence committed accidentally. But Jack got up, and in an oration of unexampled eloquence completely demolished our adversary, by proving to him what a consolation it would be to the surviving relations of any unfortunate person who might be thus killed, to think that the cause of the accident had been made to pay for his carelessness. And then an old gentleman, long resident in the village, and reputed to have been the author of some very spirited verses on the Prince Regent's coronation, which actually found their way into print, rose, and recited some poetry which he had forged for the occasion, in which Britannia was represented as bestowing crowns of laurel on each of her "commercial sons;" and this brought the meeting to a close with a storm of triumph.

OUR COUNCIL AND ITS FUNCTIONS.

On a convenient desk outside the meeting-room we had placed a large broad sheet, to which each intending "effective" member was to sign his name, and before the lecture-hall was closed we had seventy signatures. The seventy pledged ones met the next day and elected their officers—Jack Heatly, of course, being chosen captain; his brother, lieutenant; and I myself receiving the distinguished post of ensign. To any gentleman content with moderate exercise and a good position, I recommend the ensign's berth; his lungs are left intact, for he never has to shout the word of command; he is never in that awful doubt which seizes upon the other officers as to whether they are "on the right flank," as he has simply to walk behind the rear rank in the centre of the company; he is not liable to be shot by the enemy, or by his own men; and he can gain a character for smartness with little trouble, by merely occasionally uttering the caution, "Steady, now!" "Easy in the centre!" "Keep your fours in the wheel!" and such-like mandates, delivered in an admonitory voice. He is, in fact, the Lord Burleigh of the company, and best comports himself by grave silence and stern military aspect.

When the selection of officers had been made, we set to work and chose certain gentlemen to be members of council. We had seen that other corps had a council, and it was therefore necessary that we should have one; but, beyond checking the expenses of the regiment, we were not at all clear as to what were the council's functions. We soon found out. The members of the council were exclusively privates, and it appeared that their first and most urgent duties were to oppose every arrangement made by the officers, and to endeavour in every possible manner to set the corps by the ears. Did Jack Heatly, as captain commanding, issue an order, the council was down upon him like a shot, had him up like Othello before the Senate, and harangued him with Old-Bailey-like politeness and Central-Criminal-Court etiquette. Did the lieutenant, a shy and retiring young man, make a mistake in his word of command, he was summoned the next day before the Vehmgericht, had his error pointed out to him, was told to make himself immediately master of the few instructions contained in very small type in a fat red-covered quarto volume of some eight-hundred pages, and was dismissed with a rather more severe reprimand than if he had stolen a watch. Did I endeavour to come to the rescue, I was received with bland smiles and disbelieving shoulder-shrugs, and with pleasant hints that "the subaltern officers had really better not expose themselves." Now this was trying to all, especially to Jack Heatly, who is as explosive as a volcano, and who used to make a light meal off his lips and tongue in endeavouring to maintain his reticence; but as the members of the council were indefatigable in their zeal at drill, punctual in their attendance, and showed thoroughly that they had the welfare of the corps at heart, we put up with it all, and got rapidly under weigh.

Of course it was necessary that we should accumulate as ample funds as possible, besides the subscription of the members; and with this view the council determined that a select few of us should call upon the inhabitants and ask for donations. The list of names was divided into three portions; and I as junior officer had the most implacable enemies of the movement allotted to me to visit. Now it has been my fate to have been placed in many humiliating positions during my life. I have been compelled to act a knight in a charade with a tin-pot on my head for a helmet and a towel-horse for my charger, and in this guise to make love to a very stout old lady before the grinning faces of deriding friends. I have been asked to "do" an orange "nicely" for a young lady at dessert, and, owing to my having blind eyes and utterly immobile stiff fingers, have bungled thereat in a manner contemptible to behold. On the King's Road, at Brighton, I have ridden a flea-bitten gray horse formerly a member of a circus, which, in the presence of hundreds of the aristocracy then and there assembled, persisted in waltzing to the music of a German band. But never was I so thoroughly ashamed of myself as on the errand of requesting donations for the Grimgribber volunteers. In ten places they told me plainly they would not give any thing; and next to those who gave willingly, I liked these best: in others, they shook their heads and sighed, and said it did not augur well for any movement which began by sending round the begging-box. Some were virtuously indignant, and denounced us as openly inciting foreign attack by our braggadocio; some declined to give because they were comfortably persuaded that the end of the world was so close at hand that our services would never be required; one old farmer, known to be enormously rich and horribly penurious, offered us a threepenny-piece, a brass tobacco-box, and a four-bladed knife with a corkscrew in the handle.

But perhaps my noblest interview was with Mr. Alumby, our senior churchwarden, who lives at The Hassocks, close outside the village, and who has the credit of being the best hand at an excuse of any man in the county. Overwhelmingly polite was Alumby, offered me a chair with the greatest hospitality, spoke about our Queen, our country, our national defences, and the patriotic body of men now coming forward, in a way that made my ears tingle; but he declined to subscribe, on principle, on principle alone. In any other possible manner that he could aid us, he would, but he could not give us money, as he thought such a proceeding *would deprive the movement of its purely voluntary character!* I was so staggered that I paused for a moment, overcome; then I suggested that this feeling might not prevent his helping us in another way: we wanted a large space to drill in—would he lend us his field? He hesitated for a minute, and then asked if I meant his field in Grimgribber, at the back of his house. On my replying in the affirmative, his face expressed the deepest concern; "he could not spare a blade of that grass, not a blade—he required it all for grazing purposes, and it must not be trampled upon; but he had considerable property in South Wales, and if that had been any use to us, he could have put hundreds of acres at our disposal." However, notwithstanding these rebuffs, we collected a very respectable sum of money, and thought ourselves justified in really commencing operations. Of course the first and most important operation was

OUR DRILL.

He to whom our military education was confided was a sergeant in the Welsh Bombardier Guards, and he brought with him a corporal of the same regiment as his assistant.

The sergeant was short and stout; the corporal tall and thin; both had hair greased to the point of perfection, and parted with mathematical correctness; perched on the extreme right verge of his head the corporal accurately balanced a little cap. Off duty the sergeant was occasionally human in his appearance and manners, but the corporal never. In his mildest aspect he resembled a toy-soldier; but when, either in giving command or taking it from his sergeant, he threw up his head, stiffened his body, closed his heels, and stuck out his hands like the signs at a French glove-shop reversed, I can find no word to describe his wooden nonentity. I think we all felt a little awkward at our first introduction to our instructors. They surveyed us, as we were drawn up in line, grimly and depreciatingly; in obedience to a look from his superior, the corporal then fell a pace or two back and assumed the statuesque attitude; while the sergeant rapped his cane against his leg, and exclaimed, "Now, gen'l'men, FALL IN!" the first two words being uttered in his natural voice, the last two in an awful sepulchral tone, and sounding like a double rap on a bass kettle-drum.

We "fell in" as we best could—that is, we huddled together in a long line—and were then "sized" by the sergeant, who walked gravely down the rank, and inspected us as though we had been slaves in the market of Tripoli, and he the Dey's emissary with a large commission to buy; and then commenced our preliminary instruction. The first manœuvre imparted to us was to "stand at ease"—a useful lesson, teaching us not only the knowledge of a strategic evolution, but giving us quite a new insight into the meaning of the English language. In our former benighted ignorance we might possibly have imagined that to stand at ease meant to put our hands in our pockets, to lean against the wall, or to lounge in any easy and comfortable manner; but we now learned that, in order to stand really at ease, we should strike the palm of our left hand very smartly with the palm of our right, then fold the right over the back of the left in front of us, protrude our left foot, throwing the weight of the body on the right, and, in fact, place ourselves as nearly as possible in the attitude of Pantaloon when he is first changed by the fairy, minus his stick. It is an elegant and telling manœuvre this, when properly executed, and possibly not very difficult of acquirement: but we did not fall into it all at once; there was a diversity of opinion among us as to which was the proper foot to be advanced; and when that was settled, we were at variance as to which was our right foot and which our left; so that it was not until the sergeant had many times sarcastically assured us that "he couldn't hear them hands come smartly together as he'd wished—not like a row of corks a-poppin' one after the other, but all at once;" nor until the stiff corporal had paraded up and down behind us, muttering, in a low tone, "Them left feet advanced—no, no! them *left* feet advanced," that we were considered sufficiently perfect in this respect, and allowed to pass on to grander evolutions. The same difficulty was attendant upon these. On being told to "right face," two gentlemen, of diametrically opposed views on the subject, would find themselves face to face instead of being one behind the other, and neither would give way until they were set right by the sergeant.

It was not until after some time that we hit upon the golden principle of drill, which is—NEVER TO THINK AT ALL! Listen, pay attention to the word of command as it is given, and then follow your first impulse; it will generally be the right one. But the recruit who hesitates is lost. Under the present system the simplest movements are taught—not by example, but in directions composed of long sentences abounding in technical expressions, listening to which the unhappy learner, long before the sergeant has come to the middle of his direction, is oblivious of the first part, ignorant of the meaning of the last, and in a thorough fog as to the whole. These directions are learnt parrot-wise by the sergeants, and repeated in a monotonous and unintelligible tone; the men who make use of them know no more what they are saying than those who are addressed; and an example two minutes long does more good than an hour's precept. It is perfectly true that to the educated intelligence of the volunteers is due the superiority which, so far as rapidity of progress is concerned, they have shown over the ordinary recruits; but a very slight exercise of this educated intelligence will suffice for most of the evolutions.

When the command has been received on the tympanum, act upon it at once, without pausing to reflect. You will see many intelligent men bring upon themselves the wrath of their sergeant, simply because, in analysing and pondering on his instructions, they have missed the right time for action, and are half a minute or so behind the rest of their company. For instance, the command is given: "At the word 'Fours' the rear-rank will step smartly off with the left foot, taking a pace to the rear—Fours!" Or, in the sergeant's language, "Squad! 'shun! at th'wud 'Foz' the rer-rank will stepsma't lyoffwi' th' leffut, tekkinapesstoth' rare—Fo-o-o-res!" the last word being uttered in a prolonged and discordant bellow. A reflective gentleman in the rear-rank first translates this dialect into the ordinary language of civilised life, and then proceeds to ponder on its meaning; and when he has discovered it, he probably finds himself deserted by his comrades, who have taken up a position a pace behind him, and an object of disgust to the sergeant, who, looking at him more in pity than in anger, says, in a hoarse whisper, "Now, Number Three, what, wrong agin!"

When I remember the unique series of performances that inaugurated our first lessons in marching, I cannot imagine that we were then the same set of Grimgribber volunteers who defiled so steadily before her Majesty the other day, amidst the bravos of enthusiastic crowds. I think our original evolutions were even sufficient to astonish our sergeant, a man not easily overcome; for, at the conclusion of the first lesson, I observed him retreat to a distant corner of the parade-ground, strike himself a heavy blow on the chest, and ejaculate, "Well, if hever!" three distinct times. I recollect that two-thirds of our number had peculiar theories of their own, and that each trying his own plan led to confusion. For instance, the gentleman who would step off with his right foot, at the third step found his leg firmly wedged between the ankles of his precursor, and utterly lost the use of that limb; the light and swinging gait which was admirably adapted for the pursuit of a country postman was found scarcely to tally with the sober, slodgy walk of two-thirds of the corps, who were accordingly trodden down from the calf to the heel, and who did not view the matter with all the equanimity which good fellowship should engender. A third step, of a remedial tendency, consisting of a wide straddling of the legs, and an encircling of the feet of the person immediately in front of you by your own, was not agreeably received by the sergeant, and had to be abandoned: so it was some time before we presented that unanimity of action which is necessary to satisfactory marching.

But we stuck to it manfully, and progressed well. The sergeant, who at first seemed disposed to give us up in despair, because he could not swear at us as was his custom, began to take an interest in us; and when we had overcome what he called the "roodymans" of drill, we took an interest in our instructions. We had a very stormy debate about our uniform, discussed every variety of gray and green, lost an exceedingly efficient member by declining to adopt what he called a "Garibaldi shako," but which, in plain English, was a green wagoner's hat with a cock's feather at the side; and finally settled upon a very quiet and inexpensive dress. Then, of course, after a very long delay, we received our supply of rifles from the Government, and all the difficulties of drill were renewed; but we overcame them at last, and even settled the great question as to which was the best and most intelligible word of command for shouldering arms—"Shalloo humps!" as given by the sergeant, or "Shoolah hice!" as dictated by the corporal. We decided for "Shalloo humps," and have stuck to it ever since.

OUR RECEPTION IN PUBLIC.

It is almost unnecessary to say that our formation has made an intense impression on the Grimgribber mind, and that the first day of our appearance in public was anxiously looked forward to. We had purposely kept ourselves unseen by any save our own immediate relatives, and the unveiling of the Great Mokanna never caused greater astonishment than did our first outburst, preceded by the drums and fifes of the United Order of Ancient Buffaloes. We filed out two by two from the lecture-hall, and marched away to a field in the neighbourhood, there to perform our evolutions. Grimgribber was present in its entirety—the richest and the poorest; the men of peace and fighting ruffians from the beer-shops; crinoline petticoats bulged against drab shorts and white stockings; short clay pipes leered over Cashmere shawls. A roar of delight burst forth as we turned out; we grasped our rifles firmly, raised our heads, inflated our chests, and threw out our sixty left legs like one. It was a proud moment; but we were made to feel that, after all, we were but mortal, and the check we received was given to us by a very small boy, who looked at our ranks with a calmly critical eye, and hit upon a fatal blot. "Ah! and ain't they all of a size, neither!" he exclaimed. His remark was greeted with laughter; for our tallest man is six feet one, and our shortest (whom we hide away in the centre of the company) is only five feet two. However, we bore up nobly; we felt that even the great Duke of Wellington had been insulted in the streets; and that we, who had not yet quite arrived at his eminence in military matters, ought to treat our aggressors with placidity and good humour. So we marched on to the field, and there went through all our evolutions with a steadiness and precision which entirely disarmed the boy, and changed him from a jeering ribald into an admiring spectator.

So it has been ever since; we have made quiet and steady but efficient progress; our ranks have been swelled by daily additions; we are labouring away at our target practice long before the drowsy drabmen have moved from their pillows; and I hope that at the next time of writing I shall have to record that a prize at the meeting of the National Rifle Association has been gained by one of the Grimgribber volunteers.

CHAPTER XIII.

MORE OF THE GRIMGRIBBER RIFLE CORPS—OUR NEW CAPTAIN.

AUTUMN being, according to the almanacs, close at hand, and many members of our corps feeling bound to absent themselves from the neighbourhood of the metropolis and to disport in sylvan or sea-side regions, I see some chance of being enabled to get an evening to myself to chronicle our doings since the earliest stages of our formation. Up to this time it has been impossible. I thought that when I had mastered the difficulties of drill my labour would be at an end; that I might once a week lead or rather follow the regiment to our parade-ground; that on the other six days my helmet might have been used as a hive for bees, or any other rustic and pacific receptacle; that our bugler would "sing truce" as soon as the Saturday night cloud had lowered, and would not call us again to arms for the entire space of a week;

in fact, that so long as we were well up in our manual and platoon, and could put our men through the ordinary evolutions of company and battalion drill, more would not be required of us. I was mistaken—as I often am, and always to my cost. I daresay that, had we remained as we originally formed ourselves, I could have arranged things with Jack Heatly and his brother, and we should have restricted our military ambition within proper limits; but our corps increased so tremendously, so many fresh recruits came flocking to our standard, that we were obliged to form a second company, who, in their turn, elected their officers, and who chose for their captain a gentleman who, from his punctuality, exactitude, and strict attention to business, seems intended by Nature to supply the place of the late Duke of Wellington in these dominions. He was elected because he was a pleasant, strong, active young fellow, a good cricketer and oarsman, and such a maniac for dancing that he might have been a male Wili, or a victim to the bite of the tarantula. He was elected, and he thanked us. The next day on parade his true character burst forth! He made us a speech, in which he said he had observed with regret that the discipline of the regiment was not such as could be wished. He was aware, he said (glancing at Jack Heatly, who was sitting on a camp-stool smoking a short pipe)—he was aware that we had been somewhat loosely looked after; but that we might depend upon a strict supervision in future. You may be astonished to hear that there were certain men who applauded this harangue: rash young men who talked about "sticking to the thing" and "having no child's-play;" but I myself trembled in my varnished gaiters. The next day Jack Heatly took a month's leave of absence and went out of town, and the new captain, De Tite Strongbow, became our commander-in-chief. I shall never forget that day! it was a Saturday, and we had just gone through a series of the most complicated evolutions in a pouring rain; I was in the armoury divesting myself of my soaked uniform and rusted sword, and privately wondering why I had voluntarily exposed myself to so much inconvenience, when the senior sergeant of the regiment presented himself before me. A pleasant man is Sergeant Piper, with a jolly round rubicund face, a merry black eye, and a nose that attests the goodness of the port-wine at the Sternsail and Tiller on the Essex shore; which hotel he makes his summer residence. But dull was his appearance and solemn his expression as he made his military salute, and, merely saying "From the captain, sir," placed in my hands a large square printed paper. It was headed with the royal arms, and ran as follows:

GRIMGRIBBER RIFLE CORPS.

Arrangements for the week.

MONDAY.—Second squad drill at 2 P.M. by Ensign Rivers.
TUESDAY.—Platoon drill by Ensign Rivers, 2 P.M.
WEDNESDAY.—First instruction in musketry, 7 P.M., by Captain Strongbow, assisted by Ensign Rivers.
THURSDAY.—Second squad drill by Ensign Rivers, 2 P.M.
FRIDAY.—Lecture on the dissection of the lock, by Captain Strongbow, assisted by Ensign Rivers, 4 P.M.
SATURDAY.—The regiment will march out for battalion drill on Squash Common. All the officers will attend. Gaiters *if wet*, but no greatcoats on any account.

Ensign Rivers is officer of the week; and any gentleman requiring any information on any point must apply to him.

DE TITE STRONGBOW.
Captain Commanding.

I, the present writer, am Ensign Rivers, whose name is so frequently mentioned in this abominable document! I rushed off to Strongbow's rooms—he lives with his father, the eminent drysalter, but has a little outbuilding next the stables especially appropriated to his use. As I neared this pavilion I heard strange sounds of stamping, mingled with thwacking of weapons, and cries of "Ha! ha! had you there!" Entering, I found Strongbow stripped to his shirt, and busily engaged in belabouring the corporal, who, wooden as ever, solemnly defended himself with a single-stick. "Hallo!" says Strongbow, "come for more orders, Ensign?" I boil over, I object, I appeal—all in vain. "What will the men say when they see their officers shirking duty?" Fruitlessly do I urge that I know nothing of the musketry instruction, or the dissection of the lock; he gives me books—enormous volumes—which he bids me study. For a moment I waver in my allegiance; I have a faint notion of requesting Her Majesty to be graciously pleased to accept my resignation of my commission; but better thoughts prevail, and I go to work. I drill the second squad; I pass a bright afternoon in the dull lecture-room of the Mechanics' Institute, where the Map of Europe glares feebly at me from the damp-stained wall, and where the mullioned windows rattle dismally at the tramping of the recruits. Painfully and wearily do I go through the different evolutions, and tight and gordian-like is the knot into which I once or twice get myself and all the men, and have to summon the stiff corporal to my assistance, amidst furtive grins and whispered hints of "try back." But I did get through it at last, and next day accomplished the platoon drill, with directions, and in a manner that struck the corporal mute with horror. It has been malevolently remarked that the gentlemen who benefited by my instruction have since been recognisable principally by a habit of invariably carrying their rifles at full cock, and secondly by the slight omission of neglecting to withdraw their ramrods after loading with blank cartridge: a disadvantage which is apt to be unpleasantly felt by their comrades when they are placed as "a rear-rank standing." But this is mere envy.

THE FIRST INSTRUCTION IN MUSKETRY.

It was so called in the Orders for the week, because it is rather a fine phrase. I believe, however, that the real technical unvarnished name of this performance is "Preliminary Drill for cleaning Arms." A select class attended Captain Strongbow's first instruction-lecture on the Wednesday evening; but I shall better be able to give an account of their proceedings by adopting the dramatic form.

SCENE—*Captain Strongbow's rooms. Evening. Moderator-lamp alight in centre. Captain Strongbow at head of table; a long Enfield Rifle and two very ominous-looking red books by his side. Privates and sergeants of the corps gathered round him. Ensign Rivers standing immediately behind the Captain, where he has the least chance of being seen by him, and looking doubtfully on. The opening portion of the lecture has already been given.*

Captain Strongbow (*proceeding*). Now, gentlemen, I will once more run through what I have said, before questioning you. Now, gentlemen, the principal parts of the rifle are the stock and the barrel. (*He takes up rifle, and points to each part as he names it.*) The stock is divided into the nose-cap, the upper, middle, and lower bands, the swell, projections, lock-side, head, small, trigger-guard, trigger-plate, trigger, butt, and heel-plate. Once more! (*He repeats all the names.*) Now,

Mr. Lobjoit, what is this called? (*Laying his hand on the nose-cap.*)

Lobjoit (*who is a horsy man, and is always wishing we were cavalry*). Nose-bag!

Capt. S. (*disgusted*). What do you say, Mr. Pruffle?

Pruffle (*a slow, middle-aged gentleman, who has entered the force with the sole object of learning how to defend his large family*). Night-cap!

Capt. S. (*more disgusted*). Now, Mr. Skull, what is it?

Skull (*looking blankly at it through his spectacles*). 'Pon my soul, I don't know!

Capt. S. (*profoundly disgusted*). Really, this is too bad! Is there no gentleman present who can remember what this is called?

Sergeant Fluke. Eh? of course; yes! I can! It's the—the—the nose-cap, of course! (*Aside, to next neighbour.*) Gad! what a good shot!

Capt. S. (*overjoyed*). Very good; very good indeed, Sergeant Fluke! Ensign Rivers, I must trust to your honour not to prompt the gentlemen!

Ensign R. You may rely upon my doing nothing of the sort, sir! (*N.B. This is strictly correct, as Ensign Rivers knows rather less about it than any one in the room.)*

Capt. S. Now, Sergeant Fluke, can you touch any other parts of the stock, and tell me their names?

Fluke. Oh, yes, of course! (*Glibly.*) This is the barrel, and—

Capt. S. Parts of the *stock*, I said. The stock and the barrel are two distinct things.

Private J. Miller (*the funny man of the corps—aside to his neighbour*). Not at a cooper's or a brewer's; there, the barrels constitute the stock!

Private Miller's neighbour (*derisively*). Ho! ho! ain't you funny!

Capt. S. Silence, gentlemen, pray! Now, Sergeant Fluke?

Fluke. Well, you know, this is the trigger, and this is the butt.

Capt. S. Which is the heel of the butt, Mr. Pruffle?

Pruffle (*touching the wrong end*). This, sir.

Capt. S. No, no! that's not the heel; that's the toe!

Private Miller. Heel and toe! I say, Pruffle, my pimpkin, which is the double-shuffle?

Capt. S. Mr. Miller, I shall be compelled

to call upon you to retire, if you persist in this buffoonery! (*Private Miller makes a grimace of preternatural ugliness behind his neighbour's back, hums the Dead March in Saul, and crosses his hands to simulate a handcuffed deserter about to be shot.*)

Capt. S. Now, then, let us take the barrel.

Private Miller. Ah! some of us have taken to that kindly.

Capt. S. Taken to what?

Miller. To the barrel, sir! Don't mind me! Go on!

Capt. S. (*touching them*). The muzzle, fore-sight, back or elevating sight, nipple, breech, breech-pin. Component parts of the breech-pin: face, tang, and breech nail-hole. What are the component parts of the breech-pin, Mr. Lobjoit?

Lobjoit (*rapidly*). Face, fangs, and breeches-nails!

Capt. S. (*in despair*). This is dreadful! I don't know what they'd say to you at Hythe!

Miller. He'll never go there, sir; no more shall I. I say, Lobjoit, old boy, fancy their catching us playing at Hythe among the Sikhs.

Capt. S. (*with dignity*). I shall leave you out of the course, Mr. Miller! (*Miller feigns to weep, and dry his eyes on the back of his hand.)* Now, once more, before I give up. The component parts of the back or elevating sight are the flanges, flap, slider, spring, and bed. Name them, Mr. Skull.

Skull (yawning). The principal part of the back-sight is the spring-bed.

Capt. S. (*rising in disgust*). No more at present!

(*Exeunt all but Strongbow, who sits up half the night studying the theory of trajectories.*)

THE PRESENTATION OF OUR BUGLE.

We had attended the Wimbledon meeting and the Chiselhurst sham-fight, and had covered ourselves with glory at both; but there was nothing to look forward to, and the perpetual platoon exercise and theoretical musketry instruction began to grow monotonous. The attendance of men was a trifle falling off; and I had suggested to Captain Strongbow that he should hurry on the preparation of our butts, and get us out to "judging distances" and firing with ball-cartridge as speedily as possible, when we received intimation of an approaching event which brought back all those who were beginning to lapse. When our numbers increased, and we grew too large for the Mechanics' Institute or Toddler's Yard, we looked about for some suitable drill-ground; but there was no place to be had, and we were in despair, when the Principal of Dulciss's Grimgribber College, hearing of our extremity, came forward in the kindest manner and placed the grounds of that establishment at our disposal. Dulciss's College is not, as you may probably imagine, a scholastic institution for young gentlemen; it is a retreat, a refuge, a harbour for elderly gentlemen who have been broken and buffeted by the tempests of the world: a roadstead where they may ride safely at anchor for the remainder of their lives, comfortably housed and tended, and provided with a small income to supply themselves with necessaries. The only qualifications for candidates are, that they shall have been born in Grimgribber, shall have exceeded sixty years of age, and shall be without pecuniary resources. It is not difficult to find many who can fulfil these requirements, and the college is always full; there, slowly pacing up and down the shady cloisters, or sitting sunning themselves on the wormeaten old benches outside the porch, are the old fellows constantly to be seen, wearing their old black cloaks and queer shovel-hats as decreed by the founder, old Sir Thomas Dulciss, who died two hundred years ago. Attached to their prettily-terraced garden is a fine open meadow of several acres; but the old collegians rarely stroll so far; and when, under the permission of the principal, we held our first drill therein, none of them even came out to look at us, or took the trouble to inquire what we were doing. But a little later, on a fine spring day, they came down in a knot and stood close by, watching our movements; and as the words of command rang out, two or three of them, evidently old soldiers, straightened their poor bent backs and cocked their shovel-hats with the ghost of a military swagger; and one, a very old man, hobbled back to the college, whence he returned with his black cloak thrown very much back, and a Waterloo medal gleaming on his brave old breast. When drill was over, we gave him a cheer that brought the fire into his dim eyes and the flush into his withered cheeks. Then Mrs. Principal, a benevolent old lady, and the two Miss Principals, very dashing girls, got in the habit of coming to watch us; and the Miss Principals brought their friends, and the friends brought their cavaliers; so that at last we used to exhibit before quite a bevy of spectators. One day Sir Gregory Dulciss, the present representative of the great family, was at the college on business; and hearing of this, we formed on the terrace and saluted the great man, presenting arms to him as he came out. Sir Gregory was greatly touched at this, called it audibly a "dayvlish gratifying mark of 'tention," made us several bows modelled on those of his great friend the late King George the Fourth, and hoped to meet us again. And a few days afterwards it was officially announced that Lady Dulciss intended presenting us with a silver bugle.

This it was that caused the new excitement; this it was that brought up the few laggards, and caused the many who had hitherto been indefatigable to show even greater attention. It was determined that we should have a great day; it was understood that a select company would come over from the Radishes, Sir Gregory's house; that the neighbourhood generally would attend; and there was to be a tent with a cold collation for the corps, while the officers were invited to a champagne luncheon at the principal's. Such furbishing-up of arms and accoutrements, such worrying of tailors and armourers, such private drill among the men, and such minute inquiries among the officers as to the exact meaning of "recover swords!"

The day arrived and the hour. Headed by our band (their first appearance in public —rather nervous and shaky, a trifle agitated in the trombone, and a thought Punch-and-Judyish about the big drum, but still playing capitally), we marched through the village and into the field. The profane vulgar were not allowed to come inside, but they clustered thickly round the gates, and swarmed about the palings like bees. Very good and searching were the remarks of the boys. "Walk up! walk up! just agoin' to begin!" shouts one, as the band passed. "Hooray for the Workus Corps!" says another, in allusion to our neat gray uniform. "Here's the pauper lunatics with their throats cut!" says a third, hinting at the red stripe on our collars. "Hallo, Bill," says a boy perched on the gate, "here's your huncle!" "I see him," responds Bill, a grimy-faced cynical young blacksmith—"I see him, *but I never takes no notice on him when he's with his Wolunteers!"* And we passed on into the field. The white tent glimmered in the sun, and the ground was covered with company. The Dulciss people had brought some great acquaintances with them, country grandees in their carriages, dashing girls on horseback, and three or four young Guards' officers who came to scoff, and remained to prey—upon the luncheon. To pass this lot was the great ordeal. "Keep up, rear rank!" "Steady in the centre!" "Touch to the left, Jenkins; where the deuce are you going to?" The first and second companies went by splendidly. "Weally, not so bad, now, for quill-drivers and mechanics," says young Lithpson of the Bombardiers to Jack Gorget of the Body Guards, mauve. Jack nods approvingly; then, as the third company advances, headed by Tom Exlex, who was in the Spanish service under General Evans, and wears his Sebastian medal and San-Fernando cross on his breast, Jack says earnestly, though ungrammatically, "Hallo, what's this swell's decorations?" "'Pon my soul, I can't say," answers Lithpson; "pwobably some weward for supewiour penmanship."

But we could afford to laugh even at such bitter sarcasm as this, so well were our evolutions performed, and so heartily were they applauded. Finally, we were drawn up in line, and, amidst the cheers of the populace, Lady Dulciss advanced, followed by a portentous servant bearing the bugle on a cushion. Lady Dulciss is a very fine woman: a kind, benevolent, motherly-looking lady, and I've no doubt she made an excellent speech. It was intended for the entire regiment, but she delivered it in a confidential tone to Jack Heatly, who stood in front of her, and all we caught was "Britannia," "bugle," "Grimgribber," and "call to arms." Then she presented the bugle gracefully to Jack, who, in his intense nervousness, instantly dropped it, and she and he and Sir Gregory and the portentous footman all struggled for it on the ground. Then the band played "God save the Queen," the people cheered louder than ever, and we broke off and went in to lunch.

CHAPTER XIV.

GRIMGRIBBER POSITION-DRILL.

In the spring, according to Mr. Tennyson, the wanton lapwing gets himself another nest, a brighter iris changes on the burnished dove, and a young man's fancy lightly turns to thoughts of love. These are unanswerable facts; but here is another vernal incident, which, probably because Locksley Hall was written before the institution of the volunteer movement, has been unnoticed by the poet. In the spring the gentlemen attached to the various rifle corps, whose ardour has been chilled by the dreary winter, and whose time has been consumed in festivity, suddenly recal the fact that the eyes of their country are earnestly fixed on them for its defence. I am proud to say that we of the Grimgribbers were, theoretically, early in the field. No one who knows Captain de Tite Strongbow will imagine that he would have allowed us to be laggards. This indefatigable young man has never relaxed in his exertions. After the presentation of our bugle, recorded in the previous Chapter, the ardour of the members thawed, and the general voice resolved itself into a-dieu; that is to say, half the men went to the Continent, and the other half to the seaside. Before we broke up, Captain Strongbow called a battalion drill, when the prevalent disorder showed itself in an eruption of moustaches of a week's growth, and in the bulging of Continental Bradshaws from uniform pockets. Strongbow noticed this, and, as I may express it in the language of the Wardour-Street Elizabethan drama, "advantaged himself of the occasion." He put us through some of the most difficult and most perspiration-causing movements in the Field Exercise-book, and then, having formed us into a square, and faced us inward, he solemnly addressed us. He said that he grieved to find a general disposition for a holiday, a disposition by no means in accordance with that solemn pledge which we had given when we voluntarily placed our services at her Majesty's disposal. He mildly hinted that any one declining to attend parade or drill when summoned, was guilty of perjury in its grossest form; and he asked us where we expected to go to? Through the dead silence which followed this appeal, the voice of the ill-conditioned private J. Miller was heard, suggesting "Margate;" but the ribaldry had effect on none but a few hardened scoffers. However, it was useless attempting to stop the threatened exodus; and, after suggesting that those who visited the Continent should keep a sharp eye upon the foreign troops, "with whom they might be called upon to cross bayonets" (an idea which made a profound impression on private Pruffle); and that they should take measures for becoming generally acquainted with the defensive works of such foreign fortresses as they might happen to come across; and after recommending the stay-at-homes to attach themselves to the garrison of the seaport town where they might be staying, and pass an easy month of relaxation in attending three drills a day and perusing the Field Exercise-book in the evening, Captain Strongbow dismissed us with a benediction.

I do not believe that any one, save Strongbow himself (who went first to Hythe and then to Shorncliffe, and passed the remainder of the autumn in endeavouring to improve the

Armstrong gun), paid the smallest attention to the recommendation. Pruffle was seen with a wideawake hat and a telescope on Southend pier. Lobjoit broke three colts and his own leg among the Yorkshire spinneys. Skull went to Worthing, and fell into a chronic state of sleep and seaweed. Private Miller, though he certainly visited Aldershot, only went for one night to assist at the military theatre in an amateur performance. We all went away, and did cathedrals, and mountain passes, and ruined abbeys, and lay on beaches, and swam, and mooned, and enjoyed ourselves; and by the time we returned to Grimgribber we had nearly forgotten the existence of our noble corps.

The Quakers were in ecstasies; they knew it; had they not prophesied it? "Friend, did I not tell thee?" &c. &c. All of which so roused the ire of De Tite Strongbow, that one day early in October, every dead-wall, tree, and post in Grimgribber blossomed with a blue-and-red announcement of a "Parade on the Common on Saturday next."

The day came and the hour, but not the men; that is to say, there was not a very great muster. Parties of two and three came straggling up the lane, evidently intending merely to look on; but they were spied by the vedettes posted by Strongbow at available situations, and immediately hailed by that energetic officer in stentorian tones and appealing phrases, all of which commenced, "Hallo! you sirs!" The persons addressed, recognising the voice, generally feigned total deafness, looked round in a vacant manner, and commenced a retreat; but Strongbow was by their side before they had gone three paces, and by coaxing, wheedling, and bullying, induced most of them to proceed to the Common, so that at last two-thirds of our total number were present.

That day will be for ever remembered by the Grimgribber Volunteers; on it they were initiated into the mysteries of rifle-shooting; on it they laid the foundation of that system of skill which will, I doubt not, enable them to carry off the Queen's prize and a few other trifles at the forthcoming Wimbledon meeting; on it they commenced the practice of a series of fearful gymnastics, compared with which the crank is a light and easy amusement, and the stone-excavating at Portland a pleasant pastime.

We had executed our "company-drill" in a singularly fanciful manner, remarkable chiefly for its divergence from prescribed rule. Long absence from parade had rendered us rusty and entirely oblivious of the meaning of the various commands. Thus, at the word "fours," the rear-rank, instead of stepping smartly back, remained perfectly stationary, while a pleasant smile overspread the faces of most of its members at what they considered the extraordinary conduct of the two or three knowing ones who moved. In wheeling, the difference of opinion between the men was even more plainly exemplified; for, while some clung close to the pivot man, others ambled away into the far distance, while the centre portion distributed their favours equally between the two, rushing sometimes to the one end, sometimes to the other; so that, instead of coming up "like a wall," as had so often been urged upon us, we serpentined about in a very graceful festoon, and resembled nothing so much as the letter S. From my ensign's position in the rear I had watched Captain Strongbow's face during the performance of these manœuvres, and had every moment expected to see it overcloud; but, to my astonishment, he remained perfectly calm, and, at the conclusion of the drill, he called us together, told us we should soon "pick up our movements," but that he had something of far greater importance in store for us. He here stated that it was most important that we should perfect ourselves in the practical portion of shooting; that he had already prepared four sergeants who would undertake to instruct various sections of the corps; and that on that evening the first meeting for position-drill would take place at his (Strongbow's) rooms. He hoped he should have a good attendance, and concluded by telling us to bring our rifles, and not to eat too much dinner. What could that last caution mean? Alas, in a very few hours we knew its value!

OUR INSTRUCTION IN POSITION-DRILL.

SCENE—*A barn attached to Captain Strongbow's house. Rather a bleak and cheerless place, with targets painted in black-and-white on the walls. A flaring lamp on a bracket lights only the end portion of the place. Some ten members of the corps, sergeants and privates, are lounging about, waiting to begin business. Captain Strongbow by him-*

self, aiming at a painted target with marvellous precision.

Enter Private Miller, smoking a short clay pipe; he stares round at the painted targets on the walls, and then shouts in a hoarse voice: "Here y'ar! Now's your time! Three shots for sixpence! Try your fortune at the Little Vunder, gents! Pint o' nuts for him as hits the bull's-eye!"

Captain Strongbow (*aghast*). For Heaven's sake, stop this most discreditable noise, Mr. Miller!

Miller (*in broken and melodramatic tones*). Pardon me, noble captain, but the sight of these targets reminded me of the Greenwich fairs of early youth!

Strongbow. Pray, silence, Mr. Miller! It is impossible to get on if you indulge in buffoonery. Now, gentlemen. Fall in! (*Sergeants and privates range themselves in line.*) I am about to put you through position-drill; a course of instruction which habituates for the correct position of firing, and teaches you the natural connection between the HAND and the EYE. What are you smiling at, Mr. Skull?

Skull. Nothing, nothing; only Miller——

Strongbow. Miller; what?

Skull. Miller said that Mr. Mace in the last prize-fight taught Mr. Hurst the natural connection between the hand and the eye!

Strongbow. This is most disheartening! Now! There are three practices. The first word of command in the first practice is, "As a rear-rank standing at three hundred yards, Ready." On the word ready, make a half-face to the right, feet at right angles, grasp the rifle firmly with the left-hand, fingers of right-hand behind the trigger-guard, body erect, left side perpendicular, left breast over left foot, shoulders——

Private Pruffle. Stop, sir, pray stop (*confusedly*). I can't recollect half that! I've a short memory! What did you say after making a face?

(*Captain Strongbow repeats the instructions. All listen attentively, especially Private Miller, who places his hand behind his ear, bends forward, and assumes the attitude of the stage savage expecting the "pale-face."*)

Strongbow. Now, as a rear-rank standing at three hundred yards, ready! (*all move except Skull*). Did you hear me, Mr. Skull? Ready!

Miller. Don't you hear, Skull? Ready!

Present! Fire! (*kicks Mr. Skull just above the calf of his leg, and nearly brings him to the ground*).

Strongbow. Try that again! (*motion repeated several times*). Now, at the word "Present," without moving the body, head, eye, or hand in the slightest degree, throw the rifle smartly to the point of the right shoulder, at full extent of the left arm——

Lobjoit (*a coarse person*). Gammon!

Strongbow. What, sir?

Lobjoit. Stuff, sir! Can't fling a rifle about without moving your hands! Don't believe in that!

Strongbow. Pray don't interrupt; it's all correct; done at Hythe; perfectly possible. Now—*P'sent!*

(*Five men throw out their rifles bravely to the front, three bring up theirs slowly and sneakingly, two boldly support their elbows on their knees, and look as if they were performing a rather meritorious action than otherwise.*)

The position-drill proceeded, but it was very hard work. We speedily noticed that when Strongbow had any instruction to give, he invariably chose the time when we were at the "Present," *i. e.* when the strain upon our muscles in holding out the rifle was tremendous. After two seconds you would perceive the muzzle of the extended rifle begin to quiver in a very singular manner, then the body of the gentleman holding it would begin to rock about from the knees upwards, and finally, when he received the grateful command to "ease springs," he would give vent to an exclamation something between the ejaculation of a pavior, and the "characteristic 'hugh'" of Mr. Fenimore Cooper's Indians, and add, "'Gad, I'm nearly done up!"

The art of comporting oneself as a "rear-rank standing" having been acquired, we were initiated into the mysteries expected from a "front-rank kneeling;" and these gymnastics proved even yet more serious and invincible. For a gentleman of large frame, and accustomed to a well-stuffed easy-chair, to have to sit for five minutes on *his right heel*, and that alone, is by no means an easy matter; but the difficulty is considerably aggravated when he has to perform, while in this attitude, feats of manly strength in connection with throwing out a rifle to the full extent of his left arm. He has then to take aim at the target on the wall; and about this time, and just when he begins to puff dreadfully, he will hear a stentorian shout from the instructor, "What are you doing, sir? restrain your breathing! restrain your breathing, for Heaven's sake!" The unhappy man endeavours to do this, and to follow all the other directions given him in the slowest time, thus: "P'sent! to—oo—ooo! thre—ee—eee! fo—o—war! f—'ive!" until at the end, when he is called upon to spring smartly up to "Attention!" what with breath-holding and extra exertion, he resembles a boiled lobster in colour, and is shaking in every limb.

The judging-distance drill is an equally humourous but considerably less fatiguing evolution. Its object is to enable the soldier to note the difference in the appearance of men at different distances: a happy result, which is apparently accomplished by sending several of the persons to be observed completely out of the range of any but the sharpest sight. Points are thrown out at certain allowed distances up to three hundred yards, and the men under instruction are told the distance, and made to observe the appearance of the "points." Then the "points" are sent out at unknown distances, and the men have to give their opinion of the distance at which these points are placed, the answers being noted in a register. We had some little difficulty at first in preventing the "points" from running away altogether, or slipping into the public-house when the instructor's back was turned. The guesses of some of the men were perfectly miraculous in their inaccuracy; and it was observed that whenever private Miller whispered his ideas on distance to the sergeant, that functionary would be convulsed, and rendered so oblivious of decorum as to attempt to write without any ink, and to make futile scratches on his register. It was afterwards discovered that the ill-conditioned Miller, instead of giving his ideas of distance, was whispering the latest riddle in the ears of the instructor. Even he, however, owned to the value of the judging-distance practice, declaring that after a few lessons he should be able to recognise, and consequently to avoid, his tailor, if he saw him at the other end of Pall-Mall.

So we progressed through our difficulties, until we numbered some excellent shots among us. We are to be inspected by Colonel M'Murdo very shortly, to take part in the

Wimbledon rifle contest and in the grand review, where we shall have plenty of opportunities of distinguishing ourselves. I shall not fail to chronicle our movements.

CHAPTER XV.

WARLIKE WIMBLEDON.

He was a discontented man, the omnibus-driver, and he said generally that he didn't like it. Wollunteers might be good, he said, and they mightn't — leastways, what noise they made, frightening horses with bangin' bands and such-like, wasn't much 'count: lawyers they was, and clurks, and ribbing-coves (understood by present writer to be drapers' assistants), and such-like. Rifle-matches — ah! well, he'd heard tell, but hadn't seen much of that game, further than the Red House at Battersea, and for nuts at Greenwich Fair. If they was any good—as men—do you see? they'd come up to Copenhagen House, or the Brecknock, at Easter Monday, and have a back-fall with those parties that came up from Devonshire and the North. Wollunteers! he thought he knew a young man in the public line not far from Tottenham, which—he was all fair and 'boveboard—which it was at Wood Green, his name being Obble, what could show them Wollunteers *something* at knurr-and-spell: let 'em come with their fur-caps and all their fandangoes! Here he grew defiant, and elbowed me fiercely with his whip-arm. The whole affair was bellicose. I was on a Waterloo omnibus, going to the Waterloo station on my way to Wimbledon, then under martial law; and seeing that the taint had got into the driver's blood, and fearing lest he should kick me with his bluchers, I remained silent, and never opened my mouth until I asked for my railway-ticket.

But when I had curled into my corner in the railway-carriage, and had taken stock of the arms, accoutrements, and general appearance of the three privates and the ensign who went down with me, and had weaned my ears from drinking in the pompous rhetoric of the other occupant of our compartment, a gentleman of very imposing appearance, to whom, according to his own account, Wimbledon was indebted for its tenure of existence, I began to ponder over the omnibus-driver's remarks; and his reminiscences of Battersea Red House, and the nuts at Greenwich Fair, reminded me of what my idea of a rifle-match was, as embodied in the last one in which I took part. Sixteen years, I thought, have passed since I went down, rifle in hand, to a long strip of meadow bordering the Rhine, and paid my money to become a competitor at the Düsselberg Schützen Fest. A pretty quiet spot, flanked on one side by other meadows filled with large-uddered mild-eyed cows, whose bells tinkled pleasantly in the ears of the competitors, and on the other by the rapid-rushing river. There were some half-dozen painted wooden targets, arranged on the Swiss system; while a little distance apart, on the top of a high pole, towered a popinjay, to hit which was the great event of the day. The spectators of the friendly contest, varying, according to the time of day, from one to three hundred, were all townspeople well known to the marksmen and to each other, and occupied their time either in coming to the firing-posts and giving utterly vague and incoherent advice to their favourites, or in examining with deep reverence the prizes, consisting of two silver-mounted biergläser, and a few electrotyped Maltese crosses bearing the name of the Schützen Fest and the date, one of which I saw the other day in a dressing-table drawer, with a few old letters, an odd glove or two, a hacked razor-strop, a partially-obliterated daguerreotype, and such-like lumber. I don't think we shot well; I know that an enlightened public would not have liked our appearance, and that General Hay would have objected to our attitudes, which were anything but Hythe-position. I am certain that the merest tyro of a recruit would have scorned our rifles, which required several seconds' notice before they went off; and I have no doubt that we were supremely ridiculous; but I am equally certain that we were undeniably happy. The great charm, I thought, of such a meeting as that which I am recalling and that to which I am going, is its quiet—the change from the bustle and roar of ordinary life to the calm tranquillity, the noiseless serenity, of open country space. If I felt it then, when merely straying from the monastic seclusion of my university, how shall I enjoy it now, when flying from the ceaseless hum of London! How pleasant will be the open heath, dotted here and there with rifle-ranges and marksmen, the freedom from bustle and noise, the picturesque surroundings, the fresh turf, the elastic air, the—PUTNEY! The voice of the guard announcing my destination breaks upon my reverie. I jump out of the carriage, and, ascending the steps of the station, I emerge.

Into Pandemonium. Into a roaring, raving, shouting crowd; into a combination of the road to the Derby and Aldershot Heath on a field-day in June; for you have every component part of both. Enormous rolling clouds of dust, a heterogeneous mass of carriages open and shut, some regularly licensed, other improvised for the occasion and bearing a paper permit obtained impromptu from Somerset House and gummed on to the panels; the drivers of the vehicles shouting, shrieking, touting, beckoning, and gesticulating with whips, carnying weak-minded and hustling feeble-bodied persons into becoming passengers; gipsies, beggars; imps, with the bronze of the country on their faces and the assurance of London in their address, vending cigar-lights, showing the way, turning "cart-wheels," and being generally obstructive; volunteer-officers clanking a good deal, and volunteer-privates unbuttoning their tunics and showing more shirt-front than is provided for in the regulations; public-houses crammed and overflowing into the road with drink-seeking wayfarers; station-porters giving up all idea of business, and flitting from one knot of people to the other, sipping here, sporting there, like butterflies in velveteen. The inhabitants of Putney evidently divided into two sections—the natives, who gathered together in grinning masses, who chuckled fat-headedly, and sniggered, and saw a grand opportunity for shirking work and passing the entire day in vacant staring; and the affiliated, acclimatised, or naturalised Putneians, who are grubs in the City from nine till five, and butterflies at Putney for the remaining portion of their lives, and whose wives and daughters looked upon the whole thing as "low," and glared balefully at us from their plate-glass windows. I managed to survive even their scowls, and installed myself as one of a cheerful though perspiring party of seven, in a carriage intended to hold four (and looking, in its check-chintz lining, as though it had come out in its dressing-gown), which, after five minutes' dalliance with a knotted whip, a very flea-bitten gray horse was persuaded to drag up the hill towards the camp.

As we neared the spot, I was reminded of my friend the omnibus-driver's observations anent Greenwich Fair and shooting for nuts; for I am bound to say that, in the course of a long and varied experience, I never saw anything so like a fair as the Wimbledon camp seen from the outside. A wooden railing, shabby enough in itself, and rendered more shabby by the torn and ragged bills sticking to it, surrounds the camp; from within float sounds of distant bands, popping rifles, and cheering populace; while immediately outside stands that selvage of nothing-doing, lounging, thieving, drunken scum invariably to be found in the immediate vicinity of all fairs. On first entering, the same idea prevailed, for there were a few miserable little booths, in front of which one expected to see painted canvases of the giantess, the armadillo, and the tiger that devoured the Indian on horseback. But as I progressed up the ground, and passed wonderingly through the long line of tents, this notion vanished entirely, and instead of being in a fair, I found myself in a very village of canvas. An hour's stroll showed me that this village was a town. The early Australian gold-diggers had their canvas town; and here we had ours, within a twenty minutes' run from London. Canvas Town, by all means! for in what town could you find more completeness, or in what town would you require more than is here to your hand? For in the course of my survey I have lighted upon a newspaper-office (*Volunteer Service Gazette*), a police-station, a post-office with the hours of the arrival and despatch of mails duly placarded outside, a telegraph-office with temporary wires communicating with—everywhere, whence you could send the name of the winner of the Queen's Prize to your friend Ryot in the indigo trade at Suez, or utterly depress Sneesh of M'Mull, yachting off Malta, with the tidings that the Scotch were beaten in the International Match; many taverns and restaurants; many gunsmiths' and shops (tents) for kindred matters; a club, where four copies of the *Times* are to be found, with other journals in proportion, and from which issuing the sound of a grand-piano and a musical voice, proved that a great step in advance had been made in club matters, and that lady-members were admitted. Further on, here and there, I found public boards whereon printed matters affecting the common weal might be—and were—read; "Lost" and "Found" (rare the latter) notices, shooting-scores for great prizes, and other documents, very like the inscriptions on pounds and such-like country-town institutions. I am not much of a reckoner in such matters, but from my observation I should imagine that Canvas Town covers many acres; it is duly fenced-off from the outlying grounds, and it has streets and a square regularly arranged. In what might be called the market-place, at the back of what I choose to consider the town-hall (which, to vulgar minds, is the "Grand Stand"), I find the public clock, a monster Bennet, and a little further off the public thermometer, which tells you every thing scientific which you cannot possibly want to know, and which, while being, I understand, excessively useful to the erudite, is so exact and so complicated, that even my very cursory inspection of it sends me away headachy and discomfited.

The whole of this city, which teems with an ever-busy, running, pushing, shouting, gun-carrying, band-playing, red, green, gray, and brown population, is under canvas, save in a few instances where canvas is supplemented by wood. Far and away, right and left, stretch the long lines of tents, looking somewhat ghostly even in the bright afternoon sun, and suggesting a very spectral appearance at night. The tents are of two shapes — some like Brobdignagian dishes of blanc-mange, others like inverted monster pegtops without the pegs. Strolling on, I come upon a little oasis of painted brick, a small house belonging to the miller, whose mill looks like a huge genie with arms outspread, protecting the phantom-village he has called into existence — a little house which seemed quite ashamed of its conventional appearance, and had done its best to hide it by having tents in its garden and right up to its very door-step; and as I skirt the garden I become aware of something couchant in the grass—something which I imagine at first to be a snake, but which turns out to be nothing more than a harmless policeman off duty, who is lying supine on his back looking up at the sky, rural, happy, contemplative—as though there were no such things as bad "beats" or Irish navvies with homicidal tendencies. Recalled to sublunary matters by my approach, he sits up and gives me good-day; and sitting down beside him, I enter into conversation, find him a very pleasant fellow, and learn from him, amongst other things, that Canvas Town has a place for public worship, divine service being performed on Sunday in the Grand Stand to a large and attentive congregation, and a school—where, however, the "instructors" are, to a man, from Hythe.

On leaving my policeman, I strayed pleasantly into the arms of some of my old companions the Grimgribber rifles, and who received me with the greatest cordiality. From them I learnt that the most interesting feature in Wimbledon life was the camp-fire and its gathering, which was decidedly a thing to be seen. It sounded well—a camp-fire, with plenty of punch, and singing, and ladies' company, to be preceded by a dinner with my old corps, and to be concluded with a dog-cart drive to London—so I agreed to stop; and very glad I am I determined on this arrangement, for the camp-fire was the end which crowned the day's work, and crowned it royally.

After a capital dinner, we moved out about nine o'clock to the "meeting," which was held in a large open space, a circle, surrounded by a rising mound, forming a perfectly natural amphitheatre. In the middle of the circle blazed a large fire of dried heather; on the mound—some on chairs (ladies these mostly), some couchant at full length, some squatting on their hams like Indians at a council-fire—sat a motley assemblage, composed of volunteers in all uniforms and from all counties, natives of Wimbledon, neither pure nor simple, gaping people from town, and people from the neighbourhood: the ladies muffled in pretty capes and fantastic hoods and ravishing yachting-jackets; the gentlemen in that stern simplicity of white neckcloth and black every thing else, which gives such picturesque dignity to the dining Briton. Nor was Scotland Yard without its representatives. Not possessing the advantages enjoyed by caricaturists, I have never seen a policeman at supper in my kitchen, and consequently have never been a spectator of that hilarity to which the "force" abandons itself when it is off duty. Certainly, at Wimbledon the police never entirely forgot that they were not as other men; they smiled, they spoke, they sang; but I imagine the singer only let out his stock by one hole to suffer his high C to have scope, and that in no moment of delight did any one of them cease to give an occasional slap at his coat-tails, to assure himself that his truncheon had not been purloined. But it was very jolly. When we arrived (and we had scented the burning heather and the tobacco a quarter of a mile off), Lord Bowling was just finishing a comic song, which, so far as I could make out, was about some transaction in which a Jew and some poached-eggs were equally implicated; and when the roar of applause which followed the termination died away, Lord Echo, who was apparently the president of the evening, called upon "A 395;" and that "vigilant officer," as, no doubt, he has been often described in print, set to work with a will, and piped us a sentimental ditty with a good voice and much real feeling. While he sang I looked round me in wonder. Rembrandtish, or rather more after the wild dash of Salvator Rosa, was the scene: in front the fitful glare of the fire lighting up now, leaving in dusk then, uniforms of various sombre hues, relieved here and there with a sharp bit of scarlet stocking, the top of which, surrounded by the dark knickerbocker, glowed like a fire in a grate; incandescent tips of cigars dotting the black background, illumined now and then in a little space by a Vesuvian match; further still, the long, weird, gaunt common, stunted, blank, and dreary, with a ghostly fringe of waning spectral tents. This was a quiet night. "Not one of our great meetings," said a Victoria rifle to me; and yet there must have been between three and four hundred people present. Close by me is a family party, evidently from one of the houses hard by, consisting of papa, bland and full of port-wine; mamma, half-sedate, half-anxious; two noble sons of sixteen and fifteen, braving papa in the matter of tobacco, and entirely absorbed therein; some very pretty daughters and dining friends. As policeman A 395 warbles forth his ditty, one pretty daughter (the auburn-haired daughter) and one dining friend (with the shaved face and the heavy Austrian moustache) want "to see better"—happy A 395, to be the attraction of so much curiosity!—so they gradually edge off until they are quite by themselves, and then they no doubt see admirably, for the gentleman looks down at the lady, and the lady looks down at the turf and draws figures on it with her parasol. Never mind, A 395;

you are not the first person by a good many who has stood innocent godfather to this kind of business; and you quiver so nicely and make such a prolonged shake on the last note of your song, that you deserve all the applause and the glass of punch bestowed on you, as you make a stiff bow and retire.

Who next, my Lord Echo? Who next? Who but Harrison? And so soon as the name is heard, the welkin (what is the welkin? you don't know! I don't! but it's a capital phrase), the welkin rings with shouts of delight. A prime favourite Harrison, evidently. Doubtless a buffo-singer, short, fat, broad, genial, and jolly, as all comic men should be. No! Harrison is a slim handsome fellow of middle height, with a bright eye, a mellow voice, and a lithe agile figure. "Capital fellow," says the man of the Victorias next to me; "*tremendous* favourite here; sings like a lark, talks like a book, and starts next week to join his regiment in India." Bravo, Harrison! Well sung, young friend! After Harrison has sung his song, he gives us (being loudly encored) an imitation of a "stump oration," which, truth to tell, is a dull affair. At its conclusion, to our astonishment, Lord Echo calls upon General M'Mortar for a song. We think it is a joke, and have no idea that the gallant Inspector is among us. But lo! like the ghost of Banquo, the well-known form of General M'Mortar rises amidst the smoke, and the well-known voice commences. Not a song! no, a speech! The old story of volunteers being descended from those old English bowmen (who have done such enormous service to writers and speakers on this matter), and of pluck, and valour, and of being called upon to resist an enemy; and, in fact, a choice selection from the speeches which the good general has delivered at inspections for the last three years. This is a damper! Men begin to scuffle off; ladies shiver and clasp their cloaks tighter round them: the evening is evidently finished — thanks to General M'Mortar.

Off we go then, making towards the road as best we may: one minute's halt at the Grimgribber tent, for what is known as a "nip;" and then home in my friend's dog-cart, with a very happy reminiscence of the day's loitering and the night's camp-fire.

CHAPTER XVI.

KENSAL GREEN.

IN a novel by M. Paul de Kock, it is stated that the principal promenades of the English people take place in cemeteries, which are congenial places of resort to a nation suffering from the spleen. So far as I, an unit in the nation, am concerned, the French author's assertion is to some extent correct. I do not exactly know what the spleen is, and consequently I may be suffering from it unconsciously; but, whatever may be the motive power, I have a taste for wandering in churchyards, and looking at those houses which the gravemaker builds, and which "last till doomsday." Both in Germany and in England there is a certain due sense of solemnity about the churchyard; walking in them, one feels with the man of Uz, that "there the wicked cease from troubling, and there the weary be at rest. There the prisoners rest together; they hear not the voice of the oppressor. The small and great are there, and the servant is free from his master." They are essentially places for meditation and reflection, and as an antidote against an overweening sense of worldliness, I would back an afternoon spent in one of certain churchyards which I know—say, haphazard, Hendon, Stoke-Pogis, Stratford-on-Avon—against most of the trenchant homilies I have listened to. As old Thoresby the antiquarian says, "One serious walk over a churchyard might make a man mortified to the world, to consider how many he treads upon who once lived in fashion and repute, but are now quite forgot. Imagine you saw your bones tumbled out of your graves as they are like shortly to be, and men handling your skulls, and inquiring, 'Whose is this?' Tell me of what account will the world be then?"

Of the English Cemetery, however, I knew nothing, until, on a blazing July afternoon, I set out for Kensal Green.

Just as a town has its suburbs, an army its pioneers, and a village its outskirts, so the great cemetery of Kensal Green (dedicated appropriately enough to All Souls) makes its vicinity felt some time before it is actually in sight. Once past the turnpike on the road, though yet a good half-mile from the nearest entrance, you are struck with certain signs and tokens which speak significantly of the region. The building to the right, just by the turn in the road, is an establishment for the sale of tombstones, and that monotonous grinding sound, which so grates on the ear, is occasioned by the polishing or the smoothing of the surface of a huge slab destined to be sacred to the memory of some person unknown, who is not impossibly at this moment alive and well. As you trudge along, and before you have done speculating how often the muddy canal to your left has been compared to the Styx, and whether a certain yard or field, also on the left, has been made a receptacle for carts and wagons which have departed this life, solely because of its locality, and, if not, why so many broken-up vehicles are there congregated, you come to more tombstone establishments. Statuary and mason are inscribed after the dealers' names on the façade, but this is a mere euphuistic fencing with the subject. The only statuary sold is for the graveyard; the only masonry dealt in is for the crypt or mausoleum. Past the snug-looking Plough Inn, at the old-fashioned entrance to which stands an empty hearse, and at the windows whereof several professional gentlemen, arrayed in solemn black, are indulging in bibulous refreshment; past an elaborate monument on which mortuary emblems are crowded in great profusion — an hour-glass surmounting two dead lions, and a couple of weeping females supporting an affecting tablet, whereon a trade advertisement is inscribed; past several shops where even the pictorial literature assumes a mournful character, the nearest approach to humour being a "ladder of matrimony," which commences with "hope," and ends in "despair," such end being typified by the cheerful emblem of a foundering ship; past the shop-window full of white and yellow immortelles, which look like so many wedding-rings from the fingers of departed Brobdignagians; and, duly armed with a courteous letter from the secretary of the company, I present myself through the arched entrance to the cemetery.

Having conferred with the pleasant-looking rubicund gatekeeper, an evidently cheerful philosopher, who supplies me with an Illustrated Guide to Kensal Green Cemetery, and requests me to wait until the clerk is disengaged, I stroll into the garden and sit down. A Frenchman, with wife and family, are chattering on the adjoining seat, eating bon-bons, and gazing round the cemetery with a critical air, as comparing it with cemeteries of their own land. It is some time before I see any other visitors, and it may be worth stating that during the whole time I was in the cemetery (some hours) I met with only one person in mourning: a widow, whose scarlet petticoat, I may be excused for mentioning, contrasted gracefully with her looped-up black dress, making a tasteful setting to a remarkably neat pair of feet. Three or four damsels from the neighbourhood, a tender couple apparently on the first round of the ladder of matrimony aforesaid, a couple of carriages with provincial occupants, and one or two people who were selecting ground, were, besides the gardeners and servants employed by the company, my only fellow-explorers on the day I devoted to the city of the dead. "The clerk" was not, as I had hastily concluded, a clerk of the works, a sort of overseer who looked after the persons employed, and kept the books of the company, but the severe ecclesiastical official who reads the responses, and says "Amen!" after the clergyman. His engagement was of course a funeral, or, as he termed it, when politely apologising for having kept me waiting, "an interment." Both these words mean the same thing, of course; but as I have remarked that undertakers invariably use the latter, I have long inferred that its enunciation is, in some inexplicable way, considered to be more palatable to survivors. Be this as it may, an interment had detained the clerk, whose name I have not the pleasure of knowing, but whom I mentally christened Mr. Dawe. He was a little man, dressed in black, with the conventional white tie, and his daily occupation had left its trace both upon his bearing and his voice. The one was sympathetic, and the other soft, and his general demeanour was that of sparing your feelings. Both communicative and intelligent, he never wearied, either of ministering to my inquisitiveness, or accompanying me on my rounds, but he was consistent throughout, and furnished me with statistics in a manner which impressively said all flesh is grass. The conservatory to the right, Mr. Dawe informs me, has only been in existence this year, and was started by the cemetery company, to supply an increasing demand for flowers on graves: a demand which the adjacent nursery gardeners were not always able to meet. Would I like to see the inside of it?

Not greatly different from other buildings of the same character: flowers, blooming in their several pots, and the usual paraphernalia of a greenhouse lying about. Each of these plants is destined to be transferred to a grave; but as the end for which they are tended and nurtured is their only speciality, we leave the greenhouse, and proceed up the centre road. Those wooden "sleepers" reared against the wall are of seasoned wood, and are used during the formation of earthworks and in building brick graves. On our way to the chapel, disturbed neither by the constant whizzing past of trains on the divers lines adjacent, nor by the incessant "Crack, crack," from the riflemen at practice on Wormwood Scrubs, Mr. Dawe informs me that the cemetery is vested in a joint-stock company of proprietors; that it has been in existence more than thirty years; and that from fifty to sixty thousand persons are interred herein. This he considers a low estimate, as there are some eighteen thousand graves, and an average of three or four bodies in each. How many burials does he consider the rule per week? Perhaps seven a day in summer, and eight in winter; he has known as many as twelve in one winter's day, but that was exceptional. No, this cemetery never inters on Sundays. It used to do so formerly, but has given up the practice for years; the Roman Catholic one adjoining it to the west does, and also, he believes, the one at Willesden; and if I should ever attend the chapel of Lock Hospital, and hear of, or see, irreverent burial processions passing on the road, perhaps I will remember that they are not coming here, but to one of the two grounds adjacent.

What is the size of the cemetery? Well, between seventy and eighty acres. Forty-seven acres are at present in actual use, but thirty additional acres have been recently consecrated, the party-wall having just been taken down; and workmen are now employed in making roads and laying out the ground. A portion of the original forty-seven acres is unconsecrated, and appropriated to dissenters. This portion has its separate chapel and catacombs; and a dissenting minister, provided by the Company, attends the funerals therein.

Any other minister preferred by the friends of the deceased is permitted to officiate, and, if desired, the body may be consigned to earth without any ceremony. Perhaps I have read in the papers of the Indian princess brought here the other day, and whose remains some of her Sikh servants wished to have burnt? Well, this was a case in point. The coffin was placed in the dissenters' catacomb, and, though a speech was delivered which Mr. Dawe, though not speaking the Sikh tongue, believes to have been on the virtues of the deceased, the burial is described in the Company's registry-book by the words "no ceremony." It was a large funeral, with many carriages. No, not the largest he had seen; perhaps one of them; but then he had only been here a few months, and it is in place of the superintendent, who is away, that he is acting as my guide. The most numerously-attended interment coming under his own observation was that of the secretary to the Young Men's Christian Association; and the next that of Sir Cresswell Cresswell, who lies under the plain slab before us. There has not been time to procure a monument, explains Mr. Dawe; but you will be interested to learn, sir, that the poor gentleman came up here and selected that bit of ground for himself, not ten days before he met with the accident from the effects of which he died. What constitutes a dissenter in the eyes of the Company? Well, nobody can be buried in consecrated ground unless the "Committal Service" is read by a clergyman of the Church of England. That is the only stipulation, and other rites may be, and sometimes are, previously performed elsewhere. The Company has nothing to do with that: only, if the Church Service be objected to, the burial must be in the dissenters' or unconsecrated portion of the cemetery. Are there any quaint out-of-the-way epitaphs or inscriptions on any of the tombs? No, Mr. Dawe does not know of one. You see, nothing can be inscribed upon any tomb until it has been submitted to, and approved by, a sub-committee of the directors, which meets every month; and any ludicrous or unseemly proposition would be at once refused. Does he know of many instances in which it has been fruitlessly attempted to put up questionable inscriptions? Of none; and he believes that an out-of-the-way country churchyard might be found which contains more of these curiosities of bad taste than have ever been even "tried on" since the formation of the cemetery. This, Mr. Dawe attributes to the spread of education, and to the cemetery being devoted principally to the well-to-do classes. Nothing would have tempted me to shake a standard of taste shared in by so many people besides this worthy clerk; so, agreeing that the possession of money invariably elevates the mind and purifies the heart, I asked in all reverence which was considered the most costly tomb in the grounds? I was taken to a sort of temple in gray marble, the peculiarity of which is, as I was begged to observe, that on entry you go up a step instead of down one, and the graceful shape and the polished sides of which are decidedly handsome and a little heathenish.

This, I was told, cost some three thousand pounds, and I uncovered my head accordingly. The one nearly opposite, not yet finished, would come to about two thousand pounds; while the foundations just laid down were for a vault to hold twelve people, and to cost more than a thousand pounds. What is the bricked pit in the centre for—the coffins? Oh dear no! A grating would be placed over that, and would form the flooring of the vault, while the coffins would be ranged round the walls at the sides. Did I observe the thickness of the masonry? Well, this pit was designed to receive the ashes of the people interred, if—say a thousand years hence—these walls should crumble and decay. It was being built by a gentleman for himself and family, who, when in town, takes the deepest interest in the work, coming here every day to see how the building progresses. No time to meditate upon the strangeness of this idiosyncrasy, for we have arrived at the chapel, and Mr. Dawe hands me over to another official, while he transacts some business with a fat and jolly-looking couple who "want to look at a bit of ground." Again, as when in the conservatory, a singular feeling arises as to the speciality of the building. As in every other instance flowers are associated with joy and life, so in every other sacred edifice bridals and christenings, with their attendant prayers, and hopes and fears, are as germane as the last rites to the dead. But there is no altar here wherefrom to pronounce the marriage blessing, no font round which parents and friends have clustered, and the double row of seats at each side have been used by mourners, professed or real, but by mourners only. It needs no guide to explain the use of the black trestles in the centre of the building. Some thousands of coffins have probably rested on them, though they are only used for the burials in the grounds. For the coffins deposited in the catacombs below, these trestles are not required. They are placed on a hydraulic press, and lowered through the floor by machinery, as the clergyman reads the service.

We go down by a stone staircase, and I am speedily in the centre of a wide avenue, out of which branch other avenues; and on stone shelves on each side of these rest coffins. This is Catacomb B. Catacomb A is away from the chapel, and has long been filled. This present catacomb has room for five thousand bodies, and my companion (who has been custodian of the vaults for the last thirty years) considers it about half full. I am therefore in a village below ground, of some two thousand five hundred dead inhabitants, and I can (not without reproaching myself for the incongruity) compare it to nothing but a huge wine-cellar. The empty vaults are precisely like large bins, and were it not for the constant gleams of daylight from the numerous ventilating shafts, my guide with his candle would seem to be one of those astute cellarmen who invariably appear to return from the darkest corners with a choicer and a choicer wine. The never altogether absent daylight destroys this illusion, and I proceed to examine the coffins around me. They are, as a rule, each in a separate compartment, some walled up with stone, others having an iron gate and lock and key, others with small windows in the stone; others, again, are on a sort of public shelf on the top. The private vaults are fitted up, some with iron bars for the coffins to rest on, others with open shelves, so that their entire length can be seen. The price of a whole vault, holding twenty coffins, is, I learn, one hundred and ninety-nine pounds; of one private compartment, fourteen pounds; the cost of interment in a public vault is four guineas; each of these sums being exclusive of burial fees, and an increased rate of charges being demanded when the coffin is of extra size. Rather oppressed with the grim regularity with which every one of these arrangements is systematised, I am not sorry to ascend the stairs, and ask my companion how he would find a particular coffin buried say twenty years before. By its number—and he shows me a little book wherein all these matters are methodically set down, and in which, in case of burials out of doors, under the head of "remarks"—I find the locality of each grave thus described: "Fifteen feet west of Tompkins;" or, "three feet south of Jones," as the case may be. "We have so many of the same name," exclaims the catacomb keeper, "that we should never find them unless the whole place were planned out into squares and numbers." Here Mr. Dawe joins us, and I ask to be taken to the dissenters' catacomb, that I may see for myself the last resting-place of the poor woman whose ashes have been squabbled over, and written on by Sikh and Christian. On the way, I inquire how many men are employed at the cemetery? Mr. Dawe has difficulty in saying, as so many labourers are occasionally employed. Night watchman? Oh yes, there is a night watchman, who is armed with a gun, which he fires every night at ten. He is accompanied by a faithful dog, and patrols the cemetery the whole of the night. No, he has no particular beat. Formerly, he had to be at the entrance to each catacomb (they are situated at the two extremities of the grounds) at stated hours during the night, and "telltales" were provided, to test his punctuality, but these have not been used for many years. The directors having perfect confidence in their servant, think it better that he should be left free, than by compelling him to be at one place at a particular time, enable possible depredators to make their calculations accordingly.

No, he is not aware of any attempt ever having been made to rob the cemetery. It is thoroughly known that an armed man patrols throughout the night, and it is not known where he is likely to be. The lead on the roof of the catacombs and chapels is of many hundred pounds value, and the marble of many of the statues and tombs is very costly; but these things are heavy to move, and Mr. Dawe thinks the existing arrangements a sufficient protection against robbery. When the wall was being taken down, and the recently consecrated thirty acres added, two extra men were employed as sentries to guard that point, but it is no longer a weak one, and the original watchman is once more held to be sufficient. There are two gate-keepers, several gardeners, a messenger, who takes a duplicate "sexton's book" and other papers to the London office every day, and others. Two of the gardeners and this messenger are sworn constables, and on Sundays assume a policeman's dress and keep order among the visitors. The graves are not dug by servants of the company, but by contract with one of the tombstone-makers, whose house I passed outside. This end of the centre walk is not occupied near the gravel, because it is only let on the condition of the lessee spending not less than from two to three hundred pounds on a monument, and such people have hitherto preferred to be at the end nearest the chapel. The "monumental chambers" above the catacombs are devoted to tablets containing the names and descriptions of many of the people buried below. Yes, there is an extra charge of a guinea a foot for all space thus occupied. (As we walk their length, I discern more than one piece of mortuary work having a cramped look, as if the statuary had been restricted in his scope. Again I had to reproach myself for an incongruous simile, but the "guinea a foot" and the closely covered walls reminded me strangely of advertisement charges, and of the bill-stickers hoardings which deface our streets.) I stoop to look for the inscription on an elaborate piece of sculpture occupying a prominent position at one end of the chamber, and am told it is not put there in memory of any one. "Ordered by a lady, sir, to commemorate the death of a male relative, but she died before it was finished, and her heirs declining to take it, it was thrown on the sculptor's hands, and as he happened to be one of our directors, he had it brought here" (perhaps as a not unlikely place to attract a purchaser), "and now *he's* dead; so here it's likely to remain." On admiring the foliage in the grounds, I am told that all trees are, from their rain-droppings, injurious to tombs, and that the weeping willow is the most detrimental of all; but for this, there would be many more planted; but, notwithstanding this drawback, many people like the vicinity of the last-named tree. What is that little bed of fine soil, destitute of shrub or plant, and decked out with empty cups and saucers, irrelevant and misplaced? A grave. The cups are for choice flowers, the bed is for rare plants; but the heirs of its occupier are abroad, so it remains bald and shabby-looking, without even its natural covering of turf. Such cases are not uncommon, says Mr. Dawe: all melancholy enthusiasm at the funeral; flowers ordered and the company engaged to keep them in order, at the regulation charge of a guinea a year. Two years generally find enthusiasm cooled down, and the guinea discontinued. For ten guineas the company undertake to keep up the flowers for ever; and I agree with Mr. Dawe, that, the weakness of human nature considered, this is the best plan. The price for merely turfing is half-a-crown a year, or four guineas in perpetuity: the contract for flowers being only ten times the annual subscription, that for turf more than thirty times. This, however, is explained by the fact that flowers add to the general beauty of the cemetery, and that it is the interest of the directors, even at a slight pecuniary sacrifice, to encourage their growth.

But here are the dissenters' chapel and catacombs. Both somewhat dingier and smaller than the other, but managed on a precisely similar plan. And down here, in a coffin covered with white velvet, and studded with brass nails, rests the Indian dancing-woman, whose strong will and bitter enmity toward England caused Lord Dalhousie to say of her, when in exile, that she was the only person our government need fear. I place my hand on the coffin, and holding the candle obliquely see a large gilt plate, whereon her name and titles are engraved. And now, a hasty visit to the office of the company at the gateway; a glance through the registry-book; another at the sexton's books—thirty-five fat volumes, with the particulars of every burial since the establishment of the company; another at the huge brass-bound heap, whereon the entire burial-ground is to be found in sectional divisions, each name being written in; and I say good-by to Mr. Dawe.

CHAPTER XVII.

A TRIAL OF JEWRY.

DON'T talk to me about November! Don't point with triumphant finger to your Letts's Diary, or hunt out that Almanac which the never-dying Francis Moore, Physician, still persists in producing in alternate black and red letter, and which he calls *Vox Stellarum!* They may make this present month November, if they like; it comes after October and precedes December, I know; but I am not to be put down by mere book-learning and meteorological statistics. I go by the weather, and I see no fog, no Scotch mist, no heavy atmosphere and incessant rain, which, as a Briton, I have a right to expect; produce for me, if you please, that pea-soup cloud, which, descending on earth, immediately gives rise to an epidemic of "spleen," and causes men to attach themselves to lamp-posts, and hurl themselves from bridges! I defy you. I decline to accept your—even to my ignorant mind—unscientific explanation of there being "a peg out" in the harmony of the seasons, or that "something has slipped" in the grand mechanism; but I am with you in your avowal that an April morning has accidentally "turned up" in the middle of the dreary autumn, and very much regret that "a previous engagement," to use the language of society's vortex, prevents my enjoying it as I should wish.

I ought to stop here in my garden for at least an hour more on this Sunday morning, lolling about, and patting my dog's big head, and caressing the cold nose which he thrusts into my hand as he walks gravely by my side, and gazing vacantly but with great delight over the broad green meadows and the purple-tinted cultivated land; over the fertile pastures and the big sweeping gardens, so trimly kept; over the red-roofed houses and the well-thatched ricks, and the tiny threads of the silver Brent, and the whole glorious landscape that lies between me and Harrow Church far away on the horizon. The church-bells are silent yet, and there is not one sound to break the stillness. Looking over the hedge (which within the last few days has become very bare and ragged, and which has concentrated all its few remaining leaves on one spot, like an elderly gentleman conscious of baldness), I see the farm-horses keeping holiday by blundering gravely over their pasture-field, only diversifying their never-wearying amusement of eating by an occasional grave and decorous roll upon their backs, from which they arise with a very astonished look around, and an apparent consciousness of having been betrayed into a temporary abnegation of dignity; I see the ducks all gathered together in a cluster at one corner of the pond in a farm-yard, and the geese, who immediately take affront at Nero's appearance, and hiss, like a theatrical manager's friends who have come in with orders and don't get front places; and—woe is me!—crossing the edge of the farm-yard, by the footpath in the Fair Meadow, I see the vicar of the parish, who gives me a cheery "Good morning," and, pointing towards the church, says he shall see me presently. Which statement is, though my excellent friend doesn't know it, the reverse of truth! He will *not* see me presently! To-day, the square pew with the red-covered seats, and the hassocks which want binding, and always go off like dusty fireworks whenever they are touched, will not contain me. To-day, the charity children who sit behind us will sniff unscared by my occasional remonstrative glances; to-day, the clerk will have it all his own way with the responses, and the vicar will miss his churchwarden; for, as I have before remarked, I have a previous engagement, and as I have not before remarked, I am going to make a trial of Jewry.

For the first time for many years, but not for the first time in my life. My first trial of Jewry was, if I mistake not, in connexion with a pressing call for money on my part, and the production of a stamped piece of paper on the part of Jewry. Ten pounds was the sum required; but after Jewry—sitting in his own private house in Burton Crescent—had read the letter of introduction which I presented to him (and which had been given me by Uptree, of the Tin-tax Office), and had made me sign the stamped paper acknowledging myself his debtor for *twelve* pounds, "value received," he proceeded to explain that he had only a five-pound note in the house. Aghast at this information, I asked him what I was to do. He frankly confessed he did not know; at length, smitten with a sudden idea, he pointed to an oil-painting of a Spanish boy, which stood against the wall, and told me I might "take the Murillo." I represented to Jewry that my want was money, not Murillos; upon which he suggested the pledging of the Murillo for five pounds. "Dicks 'll do it for you in a minute," Jewry said. "Here, Dicks!" And Dicks presenting himself, in the shape of a very evil-looking clerk, was told to take "that round the corner," and to bring five pounds back. Dicks returned in three minutes without the Murillo, and with three pounds, which was all, he said, he could get for it. As Jewry handed me the money, he said, "About the ticket now? That's no use to you! You'll never take the picture out; and if you did, you wouldn't know what to do with it! Come; I'll give you ten shillings for the ticket!" And he did; and eight pounds ten was all I ever got for my twelve-pound bill, which I had to pay at the end of the month.

But the trial of Jewry which I am now about to make is of a very different kind. It involves my leaving behind me my watch and my purse, my putting on an unobtrusive garb and a wide-awake hat, my stealing out at the back gate so as to be unobserved by the servants, and my making the best of my way to an adjacent railway station. There, after a minute's interval, I am picked up by a train all blossoming with male and female specimens of "Sunday out," and, after making a circuitous journey, calling at Kentish Town and Hampstead Heath, dallying in that Utopia the Camden Road, flitting from Kingsland to Hackney, glancing at Victoria Park, and getting a glimpse of distant masts at Stepney, I am landed at Fenchurch Street, scud rapidly down Billiter Street and St. Mary Axe, and, opposite Bishopsgate Church, into which are crowding the denizens of the neighbourhood, find my intended companions awaiting my arrival. Two in number are my companions; one, Oppenhardt, my friend, whose innate patrician feelings were outraged by having allowed himself to come east of Temple Bar, and who was standing, with an acute expression of hurt dignity in every feature, contemplating the back of Inspector Wells, who was to be our guide in the trial of Jewry which we were about to make. As I crossed the road, I looked at those two men, and mused, for twenty seconds by the clock, upon the falsity of appearances. There was Oppenhardt—whose paternal grandfather was, I believe, a worthy German sugar-baker at Hamburg—looking, with his blue greatcoat, and his black beard, and his perpetual expansion of nostril, like a peer of the realm at the very least; and there was Inspector Wells, a pallid round-faced man, with a light fringe of whisker, and a sleepy boiled eye, and a stout idle figure; and yet I believe the Custom House possesses no clerk having a more acute knowledge of drawback and rebate, of allowances and landing dues, than Oppenhardt; nor has the City of London Police an officer so sharp and painstaking, so unwearying and intelligent, as Inspector Wells. With very few words I make my companions known to each other; and then, obedient to the inspector's suggestion, we cross the road and prepare for our plunge. "It's going with the stream, gentlemen," says our guide, "and taking the rough with the smooth. You've brought nothing of any value with you, I suppose? Handkerchiefs in an inside pocket, if you please! You'll soon see why!" "Do they know you, Wells?" I asked. "Some of 'em, sir; but not all. I thought of putting on my uniform coat, but then they'd have made way, and you'd have seen the place under rather a false view, perhaps! It's better we should rough it with the rest."

As he finished his sentence, we turned short round to the right, up a street called Sandys Row, and were in the thick of it. Jewry, which I have come to make trial of, lies in the heart of the City of London, in the corner of the angle made by Bishopsgate Street and Houndsditch. In the midst of it stands a huge black block of building, for the most part windowless, but crane-bearing, and having odd trap-doors, some near the roof, some near the basement, for the swallowing in or giving out of goods. For this is where the defunct Company which had its head-quarters in the Street of the Hall of Lead—the Company which had an army and a navy of its own, and ruled kings and princes, but which has now dwindled down into a mere appanage of Downing Street, and has shrunk into a "Board"—used in the old days to store the costly silks which had been brought from its dominions in the far Ind. This hideous building was then filled with the rarest specimens of Eastern handicraft, and looked then just as it looks now, when, from its appearance, you would guess that turmeric, or sago, or starch, or any thing equally commonplace, was its contents. Round it seethes and bubbles Jewry, filling up the very narrow street, with small strips of pavement on either side, and what ought to have been a way for vehicles, between them; every bit of space, however, covered with mob—dirty, pushing, striving, fighting, high-smelling, higgling, chaffering, vociferating, laughing mob. Shops on either side, so far as can be seen above mob's head; tool-shops, files, saws, adzes, knives, chisels, hammers, tool-baskets, displayed in the open windows, whence the sashes have been removed for the better furtherance of trade; doors open, sellers and buyers hot in altercation, spirited trade going on. Hatters', hosiers', tailors', bootmakers' shops, their proprietors forced by competition to leave the calm asylum of their counters, and to stand at their doors uttering wholesome incitement to the passers-by to become purchasers: not to say importuning them with familiar blandishments. For, in what should be the carriage-way is a whole tribe of peripatetic vendors of hats, hosiery, clothes, and boots, hook-nosed oleaginous gentry with ten pair of trousers over one arm and five coats over the other; with Brobdignagian boots (some with the soles turned uppermost, showing a perfect armoury of nails), which are carried on a square piece of board, and which look harder than the board itself; a few hats; an enormous number of cloth caps of all shapes and sizes—made, so Wells tells me, from the skirts or otherwise unworn parts of old coats. Jewry will stand any trial you like to make of her in the way of actual requirements, I'll warrant it. Are you in search of mental pabulum? Here it is! Trays full of literature of all kinds, gaudily-bound books of shilling lore, or tattered copies of the Hebrew Law. Engravings, coloured or plain? Here shall you see how Herr Jakobs in the Hoher Strasse, Berlin, has copied, or thinks he has copied, some old English prints of fox-hunting scenes; and here shall you see the marvellous horses, and the more marvellous riders, and the more marvellous leaps which the German artist has probably evolved from the depths of his internal consciousness, as his countryman did the camel; here shall you see Abraham offering up Isaac: the former in all the glory of the grand old Jewish type, dignified and bearded, than which, when good, there is scarcely any thing better; but Isaac a little too nosy, and rather too oily, and considerably too lippy, and, on the whole, too much like the young Jew-boy who just now tried to steal a bit of liver out of the frying-pan in which a quantity of it is hissing, and who so nearly received in his eye the point of the steel fork which the Jewish maiden, watching over it earnestly, prodded at that feature. For eating is by no means neglected in Jewry; in the glassless windows of many of the houses the frying-pans are hard at work, presided over by Jewry's daughters, bright-eyed, dark-skinned, nimble-fingered, shrill-tongued. Pleasant to look upon are Jewry's daughters, despite a certain oiliness, which is probably attributable to contact with the contents of the frying-pan. It is in the contemplation of Jewry's mammas that you begin to doubt the beauty of the race: for, when you behold Jewry's mammas in the flesh, you generally behold them in rather too much of it, and they have an objection to buttons, and hooks-and-eyes, and other ligaments; a hatred of corsets and chemisettes, and other womanly neatnesses; a tendency to bulge, and an aversion to soap and water—all of which peculiarities detract from their charms in the impartial eye (meaning mine).

Liver and fried fish are the principal, but by no means the only, edible articles for sale; through the crowd come wending men with glass dishes on their heads, containing long gelatinous-looking fruits. "Pickled cucumbers," says Wells, as they pass; "pickled cucumbers, never eat by any body but Jews, and never seen elsewhere; they're said to be reg'lar good eating, but I never heard tell of a Christian who tried one. But the Jews—Lor' bless you—they hold 'em in their fists, and bite away at 'em like boys do at lollipops!" Wells also tells me that pickles of every kind are in high favour in Jewry; that the denizens thereof will eat pickles at any time, no matter whether onions, cauliflower, cabbage, or what not, and will drink the pickle-liquor "as you would a glass of sherry." I think I can understand this. I can imagine that a pickle must be, in some conditions, a fine setter-up! Say, at a bargain, for instance. How, just before asking your price, a fine stinging acrid pickle must sharpen your faculties, and clear your brain, and set your nerves, and string your persuasive powers! How, if you be purchaser, it must lower your tone and your aspects of human life, and degrade the article in your views, and render you generally unpleasant and morose and disinclined to deal, and so eventually successful! No wonder pickles are at a premium in Jewry.

All this time we are slowly struggling through the crowd, which, never ceasing for an instant, surges round us, reminding one more of an illumination-night mob in its component parts than any thing else. And it is curious to see how the itinerant vendors of goods, be they of what sort they may—whether sham jewelry, cheap music, pipes and cigars, bulfinches, boxes of dominoes, bird-whistles, or conjuring tricks—are whirled about in the great vortex of humanity; now, in the midst of their "patter," caught upon a surging wave and carried away long past those whom they were but this moment in the act of addressing. So, we pass through Cutler Street and Harrow Alley, borne along with scarcely any motion of our own, the crowd behind us pushing, the crowd before us shoving; and we, by dint of broad shoulders and tolerable height, making our way with occasional drifting into out-of-the-way courses, but always looked after by Inspector Wells. I don't suppose there is the smallest danger of our coming to grief, for indeed I never saw a better-behaved mob: thieves there are in scores, no doubt, from burly roughs with sunken eyes and massive jaws, sulkily elbowing their way through the mass, to "gonophs" and pickpockets of fourteen or fifteen, with their collarless tightly-tied neck-handkerchiefs, their greasy caps and "aggrawator" curls—indeed, we have not been in the crowd two minutes, before Oppenhardt has the back pockets of his greatcoat turned inside out, and I felt myself carefully "sounded" all over by a pair of lightly-touching hands. But there is no ribaldry, no blackguardism, no expression of obnoxious opinion. One gentleman, indeed, wants to know "who those collared blokes is," in delicate allusion to our clean shirts; but he is speedily silenced; and one Jewish maiden, who, with much affection, addresses us as "dears," and advises us to "take care of our pockets," is sternly rebuked by an elderly matron, who says, "Let 'em alone: if they comes here, they must suffer." But, generally, Mob is thoroughly good-tempered. Mob like Oppenhardt very much, and make numerous inquiries as to what he'll take for his beard, where he lives when he is at home, whether he ain't from furrin parts, brother to the Princess Hallexandry, a Rooshan, &c. One young gentleman, with a potato-can, points to his fruit, and says, invitingly, "'Ave a tightener, captin:" at which Oppenhardt is pleased. Mob is more familiar with me, as being humbler, and more akin to its own order; in one tremendous struggle, a lad puts his arms round me and cries out, "Here we are! All together, guv'nor!"

So, onward with the stream, catching occasional glimpses of Hebrew inscriptions against the walls, endless repetitions of a handbill issued by the Jewish Society for the Diffusion of Knowledge, and announcing a Sabbath lecture by Brother Abrahams over Brother Lazarus recently deceased, noticing here and there huge rolls of edible stuff hung up called "swoss," which is apparently divided by the thinnest line of religious demarcation from sausage-meat; onward amidst constant cries of "Pockets, pockets, take care of your pockets!"

and occasional rushes, evidently for pocket-picking purposes, until we make our way to where the crowd becomes even denser, and our progress is slower and harder to fight for, till at last, down a very greasy step, we make our entrance into the Clothes Exchange. This is a roofed building, filled round every side and in the centre with old-clothes stalls; and here, piled up in wondrous confusion, lie hats, coats, boots, hobnailed shoes, satin ball-shoes, driving-coats, satin dresses, hoops, brocaded gowns, flannel jackets, fans, shirts, stockings with clocks, stockings with torn and darned feet, feathers, parasols, black-silk mantles, blue-kid boots, Belcher neckerchiefs, and lace ruffles. This is to what my lady's wardrobe comes, Horatio; this is the ante-penultimate of flounce and furbelow, of insertion-tucker and bishop-sleeve. Mamselle Prudence has my lady's leavings, and Abigail looks after her perquisites, and thus the trappings of fashion come down to Jewry, and are refreshed and retouched, sponged and lacquered and refaced, and take their final leave of life amid the fashionable purlieus of Whitechapel, or the nautical homes of the blessed at Shadwell. No lack of customers here; stalwart roughs being jammed into tight pea-jackets by jabbering salesmen, who call on the passers-by to admire the fit. "Plue Vitney, ma tear! Plue Vitney, and shticksh to him like his shkin, don't it?" "Who could fit you if I can't!" "Trai a vethkit, then!"—this to me —"a thplendid vethkit, covered all over with thilver thripes!" While, after declining this gorgeous garment, I find Oppenhardt in the clutches of a lithe-fingered Delilah, who is imploring him to let her sell him "thutch a thirt!" Every where the trade is brisk, and the sales progress through an amount of fierce argument, verbal and gesticulatory, which would be held fatal to business any where else in London, but which is here accepted as a part of the normal condition of commerce.

In and out of the rows of stalls we dived, Wells in front, recognised occasionally, sometimes by a tradesman seated in solemn dignity at his stall, who insists on a friendly handshake. Sometimes the inspectorial presence is acknowledged by a sly nod or a wink, as much as to say, "No uniform! Then you don't want to be much noticed! How are you?" and sometimes by a half-chaffing shout of "Vot, is it you, thargent! now'th your time for a hovercoat!" We see plenty of public-houses, all with Jewry signs; and we suggest to Wells that, being half suffocated, perhaps we ought to have "something" after this protracted struggle and the swallowing of this dust. But he says, "Not yet, sir;—in a jewel-house!" and with that mysterious hint proceed we to clear the way out of the Exchange.

In a jewel-house! As I ponder on the words, my mind rushes away to the regalia in the Tower and Colonel Blood's attempt thereon; to Hunt and Roskell's shop, and the Queen of Spain's jewels, which were in the old Exhibition of '51; to the Palais Royal at Paris, and the Zeil at Frankfort; to a queer street at Amsterdam, where I once saw a marvellous collection of jewelry; to a queer man whom I once met in a coffee-shop, who told me he "travelled in emeralds;" to Sinbad's Valley of Diamonds, and —— Wells breaks my reverie by touching my arm. I follow him across a square, in the centre of which are several knots of men in discussion; opposite us stands the door of "The Net of Lemons," apparently closed, but it yields to Wells's touch; and, following him up a passage, I find myself in a low-roofed square-built comfortable room. Round three sides of it are ranged tables, and on these tables are ranged large open trays of jewelry. There they lie in clusters, thick gold chains curled round and round like snakes, long limp silver chains such as are worn by respectable mechanics over black satin waistcoats on Sundays, great carbuncle pins glowing out of green-velvet cases, diamond rings and pins, and brooches and necklaces. Modest emeralds in quaint old-fashioned gold settings, lovely pale opals, big finger-rings made up after the antique with cut cornelian centre-pieces, long old-fashioned earrings (I saw nothing in any of the trays in modern settings), little heaps of loose rubies, emeralds, and turquoises, set aside in corners of the trays, big gold and silver cups and goblets and trays and tazzas, here and there a clumsy old épergne, finger-rings by the bushel, pins by the gross, watches of all kinds from delicate gold Genevas down to the thick turnipy silver "ticker" associated with one's school-days, and shoals of watch-works without cases. "They've melted down the cases," says Inspector Wells to me in a fat whisper, "and can let the works go very cheap." Such trade as is being done is carried on in a very low tone; the customers, nearly all of whom are smoking cigars, bend over the trays and handle the goods freely, sometimes moving with them in their hands to another part of the room, to see them in a better light, and the vendors making not the least objection.

I thought I noticed a whisper run round as we entered, but the sight of Wells was sufficient, and no further notice was taken. We were afterwards told, however, that a stranger is generally unceremoniously walked out, and informed that "it's a private room." After a few moments we were introduced by Inspector Wells to Mr. Marks, the landlord of the house, who wore a pork-pie hat, and had a diamond brooch in his shirt, and two or three splendid diamond rings on his not too clean hands, and whose face struck me as being one of the very knowingest I have ever met with. Very affable was Mr. Marks, answering all my questions in the readiest manner. No! he didn't consider it a full morning; you see, the great diamond sale at Amsterdam was on just now, and many of his frequenters were away at it. Had any great bargains been made that morning?

Well, there had been a set of diamonds brought in, which were sold about ten o'clock for seventeen hundred pounds, and which, up to the present time (it was now about twelve), had been re-sold in the room nine times, and each time at a profit. Some men had made two pounds profit, some three, one as much as thirteen pounds—but each had re-sold his diamonds at a profit. "That's the vay vith our people!" said Mr. Marks; "any thing for a deal! Ve mustht have a deal, and in a deal ve mustht have a leetle profit. Latht veek I had a thouthand poundth tranthaction—I rethold the goods the thame day. Vot vos my profit? Fifty poundth? No! Theven and thicpeth! Thtill, there *vos* a profit. Look here now" (pulling a handful of various coin, perhaps four pounds fifteen in value, out of his left-hand trousers-pocket), "that'th vot I made on my little tranthactionth thith morning! Committhion money I call it."

I asked Mr. Marks if there were any celebrated characters at that time in his house, and he begged us to walk into his sanctum: a cheery well-appointed kitchen, arrived at by passing through the bar. There he introduced us to Mr. Mendoza, one of the largest diamond-merchants in the world, and a gentleman who had been consulted as to the cutting and setting of the Koh-i-noor. A quiet-looking man Mr. Mendoza, with a sallow complexion and an eye beaming like a beryl. Told by Mr. Marks that we are curious strangers without any objectionable motive, Mr. Mendoza was truly polite, and on being asked if he had any thing of price with him, produced from the breast-pocket of his overcoat a blue paper which looked like the cover of a Seidlitz powder, but which contained large unset diamonds to the value of four hundred and seventy-five pounds. As these were exposed to our view, Mr. Marks took from his waistcoat-pocket a glittering pair of fine steel pincers, and, selecting three or four of the largest diamonds, breathed on them and then put them on one side, with a view to purchase. "You use pincers, I see, Mr. Marks?" I remarked. "Vell, thir," says that urbanest of men, with a wink that conveys volumes, "fingerth is thticky, and dimonth cling to the touch. Mr. Mendoza knowth me and don't mind vot *I* do, but he vouldn't let everybody try his dimonth. You thee, the vay to try a dimonth ith by breathin' on him.

Vell, ven *thum* folkth trieth 'em, they inhaleth inthed of ekthalin, and thoveth out their tongueth at the thame time, tho that ven they put'th their tongueth back again, there ain't qvite tho many dimonth in the paper ath there voth at firth!" I asked Mr. Mendoza if he had ever been robbed, and he told me never. Was he not well known? Yes, but he kept to the broad thoroughfares, and never went out at night. He showed us several other papers of diamonds of greater or less value, and several stones handsomely set in rings.

Hospitable intentions overcome Mr. Marks (a really sensible, good-natured, most obliging man), and he insists upon our having a bottle of wine. Clicquot he proposes. We decline Clicquot, but as he will not be balked, and insists upon our "giving it a name," we stand sponsor to sherry. And very good sherry it is, and very good is Mr. Marks's talk over it. He tells us what sober people they are in Jewry, and how they never, by any chance, have more than one glass of brandy-and-water at a sitting; how they leave his rooms at two and go home to dinner, not returning until six in the evening, when they have coffee and sit down to whist, playing away till eleven; "when," says Mr. Marks with a terrific wink in the direction of Inspector Wells, whose back happens to be turned, "when thith houth alwayth clotheth to the minute, accordin' to the Act o' Parlyment." Every word of which talk is, as the Inspector afterwards pithily informs me, "kidment:" a pleasant dissyllable, meaning, I believe, in pure Saxon, playful flight of fancy.

END OF VOL. I.

CPSIA information can be obtained
at www.ICGtesting.com
Printed in the USA
LVHW040403200422
716646LV00005B/238

9 783752 589849

Motorcycle Smarts

Overcome Fear
Learn Control
Master Riding Well

Copyright and Disclaimers

Motorcycle Smarts: Overcome Fear, Learn Control, Master Riding Well

Disclaimer

Contents

Warning

Every time I suit up to ride, I weigh my options and evaluate my risks. As long as the pleasure of riding overshadows the additional exposure, I'll continue to throw a leg over and strap on my helmet.

When it doesn't, I'll stop riding.

The risks are real. Motorcycle crashes —often caused by negligent motorists— can cause serious injuries, even death.

In this book, I attempt to present accurate information that will ultimately make you a safer rider. But I'm human. My advice may not apply to every rider in every situation.

No book, including this one, can teach you how to ride a motorcycle proficiently. Please seek lessons from a licensed instructor.

Ride safely and at your own risk.

Foreword

The Author's Motorcycle Mentor

I once read that we each have a gene that controls how we relate to our environment in terms of our excitement level.

I knew a fellow once who needed to ride his motorcycle at insane speeds to feel a satisfying level of fun My excitement gene isn't like that. It doesn't take much speed for me to be thrilled, whether in a car, on a bike, or snow skiing.

Maybe that makes me a conservative rider.

When David approached me in 2005 about helping him get into this amazing hobby, I took the same careful approach I did when riding. My primary concern for David was safety, but I also believe that riding safely is an outcome of knowledge and preparation.

At the time, I had ridden well over 100,000 miles without going down—unless we count the time in my driveway when I thought the side stand was out (it wasn't) and pushed the bike over.

I put out my hand to save my head and broke my wrist.

When David came to me for advice, his enthusiasm was something to behold. He was the perfect student, and I was glad to help him.

I wanted him to understand the basics (my favorite examples being countersteering and seeing) so he could safely ingrain good riding techniques and then begin to enjoy the feeling of freedom that comes from riding. I believe he reached that goal and more.

David truly understands motorcycles, and I am honored to have been his motorcycle mentor.

feel a satisfying level of fun. My excitement gene isn't like that. It doesn't take much speed for me to be thrilled, whether in a car, on a bike, or snow skiing.

Maybe that makes me a conservative rider.

When David approached me in 2005 about helping him get into this amazing hobby, I took the same careful approach I did when riding. My primary concern for David was safety, but I also believe that riding safely is an outcome of knowledge and preparation.

At the time, I had ridden well over 100,000 miles without going down—unless we count the time in my driveway when I thought the side stand was out (it wasn't) and pushed the bike over

I put out my hand to save my head and broke my wrist.

When David came to me for advice, his enthusiasm was something to behold. He was the perfect student, and I was glad to help him.

I wanted him to understand the basics (my favorite examples being countersteering and seeing) so he could safely ingrain good riding techniques and then begin to enjoy the feeling of freedom that comes from riding. I believe he reached that goal and more.

David truly understands motorcycles, and I am honored to have been his motorcycle mentor.

Introduction

THE TRUTH IS THIS. RIDING A MOTORCYCLE WELL IS PART SKILL, PART WILLING TO LEARN, PART UNDERSTANDING OF BASIC PHYSICS, AND PART GIVING A DAMN ABOUT YOUR SAFETY AND THE SAFETY OF THOSE AROUND YOU.

Two men spent a considerable amount of time mentoring me when I first started riding a motorcycle.

They nurtured my passion for learning how motorcycles work. I studied everything I could find, and I practiced everything I learned. The *Motorcycle Smarts* book series is my attempt to pay that forward.

I wrote this book because I couldn't find one like it when I started riding. Motorcycle magazine columns converted into books are hard to follow—while other motorcycling books tend to focus on the wrong topics. Even with my engineering background, reading 300-plus pages attempting to explain everything about motorcycling feels painful.

You don't have to know everything to ride well.

You don't need to know how to change a tire, replace a headlight, or understand that rake angle affects how quickly you can flick your bike in a turn. You don't need to understand how your engine works.

And you certainly don't need to understand gyroscopic precision.

On the other hand, there are topics that every rider should understand in order to REDUCE THEIR CHANCES OF CRASHING.

This book tackles *these* topics in seven main sections:

PART ONE explores a rarely talked about phenomenon that most riders experience called *rider fear*. What is it? Who has it? What can you do to make it go away? What should you do if it doesn't?

Rider fear is real, and it shouldn't be ignored.

PART TWO introduces the importance of *YOU*. You can't become a proficient rider if you don't take ownership of improving your riding skills. Learn with your head, first, then practice until you develop the muscle memory to perform the movement correctly.

YOU are the most important part of your riding safety.

PART THREE defines and explains *countersteering*. This is one of the most important, yet often misunderstood, topics in the motorcycling community. I'll explain why and hopefully convince you that countersteering is the single most important way you control your motorcycle. Once you master it, you'll be able to make your motorcycle go where you want it to go (instinctively) with small inputs to the handlebar.

PART FOUR explains *lowside* and *highside* crashes. What are they? What causes them? What can you do to avoid them? I've included illustrations of real crashes (captured on video) and break them down frame-by-frame so you can understand what's happening.

PART FIVE covers *braking, electronics,* and the *Hurt Report*. In this section, I'll unpack ABS (along with Traction Control) and tackle the myth that you should avoid using your front brake. We'll also look at the Hurt Report—the most comprehensive study of why riders crash.

The Hurt Report will change the way you ride. I promise.

PART SIX has a few closing thoughts and my personal challenge.

And finally, in the APPENDIX, I introduce my motorcycle mentors, give a sneak peek of my next book in the *Motorcycle Smarts* book series that documents my ride from Alabama to Alaska with my best friend, and share what listeners have said about the *Motorcycle Mentor Podcast*.

As a bonus, I've added several chapters on more lighthearted topics and sprinkled them throughout the book to give the reader a break.

My goal isn't for you to agree with everything I profess.

Some will say I'm over the top in certain areas—by nagging you to practice for every possible situation, and obsessing over ABS as though it solves all the world's problems. But others will say I'm too lax in other areas—by not preaching that you should wear a full face helmet.

What you wear on your head is your business.

Hold on Tight

I have to warn you. There's a lot of information packed into this book. Stick with me, though, because once you understand and incorporate this material, I honestly believe you'll be less likely to crash.

Am I saying you can reduce your risk to zero? NO!

Skilled riders crash and die every day when there was NOTHING they could have done to avoid it. But it is also true that under-skilled riders crash and die every day when there WAS something they could have done to avoid it.

In the end, I believe with all my heart that …

ALL RIDERS CAN CHANGE THEIR CHANCES OF CRASHING.

Who Should Read This Book?

This book isn't just for riders starting out.

This is the book I'd hand to someone who's been riding for decades and wants to reduce their risks of crashing. It's also the book I'd give to my son if he told me he wanted to learn how to ride.

Back in 2007, I invited my mentors to my house for an evening of motorcycle talk in my basement. After a few minutes of light conversation, I pulled out a stack of notes, looked them in the eyes, and said:

"Someday, I want to explain motorcycles my way."

THIS BOOK IS THAT VISION.

It took me more than ten years. I did everything I could to put it off. But I knew deep in my soul that I had to finish this book, so I did. If it helps just one rider, I've accomplished what I set out to do.

I want this book to change the way you think about motorcycling.

I want this book to change the way you ride.

You're in the right place, and I'm thrilled you're here.

Wait. There's one last thing I need to warn you about.
I call the thing I write about in this book a motorcycle and a bike.

I mostly blame my riding buddy (and friend) Mike for teaching me this. I found it strange the first hundred or so times he referred to his motorcycle as a bike. It wasn't long before I did the same.

My parents were right.
You are influenced by the people you hang out with.

Mastering the Art of Riding Well

If I didn't think I could measurably reduce my chances of being in a crash, I wouldn't ride. I believe you can reduce your chances too.
— David Mixson

Mastering the art of riding a motorcycle well is about learning how to ride the right way. It's about taking each ride seriously. It’s about enjoying the experience and making good decisions based on the laws of physics.

It’s about being confident you can avoid distracted drivers. It’s about having a plan before you need a plan. It takes effort.

It’s about understanding and overcoming rider fear, and having the head knowledge of how your motorcycle works so you can make it go where you want it to go. It’s about understanding why riders crash.

Learning how to control your motorcycle should be your primary goal when you buy your first motorcycle, or your next goal if you’ve ridden for decades. *Control* is the skill that makes you less likely to be in an accident. It’s the path to proficient riding.

Too many riders get bogged down trying to select the perfect bike and thinking that buying the right gear is the most important part of the journey. It's not. And it's the reason why I don't talk about these topics in this book—the first book in the *Motorcycle Smarts* series.

I'm not saying riding gear isn't important. I'm saying that you don't need to spend all your time selecting it. Instead, focus on overcoming rider fear and learning how to control your motorcycle.

Only then can you MASTER THE ART OF RIDING WELL.

A Fresh Approach

Every study on motorcycle crashes I've seen says the same thing:

Riders are making the same mistakes we did decades ago—even with mandatory training and plenty of books on the subject.

An NHTSA study in *2012* found that motorcyclists were 26 times more likely than car occupants to die in accidents (per mile traveled).[1] A similar NHTSA study in *2018* showed that riders are now 28 times more likely to die in motor vehicle traffic crashes.[2]

What we're doing to educate riders isn't working.

We need a fresh approach.

The *Motorcycle Smarts* book series is my attempt to do that.

The foundation of every book I've written on motorcycles begins with a core belief that every rider can change their chances of crashing.

My passion has never wavered, and I doubt it ever will.

The real issue isn't that riders get banged up when they crash. That's a given.
It's that average riders crash by themselves way too often making the same mistakes riders did generations ago.

Average riders use their rear brake way too much, don't know what lowside crashes are (and what causes them), and say there's little they can do to keep from crashing—thinking, *when my time comes, it comes*.

Average riders make errors that account for half of all crashes, don't know how to react when a driver makes a mistake, and choose whether to wear a helmet based on whether their riding buddies wear one.

Average riders consider fashion over function way too often.

Average riders do the same things average riders did decades ago.

Don't fall into the trap of thinking the way to have riders crash less is to make them wear helmets. Helmets don't keep us from crashing.

I don't care what you wear or what you ride. I care that you understand how motorcycles work so you can master why they crash. Once you do this, you can avoid triggering some of the most common types of crashes—and maybe even outlive your riding buddies.

It's time for a fresh approach to explaining how motorcycles work and how they crash—so a wife won't be left without her husband, a husband without his wife, or a child without their parent.

Something's not working.
We need a fresh approach.

Rider Fear Can be Pretty Persistent

Part One: Rider Fear

Overcoming rider fear is the first step.

This section wasn't in the original version of this book, but I knew something was missing, so I added it. Rider fear is real, it's paralyzing, and it shouldn't be ignored. If you're a seasoned rider and don't have rider fear, you might want to read through this section pretty fast. If you have severe anxiety when you ride (or merely think about riding), this section is for you.

ONE

Helmet Thoughts

Something magical happens when I put on a motorcycle helmet.

I see my life from a different viewpoint. I think of things to tell my wife and childhood stories to share with my kids. I mull over tasks I need to complete around the house and actions I need to take at work to be more effective. I ponder items to add to my bucket list.

And I feel thankful for the blessings in my life.

I'm pretty sure it's not the helmet that makes me think so clearly. Rather it's the intimacy of riding through Mother Nature.

Maybe it's the hum of the engine or the sound of wind rushing by.

Maybe it's the quiet peace of knowing I can't call someone—and that someone can't call me.

This magic doesn't happen on every ride, but it happens on some. And that's good enough. Sometimes, I wonder if I'm the only one who has these magical thoughts inside my helmet.

If that's the case, lucky me.

TWO

What Is Rider Fear?

When I pulled into traffic for the first time, I nearly freaked out.
— DAVID MIXSON

In this section, I'll explain what I've learned for myself (and from others) about the topic I call *rider fear*.

I started my first website on motorcycles more than a decade ago. Without question, I've received more emails about rider fear than any other topic. I'll share some of these emails as we go along.

RIDER FEAR is the pit in your stomach when you think about riding a moto-cycle. It's your heart racing when you venture out into traffic. It's the overwhelming sensation you're not in control.

Every rider defines it differently. Some describe it as an uncomfortable feeling, while others say it feels more like a panic attack.

Here's how one rider described rider fear:

"I have always wanted to ride a motorcycle. Six months ago I bought a used motorcycle a riding friend helped me pick out. She is a great rider and has encouraged me to fulfill my dreams of riding a motorcycle. I practiced in parking lots for the first few weeks and then took a training class. I really enjoyed the class and learned a lot. I passed the rider test on my first attempt. I was so excited. As long as I ride in parking lots and in my neighborhood, I feel fine. But just the thought of venturing out onto busy streets causes me to panic, and a fear comes over me like nothing I've experienced in my 44 years."

Here's how another rider described it:

"All my motorcycle friends have been riding for years and don't seem to understand the fear and lack of confidence I have in what I'm doing."

Do all riders experience rider fear? No. But based on the number of emails

I've received, most do—some to the point of doubting everything (including their decision to ride).

Here's how Cathy described it:

> *"I have so much fear it's a shame. When I see my motorcycle, fear comes over me. When I get on it, it's even worse. Please help me overcome this."*

My Personal Story

I vividly recall my first ride in traffic.

I had just purchased my first motorcycle, a bright red Honda VFR, and wanted to take it out for a spin. I borrowed a helmet and riding jacket from a friend and ventured out on my own.

Everything started out fine. I did a few laps in the parking lot of an apartment complex near my house, and from there I ventured out to a side street at a nearby shopping center.

I felt a little nervous but nothing too bad.

A short time later, I decided to venture out into traffic. I exited the shopping center and turned right onto Highway 72 heading west. My heart started racing. Cars were all around me. I felt anxious, awkward, and incredibly small. My mind became overwhelmed.

What if I dropped my motorcycle at a busy intersection?

What would it feel like if I crashed?

What would I do if someone came into my lane, or pulled out in front of me, or stopped abruptly?

Is this really a good idea?

Did I purchase the right motorcycle?

Am I selfish for wanting to ride, especially since this whole thing makes my family nervous?

Do I even enjoy riding?

And then I thought: If I die in an accident today, my motorcycle mentor (an avid reader) will certainly find out. The headline reads:

"Beginning Rider Crashes During First Ride in Traffic."

I rode a five-mile loop that afternoon, making only right-hand turns because left-hand turns seemed too hard. How could it be that such a short ride physically and mentally consumed me?

I felt under-skilled and vulnerable. When the ride was over, I took off my helmet and made this promise to myself.

If this fear doesn't go away, I will sell my motorcycle and stop riding.

RIDER FEAR IS REAL. IT'S FRIGHTENING. AND IT POKES ITS HEAD OUT WHENEVER IT WANTS.

Key Points

1. Rider fear is real. My email inbox proves it.

2. Rider fear can range from anxiety to debilitating panic.
3. I had never heard of rider fear before I experienced it for myself. That's why I think it's important we talk about it.

THREE

Who Has Rider Fear?

If you have at least some level of rider fear, you're probably normal.
— David Mixson

Now that we've defined rider fear, let's talk about who has it.

Rider fear isn't biased. Men and women can have rider fear, as can young riders and old riders, beginning riders and experienced riders.

Beginning riders, however, seem most likely to experience it. I estimate that well over half (maybe more) of all beginning riders experience a heightened level of fear and anxiety when they first start riding. While experienced riders can also encounter this same fear, it's usually less intense.

Here's what Betty wrote:

> *"I hate to admit this, but my motorcycle seems more like an enemy than a friend. I'm paralyzed with fear. I'm frustrated. Practicing in parking lots and my neighborhood isn't much fun. How do I get through this fear? Please help."*

Over the years, I've noticed a special group of riders that struggles with rider fear—riders who feel pressured to ride. Often it's a woman who's ridden as a passenger and decides she wants to ride on her own bike. When this happens, her husband does what any good husband should do. He encourages her.

Everything usually starts out fine. It's a logical (simple) step to go from passenger to rider, right? Not always.

Here's what Helen wrote:

"I have ridden as a passenger with my husband for almost 15 years. This past spring, I decided I wanted to ride my own bike. Almost immediately, a fear overcame me. Even after taking the MSF course twice (and passing both times), I still don't feel comfortable riding. I start dreading our rides the night before. My husband doesn't understand how I feel because he's been riding since he was a kid. He wants us to take a trip on our motorcycles this summer, but I don't want to. I hate myself for feeling this way. I don't want him to be disappointed. I feel stuck."

Helen wants to overcome her fear and please her husband.

But rider fear is telling her something different.

Why am I highlighting this group of riders?

Because Helen isn't the only one in this predicament who's contacted me, and because feeling pressured to ride can make you do things you probably shouldn't.

On the one hand, your body is telling you to stop riding. On the other hand, your spouse (or friend) is telling you to battle through your fear and not give up. This can be a dangerous combination.

Don't let others silence your inner voice.

Don't mistake encouragement for pressure.

Don't ride just because someone else wants you to.

It's wrong, and it's dangerous.

Key Points

1. Rider fear isn't biased. It likes all riders.
2. Beginning riders should expect rider fear.

3. Don’t ride just because someone else wants you to.

FOUR

How to Overcome Rider Fear

Rider fear is usually rooted in a lack of confidence in your riding skills.
— DAVID MIXSON

Now that you know what rider fear is and who usually has it, let's take a look at the best ways to overcome it.

When I first started riding, all my attention was focused on operating my motorcycle. I didn't have anything left to prepare for *what-if* scenarios, and I certainly didn't have the riding skills to avoid stupid driver mistakes.

My anxiety decreased as my skills improved.

It wasn't immediate, but it was steady. After every new experience (rain, cold, traffic, interstate), I became more confident in my abilities.

As the mechanics of operating my motorcycle became easier, I was able to devote more of my attention to riding defensively and enjoying the beauty of Mother Nature around me.

Making Rider Fear Go Away

For most, rider fear will disappear or become more manageable as your riding skills improve. But for some, rider fear will never go away.

In fact, it might even become more intense.

Unfortunately, there's no magic quick fix that will make rider fear vanish. But here are some things you can do that will usually help.

1. Overcome rider fear by learning how motorcycles work.

I strongly believe that all riders should learn the basics of how motorcycles work. Learn how motorcycles work (with your head first) and good things will usually follow.

Here's what Joe said:

> *"The MSF class was worth every dime and a lot of fun. However, two weeks after my class I went riding with some friends from work on a busy street. Making a wide right turn, I got tunnel vision on the median strip and went into it like a moth into a bug zapper. It was more embarrassing than anything, but all the talk during the MSF class about keeping your head up and pointed where you want to go suddenly made more sense."*

In this example, Joe fell into the trap of looking where he *didn't* want to go, instead of focusing on the path where he *did* want to go.

This is called *target fixation*, a subject I cover in more depth later. The important thing to note here is that *head knowledge* warns us of target fixation, something no amount of riding by itself could.

In my mind, you can't become a proficient rider without understanding the fundamentals of how motorcycles work. I wrote this book because I wanted to simplify (shorten) this process for riders.

It's the book I looked for (but couldn't find) when I started riding.

2. Overcome rider fear by learning control.

I firmly believe that rider fear is rooted in a *lack of confidence* in your ability to control your motorcycle. Will all rider fear magically go away once you master control? No. But learning how to make your bike do what you want it to will usually move you in the right direction.

The most important thing here is putting what you learn about motorcycles into practice. As an example, in a later chapter, you will learn that you should favor your front brake over your rear brake.

This is *head knowledge*.

Once you understand this, the next step is to use your front brake. Use the correct technique when you practice, and you'll instinctively use the correct technique when it matters the most.

3. Overcome rider fear by taking hands-on training.

One of the best ways to reduce rider fear is to take a hands-on training class. I address this topic in more depth in a later chapter.

But here, I'll make this point.

There's something really powerful about having a trained motorcycle instructor guide you in a one-on-one setting. If you have rider fear and aren't sure what to do next, take another training class.

Here's what Beth told me about hands-on training:

"I started riding in my 20s. My brothers and I learned by hitting the dirt trails and exploring. I eventually stopped riding, however, because of the fear I felt when riding in traffic. Now almost 45 years later, I got the bug again at 67, signed up for an MSF class, and passed with the help of an amazing teacher. The training showed me how to maneuver my bike and make good decisions. Without this class, the fear would have completely taken over again. Now I have [the head] knowledge of how to ride and a reasonable expectation of my limits."

4. Overcome rider fear by practicing.

Want to kick rider fear in the butt? Want to improve your riding skills? Want to MASTER THE ART OF RIDING YOUR MOTORCYCLE WELL?

Then you must practice your craft. I address this topic in more depth in a later chapter. But here, I'll make this point.

Practice in your driveway. Practice in your neighborhood. Practice in a vacant parking lot. Practice starting and stopping. Practice low-speed turns. Practice the things you learned in your hands-on training. Practice in all weather conditions.

Learn something new every time you ride.

I like Bill's approach:

> *"I'm a beginning rider at age 48, and I'm afraid. I'm taking it slow and practicing in parking lots at my own speed and comfort level. I'm less fearful after each practice session, and I try to attain a new goal during every ride. The more I ride, the more I understand what I need to work on to become a skilled and safe rider."*

Riding frequently is one of the best ways to improve your riding skills. My motorcycle mentor encouraged me to practice as often as I could, even if I only had a few minutes.

To this day, I look at every ride as an opportunity to learn something new What did I do well? What do I need to work on next time?

5. Overcome rider fear by staying in your comfort zone.

My best advice to riders struggling with rider fear is to stay inside, or just slightly outside, your comfort zone. As your skills improve, slowly expand your comfort zone.

Once you master your driveway, head out into your neighborhood. Once you master your neighborhood, find simple roads with no traffic, and from there more difficult roads with traffic.

Here's how Robin did it:

> *"At 38 I asked myself why not. I've wanted to ride a motorcycle for most of my adult life. It was hard at first. I rode in parking lots—lots and lots of parking lots. Taking a rider course really propelled me, yet that first ride*

on a real road had me trembling. I made so many mistakes that I questioned whether riding a motorcycle was right for me. I wondered if I was doing it out of stubbornness. I stuck with it and rode every chance I could. Before each ride, I would ask myself whether I was having a good day or bad and alter my route accordingly. I worked on specific skills during each ride and was amazed at how fast things improved. My confidence soared."

6. Overcome rider fear by constantly reevaluating your progress.

As you move through this journey, your riding skills should improve, and your rider fear should become less intense. Give yourself time and then reevaluate how you feel.

The most important thing to look for is steady progress.

Progress means you're on the right track.

7. Overcome rider fear by listening.

It's never a good idea to try to silence your rider fear. Instead, embrace it and listen to what it's telling you to do.

When is your rider fear most intense?

Do you dread riding or look forward to it?

Is someone encouraging you to ride?

Do you need to work on the mechanics of riding?

Would taking another hands-on training class help?

Listen to your body, and it will usually show you where you need to improve. In the next chapter, we'll talk about what you should do if your rider fear won't go away. But before we move forward, I want you to make the following commitment to yourself.

You are more than worth it.

"I [your name] will listen to what my body is telling me. I will let others encourage me, but I will not allow them to influence my decision to ride a motorcycle. I will take responsibility for my own actions. And in the end, if my fear doesn't go away, or at least become manageable, I will take this as a sign and stop riding."

Two months after my first ride in traffic, I reevaluated how I felt. The fear was less intense, and I still enjoyed riding. I was prepared to follow through on the promise I made to myself to stop riding.

And I still am.

Key Points

1. Rider fear is almost always rooted in a lack of confidence.
2. Learning how motorcycles work is the best first step in learning how

to control your motorcycle—and directly on the path to reducing rider fear.

3. Listen to what your body is telling you. It's usually right.

FIVE

My Rider Fear Isn't Going Away

Sometimes rider fear can be pretty stubborn.
— David Mixson

Let's assume you've followed the process I outlined in the last chapter, but your rider fear hasn't gone away as fast as you'd like.

In this situation, you have two options. The best course of action for most is to push through it until you master your craft. But for others, the best path forward is to stop riding.

Some are shocked when I say this. Others are relieved.

I hesitate giving specific advice to riders who can't shake rider fear. On the one hand, I believe that fear robs us of our dreams and it needs to be overcome and destroyed, regardless. I pushed through rider fear and tons of other riders have too.

Here's a rider who persevered:

"I started riding when I was 40. The third time I had my motorcycle on the road I went off the edge on a bad bend, rode down a ditch, came back on the road, and the bike flipped end over end with me still on it. Got lots of road rash and stitches in my elbow. I tried to ride it again after it was repaired, but I was shaky and scared. I sold the bike and rode with my husband. Fast forward seven years. Feeling envious when my neighbor got a Harley, I bought her Honda Rebel. This time I did the smart thing and took the MSF safety class. I quickly realized how much I didn't

know. I failed the class because I was still gun-shy and the instructors said I needed more seat time. I rode around and around the back streets of my neighborhood mastering the skills of starting, stopping, and using the clutch. Then I retook the class and passed! My husband bought me a new Sportster for Christmas. That was 13 years ago. I'm on my second Sportster now. I think the class gave me the skills I needed, and practice gave me the confidence."

Best-selling author Michael Hyatt wrote, "Discomfort is a catalyst for growth. There's no better way to grow in any area of your life than to consistently put yourself in uncomfortable situations."

He's right. Riders who overcome rider fear should celebrate.

BUT WAIT ... Rider fear can also be a friend that saves your life!

Fear is natural, instinctive, and unbiased. Fear is your body's way of telling you it's uncomfortable, out of balance, and in danger.

Fear can be a wonderful thing. It can show you where you need to improve. It can nudge you to take action. It should never be ignored.

Best-selling author Steven Pressfield wrote, "If you are paralyzed with fear, it's a good sign. It shows you what you have to do."

Here's a rider who listened:

"I have been struggling to feel comfortable riding a motorcycle for several years. After I received your kind email response, I decided that my soul (as you called it) was telling me to stop riding. Last month I sold my motorcycle. I feel so much better! I am so proud of my decision to stop riding."

Now What?

Now that we've determined that fear can be good *and* bad, each of us has to determine what we do with it.

Do we stop riding when we have rider fear?

Do we try to overcome it?

Do we put our head down and ignore it?

Here's how Christopher plans on handling it:

> *"I rode motorcycles off-road as a kid. My dad always rode a Harley. Unfortunately, a drunk driver murdered my father while he was on his bike. I bought a new Harley for myself later that same year to join him for rides (like he always wanted). Long story short, I'm 44 now, and it's been ten years. I still have my 2003 Harley, but every time I get ready to ride I find some reason or sign not to. My nerves have driven me crazy. I feel bad, but I can't give up."*

If I were Christopher, I would probably stop riding. But I'm not. Christopher is the only one who can make that decision.

In the end, you're the only one who can decide what to do next. Only you can determine if riding fulfills your dreams, fulfills someone else's dreams, or somehow rights a wrong.

When I had rider fear, I was looking for consistent improvements. I expected to have less fear this week than I did last week. I expected my riding skills to improve. I expected the mechanics of operating my motorcycle to become easier.

All this happened, so I kept riding.

My Best Advice

If you're experiencing the same intensity of rider fear after months of consistent riding, then I want you to ask yourself this simple question:

Do you really want to continue riding a motorcycle?

If you don't, take a deep breath and smile. I give you permission to stop riding. Your soul is telling you to stop, so stop.

It's not the end of the world. I promise.

Key Points

1. Consistent improvement signals you're on the right track.
2. Don't ride just because someone else wants you to.
3. There's no shame in choosing a different hobby.

SIX

Final Thoughts on Rider Fear

How can something so terrifying be so enticing?
— David Mixson

It's been more than a decade since I conquered rider fear, *or did I?*

To this day, before I put on my helmet, I pause, take a deep breath, and ask myself if I really want to do this.

Is my mind clear?

Do I feel steady and sure?

Is the reward worth the risk?

Fear can be a great motivator and guide. Fear isn't the enemy; it's our friend. Fear is how our unconscious mind steers our conscious mind. Fear is how our body prepares for peak performance. FEAR IS AMAZING!

If you're struggling with rider fear, I believe that the best path forward is for you to lean into your fear and listen to what it's telling you.

Rider fear is part of your journey.

It's how your soul tells your body it needs to improve.

Rider fear keeps you from doing things your muscles don't know how to do. It's a meter that registers progress. Rider fear is so beneficial that I feel sorry for riders who've never experienced it.

Ralph explains it this way:

"I rode motorcycles in my 20s and 30s then stopped. I started back when I turned 52. The first thing I did was take the MSF course at the local community college as a refresher.

There's always a bit of nervousness when the kickstand goes up, but for me, nervousness combined with awareness leads to heightened alertness. My grandfather owned a small plane for years but sold it when he stopped having that small butterfly knot in his belly at take-off. He thought he was becoming too confident in his abilities. He always said, 'There are old pilots and bold pilots, but no old, bold pilots.' Maybe a motorcyclist is just a two-dimensional aviator. Becoming complacent and over-confident could place you at the Pearly Gates ahead of schedule."

Ralph is right. Having at least some rider fear is probably a good thing. Don't look for rider fear to go away completely but to become more manageable as your riding skills improve.

Once you learn how to control your motorcycle, riding will seem easier. You'll be able to notice the beauty around you

—the intoxicating fragrances of spring and the cool crispness of fall.

Hal Elrod, author of *The Miracle Morning*, said:

> *"Everything is difficult before it's easy. Every new experience is uncomfortable before it's comfortable. The more you practice [your craft] the more natural and normal it will feel."*

Scuba diving is hard before it's easy.
Playing the piano is hard before it's easy.
Riding a motorcycle is HARD before it's easy.

For most riders, there's a good chance you'll look back on rider fear as a thing of the past, an obstacle you overcame, a feeling that made you get serious about learning how to control your bike. But for others, it will be a persistent guerrilla that destroys your dream of riding.

Either way, rider fear served a valuable purpose.

In the end, when your inner voice can't be silenced, it's probably time to follow her advice. If there's one thing I want you to take away from this book, it's this.

IT'S OKAY TO STOP RIDING A MOTORCYCLE.

My first ride in traffic changed the way I rode.

Rider fear showed me what I had to do to become a better rider.

Rider fear signaled when I was making progress and when I wasn't.

Rider fear probably saved my life.

And it can save yours too.

Key Points

1. Rider fear isn't the enemy. It's your friend.

2. Riding a motorcycle is difficult before it's easy.
3. When rider fear can't be calmed, it's probably time to follow her advice and choose a different hobby.

You Can Change Your Chances of Crashing

Part Two: All About You

Riding a motorcycle well begins with YOU.

In this section, we'll talk about taking ownership of your riding safety, practicing the correct way, and developing muscle memory. Nothing great happens if you don't get this part right. This section is the foundation for the how-to material that follows.

SEVEN

An Old Country Store

One of the most enjoyable parts of riding is exploring places I've never been. It's simple to do. I head north (or south or east or west) from my house and turn onto roads I've never traveled.

I'm always amazed at how things can change such a short distance from my congested life. City streets and highways turn into country roads. Walmart Super Centers disappear—and country stores appear.

When I was a kid, there was a country store about a mile from my grandparent's farm. My sister and I used to walk there to buy candy.

Banana taffy was my favorite.

The walk was always worth it, even in the blistering southern heat. With a handful of change, we could leave with a pocketful of candy that would last us all day.

The pieces seemed bigger back then.

I didn't realize old country stores still existed until I purchased a motorcycle. I'm thrilled they still do.

Find one for yourself and see what I mean. It's like stepping back in time. Imagine what it must have felt like to buy a piece of candy for a penny or a candy bar for a nickel.

That's what I do.

A few of the country stores I've discovered look like they haven't changed much in the last 50 years. Those are my favorites. There is truly something magical about getting away from the modernness of our normal surroundings to a place that reminds us of our past.

The next time you find an old country store—stop and enjoy.

EIGHT

Take Ownership of Your Safety

Motorcycle safety is a choice.
— David Mixson

Now that we've listened to what rider fear had to say, let's talk about the most important component of becoming a better rider. YOU.

It's hard for me to understand this, but some riders don't think they can reduce their chances of crashing. Instead of taking responsibility for riding better *offensively* (by improving their riding skills) and *defensively* (by looking out for the other guy), they place their faith in mathematical statistics and believe:

"When my time comes, it comes."

Don't fall into the trap of thinking this way!

Here are six things you can do to ride more safely.

1. Taking ownership of your riding safety is about believing you can reduce your risk of crashing.

In large part, the purpose of this book is to show the MOTORCYCLING COMMUNITY THEY CAN CHANGE THEIR CHANCES OF CRASHING.

Making this affirmation is the most important step in your journey to MASTERING THE ART OF RIDING WELL. This is because there is zero motivation to take action if you don't believe your actions will influence the outcome.

I realize that I'll have to convince some of you.

I'll do this by breaking down how motorcycles work, by explaining how to avoid certain types of crashes caused by rider error, by highlighting what the Hurt Report teaches us about why riders crash, and by deciphering motorcycle electronic systems that can virtually eliminate certain types of crashes.

2. Taking ownership of your riding safety is about

UNDERSTANDING HOW TO CONTROL YOUR MOTORCYCLE.

And the foundation for understanding how to control your motorcycle is *head knowledge*. Understand how countersteering works so you can use it to make your motorcycle go where you want it to go. Understand lowside and highside crashes (and what causes them) so you can avoid them. Understand how to effectively use your brakes so you can stop faster.

3. TAKING OWNERSHIP OF YOUR RIDING SAFETY IS ABOUT IMPROVING YOUR DEFENSIVE RIDING SKILLS.

I've avoided crashing on numerous occasions by anticipating what motorists might do. Like the time I was riding on I-65 heading north toward Nashville, Tennessee. I was in the right lane, and a motorist in the left lane shot across in front of me to make the exit ramp.

I had just slowed down so I wasn't beside him, just in case.

Anticipate where drivers might want to go, and be somewhere else.

4. Taking ownership of your riding safety is about improving your offensive riding skills.

One of the best ways to do this is to take a hands-on training class. No book (including this one), training video, or Internet search can substitute for hands-on instruction.

Rider coaches are worth their weight in gold. Let them help you. More on how to get the most out of your training in the next chapter.

5. Taking ownership of your riding safety is about constantly improving.

The best riders I know say they *never stop learning*. Before and after every ride, think about what you need to work on.

Better yet, write your thoughts in a journal so you can monitor your progress.

6. Taking ownership of your riding safety is about having the right mindset.

It's about engaging in the idea that you can always do more to get better. It's about staying interested long enough to read this book all the way through. It's about caring about your loved ones enough to take this stuff seriously. Here's the honest truth.

If you want to be a better-than-average rider you have to THINK DIFFERENTLY THAN AVERAGE RIDERS. You need a different MINDSET.

Riding a motorcycle is hard. Riding a motorcycle proficiently is harder. Reading this book is a wonderful first move toward ...

Mastering the art of riding well.

Congratulations. You're on the right track.

Key Points

1. YOU are responsible for your riding safety.
2. Work to improve your offensive and defensive riding skills.
3. Mindset is a catalyst that makes average riders great.

NINE

Take Hands-On Training

We've already touched on the importance of taking hands-on training. In this chapter, we'll expand on the topic and talk about how you can get the most out of your training.

Most states require that riders complete a hands-on training class as part of their motorcycle license endorsement. When I started riding again at forty, I still had my motorcycle endorsement from when I was fifteen. I took a hands-on training class anyway.

To get the most out of your training, make sure to select a program geared toward your riding level. Inexperienced riders should look for classes focused on helping beginning riders learn the basics. Experienced riders should look for classes focused on helping seasoned riders improve their riding skills.

So Many Options

The Motorcycle Safety Foundation (MSF) offers classes for riders at different skill levels. Their Basic Rider Course (BRC) is for beginner riders. If you don't have a motorcycle, that's not a problem.

The BRC supplies the bike and helmet.

The course consists of both classroom and hands-on instruction. The hands-on portion is conducted in a closed-off parking lot.

MSF isn't your only option. Since you are working toward your motorcycle license endorsement, it's a good idea to check with your Department of Motor

Vehicles (DMV) for a list of approved courses.

Training Day Tips

To get the most out of your training, take it seriously.

Think of it this way. You could learn something during class that saves your life.

Get a good night's sleep.

Show up early.

Bring the right gear to be comfortable.

I took my first hands-on course in the middle of winter. I wasn't as prepared as I should have been and struggled to stay warm. Don't make the same mistake. If it's cold, dress in layers and bring plenty of gear to stay warm. Carry gloves.

Trust me. It's hard to ride if you can't feel your fingers.

Check the course guidelines. Most require long sleeves and pants. If it's hot outside, a mesh riding jacket works great. If you don't have one, it's probably okay to improvise.

Just check first because the guidelines change.

Who Knew?

I took my first hands-on training class with a friend—the same friend I rode to Alaska with a decade later. Our instructor was great.

I now understand some of the things he was trying to get us to understand (like countersteering). I wish I could have read this book before taking the training.

He would have made more sense.

Key Points

1. Take hands-on motorcycle training seriously.
2. Read the course materials ahead of time if possible.
3. Ask questions during the class. Most rider coaches become rider

coaches because they want to help others.

TEN

Practice Everything

The more I practice, the luckier I get.
— ARNOLD PALMER

I've worked as an engineer at NASA for more than 30 years.

For nearly a decade of that time, I worked in the payload operations area conducting science experiments during Space Shuttle flights.

One of the most valuable lessons I took away from this experience is that the best way to learn how to perform a task well is to practice that task over and over again.

Before the Space Shuttle ever took off, we spent hundreds of hours in ground-simulations practicing for every imaginable scenario.

We practiced as if the experiments worked correctly.

We practiced workarounds in case they didn't.

By the time we made it to flight, the ground controllers—working with the astronauts onboard—knew how to handle most anything.

The actual missions were always easier.

Becoming proficient at riding a motorcycle is no different than becoming proficient at operating experiments in space. They both require PREPARATION and PRACTICE.

David L. Hough, author of *Proficient Motorcycling*, wrote."The moral of the story is that we must constantly practice the right skills if we expect to use them in a pinch."

How will you know how to make an emergency stop if you don't practice? How will you know how to use countersteering to avoid an object in the road if you don't practice? How will you become proficient at putting your bike on the center stand if you don't practice?

You won't.

Practice ... Practice ... Practice

Practice starting and stopping. Practice riding in the cold and the heat. Practice riding on curvy roads and straight roads, in groups and solo. Practice riding in traffic. Practice riding in the rain.

Practice riding in traffic when it's raining.

Practice using your brakes. Practice using countersteering to dodge objects in your path (more on this later). Practice staying calm when someone around you does something stupid.

Practice develops muscle memory (more on this later) and builds confidence. Practice is the foundation that makes you a better rider.

Practice the Correct Way

Before we leave the topic of practicing, I'll make this point. Practice is of little value unless you use the correct techniques while you practice.

My motorcycle mentor, Fred, insisted that I practice the right way, even when I was just riding around in my driveway.

"David, use the correct braking techniques in your neighborhood because that's what you'll instinctively use in a panic situation."

He was right.

A tennis player who swings with incorrect form while practicing will never become a great player, regardless of how much he practices.

Likewise, someone who rides a motorcycle with poor techniques while practicing will never become a proficient rider, regardless of how many hours he practices.

Take the stuff you learn in this book (and hands-on training) and practice the correct way in every situation—because that's how you'll do it when it matters.

Key Points

1. Practice makes perfect. Your parents were right.
2. Practice the big things and the little things.
3. Practice is the excuse you use to ride on the weekend. "Honey, I need to practice when it's sunny and in the 70s."

ELEVEN

Develop Muscle Memory

The trouble is very few of us can out-think our habits. In an emergency, we will do whatever we have been in the habit of doing, then think about it after the fact.

— DAVID L. HOUGH, *PROFICIENT MOTORCYCLING*

Now that we've taken ownership of our riding safety and know to practice the correct way, let's talk about what we want to happen next.

When your muscles perform a sequence of movements over and over again, the activity naturally becomes easier. In effect, your muscles memorize how to perform the motions. This is called *muscle memory*.

The Oxford Dictionary defines muscle memory as:

"The ability to reproduce a particular movement without conscious thought, acquired as a result of frequent repetition of that movement."

A simple example of muscle memory is typing.

When I first started typing, I had to think about where each letter was located. Over time with lots of practice, my fingers (with the help of my brain) learned where each letter was located. Now, I don't think about moving my fingers to the correct keys. It just sort of happens.

Typing is now a part of my muscle memory.

A more complex example of muscle memory is throwing a baseball.

My son, Drew, took pitching lessons for years. Until then, I had no idea so many body parts have to move in sequence for a baseball to fly over home plate. Both arms and legs (along with head, hips, and back) must make precise movements at specific times during the motion for the ball to travel to the desired spot.

Drew looked awkward at first, and the ball went all over the place.

After every pitch, the coach told him what he needed to fix. "Push your gloved hand out sooner and extend your throwing arm earlier."

Once Drew understood what the coach wanted (head knowledge), he practiced the complex sequence of motions over and over until his brain made it a part of his muscle memory.

Spiking a Volleyball

It was the same for my daughter, Maddie, when she played volleyball.

Just like pitching, spiking a volleyball requires a complex sequence of motions performed at the exact right time.

Maddie looked awkward at first but worked hard to improve. First, by learning how to complete the motions (head knowledge), and then by practicing the correct way over and over again until it became a part of her muscle memory.

Over time, she no longer had to think about where to position her body. It all became automatic. With the help of muscle memory, she practiced her way to a college volleyball scholarship.

We use muscle memory every day.

Do you think about what your hands and feet should do when you drive? This is muscle memory. Do you consciously think about how to walk? This is muscle memory. Can you ride a bicycle even though you haven't ridden one in years? This is muscle memory.

Nobody Said This Was Easy

Operating a motorcycle is no different. Both arms and legs have to do stuff at the precise moment for it to go where you want it to go. Your muscles won't know how to do this at first—and your conscious brain will have to work extra hard.

But as you practice, the mechanics of riding will become a part of your muscle memory. Riding will seem easier—more automatic like typing or pitching or spiking. This is what you want.

Muscle memory is your reward for relentless practice.

It Gets Better

Here's the powerful part of all of this. Once the mechanics of operating a motorcycle become a part of your muscle memory, your *conscious* brain can focus on *defensive* riding skills (like looking for distracted drivers, noticing obstacles in the road, and finding the best lane position in traffic), and on *offensive* riding skills (like working on countersteering, using correct braking techniques, and looking where you want to go).

Muscle memory is why we practice.

Muscle memory makes us better riders.

> Muscle memory frees our mind to focus on things other than the MECHANICS OF OPERATING OUR MOTORCYCLE.

When I first started riding, I had to think about operating the clutch and shifting gears. I had to think about rolling off the throttle onto the front brake. I had to concentrate on looking deep into each turn.

After tons of practice, I don't have to think much about shifting gears or operating the clutch. It just sort of happens. The mechanics of operating a motorcycle is part of my muscle memory.

Now, I can think more clearly and focus on the beauty around me.

I can notice distracted drivers.

I can resist target fixation.

I can avoid the blind spot of the guy next to me.

This is the reason we should all strive for muscle memory.

Typing Class in High School

Before we close this chapter, let's take a step back and relook at the typing example mentioned earlier. I learned how to type in a business machines class back in high school. Every Friday afternoon my teacher gave us a speed test to see how many words we could type per minute.

At first, I was the slowest typist in the class because I did what the teacher asked us to do. "Class, type without looking at your keys."

I questioned my methodology after scoring so low on the first few speed tests. I could tell my friends were looking down at the keys.

It felt like they were cheating.

But I kept doing what the teacher told us to do because I figured she knew what she was talking about. It wasn't until several years later that I thought I knew more than adults my parents' age.

Guess What Happened?

My teacher wanted us to type without looking down at the keys when we practiced so we would develop the muscle memory to—drum roll please—type without looking at the keys.

Slowly but surely, my muscles learned where the keys were located and my speed steadily improved. It wasn't long before I could type more words per minute than anyone in the class. Why? Because I practiced the correct way until it became a part of my muscle memory.

To this day, I'm benefitting from the typing class I took back in high school. I typed most of this book without looking at the keys.

The only word that slowed me down—*motorcycle*.

Key Points

1. Muscle memory is our reward for disciplined practice.
2. Use proper techniques when you practice because that’s the way your muscles will commit the task to memory.
3. As the mechanics of operating a motorcycle become easier, work on improving other aspects of your riding.

Countersteering Puts You in Control

Part Three: Countersteering

Countersteering is a wonderful thing.

It probably took me longer to understand countersteering than most. For some reason, my body didn’t believe it could really be like this.

TWELVE

How My Motorcycle Changed Me

Riding a motorcycle has changed the way I look at my life.

I notice the beauty around me more purposefully.

I anticipate the warmth of spring and the coolness of fall.

I appreciate great riding days, even when I can't ride.

I've coined a phrase in my family that describes these near-perfect days. I call them *Top Ten Days*. You know the ones I'm talking about: blue skies, low humidity, and mild temperatures.

They usually show up in the spring and fall, but sometimes they make an appearance when you least expect them.

These are the most special.

We had a *Top Ten Day* last December. It was unseasonably warm, and my family was able to do something we had never done before. We ate outside at my wife's favorite restaurant on her birthday.

"Kids, this is a *Top Ten Day*," I said.

We all smiled and appreciated the moment—in large part because we paused long enough to notice.

I don't put a limit on the number of *Top Ten Days* I proclaim in a given year. Instead, I give thanks as often as possible.

It's a way to appreciate the beauty around me.

When you own a motorcycle, you'll see nature through a different lens. You'll no longer take for granted a clear blue sky framed with cotton-white clouds. *Top Ten Days* will call out to be enjoyed, whether on two wheels or not.

Riding a motorcycle changed me. It will change you too.

THIRTEEN

Before We Begin

He who loves practice without theory is like the sailor who boards a ship without a rudder and compass and never knows where he may cast.

— Leonardo da Vinci

If I had a weekend to talk to you about riding a motorcycle more proficiently, I'd focus on the information in the next few sections. THIS IS THE MATERIAL I PASSIONATELY BELIEVE EVERY RIDER SHOULD UNDERSTAND.

If you're an experienced rider and don't understand countersteering and lowside crashes, and have never heard of the Hurt Report, you're not alone. For many riders, these concepts have been missed along the way. Not because instructors don't understand them or think they're important, and not because the concepts are hard to understand.

Unfortunately, these topics are often buried in editorial-type magazine columns or insufficiently explained in motorcycle books.

As an example, just last week I picked up a mega book on motorcycling at a local bookstore. It had exactly one tiny paragraph on the entire topic of lowside crashes.

That's simply not enough space to explain what these crashes are—and more importantly—how you can avoid them. In comparison, the same mega book had an entire section on how to get the most out of your first Sturgis rally.

None of the material I'm about to present is unique. I didn't figure out something new that's never been figured out before. I'm just going deeper on certain subjects, the ones I believe are the most important, and with more gusto than other books.

I do this at the expense of NOT writing about other topics.

I'll leave the discussion of how to select riding gear and how to get the most out of your first motorcycle rally to other authors—for now.

Heads Up ...

Some of this material might seem overwhelming at first, but I break everything down in a non-engineering way—the way I learn best.

It's not important that you fully understand how countersteering works. It's important that you understand how to use countersteering to make your motorcycle go where you want it to go.

It's not important that you understand the physics of a lowside crash. It's important that you understand what triggers most lowside crashes so you can avoid them.

The main purpose of this book is to show you how you can CHANGE YOUR CHANCES OF CRASHING.
I do the bulk of the heavy lifting in the next three sections.

THIS IS THE STUFF THAT COULD SAVE YOUR LIFE.

FOURTEEN

Countersteering

It's hard to imagine that so many so-called "experienced" riders either fail to understand the importance of countersteering or fail to recognize that countersteering is how a motorcycle really turns.

— Ken Condon, *Riding in the Zone*

Now that we've learned the importance of practicing the correct way, let's talk about how we control our motorcycle using *countersteering*.

A textbook review of countersteering would require a discussion of a phenomenon known as gyroscopic precession. While this might be interesting to some, it's not important to understand the physics.

It's important to understand how countersteering gives us control.

My simplified but just as accurate definition of countersteering ... the PHYSICS OF HOW YOU TURN your MOTORCYCLE.

If you've taken a hands-on training course or read a motorcycle skills book, you've heard the phrase "push right to go right" and "push left to go left." This is countersteering. This is how you control your bike.

See Figure 14-1 (below).

Figure 14-1 Countersteering (Push on Left Handlebar to Lean Left)

Sound Backwards?

You have probably noticed that countersteering is counterintuitive and *backward*. Pushing on the left handlebar is the same as turning (steering) the handlebar to the right. That's right, to initiate a turn you actually turn the handlebar in the *opposite* direction you want to go.

Let me say this again because I know it's hard to believe.

When you want to lean your motorcycle to the *left* (and turn left), you actually turn the handlebar to the *right* (which is the same input as pushing on the left handlebar).

This is true whether you realize it or not.

Isn't that amazing?

The motorcycle instructor gods of the past got it right when they crafted the slogan "push left to go left." They could have also said "turn right to go left," which is painfully confusing but equally correct.

If any of this sounds confusing, I understand. I struggled to make the mental connection of countersteering when I first started riding.

During my first MSF class, the instructor spent a great deal of time trying to get us to understand countersteering (with our head) and feel countersteering (with our body).

To do this, the instructor placed cones in a curve.

Then he had us ride around the curve faster and faster to force us to use countersteering to make the motorcycle turn in a tighter circle. The only way we could make the turn riding that fast was to push on the inside handlebar with purpose.

Over and over, the instructor called out, "Go faster. Make the bike lean more by pushing on the inside handlebar."

Countersteering didn't feel natural to me that day. My head didn't understand countersteering, and my body never made the connection. It wasn't until months later that countersteering made sense.

QUICK TIP: It's probably worth noting that countersteering doesn't start working until your wheels are rolling over a certain speed. There's passionate debate about the exact speed countersteering takes over. Some say countersteering starts working at about 15 mph. I say if your feet are comfortably up on the pegs, it's probably safe to assume that countersteering is at work.

Understanding Countersteering

Why do you need to understand countersteering with your head if you are using it already? You need to understand countersteering with your head so you can make your motorcycle go where you want it to go in every situation.

Countersteering is how you do normal turns.

Countersteering is how you dodge an object in the road.

It's what you use to make delicate adjustments in a sweeping turn. It's how you tighten a turn when you're running wide in a curve on a mountain pass where death is a real possibility if you run off the road.

Countersteering is powerful, but it doesn't require much input. An 80-pound woman can make an 800-pound Goldwing lean instantly.

Curves are easier once you master countersteering.

Push on your right handlebar gently to make your motorcycle lean (turn) to the right. Push on your left handlebar gently to make it lean (turn) to the left. If you need to tighten your turn radius, simply push a little more on the inside handlebar, and your bike will lean more.

Feeling Countersteering for Yourself

Once you understand countersteering with your head, it's time to feel it. In a vacant parking lot, find a spot on the pavement and practice swerving around it like it was an object in the road.

> NOTE: If you can't find a spot, make your own by pouring a small amount of water on the pavement to darken it.

Approach the spot and swerve around it. Push right, push left, push right—will get you around the object to the right. Push left, push right, push left—will get you around the object to the left.

Here's another exercise.

In a vacant parking lot, come up to about 20 mph and take your left hand off the handlebar. Next, use only your throttle hand to make the motorcycle turn. Notice how it leans to the right when you push on the handlebar with your right hand, and leans to the left when you pull back on the right handlebar?

Feel it? You are turning the handlebar in the opposite direction.

Hence the term COUNTERsteering.

Keep Working

Don't stop until you make the mental connection of countersteering. Don't stop until it becomes a part of your muscle memory. Only then will you be able to use it to make your motorcycle go where you want it to go during the stress of an emergency.

Don't get frustrated. Mastering countersteering will take time. It certainly did for me. Be patient. Let your head and muscles put it all together over time.

It wasn't until I made the connection of how countersteering works that I felt confident riding and confident that I could make my motorcycle go where I wanted it to go.

COUNTERSTEERING IS THE PHYSICS THAT PUTS YOU IN CONTROL OF YOUR MOTORCYCLE.

Key Points

1. Learn how to use countersteering with your head, first.
2. Experiment with countersteering in a vacant parking lot. Keep practicing until you think to yourself, “I feel it!”
3. Countersteering puts you in control of your motorcycle.

FIFTEEN

Body Steering

Before we continue, it's probably worth noting that some riders don't believe countersteering is how you control your motorcycle.

Instead, they believe you lean (turn) your bike by *body steering*.

Shift your weight to the left to lean (turn) left.

Shift your weight to the right to lean (turn) right.

Keith Code, rider coach at the California Superbike School, got so tired of hearing naysayers rant that countersteering doesn't work that he modified a motorcycle to prove it does.

He calls it his *No B.S. Machine*.

Code's modified motorcycle has two sets of handlebars, the regular one from the factory and a second stationary set he added that doesn't rotate with the front forks.

Here's what Code found:

> *"At this writing, we have run nearly 100 riders of all experience levels on this double-barred bike. It has made believers out of every single one in the actuality of countersteering, of course. Even at speeds of no more than 20 to 35 mph, no matter how much you tug or push or pull or jump around on the bike, the best we saw was that the bike wiggled and became somewhat unstable. Did it turn? Not really. Would it turn at higher speeds? Absolutely not. Could you avoid something in your path? No way. Could anyone quick-turn the bike? Hopeless!"*[1]

The conclusion: Body Steering is a BIG FAT MYTH.

Key Points

1. Code's *No B.S. Machine* proves body steering is a myth.
2. Countersteering is how you make your motorcycle turn.

SIXTEEN

Tighteningа a Turn

Countersteering will save your life.
— KEN CONDON, *RIDING IN THE ZONE*

Why have I devoted an entire section in this book to the topic of countersteering? Because countersteering isn't just the way you control your motorcycle under normal conditions, it's how you control your motorcycle to avoid a crash.

Let's look at a common single-vehicle crash scenario.

Suppose you're on an interstate exit ramp around a curve sweeping to the right and have misjudged your speed. You're going wide toward the outside concrete barrier.

In this situation, you need to act quickly:

(1) look where you want to go deep in the curve,

(2) push on the inside handlebar to tighten your turn, and

(3) trust your tires to carry you through.

Believe me. This won't feel natural. The first time I did this, I was certain my tires would lose traction, but they didn't. I safely exited the turn and silently thanked my motorcycle mentor for teaching me to use countersteering and trust my tires.

The Way I Look at YouTube

FULL DISCLOSURE: I've never (knowingly) watched a video on YouTube that showed a rider being seriously injured or killed. That does me no good, and I think it's disrespectful to the rider and his family.

But YouTube can be a great tool if used properly—because there's usually a lesson buried in every motorcycle crash.

You've seen the videos, right?

Rider enters a curve and drifts wide off the road and crashes.

In most of the videos I've seen in this scenario, the rider's motorcycle wasn't leaned over very far, indicating the bike had more turning potential.

See Figure 16-1 (below).

Figure 16-1 Countersteering to Tighten Turn (Push on Left Handlebar to Tighten Turn)

I can't help but wonder how many of these single-vehicle accidents could have been avoided if the rider had used countersteering and trusted his tires to tighten the turn?

Now you know why I'm so adamant that all riders UNDERSTAND COUNTERSTEERING with their HEAD.

Three Steps: Every—Single—Time

When you watch a wide-turn crash on YouTube, think about what the rider did incorrectly to be in that position.

Did he enter the curve too fast?

Did he enter on the wrong line?

Did he start his turn too early?

Regardless of his mistake, the solution is always the same: (1) look where you want to go, (2) push on the inside handlebar to tighten the turn, and (3) trust your tires.

Key Points

1. Motorcycle tires are amazingly sticky. When you get in a bind, give them a chance to carry you through.
2. When you start going wide in a turn, push on the inside handlebar to tighten the turn. Having this head knowledge has saved me from crashing numerous times.

SEVENTEEN

Testing Countersteering

Devising a system to convince myself.
— David Mixson

When I started riding, I had a hard time believing the physics of countersteering. It didn't make sense to me. How could I be steering my motorcycle by turning the handlebar in the opposite direction?

To convince myself, I devised a test.

I selected my Honda VFR (the only bike I owned at the time) as my test vehicle and a road south of town (with little traffic and a nice sweeping curve) as my test track.

Early one morning, I headed there by myself and initiated the test.

As I approached the curve, I leaned forward onto my tank bag to the point my body felt rigidly attached to the motorcycle.

The VFR had a forward riding position, which made this easy.

Absolutely Amazing

As I entered the left-handed curve, I pushed on the left handlebar to make the motorcycle lean (turn) to the left.

While I was in the curve, I made small inputs to the handlebar to adjust the turn radius—pushing on the left handlebar to make the bike lean harder, pushing on the right handlebar to make the bike lean less.

After several test runs, something amazing happened—it clicked!

Somehow, taking out all the external factors by leaning onto my tank bag multiplied the sensation, and my brain felt countersteering.

Nonsense to the naysayers who say countersteering doesn't exist. Connect with your motorcycle by leaning over your tank bag and feel what makes your motorcycle turn. COUNTERSTEERING.

WARNING: This test isn't for everyone. It can feel a little unnerving at first. If you start to feel odd, immediately sit up and ride in a normal riding position.

Key Points

1. Countersteering works.
2. Connect with your motorcycle and feel countersteering.

EIGHTEEN

Toys Without Countersteering

Countersteering only works on two-wheeled things that lean to turn.

That means countersteering does NOT work on mechanical stuff such as four-wheelers, Can-AM Spyders, and motorcycle trikes.

Two Examples

On a motorcycle (which uses countersteering), you push left to go left

—or turn the handlebar in the *opposite* direction you want to go.

See Figure 18-1 (below).

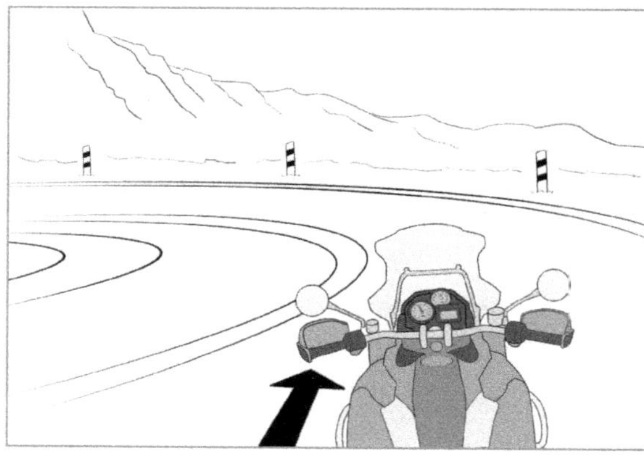

Figure 18-1 Countersteering on Motorcycle (Push on Left Handlebar to Turn Left)

On a Can-AM Spyder (which doesn't use countersteering), you push right to go left—or turn the handlebar in the *same* direction you want to go.

See Figure 18-2 (below).

Figure 18-2 Steering on Can-AM Spyder (Push on Right Handlebar to Turn Left)

If you want to feel countersteering, ride something that doesn't use countersteering soon after you've ridden your motorcycle.

You'll notice the difference immediately.

Wasn't that amazing?

The last time I rode my friend's Sea-Doo at his lake house (tough life, right?), it felt awkward. But in a matter of seconds, my brain made the adjustment.

Key Points

1. The best way to believe countersteering is to feel it.
2. Bicycles and motorcycles use countersteering. Goldwing trikes, four-wheelers, Sea-Doos, snowmobiles, motorcycles with sidecars, tractors, trucks, riding lawn mowers, golf carts, and automobiles don't use countersteering.

NINETEEN

Countersteering Wrap-Up

Countersteering is real. Countersteering is how you control your bike.

Countersteering is how you avoid crashing.

Learn how countersteering works (head knowledge), then practice using it until it becomes a part of your muscle memory. Only then can you use it in a pinch to save your life.

If you remember nothing else from this book, remember this:

When you start going wide in a curve:

(1) look where you want to go deep in the curve,

(2) push on the inside handlebar to tighten your turn, and

(3) trust your tires.

THIS DOESN'T HAVE TO FEEL NATURAL ... JUST DO IT. CONGRATULATIONS. YOU JUST PREVENTED A CRASH.

Have you heard about the 'Motorcycle Smarts' Quick Tips Newsletter? I share riding tips (some of which didn't make it into my books) and keep you informed about what's next.

Sign up at the link below.

Unsubscribe at any time.

motorcyclesmarts.com/tips

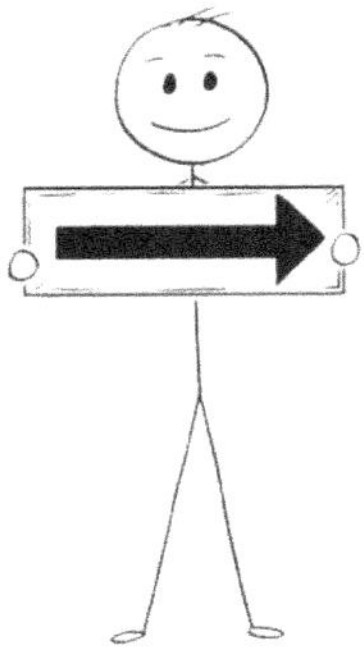

"Motorcycle Smarts" Quick Tips Newsletter

Free weekly riding tips you can consume in less than 3 minutes—delivered to your inbox for you to use and share with others.

motorcyclesmarts.com/tips

You're not doing everything you can to keep from crashing until you're signed up.

Avoid Lowside and Highside Crashes...

and

Outlive Your Riding Buddies

Part Four: Lowside and Highside Crashes

What are they, what causes them, and how you can avoid them?

This might be one of the most in-depth discussions you'll find on the subject of lowside and highside crashes—probably because it's easier to write about how to get the most out of your first motorcycle rally. The information in this section is important because I believe that most lowside and highside crashes are avoidable. I'll explain how.

> NOTE: If you become frustrated with the physics in this section, skip ahead to chapters 28 and 29. There, I'll explain how you can prevent most lowside and highside crashes.

TWENTY

Riding Off My Google Map

Fall is my favorite season of the year and my favorite time to ride.

Every year I forget how Autumn Blaze red maples glow red when the sun hits them just right, how sugar maples burst yellow-orange painting the ground with their leaves—and how the temperature can fluctuate ten degrees in the length of a football field.

I hope heaven is this good.

With a hard rain predicted for Friday, fall color at its peak, and no meetings planned at work, I penciled-in Thursday as *David's Day.* I checked and cross-checked with my wife to make sure she was point for family duties.

My goals for the day were simple: to leave early, enjoy breakfast with a friend, and explore the spectacular fall colors on two-wheels.

I didn't have detailed plans, and that's the way I wanted it.

Before leaving my house, I printed a simple Google map for my tank bag that covered a 30-mile radius. Only a couple of major roads bore numbers on my map, including I-65 that runs north and south.

Mike and I took the long way to breakfast.

We must have passed by two dozen restaurants as we headed south on Highway 431 to Guntersville, Alabama. But that didn't matter.

After a long breakfast, Mike headed to work (something about a meeting to discuss turning astronaut urine into drinking water on the International Space Station), and I headed out solo.

I didn't think much about where I was going. A little south and west seemed good enough. Thirty minutes later, I was outside the parameters of my printed Google map.

Using the inclination of the sun as my guide, I continued. When state roads turned to county, the fun really began. A sign pointed right to Clarkson Covered Bridge. I turned in.

What would normally have been a nice backdrop was no less than spectacular on this beautiful fall day. The deep blue sky and vibrant fall colors were spectacular. After a quick stop, I continued on my adventure through the rural side of Alabama, enjoying every fallen leaf and autumn fragrance. The Elaeagnus shrubs smelled spectacular.

At every intersection, I made a real-time decision to go straight, left, or right. It's hard to describe the joy that overcame me.

I was in the middle of Mother Nature without a map or a clue where I was—and it felt wonderful. I could have stopped for directions (or looked at my GPS), but I didn't want to.

I headed north, then west, then south around Smith Lake.

As I continued, the winding roads became straighter and wider, signaling I was getting close to a city. About that time, a dark green sign with white lettering read “Jasper City Limits.”

Alas, I knew where I was, even though I had never been there.

Since it was time to head back to my real life, I started looking for a meaningful road that led east. Highway 69 seemed good enough, so I turned left (heading east and a little north) and clicked up my speed.

Thirty minutes past, I found I-65 and turned left toward home.

I pulled into my garage about an hour later, just in time for my son’s Lego Robotics team meeting at my house.

My body felt fatigued. My soul felt rejuvenated.

I got lost today and enjoyed every minute of it.

The Clarkson Covered Bridge is located just off Highway 278 in Cullman County, nine miles west of I-65. The 270-foot bridge (initially built in 1904 for $1500) is one of 14 covered bridges still standing in Alabama.

TWENTY-ONE

Lowside and Highside Crashes

Now that we've mastered countersteering, let's talk about crashing.

In the next several chapters, I'm going to explain lowside and highside crashes, what causes them, and how you can avoid them.

The illustrations are from real crashes captured on video.

Most riders have probably heard of lowside and highside crashes. But I'm going to dial it up a notch and explain how you can virtually eliminate them. Talk about reducing your chances of crashing!

The concepts of lowside and highside crashes aren't that difficult to understand, as long as you don't get bogged down with the physics of how these crashes happen.

However, since there are so many possible scenarios for what triggers these crashes, this section might be the most difficult one to power through in the entire book.

Power through with me.

It's also one of the most important.

Quickie Definitions

Before we get started, here's an introductory definition for each.

In a nutshell, a *lowside* crash is when your motorcycle slides on its side, and you slide on the ground behind it. A *highside* crash is when your bike tosses you up and over the handlebars.

I'll explain both in more detail later in this section.

Just in case I lose you in the details, I want to tell you up-front the most important thing you need to know.

On a motorcycle, BAD THINGS HAPPEN when you lock up (skid) your tires—especially your REAR tire. I feel better knowing I got that point out. It's so important that I'll say it again.

LOCKING UP YOUR REAR TIRE IS BAD.

The topic of lowside and highside crashes is well understood by rider coaches and authors of motorcycle skills books. Yet, most riders don't understand what triggers them.[1] If this is true, our current motorcycle training programs need to be modified.

Here's one man's attempt to thoroughly explain lowside and highside crashes in simple-to-understand language. If you understand and implement the recommendations in this section, you *will* slash your chances of crashing.

TWENTY-TWO

Lowside Crashes

A lowside crash is easier to understand than a highside crash, so let's tackle that one first.

What Is a Lowside?

A lowside crash is when your motorcycle loses stability control, falls on its side sliding, and dumps you (the rider) on the ground behind it. Some refer to a lowside as a "slide-out" because that's sort of what happens—your rear end slides out.

Figure 22-1 (below) shows a rider who has just lowsided.

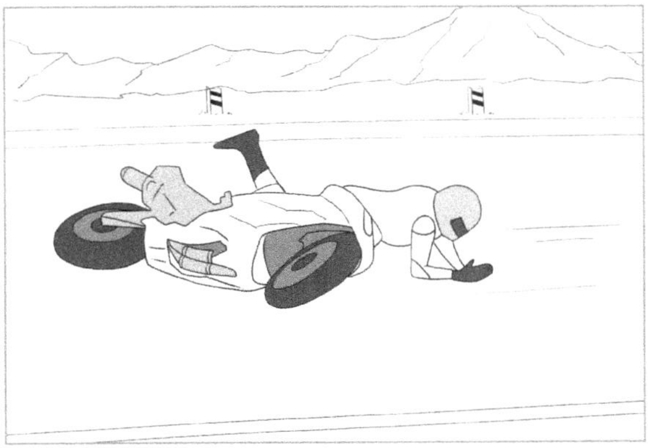

Figure 22-1 Lowside Crash (Motorcycle Slides Out and Dumps Rider)

A lowside occurs when your rear tire (more likely) or front tire (less likely) loses traction with the asphalt. This can happen when you lock up (skid) a tire using your brakes or accelerate too hard in a curve.

NOTE: A skidding tire (which has kinetic friction) has less grip than a rolling tire (which has static friction).

What Triggers Most Lowsides?

Lowside Trigger #1

Rear tire locks up (skids) due to over-braking while in a curve.

If you lock up your rear tire when you're going around a curve, you'll most likely lowside. When your bike is leaning over, it needs the rotational control and friction between the rear tire and the pavement to keep the bike upright.

See Figure 22-2 (below).

Figure 22-2 Beginning of a Lowside (Rear Tire Locks Up Due to Over-Braking in a Curve)

Once you lose static friction (by locking the rear tire), the back tire will slide out, and the bike will fall on its side —dumping you on the ground behind it.

Lowside Trigger #2

Rear tire locks up (skids) due to over-braking while going straight.

If you lock up your rear tire when you're going in a straight line, you may or may not lowside. It depends on whether the skidding back tire slides around to the side. If the back tire slides around, you'll most likely lowside. If the skidding back tire stays in line with the front tire, you won't lowside.

If you lock up the rear tire when your front brake is applied (likely the case during an emergency stop), or when you're on a road that isn't perfectly flat, the skidding back tire will tend to come around to the side, and you'll most likely lowside.

Lowside Trigger #3

Rear tire spins due to over-accelerating while in a curve.

If you spin your rear tire when you're accelerating hard in a curve (bike is leaned over), you'll most likely lowside because a slipping tire has less friction than a tire in rotational contact with the pavement. Once the rear tire starts slipping, the back end will slide out, and you'll lowside.

Lowside Trigger #4

Front tire locks up (skids) due to over-braking while in a curve.

If you lock up your front tire when you're going around a curve, you'll most likely lowside. When your bike is leaning over, it needs the rotational control and friction between the front tire and the pavement to keep the bike upright.

See Figures 22-3 through 22-5 (below).

NOTE: In the particular example below, the rider wasn't going very fast since neither the rider nor bike slid very far. This isn't always the case. I'll break down a more typical lowside crash in the next chapter.

Figure 22-3 Beginning of a Low-Speed Lowside (Front Tire Locks Up Due to Over-Braking in a Curve)

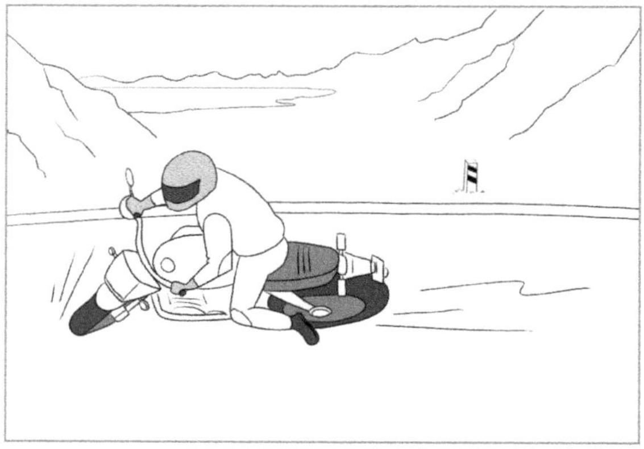

Figure 22-4 Middle of a Low-Speed Lowside (Front Tire Locks Up Due to Over-Braking In a Curve)

Figure 22-5 End of a Low-Speed Lowside (Front Tire Locks Up Due to Over-Braking in a Curve)

QUICK TIP: It's worth noting that locking up (skidding) your front tire when you're going in a relatively straight line (bike is upright) will NOT cause you to lowside. Tests have shown that a skidding front tire will continue in a straight line as long as the bike is in an upright position.[1] One motorcycle myth debunked.

Locking up (skidding) your *front* tire requires a lot of lever force because weight is transferred to the front tire when you decelerate.

Locking up (skidding) your *rear* tire requires less lever force, especially if you're applying heavy front brake pressure at the same time.

THIS IS WHY LOCKING UP YOUR REAR TIRE IS THE MOST LIKELY TRIGGER FOR A LOWSIDE CRASH.

I've never lowsided, but I've spoken to several riders who have. They all said it happened really fast. In the blink of an eye, they went from *(everything is fine)* to *(my bike is sliding, and I'm sliding behind it)*.

If you think a lowside crash sounds painful, wait until I describe what happens in a highside crash.

> UPDATE: I lowsided on a Backcountry Discovery Route in the George Washington National Forest in Virginia a few years later. The dirt road was a muddy mess. Unfortunately, my bike slid down a 10-foot embankment. My first words after the crash were, "We'll never get it out of there." Two hours later, my riding buddy and I manhandled it up the embankment—only because we didn't have another option. Right as we did, a group came along, and two of the riders lowsided in the exact same spot. I wasn't hurt. *Yes, it happened incredibly fast.*

Key Points

1. A lowside is the same thing as a slide-out.
2. Know what causes a lowside: (1) locking up your rear tire by over-braking (most likely), (2) locking up your front tire while bike is leaned over (less likely), or (3) spinning your rear tire by over-accelerating in a curve (less likely).

TWENTY-THREE

Analysis of a Lowside

Here's a frame-by-frame analysis of a real lowside crash where a rider locked up his rear tire (or over-accelerated) in a curve.

These illustrations are from a *real* crash captured on video.

In Figure 23-1 (below) both tires are in rotational contact with the ground. Everything is working as it should.

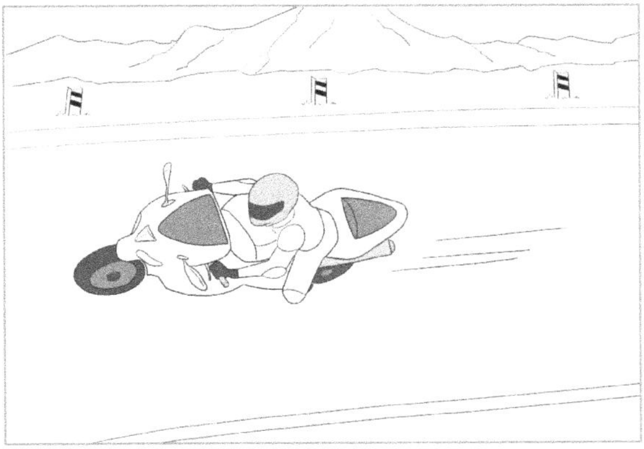

Figure 23-1 Lowside Frame #1
(Riding Around Curve Just Fine)

In Figure 23-2 (below) the rider locks up his rear tire (or over-accelerates and spins rear tire) while he's in the curve.

His rear tire loses rotational contact with the pavement.

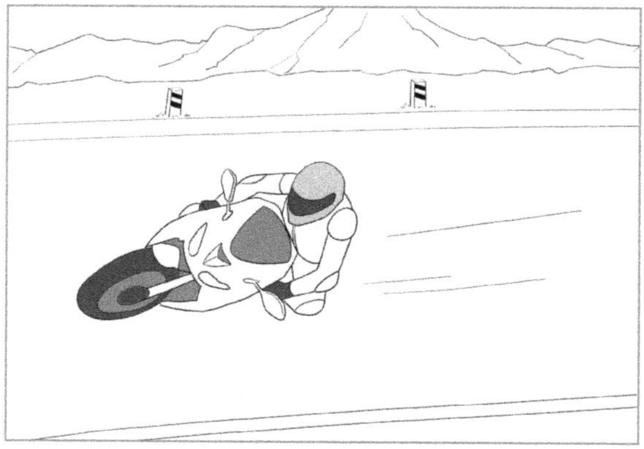

Figure 23-2 Lowside Frame #2
(Rear Tire Loses Traction)

In Figure 23-3 (below) the rear tire starts sliding around. The rider panics and puts his hand down. That won't keep him from crashing.

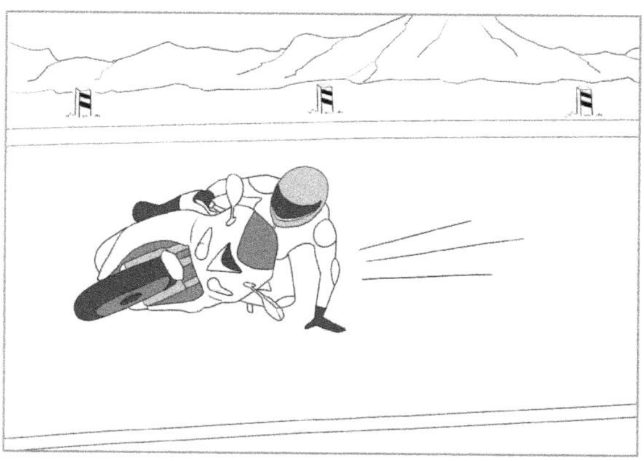

Figure 23-3 Lowside Frame #3
(Rear Tire Slides Around)

In Figure 23-4 (below) the motorcycle slides and dumps rider.

Figure 23-4 Lowside Frame #4 (Bike on Side and Rider Dumped)

In Figure 23-5 (below) the rider and motorcycle continue sliding. How far each slides depends on how fast the rider was going when he lowsided, and how easily the bike and rider slide on the ground.

Let's hope the motorcycle slides more easily (often the case) so the rider won't slide into the back of his sliding bike.

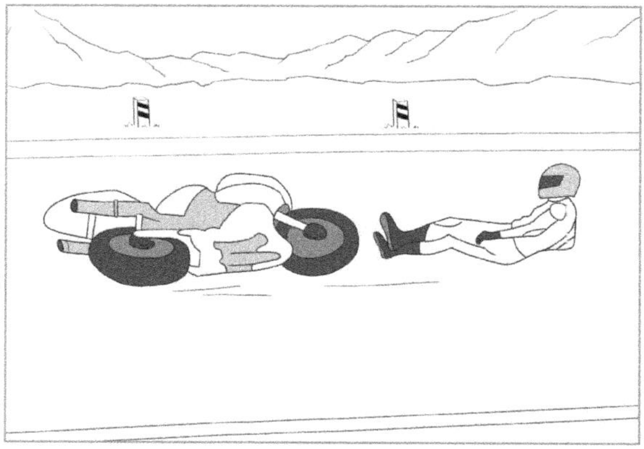

Figure 23-5 Lowside Frame #5 (Bike and Rider Slide)

In Figure 23-6 (below) the motorcycle and rider come to a stop. In this example, the rider stopped faster than his motorcycle. Good news.

Figure 23-6 Lowside Frame #6 (Bike and Rider Stop)

THERE YOU HAVE IT … A FRAME-BY-FRAME ANALYSIS OF AN ACTUAL LOWSIDE CRASH.

Key Points

1. Most lowsides end with the rider sliding behind his bike.
2. Jeans won't help much if you lowside, but abrasion-resist riding gear (jacket, pants, and gloves) could.
3. There's good news ahead. Most lowside and highside crashes can be prevented with electronics. Keep reading.

TWENTY-FOUR

Highside Crashes

The thought of highsiding makes me want to sell my motorcycle.
— David Mixson

Now that we understand lowside crashes and what causes them, let's look at highside crashes. I've spent hours going through slow-motion videos trying to understand the physics of a highside.

And this is what I've discovered.

I have to warn you. What you're about to learn is both *fascinating* and *terrifying*. The physics of a highside is fascinating!

The thought of doing a highside is terrifying!

What Is a Highside?

A highside crash is when your motorcycle loses stability control and catapults you over the handlebars. You eventually hit the ground, often headfirst, and your bike tumbles toward you.

Figure 24-1 (below) shows a rider in the middle of a highside.

Figure 24-1 Highside Crash
(Motorcycle Catapults Rider)

Yeah, I know. Freaking scary, right?

A highside occurs when a skidding rear tire, which has slid out of alignment with the front tire, is released and allowed to rotate again.

Why It Happens

When the rear brake is released, the skidding rear tire (which has now slid out of alignment with the front) starts rotating again and immediately tracks inline behind the front tire. When this happens, the bike instantly sits up to a vertical position.

Since the motorcycle was leaned over (squatted) because the rear tire was sliding, the motion of the motorcycle snapping to a vertical position is like releasing a coiled-up spring.

This combination launches the rider into the air.

NOTE: I know this is a hard concept to understand. It's also a hard one to explain. I must be on my hundredth edit of this section. Stay with me. I have real examples (below and in the next chapter) that I think will help.

In Figure 24-2 (below) the skidding rear tire has moved out of alignment with the front. If the rider releases the rear brake and allows the tire to rotate again, he will most likely highside.

Figure 24-2 Rear Tire Slides Out

What Triggers Most Highsides?

Highside Trigger #1

Locking up rear tire (and then releasing it) while in a curve.

If you lock up (skid) your rear tire (by over-braking) while going around a curve, then release the rear brake and allow the tire to rotate again, you'll most likely highside.

QUICK TIP: The faster you're going when you lock up your rear tire (and the farther out the skidding rear tire gets while it's locked up), the more abruptly the rear end will snap up once the rear tire is allowed to rotate again. If you're going slowly when you trigger a highside, it's unlikely that the highside snap will have enough energy to throw you off your bike.

Highside Trigger #2

Spinning rear tire (and then backing off throttle) while in a curve.

If you spin your rear tire (by over-accelerating) when going around a curve, then back off the throttle and allow the tire to regain traction, you'll most likely highside.

Highshide Trigger #3

Locking up rear tire (and then releasing it) while on a straight road.

Unfortunately, you don't have to be in a curve to highside.

Let's assume you're making an emergency stop and applying both front and rear brakes. Since you're stopping so quickly, weight is transferred to the front of the bike.

Good, because it gives your front tire more stopping power.

Not so good, because it takes load off your rear tire (which makes it easier to lock up).

If you lock up your rear tire while you are braking hard with your front brake, the skidding back tire can skid around to the side because the front tire is braking hard and the skidding rear tire lost directional control and static friction.

Now you're in trouble. If you then release the rear brake and allow the tire to rotate again, you'll most likely highside.

Here's the dilemma. Once your back tire starts skidding (by over-braking), or spinning (by over-accelerating), one of two things is likely to happen: You'll either LOWSIDE or HIGHSIDE.

I'm getting depressed thinking about my options.

While I have your attention, let me say it (again) because it's one of the most important points in this entire book.

LOCKING UP YOUR REAR TIRE IS BAD BECAUSE IT TRIGGERS MOST LOWSIDE AND HIGHSIDE CRASHES.

Key Points

1. A highside almost always starts the same way as a lowside.

2. I know this is a hard concept to understand. That's why I'm going to take two real examples and break them down (frame-by-frame) in the next chapter.

TWENTY-FIVE

Analysis of a Highside

Here's a frame-by-frame analysis of two real highside crashes where the rider locked up his rear tire (or over-accelerated) in a curve and then allowed the tire to start rolling normally again (by releasing the brake or backing off the throttle). Remember, these are freeze-frame illustrations of *real* crashes that were captured on video.

Highside Crash Example #1

In Figure 25-1 (below) both tires are in strong rotational contact with the ground. Everything is good.

Figure 25-1 Highside Frame #1
(Riding Around Curve Just Fine)

In Figure 25-2 (below) the back end starts to slide out in the curve because the rear tire has lost rotational contact with the asphalt. This is because the rear tire is either locked up (from over-braking), or spinning (from over-accelerating).

Figure 25-2 Highside Frame #2
(Rear Tire Slides Around)

In Figure 25-3 (below) it looks like the rider has released the rear brake (or let off the throttle) and allowed the rear tire to rotate again. The rear tire is trying to get back in alignment with the front tire.

Figure 25-3 Highside Frame #3
(Rear Tire Regains Traction)

In Figure 25-4 (below) the rear tire is rotating again, and the bike has snapped up into a vertical position. This motion catapults the rider up into the air off his motorcycle.

Figure 25-4 Highside Frame #4
(Bike Launches Rider)

In Figure 25-5 (below) the fun doesn't stop. The rider flies over the handlebars, and his motorcycle becomes unstable.

Figure 25-5 Highside Frame #5
(Bike Becomes Unstable)

In Figure 25-6 (below) the rider heads toward the asphalt, and his motorcycle starts tumbling.

Figure 25-6 Highside Frame #6
(Rider Prays)

In Figure 25-7 (below) the rider reaches the ground, and his bike tumbles toward him.

Figure 25-7 Highside Frame #7
(Rider Lands)

Doing a highside doesn't look very fun, but studying the physics sure is. Let's take a look at another one!

Highside Crash Example #2

This highside is a little different but just as real. In Figure 25-8 (below) both tires are in solid rotational contact with the ground.

Everything is good.

Figure 25-8 Highside Frame #1
(Riding Around Curve Just Fine)

In Figure 25-9 (below) the back end starts to slide out in the curve because the rear tire has lost rotational contact with the asphalt. This is because the rear tire is either locked up (from over-braking), or spinning (from over-accelerating).

Figure 25-9 Highside Frame #2
(Rear Tire Slides Around)

In Figure 25-10 (below) the rear tire is rotating again, and the bike has snapped up into a vertical position.

This motion catapults the rider into the air.

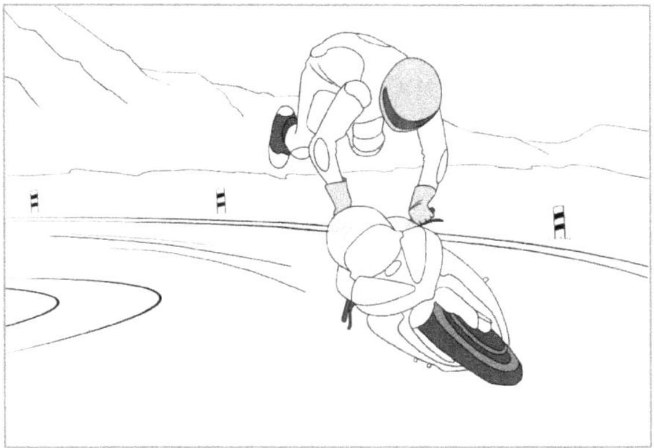

Figure 25-10 Highside Frame #3
(Bike Launches Rider)

In Figure 25-11 (below) the fun continues. The rider flies over the handlebars, and his bike keeps going.

Figure 25-11 Highside Frame #4
(Bike Remains Stable)

In Figure 25-12 (below) the rider lands, and his bike heads away from him (fortunately).

Figure 25-12 Highside Frame #5
(Rider Lands)

There you have it ... a frame-by-frame analysis of two real highside crashes. I suppose there are worse things in life than doing a highside, but exactly what those might be escapes me.

Key Points

1. Most highsides end with the rider being thrown into the air off his motorcycle.
2. Highside crashes look incredibly uncomfortable. Thank goodness, I can base that only on speculation.
3. There's good news ahead. Most lowside and highside crashes can be prevented with electronics. Keep reading.

TWENTY-SIX

Lowside and Highside Examples

Now that we understand what lowside and highside crashes are, let's look at more examples. The scenarios below are my attempt to think through what might happen in a lowside or highside crash.

I'm confident not everyone will agree with my assessments. They're not meant to be absolutes of what will happen. Instead, they're meant to help us understand what causes most lowsides and highsides.

Once we understand the causes, we can better avoid them.

Scenario #1

In this example, let's assume a rider is on a straight, flat road and is NOT using his front brake. The rider could probably lock up his rear tire and skid to a stop without lowsiding. This is because the back end has no force (front-tire braking or uneven road) to make it slide to the side of the bike when it's skidding.

The rider could most likely release his skidding rear tire without highsiding. Why? Because as long as he can keep the skidding rear tire in line (behind) the front tire, nothing significant will happen when the rear tire is allowed to rotate again.

NOTE: While it might sound like I m suggesting that using *only* your rear brake might be a good thing, *I'm not.* Without going into all the details here (more on braking comes in later chapters), I'll quickly make the point that stopping power on your rear tire is only a fraction of your front, making it incredibly easy to lock up your rear tire under heavy braking (the exact thing we're trying to avoid because it initiates most lowside and highside crashes).

Scenario #2

In this example, let's assume a rider is on a perfectly flat, straight road and is applying heavy braking (both front and rear) to avoid an object. If the rider locks up his rear tire, the back end will most likely slide around to the side of the motorcycle because the front tire is under heavy braking.

At this point, if the rider keeps the rear tire locked up, he will most likely lowside. If he releases the rear brake after the rear tire starts skidding, he will most likely highside.

Scenario #3

In this example, let's assume a rider is on a straight road that is slanted to allow water to runoff, and that he is NOT using his front brake. If the rider locks up his rear tire, the back end of the motorcycle might slide around on the downhill side of the road.

If the back tire slides to the side and the rider keeps the rear tire locked up, he will most likely lowside. If he releases the rear brake after the back tire has slid to the side, he will most likely highside.

In this scenario, I can also imagine a situation where the skidding rear tire didn't go around to the side, and instead tracked behind the front tire. If this happens, no lowside or highside.

Scenario #4

In this example, let's assume a rider is in a sharp curve. If he locks up his rear tire, he will most likely lowside immediately because the rear tire will slide out quickly in a curve. If he is quick enough to release the rear brake before he lowsides, he will most likely highside.

WARNING: It's difficult to recover from a locked-up rear tire when you're going around a curve because the back end tends to slide out so fast. If you're quick enough to save a lowside, you'll be greeted with an energy-packed highside launch. This is because the motorcycle is leaned over and low to the ground (like a coiled-up spring) when it highside-snaps.

QUICK TIP: It's probably worth noting *again* that your *speed* when you lock up your rear tire determines how likely you are to lowside or highside. Speed translates into energy. If you're only going 20 mph, it's unlikely the energy of the highside-snap will be enough to throw you off your bike. Highsides for MotoGP racers going 200 mph look entirely different. The highside snap is brutal and nearly instant.

Key Points

1. These examples are intended to make you think. It's difficult to know exactly what would happen in each scenario because there are so many external factors.
2. If you lock up your rear tire in a curve, chances are higher that you'll lowside (or highside) than if you lock up your rear tire riding in a straight line on even pavement.

TWENTY-SEVEN

Recovering Options

The prospects aren't very promising.
— David Mixson

Now that we understand what lowside and highside crashes are (and what causes them), let's take it a step further and answer the question:

What should you do if your rear tire starts to skid?

You have several options.

Option #1

Since a highside is worse than a lowside, some suggest that you keep your rear wheel locked up until you either regain control (less likely) or do a lowside (more likely). While this doesn't sound very appealing to me, I can understand the logic.

I suppose.

Option #2

Some suggest that turning the handlebar in the direction the rear tire is sliding out will increase the chances you might recover.

This might be true, but I've seen numerous videos where the rider did this and still lowsided or highsided.

Option #3

Some suggest that if you release a skidding rear tire immediately after it starts skidding (by releasing the rear brake or getting off the throttle), you might be able to avoid a lowside and highside crash.

> QUICK TIP: The likelihood of this working depends on how fast you're going, whether you're using your front brake at the time, and how far out of alignment your rear tire has gotten during the skid. Remember, as long as your skidding rear tire tracks behind your front tire, it's unlikely that you will lowside or highside.

Option #4

Some suggest that putting your weight on the outside peg (loading it) right when your rear tire locks up might keep you from highsiding.

I contacted a rider that I saw highside crash on YouTube. He told me that he put all his weight on the outside peg right when his rear tire started skidding. He highsided anyway.

NOTE: While the options above might help, I'm just not convinced they'll keep you from crashing if your skidding rear tire has gotten out of alignment with your front tire.

Here's the dilemma that plagues me at night.

Once you've locked up your rear tire (the trigger in most lowside and highside crashes), you must decide (quickly) what to do next.

If you immediately release the rear brake, you will either recover or highside —and probably hit the object you're braking for.

If you hold the rear brake, you will either recover or lowside.

What should you do? I can't answer that question for you. Mostly because I can't answer it for MYSELF.

Key Points

1. If you lock up your rear tire, what are you going to do?
2. There's good news ahead. Most lowside and highside crashes can be prevented with electronics. Keep reading.

TWENTY-EIGHT

Preventing Lowside and Highside Crashes

In this section, we've established two things: (1) a skidding rear tire is the trigger that causes most lowside and highside crashes, and (2) once your rear tire starts to skid, you don't have any plausible options to keep from crashing.

Now that we understand this (head knowledge), we need a way to keep from skidding (over-braking and over-accelerating) our rear tire.

Well, there's the obvious: maintain your tires, ride with margin, slow down before the turn so you won't have to brake in the turn, and be easy on the throttle while you're in a turn.

But even better, there's something else you can do that will significantly reduce the chances of a lowside or highside crash.

RIDE A MOTORCYCLE EQUIPPED WITH AN ANTI-LOCK BRAKING SYSTEM (ABS).

ABS is an electronic system that prevents your tires from locking up. When the ABS detects that a tire is about to lock up, it automatically reduces brake pressure to that tire.

ABS has been standard on cars for years.

While ABS virtually eliminates most lowside and highside crashes due to over-braking, it doesn't keep you from spinning (over-accelerating) your rear tire in a curve.

But the story doesn't end here.

There's another piece of electronics, called *Traction Control*, that keeps your rear tire from spinning-out while accelerating.

Isn't this great news!

Traction Control uses the ABS sensors on both tires to detect when the rear tire starts to rotate faster than the front tire. When this state is detected, the system cuts power to the engine to prevent the rear wheel from spinning out. I'll explain Traction Control in a later chapter.

Here's the awesome truth: ABS and Traction Control can prevent certain types of crashes—and almost certainly save lives!

If this is true, why doesn't every motorcycle have them?

Good question. I'll attempt to answer that a little later.

WARNING: ABS and Traction Control can't overcome physics. If you're going around a curve faster than your tires can handle (or hit a slippery spot), you're going down.

ABS and Traction Control don't give you more friction, but they do significantly reduce your chances of crashing.

Key Points

1. The best way to eliminate most lowside and highside crashes is to ride a bike with ABS and Traction Control.
2. Don't listen to the naysayers who say otherwise.

TWENTY-NINE

Lowside and Highside Wrap-Up

This section was my best attempt to explain what I think every rider should know about lowside and highside crashes.

If you're mentally exhausted, I feel your pain.

The subject of lowside crashes and highside crashes (what are they, what triggers them, and how you can prevent them) is one of the most *glossed over* topics in motorcycling. I spent a great deal of time writing this section because I think the information can make you a safer rider.

I know I can't convince everyone to purchase a motorcycle with ABS and Traction Control, but I wish I could. Two little pieces of electronics could eliminate most lowside and highside crashes.

I'm a believer.

If you're serious about avoiding lowside and highside crashes, ride with margin, maintain your tires, watch your speed when entering a curve, be easy on the throttle, and ...

RIDE A MOTORCYCLE EQUIPPED WITH ABS AND TRACTION CONTROL (or ESC).

If you do these things, you *will* reduce your chances of crashing.

And you *might* even outlive your riding buddies.

Crashes Leave Clues

Part Five: Electronics, Braking, and the Hurt Report

Now that we understand lowside crashes and highside crashes—and what causes them—let's move on to something a little easier. While this section isn't as technical, the information is just as important.

In the next several chapters, I'll expand on our earlier discussion of how electronics can help us ride more safely. I'll also discuss proper braking techniques and how we can all reduce our risk of crashing by learning from riders who have already crashed.

Congratulations for sticking with me.

We're on the downhill side of the mountain now.

THIRTY

Mid-Life and Motorbikes

I'm not sure there's any truth to the hypothesis that men buy motorcycles during their mid-life crisis.

Sure, I was 40 when I purchased my first motorcycle, but I don't think I was going through a mid-life crisis. That came later. I was merely at a point in my life where owning a motorcycle made more sense. My kids were older, I wasn't getting any younger, and my bank account said I could pay cash and still keep my life insurance current.

Apparently, I'm not the only one coming to this conclusion.

I get emails often from listeners of the *Motorcycle Mentor Podcast* who have decided to take up riding later in life—some in their 40s, some in their 50s, and some even in their 60s.

It makes sense when you think about it. We all reach a point in life (hopefully) when our kids can take care of themselves, and we are still in good enough mental and physical health to explore.

This season in life begs to be enjoyed.

On second thought, maybe buying a motorcycle during your mid-life crisis is the perfect time.

The excuse certainly helped me convince my wife.

THIRTY-ONE

Arguments Against ABS

If you've listened to the *Motorcycle Mentor Podcast*, you know I like to present both sides of every argument. I've already presented the *advantages* of ABS. In this chapter, I'll present the *disadvantages*.

Nearly all new cars and trucks sold in the United States come with ABS as standard equipment.

The technology is simple, mature, and relatively inexpensive.

So why haven't motorcycle manufacturers embraced ABS like the automotive industry?

Simple economics suggests it's because riders aren't demanding it.

Hopefully, this book will change a few minds.

Before we dive in, let me assure you that none of the arguments I'm about to present sway my strong belief that motorcycles equipped with ABS are significantly safer than motorcycles without.

ABS Disadvantage #1

The argument against ABS I hear most often is this.

"A friend said my first motorcycle shouldn't have ABS because it encourages poor braking habits."

MY THOUGHTS:

ABS allows you to grab (squeeze) more brake than you could with conventional brakes. But just because you have ABS doesn't mean you will be forced to brake incorrectly. ABS doesn't change the way you brake; it just keeps you from locking up your tires.

The most important thing to know about motorcycle braking is that you should *predominantly use your front brake.* A bike without ABS won't teach you this, and it certainly won't slap you on the butt when you use your rear brake too much. The second most important thing to know about proper motorcycle braking is that you should *avoid locking up your rear tire.* ABS keeps you from doing this.

Proper braking techniques are first learned with your head and then developed with practice and repetition until the "correct way" becomes a part of your muscle memory.

This process is the same whether you have ABS or not.

More on correct braking techniques in a later chapter.

ABS Disadvantage #2

The second argument against ABS I hear is this.

"Some riders can stop faster on a motorcycle without ABS than they can on the same motorcycle equipped with ABS."

My Thoughts:

This might be true for top riders. But while we would all like to believe we're in the top rider category, few of us are. I'm certainly not, and I presume you're not either. I'm not particularly motivated that MotoGP champion Valentino Rossi can stop faster *without* ABS.

I'm more moved that you and I can stop more quickly *with* ABS.

Every study I've seen shows that most riders (from beginning to experienced) can stop more quickly in panic situations with ABS than without it. As ABS technology improves, I predict that even MotoGP racers will use it. I promise they understand what's going to happen if their rear tire loses traction at 200 mph.

Hello, highside!

ABS Disadvantage #3

The third argument against ABS I hear is this.

"Motorcycles with ABS don't perform as well in dirt and gravel."

My Thoughts:

There's some truth to this argument, but it's not always the case. Some tests actually show that motorcycles with ABS stop just as well or even better than their non-ABS cousins in off-road situations.[1]

Many adventure motorcycles like the BMW R1200GS Adventure (my current bike), allow the rider to disengage the ABS.

Perfect. Turn ABS "off" when you go off-road—if you want to.

> NOTE: I usually keep my ABS "on" even when I'm riding in off-road conditions. But that discussion is for another book.

The Bottom Line

I don't profess that current ABS technology is perfect. But the advantages—shorter stopping distances, fewer lowside and highside crashes, easier to use in panic stops—far outweigh the disadvantages. So much so that I've made a personal commitment never to own a modern bike that doesn't have ABS.

Just last week I spotted a beautiful used Ducati ST4 for sale. The owner really wanted to sell it and marked it down to a great price.

I wanted it, but it didn't have ABS.

I had a serious conversation with myself and decided not to buy it.

I'll wait for one that has ABS.

Stop for a moment and think about it this way. If a car spinning out of control is coming across your lane in front of you, do you really want to worry about grabbing the *correct* amount of front and rear brake—the amount that stops you in the shortest distance but doesn't lock up your rear tire?

I don't ... and I won't ... because I have ABS.

I can grab both brakes and let ABS do its thing.

My Best Advice ... CHOOSE A MOTORCYCLE WITH ABS.

BMW embraced ABS before most. When I started looking for my first motorcycle, the only used motorcycles with ABS in my price range (motorcycles old enough) were BMWs.

I didn't fully understand the advantages of ABS back then, so I ended up buying a motorcycle with conventional brakes.

BMW continues to lead the way. In 2013 BMW Motorrad was the first manufacturer to equip all new motorcycles with ABS as standard equipment. Way to go BMW.

ABS has been available on most touring and sport-touring bikes for years. Recently, other manufacturers (including Harley Davidson) have started offering models with ABS—sometimes as standard equipment and sometimes as an upgrade.

That's awesome.

I want my Harley friends to have the same advantages that I do.

If you want to significantly reduce your chances of crashing, DITCH the LOUD PIPES and RIDE A HARLEY WITH ABS. Your neighbors might even love you for it.

Key Points

1. Embrace ABS. The advantages outweigh the disadvantages.
2. The worst braking habit is overusing your rear brake.
3. Don't listen to anyone who says ABS is bad. You don't have to argue with them. Just ignore them. Better yet, hand them a copy of this book and smile.

THIRTY-TWO

The Wrong Argument for ABS

Now that we've established that ABS is a beautiful thing, let's take a look at why some riders still don't see its benefits.

ABS proponents argue that ABS shortens their stopping distance, while anti-ABS proponents argue that top riders can stop more quickly with conventional brakes.

In this case, neither side wins because both sides are right.

WE'RE LOSING THE ABS DEBATE BECAUSE WE'RE USING THE WRONG ARGUMENT.

The main reason I like ABS has nothing to do with stopping distances and everything to do with something we discussed earlier—crashing. In my mind, the real benefit of ABS is that it *eliminates most lowside and highside crashes*.

Another benefit I rarely hear mentioned is that riders with ABS feel less stress in panic stops because they don't have to worry about braking correctly. In other words, they can squeeze both brakes firmly without fear of locking up either tire.

This allows riders to focus more on avoiding the obstacle they're braking for in the first place.

According to an NHTSA study:

> *"Anti-lock brake systems not only prevent rider and motorcycle from harm and damage by increasing active safety, but also reduce significantly [the] mental strain while*

riding and braking. In case of a critical riding situation, this higher remaining mental reserve would help the rider to develop and wishfully realize alternative emergency strategies that additionally could help the rider to prevent a crash."[1]

NOW YOU KNOW THE REAL REASON I ONLY OWN MOTORCYCLES WITH ABS

Key Points

1. Want to win the ABS debate? Instead of arguing that ABS will shorten your stopping distance, argue that ABS will eliminate most lowside and highside crashes, and reduce mental strain in emergency situations.

2. Don't be the guy who lets pride stand in your way of getting a bike with ABS. Having ABS doesn't make you a wimp. It signals that you know what you're talking about. It shows that you give a damn about your riding safety.
3. Once you've MASTERED THE ART OF RIDING WELL, the single best thing you can do to reduce your chances of crashing is to ride a motorcycle equipped with ABS.

THIRTY-THREE

Insurance and Mandatory ABS

I'm not the only one who likes motorcycles with ABS.

Insurance companies love them too because riders on motorcycles with ABS file fewer claims than riders on motorcycles without ABS.

That's saying something.

The statistical data is so overwhelming that the Insurance Institute for Highway Safety and the Highway Loss Data Institute have asked the NHTSA to make ABS mandatory on all street motorcycles manufactured in the United States.

> *"The letter addressed to David Strickland, NHTSA Administrator, included a recent IIHS study on the effects of ABS on motorcycle fatal crash rates. The report found that ABS technology reduces the rate of fatal crashes by 31 percent, while collision claim rates were 20 percent lower with ABS-equipped motorcycles."*[1]

Beginning in 2016, the European Parliament approved regulations that made ABS mandatory on all new street motorcycles over 125cc. India, Japan, and Brazil have also approved legislation to make ABS mandatory on certain sizes of motorcycles.

Meanwhile, ABS legislation for motorcycles pops up on the political agenda in the U.S. and Australia from time to time.

Mandatory ABS for motorcycles is coming soon to a country near you. As far as I'm concerned, this is EXCELLENT news.

Key Points

1. Insurance companies have studied the data. Motorcycles with ABS crash less often than motorcycles without ABS.
2. I predict that ABS will someday be required on all street motorcycles sold in the United States. In my lifetime?

THIRTY-FOUR

Traction Control and Stability Control

Now that we understand the importance of ABS on motorcycles, let's talk about other electronics that can reduce your chances of crashing.

Recall that ABS keeps you from skidding your tires when braking (a leading trigger of lowside and highside crashes), but it doesn't keep you from spinning your rear tire when over-accelerating in a curve (also a trigger of lowside and highside crashes).

I have good news. *Traction Control* will.

Traction Control is an electronic system that prevents your rear tire from spinning (losing rotational contact with the asphalt) when accelerating. The system uses the ABS sensors to detect when your rear tire is slipping. When it does, it reduces torque to the rear wheel by cutting engine power.

Traction Control can also help you maintain control in low-speed situations like pulling out from a side street over a high lip of asphalt.

Remember, your rear tire has less friction once it starts spinning and wants to slide around to the side of least resistance.

QUICK TIP: If a motorcycle has Traction Control, it also has ABS. But just because a motorcycle has ABS doesn't mean it has Traction Control.

Here's where it gets a little confusing. There's another piece of electronics called *Electronic Stability Control* (ESC) that helps you ride even more safely. Stability Control combines ABS, Traction

Control, integrated brakes, and lean angle sensors into one system.

When the system senses that an *out-of-control state* is imminent (slide-out, over-acceleration, rear tire lock-up, etc.), it applies one or both brakes (and/or reduces engine power) to keep the bike stable.

ESC is like Traction Control on steroids.

Traction Control for MotoGP

MotoGP racers have experimented with Traction Control systems with mixed results. Some like it. Some don't. When asked what he thought about Traction Control, MotoGP champion Valentino Rossi said:

> *"Having the Traction Control system makes riding the motorcycle much easier, and allows me to open the throttle more rapidly without launching me into a highside. Unfortunately, it takes away from the rider's natural ability and feel for the*

motorcycle, and makes it easier for people to compete with those who they couldn't before having this rider aide. It is basically cheating."[1]

At some point in the future, I predict we will all be riding motorcycles with Stability Control. When this happens, the naysayers—the same riders who don't have a clue what triggers lowside and highside crashes—will still be moaning that they don't need any electronic aids on their motorcycles.

In the end, it's your choice. Choose wisely.

QUICK TIP: It's important to remember that ABS, Traction Control, and Stability Control can't overcome the laws of physics. If you ride outside the limits of available friction, you will lose control. But most motorcycle crashes could have been avoided well within these limits. Remember what my motorcycle mentor used to tell me. TRUST YOUR TIRES.

RIDE A MOTORCYCLE WITH TRACTION CONTROL or STABILITY CONTROL (both include ABS) ... and say goodbye to most single-vehicle lowside and highside crashes.

Key Points

1. Traction Control prevents your rear tire from spinning when accelerating by reducing engine power.
2. Some riders will never embrace electronic aids on their motorcycle. Bad call.
3. ABS, Traction Control, and ESC can't overcome physics, but they can certainly reduce your chances of crashing—and that's good enough.

THIRTY-FIVE

Misinformation on Braking

Now that we have the head knowledge of how ABS, Traction Control, and Stability Control can keep us safer, let's talk about *braking*.

Warning: There's probably more misinformation on how to CORRECTLY USE YOUR BRAKES than on any other topic.

The forums are the worst. I just spent thirty minutes looking online for how to properly use motorcycle brakes, and every forum thread I read was plastered with incorrect information. In each forum, the most incorrect posters were the loudest and crudest.

It's hard to argue with an idiot who thinks he's right.

THIRTY-SIX

Use Your Front Brake

Stay in the habit of using the front brake every time you brake, even if your machine has integrated front/rear brakes or anti-lock brakes.
— David L. Hough

NOTE: This chapter is for normal motorcycles—the ones designed by engineers. If you ride a homemade chopper, skip ahead because the physics here probably doesn't apply. *Do choppers even have front brakes?*

The first thing to know about motorcycle braking is that you should mostly USE YOUR FRONT BRAKE. Rider coaches know this, but somehow some riders don't.

A ton of test data shows that 70 to 90 percent of a bike's stopping power comes from the front tire (front brake). This is because weight is transferred to the front of the motorcycle when you apply your brakes. When this happens, the front tire has more stopping power (friction), and the back tire has less.

Pure physics.

> HERE'S the SIMPLE TRUTH. IF YOU ONLY use your rear brake, it's going to take you LONGER TO STOP than me. EVERY–SINGLE–TIME.

It's the same way on a car. The front tires provide the vast majority of the stopping power. Have you ever driven with your emergency brake engaged (by accident) and hardly noticed it? That's because most emergency brakes on automobiles only engage the rear brakes.

Cruiser Magazine said it best:

> *"Hopefully, deliberate avoidance of the front brake [only using the rear brake] is limited to a few dinosaurs (who are likely to be extinct rather quickly). The don't-use-the-front-brake concept shares one thing with all those other [misguided] braking theories: it's wrong."*[1]

Key Points

1. USE YOUR FRONT BRAKE.
2. During emergency stops, the rear brake does very little.
3. If you mostly use your rear brake, change your habit.

THIRTY-SEVEN

How Much Rear Brake?

The rear brake is one of the most misused controls on a motorcycle, which is why it's important to better understand its benefits in different situations.
— *Sport Rider* Magazine

Most experts generally agree that you should predominantly use your front brake. From there, things get a little muddy.

Some suggest that you use a small amount of rear brake, and some suggest that the situation dictates how much rear brake to use—if any.

There's one school of thought that says you're better off using your front brake exclusively during emergency stops because the back tire gets so light and prone to lock up. We all know by now that a locked-up rear tire usually leads to a lowside or highside crash, right?

Just checking.

Before you turn up your nose at the idea of using your front brake exclusively, consider what one thought-leader in the riding community thinks. Keith Code, one of the best known and most successful on-track motorcycle instructors in the world, said:

"The obvious mathematics of the situation is that the front wheel can do 100 percent of the braking and the back, at that point, just locks up no matter who you are. Learn to totally rely on the front brake for quick, clean stopping; then, if you still have a use for the rear, go ahead and use it. But realize that the rear brake is the source of a huge number of crashes, both on and off the track. I'll leave the final decision up to you. While it is true that a motorcycle will come to a full stop quicker with both brakes applied, in racing, you don't come to a full stop until you're done."[1]

Keith knows what he's talking about, yet he gets blasted in online forums for his position on braking. I just spent an hour reading rude insults in three different forums. It frustrates me that so many riders think they know more about braking than Keith.

Note to the guy on the [undisclosed] forum. Keith is not the idiot; *you are*.

And the fact that you think you know more about braking than he does proves it.

More Test Data

An engineering firm, Mechanical Forensics Engineering Services LLC, conducted tests on several different motorcycles to measure the effectiveness of front and rear brakes. Tests results showed:[2]

USING THE FRONT BRAKE BY ITSELF DELIVERED SIMILAR DECELERATION G-LOADS AS USING BOTH FRONT AND REAR BRAKES TOGETHER.

The study concluded: “A motorcycle’s rear brake contributes very little (or even nothing) to the overall stopping power when efficient use is made of the front brake.”[3]

James Davis, an expert witness in Motorcycle Dynamics, said:

> *"Since you can generate nearly 100 percent of your stopping power with the front brake on almost any contemporary motorcycle (meaning that you can reduce traction of the rear wheel to zero via load shifting), there is a pretty strong argument that can be made that you should focus your entire braking attention to the task of using it [your front brake] and ignoring the fact that you even have a rear brake. I would not go that far, however, [because] the use of both brakes together will invariably slow you down more quickly than using just one of them."*[4]

NOTE: Before we go any further, it's important to make this point. Most experts agree that it's best to use *both* brakes when it's been raining, or the road is slippery. This is because less weight is transferred to the front tire when there's less friction to stop you. ABS really helps here.

The Bottom Line

Studies have shown that adding rear brake can help you stop about ten percent more quickly than using your front brake by itself.

But ... USING YOUR REAR BRAKE ALSO SIGNIFICANTLY INCREASES THE CHANCES YOU'LL CRASH.

Not because you hit the object you're trying to avoid, but because

—you lock up your rear tire and lowside or highside on your own!

WARNING: You might want to sit down before you read what I have to say next. It's going to shock some of you, but it's a point I have to make.

I believe that FEWER RIDERS would CRASH AND DIE every year if the REAR BRAKE was REMOVED on all street MOTORCYCLES.

Don't misunderstand me. I'm not advocating this.

I'm simply making the point that your rear brake is one of the most dangerous controls on your motorcycle.

Proficient braking habits begin with this head knowledge.

So, how much rear brake should you use?

If you have ABS, you're probably better off using *both brakes*.

If you don't have ABS, you're probably better off concentrating on using the *front brake* effectively.

Whether you add some rear brake is your decision.

Whatever you decide ...

PREDOMINATELY USE YOUR FRONT BRAKE!

Key Points

1. While experts don't agree on exactly how much rear brake you should use, they do agree that you should use significantly more front brake than rear brake.
2. If your motorcycle has ABS, apply both brakes.
3. Don't dismiss your rear brake yet. Using your rear brake in low-speed maneuvers can provide added stability and control. More on this in a future *Motorcycle Smarts* book.

THIRTY-EIGHT

The Hurt Report

We can reduce our risks by studying how other riders have crashed.
— DAVID MIXSON

Now that we understand how electronics can help us keep from crashing, let's take a look at a study that shows us why motorcyclists crash. The *Hurt Report* is considered by many to be one of the most comprehensive studies of motorcycle accidents ever conducted.

I read it when I started riding, and it changed everything.

Background

The NHTSA selected the University of Southern California (USC) to conduct the study entitled: *Motorcycle Accident Cause Factors and Identification of Countermeasures Volume 1: Technical Report.*[1]

The USC professor leading the study was Harry Hurt, Jr. Since the study's official title was such a mouthful, it quickly became known as the *Hurt Report*. Thank goodness.

The purpose of the Hurt Report was to determine the causes of motorcycle accidents, to analyze the effectiveness of protective gear, and to determine what riders could do to keep from crashing.

Professor Hurt's team studied every motorcycle accident in a two-year period (900+) in the Los Angeles Basin area in Southern California. The team collected data from the scene of each accident, reviewed police reports, and interviewed eyewitnesses—including the rider if he survived the crash.

Still Relevant?

A lot has changed since the Hurt Report was published back in 1981. Motorcycle tires and brakes are much better (good things), but roads seem more congested, and drivers seem more distracted (bad things).

Journalist David Hough interviewed Hurt in 1999 and asked him if he thought his study was still relevant. Hurt said:

> *"The more time that goes by, the less things look different. Riders today have the same sort of accidents as riders in the 1970s—except that today they crash much more expensive bikes."*[2]

Hurt also said this during the interview:

> *"I still do consulting for police departments and have investigated a number of police motorcycle accidents over the years. Police*

motor officers get some extensive training. I mean really good training. But even professionals make the same sort of mistakes as novices, and today's riders seem to have the same sort of accidents as those in the NHTSA [Hurt] report."[3]

Numerous NHTSA studies, published since the Hurt Report was released, continue to show similar findings.

Riders are making the SAME MISTAKES that they did nearly 40 YEARS AGO. Think about how UTTERLY INSANE this is. It's one of the main reasons I WROTE THIS BOOK. I wanted to present the information that I think is MOST IMPORTANT in a way readers could understand—a different way—the way I wanted to learn when I started riding.

From all my studies, I believe that Hurt was right.

Riders are still crashing because they aren't using their front brake; because they don't understand what happens when they lock up their rear tire; and because they don't know what do when they start going wide in a turn.

Becoming a proficient rider begins with head knowledge.

The Hurt Report is packed with useful information.

The Hurt Report reveals WHY RIDERS CRASH. It highlights the most common rider errors and shows us how to avoid the most common types of crashes.
POWERFUL STUFF.

If you're serious about changing your chances of crashing, reading and understanding the Hurt Report (and acting on the data in it) is one of the best things you can do. We'll take a deeper look at some key points in the next two chapters.

I read the Hurt Report before I bought my first motorcycle. It gave me confidence that I could reduce my chances of crashing.

It can change your chances of crashing too.

Harry Hurt passed away in 2009. He was 81.

THIRTY-NINE

Hurt Report Golden Nuggets

If you rush through the next two chapters, you're missing some of the most powerful points in this entire book.

— David Mixson

The Hurt Report isn't just a bunch of numbers. It shows us what we should focus on to reduce our risks.[1] It's more than 400 pages.

No worries. I'm going to pull out ten of the best nuggets (five in this chapter and five in the next chapter) and explain how we can use the information to ride safer.

Before we dive in, I want to congratulate you on making it this far.

I realize some of the information in this book wasn't easy to get through, but you've done it.

Thank you for sticking with me.

You're in the home stretch.

Here are five of my favorite golden nuggets in the Hurt Report.

Hurt Report Golden Nugget #1

Hurt found that 25 percent of motorcycle accidents were single-vehicle crashes (motorcycle *did not* hit another vehicle) and that 75 percent were multi-vehicle crashes (motorcycle *did* hit another vehicle).

In addition to this, a 2009 NHTSA study found that 46 percent of all motorcycle fatalities occurred in single-vehicle crashes.

My Thoughts:

When both data points are analyzed, we find that a fourth of all crashes were single-vehicle crashes, yet almost half of the fatalities were in single-vehicle crashes. This means half of the deaths were in a fourth of the accidents—when riders crashed by themselves.

It also means that if you crash all by yourself, you're more likely to die than if you're hit by another vehicle.

Surprising, but useful.

What causes single-vehicle crashes? Keep reading.

Hurt Report Golden Nugget #2

Hurt found that rider error accounted for 67 percent of single-vehicle crashes. Typical errors were:

(1) locking up rear tire and lowsiding, and

(2) running wide in a curve due to excess speed or under-cornering (not using enough countersteering to tighten the turn).

Other causes were animals, blowouts, and surface hazards.

Hurt also found that rider error accounted for about 33 percent of multi-vehicle crashes and that most multi-vehicle crashes were caused when the motorist violated the motorcyclist's right-of-way.

MY THOUGHTS:

Two-thirds of single-vehicle crashes and one-third of multi-vehicle crashes were due to rider error. This doesn't surprise me. I have seen a ton of videos on YouTube where the rider went wide in a turn (because he didn't use countersteering to tighten his turn) or locked up his rear tire and lowsided (because he didn't use his brakes properly).

Using the numbers above (along with basic math), I calculated that 17 percent of all motorcycle crashes were single-vehicle crashes caused by rider error, and 26 percent of all motorcycle crashes were multi-vehicle crashes caused by rider error.

THIS MEANS THAT 43 PERCENT (ALMOST HALF) OF THE ACCIDENTS STUDIED IN THE HURT REPORT WERE CAUSED BY RIDER ERROR.

There's another point worth considering. How many of the accidents determined to be the motorist's fault in the Hurt Report could have been avoided if the rider would have known how to control his motorcycle more proficiently?

Probably a lot.

To all the riders who say, "I can't change my chances of crashing," I say nonsense. You CAN reduce your risks of being in an accident by improving your offensive and defensive riding skills.

The Hurt Report proves it.

Hurt Report Golden Nugget #3

Hurt found that nearly 28 percent of multi-vehicle crashes involved an automobile turning left in front of (or into) a motorcyclist.

My Thoughts:

Every rider should know this tendency so they can know to look out for it. If you could take this crash scenario off the table, you would be less likely to crash on a motorcycle. Even if you could only cut your chances in half of being hit by a motorist turning left in front of you, you would meaningfully reduce your chances of being in an accident.

This statistic was a huge motivator for me when I started riding—and it continues to be something I look out for every moment I'm on a motorcycle. I scan ahead, anticipate when automobiles approaching me might be turning left across my lane, and adjust my position so I won't be in their path if they do.

Hurt Report Golden Nugget #4

Hurt found that motorists failing to recognize and detect motorcycles was the leading cause of accidents.

My Thoughts:

Reading this changed the way I ride. Now, I assume motorists have a hard time seeing me and judging my speed and distance. Be visible, install running lights, wear bright gear, and don't ride at night.

It's your responsibility to be seen.

Have you ever pulled out in front of a motorcycle when you were driving an automobile? I have many times, not because I have a thing against motorcycles, but because I didn't see them or misjudged their speed. I'm betting you have too.

Hurt Report Golden Nugget #5

Hurt found that most accidents were close to the trip's origin (usually home) and involved running an errand or meeting with friends.

My Thoughts:

Never let your guard down. Always ride with the correct gear and the proper mindset—regardless of whether you're one mile from home or a thousand miles from home.

The Hurt Report is packed with useful information that gives us clear clues on how we can ride more safely. I'll highlight five more in the next chapter.

Key Points

1. Don't be the idiot who says you can't reduce your risks. The Hurt Report proves that we can change our chances of crashing—and it shows us how.
2. Don't crash by yourself. Watch out for motorists turning across your lane. Be visible and assume motorists can't see you. Take every ride seriously—even ones close to home.

FORTY

More Hurt Report Golden Nuggets

I hope your mind is racing with ideas on how you might implement what you've learned so far from the Hurt Report

I know mine was when I first read it.

Here are five more golden nuggets in the Hurt Report.

Hurt Report Golden Nugget #6

Hurt found that riders didn't make the correct evasive maneuver to avoid crashing in most cases. Even worse, riders didn't attempt *any* evasive maneuver 32 percent of the time.

In addition, Hurt found that braking errors were frequently made during the collision-avoidance maneuver when riders attempted one. Riders overused their rear brake and locked up the rear tire (leading to a lowside), and underused (or failed to use) their front brake (leading to longer stopping distances).

Hurt said:

> *"Skidding from over-braking was the most common execution problem, and usually resulted in a loss of control of the motorcycle. Failure to use the front brake is a critical element in collision avoidance because proper use of the front brake would have avoided many of the collisions or greatly reduced the severity. [In most accidents] the ability to countersteer and swerve was essentially absent. In other words, riders didn't stop the correct way and didn't swerve to avoid the crash."*[1]

In Hough's interview back in 1999, he asked Hurt if riders should practice evasive maneuvers. Hurt responded:

"Use the front brake."

"Use the front brake."

"Use the front brake."[2]

My Thoughts:

Frankly, every time I read this finding I get mad. This one piece of information from the Hurt Report puts everything in perspective and reveals just how unskilled some riders actually are. One-third of riders didn't know enough (well enough) to even attempt to stop or make their motorcycle go in a different direction to avoid a crash.

Maybe it would be easier if I didn't care so much.

Riders are missing the fundamentals.

Don't skid your rear tire. Understand countersteering with your head, then practice using it to control your bike until it becomes a part of your muscle memory.

Why? So you can do *something* to avoid a crash. Understand what causes lowside and highside crashes so you can avoid them.

USE YOUR FRONT BRAKE.

Come on riding community. Learn enough about controlling your motorcycle so you can do something to dodge a crash. Don't just sit there like 32 percent of the riders Hurt studied.

When Something Is Coming Your Way

While we're talking about the subject, let's quickly go over what you *should* do if you're about to hit something: (1) look where you want to go (away from the object your trying to avoid), (2) apply your front brake to reduce your speed, and (3) use countersteering to swerve away from the object and toward an opening or a less dangerous object.

If you can do these things, you might be able to avoid crashing (or at least make the crash less severe).

If it sounds like I'm starting to repeat myself, you're getting it.

What you've learned in this book is the foundation of how to control your motorcycle when you're just PUTZING AROUND in your neighborhood. It's also the foundation of how to control your motorcycle when you want to DODGE A CAR spinning out of control towards you. It's the same.

Hurt was an avid motorcycle rider for most of his life and continued educating riders well after the Hurt Report was published. I find it powerful that he never stopped asking riders to use their front brake.

I believe USE-YOUR-FRONT-BRAKE is the first rule of braking because Professor Hurt told us so.

Hurt Report Golden Nugget #7

Hurt found that chest and head trauma were the leading causes of death and that the use of a motorcycle helmet was the single most important factor in the prevention or reduction of head injury.

My Thoughts:

I'll let you draw your own conclusions on the relevance of wearing a helmet and protective gear. They do what they're designed to do.

I wear both.

Hurt Report Golden Nugget #8

Hurt found that riders who took hands-on training from professionals were the *least* likely to be in an accident and that motorcyclists taught by friends and family were the *most* likely to be in an accident.

My Thoughts:

Don't ask your cousin to teach you how to ride a motorcycle. Take hands-on training from professionals.

Hurt Report Golden Nugget #9

Hurt found that riders between 16 and 24 years old were significantly *overrepresented* in crashes and that riders between the ages of 30 and 50 were significantly *underrepresented*.

My Thoughts:

Don't let your age dictate your emotions. I won't let my 18-year-old son ride a motorcycle, and I don't apologize for it. Now you know one of the reasons why.

Hurt Report Golden Nugget #10

Hurt found that nearly half of all riders killed in motorcycle crashes were under the influence of alcohol.

My Thoughts:

If you ride your motorcycle to a bar to get wasted, you're an *idiot*. I don't have a softer way of putting it. I also recognize that absolutely zero riders who do this have made it to this point of the book.

I know—I'm preaching to the choir on this one.

Key Points

1. According to the Hurt Report, riders are missing the fundamentals. Don't lock up your rear tire. Understand and use countersteering to control your motorcycle. Do SOMETHING (brake, countersteer) when you're about to crash. Wear a helmet if you want to protect your head in a crash. Don't rely on a friend to teach you how to ride. Don't drink and ride. USE YOUR FRONT BRAKE.
2. Share some of your favorite Hurt Report takeaways with your riding buddies.

FORTY-ONE

Target Fixation

Look where you want to go because that's where you're going.
— David Mixson

No book about motorcycle control would be complete without at least a short discussion of the topic of this chapter. Studies have shown (and I've proven it to myself with experiments) that your motorcycle goes where you're looking. It's kind of freaky how this works, but it does.

The phenomena is called *target fixation*. Understanding it can help you avoid a crash if you know how to use it. It can also kill you if you fall victim to its energy.

The key point here is to *look where you want to go*. Sometimes this is easy. Other times it takes extreme focus to make yourself look away from an approaching hazard. Your eyes will naturally fixate on the car sliding out of control toward you, or the huge pothole 20 yards ahead, or the rabbit that decided to stop in the middle of your lane.

When you see a hazard in the road, pick a spot that misses it and look that way. If a car is coming toward you, pick a path that misses the car and look in that direction. Then use countersteering to make your motorcycle follow your eyes.

This sounds so simple, but it can be so difficult.

Try It for Yourself

When you're riding with no traffic or hazards, pick a spot in the road ahead and look at it. Notice how your motorcycle hits the spot. It's amazing. Your body naturally steers the motorcycle in the direction you're looking.

Now you know why it's important to LOOK FAR INTO TURNS when riding around curves. I struggled with this when I first started riding, but with practice it became natural.

Key Points

1. Your motorcycle goes where your eyes tell it to go.
2. Do NOT look at hazards you want to avoid.
3. DO look far into turns in the direction you want to ride.

Nearly Half of all Motorcycle Fatalities are Caused by Rider Error

Part Six: Wrap-Up

In this section, I'll wrap things up and introduce you to *The Motorcycle Smarts*

Creed. You're awesome for making it to this point!

Honestly, this might be the best tip in this book.
Go to the link below and subscribe now.
The book can wait.

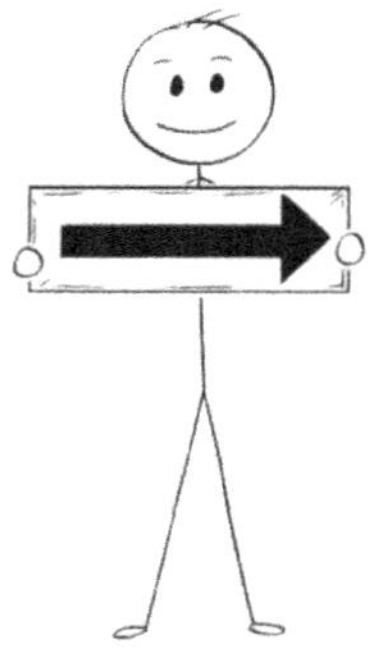

"Motorcycle Smarts"
Quick Tips Newsletter

Free weekly riding tips you can consume in less than 3 minutes—delivered to your inbox for you to use and share with others.

motorcyclesmarts.com/tips

You're not doing everything you can to keep from crashing until you're signed up.

Sign up at the link below.
Unsubscribe at any time.
motorcyclesmarts.com/tips

FORTY-TWO

The Motorcycle Smarts Creed

I wrote this to help me get into the right mindset before I ride.

It's called the *Motorcycle Smarts Creed*.

I will only ride my motorcycle on this day if my mind is clear, my body is rested, and my soul is undistracted.

Today, I will focus on improving my riding skills. I will practice doing what I do well and what I don't do as well.

don't do so well.

I will ride defensively and assume others don't see me. I will watch closely for distracted drivers and give them extra space.

I will position myself so others can see me and ride at a comfortable pace, even if this means I arrive at my destination a few minutes late.

I will represent the motorcycling community to the best of my abilities. I will wave to every motorcyclist, regardless of what they're riding.

I will stay focused on the tasks before me. I will remain patient and expect nothing from the drivers around me. If someone does something stupid, I will not blow a fuse, make a hand gesture, or yell inside my helmet.

I will notice the beauty of nature around me. I will appreciate the smells of changing seasons and the uniqueness of every cloud. I will enjoy the warmth of the sun shining on me, and the

the sun shining on me, and the different shades of green Mother Nature has painted for me.
And when my ride is done, and my thoughts are clear, I will document today in my journal— the good, the bad, and the silent thoughts that pop into my head only when I ride.
Because today is a special day.

FORTY-THREE

Final Thoughts

When I set out to write this book, I was motivated by the data in the Hurt Report to do something to help riders understand the basics of *how motorcycles work* and *why riders crash.*

Several NHTSA studies have shown that almost half all motorcycle fatalities occurred in single-vehicle crashes—when the rider crashed all by themself. The data doesn't lie.

WE'RE KILLING OURSELVES IN SINGLE-VEHICLE CRASHES BY REFUSING TO UNDERSTAND HOW MOTORCYCLES WORK AND WHY THEY CRASH.

In some ways, it would be more comfortable to blame the distracted driver who pulled out in front of us or the drunken driver who lost control and swerved into our lane.

But that's only a fraction of what's causing us to crash.

THE GUY IN THE MIRROR IS THE ONE WE SHOULD REALLY WATCH OUT FOR.

One of the main goals during my first riding season was to avoid being in a single-vehicle accident. I figured I could at least control this. I was also motivated because the last thing I wanted to do was have to tell my mentors I crashed all by myself.

I remembered this commitment every time I put on my helmet and every time I approached a high-speed curve—the skill I struggled with most in the beginning. I practiced the things I wasn't good at.

I studied what I didn't understand.

I asked my mentors for advice when something felt wrong.

Am I suggesting we can reduce our risks to zero? NO!

Skilled riders crash and die every day when there was nothing they could have done to prevent (or avoid) it.

BUT IT'S ALSO TRUE THAT UNDER-SKILLED RIDERS CRASH AND DIE EVERY DAY WHEN THERE was SOMETHING THEY COULD HAVE DONE TO AVOID IT.

In the end, I believe far too many riders cruise around with a better understanding of what looks cool than an understanding of how to effectively control their motorcycle.

This book was my attempt to change that.

It took me ten years to complete it. I did everything I could to put it off. But I knew deep in my soul that I had to finish it, and I did.

If it helps one rider, I've accomplished what I set out to do when I told my mentors, *"Someday, I want to explain motorcycles my way."*

MASTERING THE ART OF RIDING A MOTORCYCLE WELL is about learning how to ride the right way. It's about taking each ride seriously. It's about enjoying the experience and making good decisions based on the laws of physics.

It's about being confident you can avoid distracted drivers.

It's about having a plan before you need a plan. It takes effort.

It's about understanding and overcoming rider fear, and having the head knowledge of how your motorcycle works so you can make it go where you want it to go.

It's about knowing how to control a motorcycle.

Learning how to control a motorcycle should be your first goal when you buy your first motorcycle, or your next goal if you've ridden for decades. *Control* is the skill that makes you less likely to be in an accident. It's the path to proficient riding.

I honestly believe the information in this book could save your life. But only if you do something with it.

As I said in the beginning:

I believe that riding a motorcycle well is part skill, part willing to learn, part understanding of basic physics, and part giving a damn about your safety and the safety of those around you. THE BALL IS IN YOUR COURT.

Final Challenge

As our time together draws to an end, I leave you with one final challenge to BE INTENTIONAL.

Be intentional about learning how motorcycles work and how to control them, intentional about recognizing and overcoming rider fear, intentional about improving your offensive and defensive riding skills.

Don't be the rider who says you can't reduce your risks. Don't be the rider who doesn't know what the Hurt Report is, what countersteering does, or why you should never lock up your rear tire. Don't be the rider who doesn't wear a helmet because his riding buddies think helmets aren't cool.

Instead ...

Take the information given in this book and use it on your journey to MASTERING THE ART OF RIDING WELL. Practice your craft often.

Take each ride seriously. Learn something new every time you ride.

Keep a journal. Document what you did well and what you need to work on for the next ride. Find a motorcycle that fits your body and your riding goals.

Be wary of drivers turning left across your lane. Riders die every day because of this. Assume motorists don't see you because sometimes they don't—especially if you're wearing dull colors.

And if you're wearing dull colors, ask yourself why?

Know how to use countersteering to put your motorcycle exactly where you want it—regardless of how small you are and how large it is. Consider a motorcycle equipped with ABS and

Traction Control (or ESC) because the advantages far outweigh the disadvantages.

DON'T LOCK UP YOUR REAR TIRE BECAUSE BAD THINGS HAPPEN WHEN YOU DO!

Leave margin so you aren't pressured to ride faster than you want to. Practice in all weather conditions so you'll be ready in real life. And don't be the guy who brags, "My motorcycle has never seen the rain." If you can say this, you've missed out on one of the most memorable things you can do on a motorcycle.

Take a ride to nowhere just because you can. Explore roads near your home you've never been on. Take the long way to familiar places. Discover your city, your state, and your country.

I promise they'll look different on a motorcycle.

Believe you can reduce your chances of crashing because you can.

Use rider fear as a motivator to improve your riding skills or as a sign you should choose a different craft.

Know what to do when you start going wide in a turn and how to keep from lowsiding and highsiding.

USE YOUR FRONT BRAKE! USE YOUR FRONT BRAKE! USE YOUR FRONT BRAKE!

And lastly, represent the sport by being courteous to motorists, choose your riding friends carefully, and embrace the reality that rider safety is a choice—because anyone who tells you different is a liar!

MASTERING THE ART OF RIDING A MOTORCYCLE WELL is a journey, not a destination. Ask any rider who's been doing this for decades, and they'll tell you the same thing—they never stop learning.

I learn something new every time I ride. That's one of the best things about motorcycles—there's always something left to learn, something left to experience, something left to discover. I'm convinced

I'll never have it all figured out, and that's the way I want it.

In the basement of my house back in 2007, I pulled out a perfectly typed set of notes ten pages long and placed it in front of my motorcycle mentors. With more confidence than I deserved, I proclaimed:

"Someday, I'm going to explain motorcycles my way."

In my wildest imagination, I had no idea I would end up here.

I've accomplished what I promised my mentors I would do.

I'VE EXPLAINED MOTORCYCLES MY WAY.

In a deeply personal way, writing these final words feels amazing.

"I finished what I started" feels pretty darn good.

Thank you again for following along and reading what I had to say about a subject I'm so passionate about. I sincerely hope you found something that makes you a better, safer rider. — *David*

FORTY-FOUR

UPDATE: A Case for Mandatory ABS

In the first publication of this book, I was afraid to be so bold.

But this is too important to sit by and do nothing.

By now, you know that I'm a huge proponent of ABS.

So much so that I think ABS should be federally mandated on all street motorcycles sold in the United States. There. I said it.

My hope is that it's already happened by the time you read this.

But just in case. Here's why.

ABS stops most riders more quickly than conventional brakes. But that's not the point I'm going to focus on because that's debatable and has lots of naysayers.

What's even more important to understand is that ABS keeps you from locking up your rear tire and triggering a rider-induced lowside or highside crash—every single time—even when you panic and apply both brakes as hard as you can.

I wrote the *Motorcycle Smarts* book series, in large part, to explain this so all riders and politicians can understand.

It's one of the most important points in this book.

Let me say it a different way.

I WOULD STILL CHOOSE TO RIDE A MOTORCYCLE WITH ABS EVEN IF IT MEANT IT TOOK ME A FEW FEET longer TO STOP THAN RIDERS WITH CONVENTIONAL BRAKES!

The physics explains all this with clarity.

There's no doubt in my mind that ABS would reduce the number of single-vehicle motorcycle crashes. There's no doubt in my mind ABS would lower the overall number of motorcycle fatalities.

Why is this point avoided in other motorcycle skills books?

I believe many riders don't see the need for ABS because their training didn't show them. And neither have the popular motorcycle skills books. If they had, I promise I wouldn't have felt the calling to write the *Motorcycle Smarts* series.

And neither have many of the federally funded crash studies.

The engineer in me says there must be huge opposition to mandatory ABS, or it would already be in place—like it is in Europe. But for the life of me, I can't imagine a viable argument against it.

This is why I explained lowside and highside crashes my way.

Could somebody please show Congress my explanations?

I'm sure folks argued against mandatory ABS for automobiles and light trucks too. But you found a way to pass that legislation.

It's time to do the same courtesy for motorcycle owners.

And while you're mandating ABS, why not go ahead and mandate ESC at the same time? The technology already exists.

If you have ABS and ESC (or Traction Control), you won't be able to spin your rear tire even if you give her too much throttle—further reducing the chances of triggering a lowside or highside crash.

At some point, maybe before you even read this book, I believe ABS *will* be mandatory. At that point, the purpose of this chapter is to convince riders that ABS, ESC, and Traction Control are good.

I know I won't be able to convince all of you.

I just spent my morning looking online at motorcycle forums, and there are certainly some passionate folks against ABS.

Maybe some of the same riders whose bike has never seen the rain?

If the naysayers would look past the stopping distance argument and instead focus on the fact that ABS prevents rider-induced lowside and highside crashes, I think some might reconsider.

If I convert one ABS naysayer, this book series was worth it.

In the first printing of this book, I stopped short of recommending mandatory ABS. After studying the data for my third book, "Motorcycle Hacks," I changed my mind.

Today. I'm asking Congress to pass legislation that requires ABS (and Stability Control) on all street motorcycles sold in the U.S.

You did this for cars in 2012. Are motorcyclists less important?

Europe passed ABS legislation years ago. It's time we do the same.

If you want to keep everyone happy, make it so riders can manually deactivate ABS when they want to—even though most never will.

I understand that if riders demanded ABS, manufacturers would already be providing it. That’s not happening because no one seems to be talking about ABS preventing riders from triggering crashes.

The passionate arguments against ABS focus on stopping distances and the rider having full control (pop a testosterone pill, beat on chest) of his motorcycle without electronics getting in his way.

Give me a break.

FORTY-FIVE

How Can I Help?

My goal in writing the *Motorcycle Smarts* series was never financial.

I'm passionate about the sport, and I hope it shows. If someone wants to champion mandatory ABS on all street motorcycles, I'd be happy to do what I can to help.

I'm also open to sharing parts of the unique content I wrote about in my books with online and print publications—especially the parts about lowside and highside crashes.

Thanks again for following along. —
David

david@motorcyclesmarts.com
linkedin.com/in/david-mixson/

FORTY-SIX

Courtesy Copies for Rider Coaches

My vision has always been to share this book with as many riders as possible. That's my best shot at changing the crash data.

I'd like to start by sending a free copy of this book to as many rider coaches as I can. My hope is that every coach might find a nugget of useful information that they can share with their students—possibly on the topic of what triggers lowside and highside crashes.

Just a suggestion.

But I don't want to stop there.

If I can get enough company sponsorships and individual support, I'd like to provide free/discounted copies to riding clubs and rallies.

Learn more about the *Motorcycle Smarts Dream Team* below.

I can't do this alone.

motorcyclesmarts.com/dreamteam

Appendix

In this final section, I'll introduce my mentors, tell you what folks are saying about the *Motorcycle Mentor Podcast,* and give you a sneak peek of my other books in the *Motorcycle Smarts* series.

Meet My Motorcycle Mentors

I was lucky. I found two men willing to help me when I started riding. Their guidance was less about how to ride the correct way and more about the mental steps you must take to become a proficient rider.

Let's meet them.

Fred Applegate

Fred and I worked together at NASA in the late '90s training astronauts for Spacelab flights and controlling science experiments onboard the Space Shuttle.

Fred retired when he was still young and in good health. With his free time, he played golf, took tennis lessons, and continued enjoying his lifelong passion for riding his Honda ST1100.

Fred is very methodical, detail-oriented, disciplined, cautious, and patient. When I started toying with the idea of buying a motorcycle, I immediately approached him for guidance.

Fred agreed to become my motorcycle mentor.

He graciously helped me through every new challenge. Instead of giving me the answer to my problem, he always guided me toward the solution—knowing that it would have more meaning if I figured it out for myself. Fred was the perfect mentor.

Pete Tamblyn

Pete is one of the top motorcycle instructors in the country.

If you've taken a Stayin' Safe Advanced Motorcycle Training class, Pete might have been your instructor. Over the years, Pete has helped thousands of riders as an instructor at several different riding schools.

Lucky for me, Pete and Fred were roommates back in college and good friends today. Fred refers to Pete as *his* motorcycle mentor. Pete was gracious with his time and always answered my toughest questions with patience and thoroughness.

Thank you both for investing in me, for being patient, for having the heart of a teacher, for encouraging me to follow my passion to start a website, and for helping me write content for the site during the early days. Thank you for helping me ride more safely.

This world needs more MENTORS LIKE YOU!

CPSIA information can be obtained
at www.ICGtesting.com
Printed in the USA
LVHW050339210423
744868LV00002B/97

9 781806 311767